"Closing Shop"

I0549580

A Hell and Heaven Novel

by

Darren Walker

First Published in 2018 by Blossom Spring Publishing

Closing Shop Copyright © 2018 Darren Walker

ISBN 978-1-9996490-2-9

E: admin@blossomspringpublishing.com

W: www.blossomspringpublishing.com

Darren Walker has been asserted in accordance under the
Copyright, Designs and Patents Act,1988 and by British library
cataloguing in publication data. A catalogue record for this
book is available from the British Library.

Introduction

"Here we may reign secure, and in my choice
to reign is worth ambition though in Hell:
Better to reign in Hell, than serve in Heaven."

Paradise Lost,

John Milton (1674).

"What does Milton know about it? Total, complete and utter balls!"

Satan, (Every single day)

Prologue – Time Before Time.

In the darkness of night neither side could see one another, never mind the enemy. As all the warriors with vision better suited to night skirmishes tended to be at the front of any fighting columns, they had long since been destroyed. In their current blind state, they could easily march forward, stumbling over the rough and uneven ground, and both sides might pass within feet of each other and be none the wiser until dawn. Only then, looking around, might they see footprints in the mud leading in the opposite direction. Realising their mistake, they'd be forced to turn around and seek battle; back at some point where they had just come.

That's what could have happened; tonight however, there was no missing each other. The spearheads of both formations were virtually touching before foes were recognised for what they were. Then there was a joint roar, battle cries sounding as warnings were issued so those behind could join the fray. Spears were sent flying, landing in the middle of the troops, a flock of arrows could be heard, piercing the air with high-pitched whistles, but not seen until it was too late. Hitting shields or flesh, they didn't discriminate. Those in the front lines had swords, axes and spiked flails which were swung with wild vigour and enthusiasm. Those who didn't block the blows were either killed or injured, their bodies becoming a carpet for the troops behind them to stand on and continue fighting.

Incomprehensible orders were screamed, attempting to direct the battle and take advantage of any identified weaknesses in the opposing lines. Those instructions were ignored by those engaged in battle, as they had more important things to focus on than some leader's bigger plans and strategies. Often, it was a case of listening to someone giving directions, or blocking a sword aimed for their heads. They seldom had the luxury of doing both.

Over the normal din of the conflict, in the vast and black emptiness they suddenly heard it; the heavy and hard swishing of leathery wings. The winged demons were on their way. Unguarded flanks might be breached, and the ensuing chaos could make the difference between stalemate, victory or defeat. Vague orders were given and the cacophony of sounds already filling the air, were increased as the gentle whoosh of angel wings began. Many angels, although not all, could fly; but those able to do so took to the skies. Eyes strained as they attempted to catch sight of the enemy and strike first, knowing that if the demons had the advantage of height and surprise then talons would soon be ripping into flesh. Such was war, be it between humans, or the powers of good and evil, never let the enemy have the advantage. Surprise and brute force forever clashing, sometimes one element would be the deciding factor, and then on a different day, it could be another. Often luck played a greater part in a soldier's life than they liked to admit.

Back in God's encampment, temporary wooden barricades and stone fortifications had been built and were manned in preparation for possible surprise assaults. They could hear the battle in the distance, puncturing the night like faint pin pricks in the blackness but couldn't see it and they couldn't leave their posts to give aid to their brethren-in-arms. All they could do was stare into the darkness and wait. They didn't have to remain in suspense for long. A single spear was seen briefly in the light of the campfire before it struck an angel squarely in the chest. A brief scream of agony, more of pain and surprise than a call to arms, escaped his mouth and he fell to the ground. Blood escaped from his lifeless corpse; mixing with the dirt beneath him as the spear swayed back and forth, resembling a post which had lost its pennant.

Demons whooped as they scrambled over the defences. Angel guards valiantly met the assailants, unable to stem the sheer weight of numbers. The enraged demons soon found themselves on the edge of the vulnerable square, eyeing the angels like a mischief of hungry and veracious rats attacking a grain store.

One angel, Gabriel, stepped forward to meet them. His armour, once shining and bright had been left battered, blood stained and tarnished after centuries of battle. Standing before the demons, the camp fire behind him gave Gabriel's armour an unearthly red glow. With demons swarming towards him, he swung his sword, which glinted in the gloom. Closer his foes drew, ever closer, until he brought the weapon down upon the nearest. When the blade impacted with their thick hides and taut muscles, they disappeared in wisps of grey dust.

The absence of remains left the remaining, unscathed, demons wary and halted their red mist rage filled charge. They'd heard rumours about a sword with special powers, but these were unconfirmed until now, as all who encountered it in battle had never returned. Now it seemed they were face-to-face with it. The angel had it raised to his shoulder, ready for the next onslaught.

The look of invincibility and arrogant victory drained from Gabriel's face when he saw what the demons couldn't; behind them Satan stood in his full demonic form. Long, twisted, sharp horns protruded from the top of his head, his angular face was blood red with eyes which burned brighter than any fire. The tall, lean and muscular body enough to send any other angel running in fear. A spear was grasped tightly in one of his taloned hands, a sword gripped in the other. He glowered contemptuously at the angel before raising his arm and launching the spear. It flew straight, and true, leaving no opportunity for Gabriel to deflect it or move out of the way. Passing through armour, flesh, and bone, Gabriel was impaled by the weapon. He staggered backwards and fell into the flames, his death greeted with a cheer from the demon spectators. They watched Satan move into the firelight, the flickering glow dancing against his red flesh. He strode into the flames, the fire having little effect on the Master of Hell and dropped his own sword before stooping to pick up the mythical one from the Archangel's funeral pyre. Studying the blade for a moment, he lifted his gaze and stared at his pensive army. The angels staring in disbelief at what they had seen. Far superior numbers now no longer an advantage without the sword.

"Well?" he bellowed. "What are you waiting for? An invitation?" Emboldened by their dark master's words, the demons needed no further instructions and began a noisy advance, ensuring they remained a respectful distance behind Satan and the lethal sword.

Satan began to run, and he rushed through the flaps of the largest and most imposing tent in the whole encampment. God sat at a table studying a map, as if the noises outside were none of his concern. Satan knew he'd never get another opportunity like this. He raised the sword; aiming at God's neck. One brief stab and it would all be over. The war which had been fought for millennia would finally end and he would celebrate the ultimate victory.

He came to an abrupt stop as if his muscles were unable to push forward and deliver the fatal blow into unguarded flesh. The memories of what once was but had been and then lost filled his mind. The banishment from heaven and the subsequent fall into Hell, breaking his body and leaving scars in his souls. Not regrets, but recollections still tinged with sadness.

The hesitation was enough. God sensed the unwelcome guest and turned. The sword which was already in his hand struck, hitting Satan in his stomach and digging deep. Their eyes met, both showing a sorrow for what used to be but could never be again. As if momentarily frozen the devil dropped the sword only for his body to suddenly go limp and join the weapon on the floor. Lifeless as its spirit returned to his own domain, Hell.

Waking, as he did most nights, with his body drenched in a sweat that not fires of hell could ever generate, Satan's mind continued to review every detail of his vivid and all too real dream, an echo of long ago. Regrets at not acting, and anger aimed at God and everything else in creation. Attempting to go back to sleep, all he could do was wonder when the nightmares would end.

Chapter 1 – So This Is It?

Satan wasn't on his best form today. He was fed up; he'd been pensive for the past couple of decades and knew he was completely depressed. Being evil just wasn't fun anymore and he'd got bored with the whole thing. Yes, he truly believed in his heart that hate was what he should thrive on; it should fill his very soul like a forest fire. After all, that was what made people do evil things and those evil things brought their souls to him instead of going off to the other, far duller, place. But what was the point? Hate was a blanket that could be spread over everything. He could hate a fluffy golden retriever puppy, but big deal. Besides he secretly found them cute, but he would never tell his loyal demons that. They would make his existence hell, instead of the other way around. In the big scheme of things, he should hate everything – but how could he loathe a house brick or a glass of lemonade? Sure, he could easily make the brick crumble to dust or make the drink go off, but so what? Given the right amount of time nature could do that for him anyway, so it was a complete waste of his evil talents. Maintaining his enthusiasm for hatred was draining him and he couldn't be bothered with any of it.

For millennia, he had loved his position on the throne as the ultimate evil. The dark ages had rocked, the black-death a work of pure genius. And even parts of the twentieth century had its moments. There'd been so many evil leaders who had found ways to utilise modern technology, creating a hell on Earth that had almost made him redundant. No need to try and coax people into selling their souls when they were lining up to put on fancy uniforms and blindly slaughter the masses at the behest of some lunatic or other. All done because they were pathetic, and too stupid to simply stop and question their actions. It wasn't until those leaders, and their devout followers, had died before he felt anything resembling better. His creative skills were challenged, but he'd managed to dole out suitable punishments in the inner rings of Hell for the likes of Hitler,

Stalin and Pol Pot. The old classics, such as boiling in hot oil for all eternity, were far too simple and gentle for people like them.

But those heady days were gone. The new age of political correctness, international cooperation and foreign aid had taken the dark glint away from any acts of evil. After all, what kind of damnation would someone receive for telling a sexist, racist, or sick joke? An eternity in purgatory with a right shoulder that twinged slightly every other Tuesday? How about a mild migraine every now and then? No, the new world which had seemed like a good idea at the time, was so dull; his head ached at the thought of the sheer un-evilness of people. They weren't good exactly, which gave him a little relief, but for far too many of them they wouldn't know pure evil if it moved into the house next door, played Thrash Metal backwards at full volume until 4am, and sacrificed virgins on the back lawn while people were on the school run.

The occasional religious fanatic was always welcome. It made him laugh to see the surprise on their faces when they arrived – having blown themselves up along with some innocent shoppers– only to discover their act of martyrdom hadn't propelled them into heaven to receive their seventy-two lustful virgins. But once the initial laughter and joy of allocating some suitable punishment had subsided, he soon felt tired and lonely again.

And the calibre of the average damned these days? They either shamelessly enjoyed the punishments and asked for more, or they never stopped complaining, as if they had ordered a cup of low fat espresso coffee from a high-street chain and when it arrived they got 'café Americano'. They'd got so used to complaining about things, they could no longer see the irony of being in Hell in the first place. Even the English had learnt how to complain. What was Earth coming to? Even if he made it so their mouths wouldn't open, he could see the indignation in their eyes. He could imagine them saying "Excuse ME, but I specifically requested an eternity in Hell where I was NOT

2

pushing rocks up a hill and here I am, with rocks! I demand to see the manager!" Why couldn't they understand this was Hell and it was supposed to be bad! Yes, he had to admit Hell wasn't what it used to be.

This ugly mood had transported Satan to a dark place and for him that was a very dark place indeed. He probably would have spent a few more years lamenting the entire situation if not for the loud knocking on the giant oak door. It echoed around the room like a bass drum being thrown down a flight of stairs into a big bowl of strawberry trifle. Looking up from his desk Satan paused, collecting his thoughts, and tried to shake the apathy from his mind. Breathing deeply so his voice would take on the deep resonance and air of anger he certainly didn't feel, he bellowed in response. "Yes? What do you want, you pathetic maggot?"

The door opened grudgingly, groaning as if the metal hinges were being bent almost to breaking point. Satan was unsurprised to see the face of his closest and most detested assistant, Stuart, appear around the edge.

"It's just me, sir" Stuart squeaked. "I have today's reports." On announcing himself, he slowly walked across the office to Satan's desk. He kept his head slightly bowed and clutched the four-inch-thick, blood red, leather-bound ledger tightly against his chest as if he expected it to leap out of his arms and run out of the room screaming in terror. Which admittedly, was something other living visitors had tried, and failed, to do.

Heaving out a breath and tilting his head to the right, Satan watched the pathetic creature coming towards him. In any crowd, Stuart would have been the last person noticed. He was in his fifties, just below average height, skinny and had lank, greasy brown hair with grey patches. Wearing a pale blue chequered cardigan, and light brown corduroy trousers with patches sewn over holes on the knees, he was quite possibly the most snivelling excuse for a human Satan had ever encountered. His saving grace was having one of the most cunning and devious minds in the whole of Hades. Stuart's ability to go anywhere and be deemed completely insignificant made him a handy intelligence officer. Where some of Satan's fiercest and most evil demons might be afraid to tell him bad news, Stuart would gladly report every little detail without worrying about leaving the office with a red hot poker shoved in an uncomfortable position.

Stuart reached the desk and placed the heavy ledger down on it with a dull thud. "There you go Sir; I hope you find it satisfactory." He took one pace back and stood patiently, a rictus grin on his face, his arms behind his back.

Satan rubbed at his face, running his fingers through his hair and resting his hands on the back of his neck. "Stuart," he muttered.

"Yes sire?"

"Stuart…" he repeated, then paused for a second to collect his thoughts. "Are you happy here?"

"Sir does know that this is Hell, doesn't he?" Stuart responded with almost undisguised glee. "I'm not supposed to be happy and I know that if you found out someone was boasting about how happy they are here, you would go out of your way to make sure they were very unhappy for the rest of eternity."

Satan smiled. Coming from anyone else in Hell, that comment would have had him breathing fire and ripping them limb from limb, but coming from Stuart it merely seemed part of his job, a duty carried out with utmost sarcasm and disdain. He was the ultimate uncivil civil servant; in the place which might have been specifically designed by them.

"Well put, Stuart, very well put indeed."

"Thank you, sire. If you don't mind me saying, it did seem a rather strange question."

Stroking the stubble on his cheek and chin, Satan looked Stuart straight in the eyes and saw neither fear nor hatred, only expectant curiosity. How was it that he could strike pant-wetting terror into the hearts of bloodthirsty tyrants, but this lowly pencil pusher treated him like a dotty college professor asking for a fresh bottle of sherry during dinner? He decided to try again and rephrase the question.

"Stuart, you have been my closest aide for a very long time, haven't you?"

"Yes sir, ever since my predecessor accidentally made you a cup of tea and put sugar in it. I believe he is still, at this very moment, on tea brewing duties in a sulphur mine somewhere on the fifth ring. A most unfortunate mistake for him, but a very lucky day for me."

"Yes, quite," interjected Satan, "but I'm not interested in that. What I'm getting at is this place – Hell. Is it exciting any more?"

Not being the sort of question he was used to, especially coming from Satan, Stuart paused to collect his thoughts before answering. No point in rushing into a possible trap. "Wellllll," he began, "the people who come here don't get a massive adrenaline rush regarding their final destination and designated punishments. In fact, they'd probably all prefer to be anywhere but here. So, in answer to your question, no, I don't think hell is exciting. Maybe in the early days – before my time – but ever since I arrived, it hasn't been the most popular of holiday locations."

Such an attitude amazed Satan. A mixture of servility and contempt, all combined into one cold and emotionless tone. How did Stuart manage it? He'd perfected a natural voice which mocked him so politely, he had to admire him. Letting out a frustrated breath, he surveyed his office. Even here everything was decay, rot and entropy. If this was the office of some high-flying CEO on Earth, everything would be rich dark oak panelling and gleaming gold plated handles. Volumes of unread, identical looking, books discreetly lining the walls to impress any visitor with their pristine and untouched pretension. But, here in Hell, even his own private inner sanctum suffered the same fate as everywhere else. The lights were too dim to see things clearly, but not darkened enough to make the raging log fireplace seem attractive. The walls were damp and mouldy and the once thick, luxuriant carpet was stained red by oceans of spilt blood and smelt of who-knew-what. In truth, he knew exactly what it smelt of, but he didn't care to think about that! No matter how often he redecorated, or tried to get the place looking better, within a matter of days it always ended up looking and smelling the same as before. Using the damned as his interior decorators wouldn't have been his first choice, but it wasn't as if he had any alternative. The few famous fashion designers who arrived in hell had interesting ideas but they always tried to cheer the place up, or add big, glitzy crucifixes – and they just didn't work! He realised that Hell was mad, and he wasn't going to take it anymore.

"Stuart!" he snapped. "Assemble all my top-level demons in the great hall, six hours from now; I have an important announcement to make."

"Of course, sire." Stuart turned and briskly walked away.

Watching Stuart exit and hearing the massive door screeching in a futile attempt at resisting being shut, he allowed himself a loud, self-indulgent laugh. Things were going to be different, whether they liked it or not. And he was certain they wouldn't like it. But things were going to get better…

Chapter 2 – Please Feel Free To Object...

Time in hell is relative and doesn't follow the standard units adhered to on Earth. To a soul experiencing the full brunt of whatever punishment they're receiving, one minute feels like a week of excruciating agony. An experience not dissimilar to watching some soap operas on Earth television. Very much a case of time doesn't fly when you're enduring!

Therefore, six hours would be an unimaginable period to many of Hell's residents. But to the demons themselves, who mainly had the luxury of dishing out the pain, rather than receiving it, they knew roughly when they needed to arrive at the meeting. They also knew better than to risk being late, or worse, missing it altogether, so every one of them had been waiting impatiently and noisily for at least two hours. Some of the demons, waiting at the front of the hall, had rushed there as soon as they'd been made aware of the meeting, to avoid any possibility of being unavoidably detained. Any such delay would probably involve chains, a locked, dark room and a fellow demon with a grudge, snatching the opportunity to destroy one of his colleagues. Every demon was paranoid and tended to hate everyone else, and consequently, it was a tense place to be.

Although such meetings were rare, when they did occur it wasn't unknown for fights to break out and if left unattended to, small skirmishes would evolve quickly into full-scale battles as old scores were settled and new excuses for further battles were created. The tension was palpable and, the atmosphere could be cut with a large and vicious knife. And considering the number of knives that were secreted about the demons, the cutting could begin at any minute. Although he wasn't in the hall yet, Satan knew exactly what could happen and enjoyed the mental powder keg he'd created. If they did use up all their energies on a bit of playful bickering they would be more compliant and willing to listen without the need for him to rip the flesh from any of them. It was a drastic measure, but a highly successful and effective method of garnering their attention.

Satan was in an ante-chamber, getting ready. Although he could take on any form or appearance he liked, he had to admit he really did enjoy putting on a well-fitting designer suit. He knew a man in Savile Row who'd sold his soul for the love of a woman who went on to cheat on him. In exchange for delays in the payment of his dues, he could stay alive, as long as Satan was kept supplied with smart attire. This deal had been in place for the last one hundred and twenty-three years, but for some inexplicable reason, nobody on Earth had noticed how long the little tailors shop had been owned and run by the same person. Satan studied himself in an ornate full length mirror. The mirror was tarnished, the gilt peeling and his reflection was speckled in the old glass, but he had to admit he looked very stylish and handsome in his well-made grey suit, subtle burgundy tie and shiny, plain black shoes. The sin of pride, but he didn't mind. After all, who was going to punish him for it? Besides, he invented the seven deadly sins and if he'd given himself more time, he could have come up with a lot more. But God had a thing for the number seven, so he'd found it easier to get them all accepted by sticking with that number.

Taking one last look in the mirror, he considered one final detail of his appearance – horns, or no horns? They were a cumbersome accompaniment and gave him a neck ache, so he decided that in this instance, they were inappropriate and unnecessary. He commanded enough fear and abject terror without the pointy, but pointless, showmanship. He could soon make them appear, if he needed to eviscerate any demon that didn't display the right level of respect. Besides, they ruined his immaculately trimmed hairstyle. Panache was important and must be maintained to ensure he received full homage. Antlers, no matter how menacing, just made the crowd feel as if they were standing before a dapperly-dressed antelope or mountain goat.

When he was sure he looked perfect, he turned and made his way to his own private entrance to the grand hall. The door was guarded by two small, hunchbacked cacodemons, dressed only in loincloths and holding spike-headed maces in their immense hands. On his approach, they bowed their heads and one of them pulled the door open for him. He walked nonchalantly through the doorway, and once he was through, the door closed behind him. The hall itself was vast, large enough to accommodate every demon and still have room for a game of football at the back. Gnarled, glowing red rock stalactites hung from the ceiling and the walls were created from the same rough material. The light they produced wasn't very bright, but it was enough for everyone to see each other and any weapons if they were drawn in anger. The stage, where he stood at the front of the hall, was ten feet above the massed audience and undecorated, except for a large wooden lectern engraved with images of decapitation and mutilation. It was illuminated by raging fires at either side, ensuring there was no danger of him not being noticed when he chose to get the audience's attention.

Glaring at the massed throng of loud, jostling demons he walked to the lectern unnoticed. He climbed a couple of steps and, grasping it, looked down at the audience knowing that no matter where they were in the hall, they could see him. Resting his arms on the top of the lectern he inhaled a deep breath and exhaled a massive tongue of flame, which reached out 500 yards in front of him, fanning over the heads of any demon within range, and scorching the horns of those unfortunate enough to be particularly tall.

"Silence!" he bellowed.

With that single word, the entire hall fell silent. The scattered groups who'd been fighting froze, arms held in mid-punch. Those in neck holds were unceremoniously released and fell heavily to the floor. Any daggers or pointed weapons were removed from opponent's bodies and returned to their scabbards or sheaths and an uneasy, anger filled armistice followed. All eyes focused on Satan, every demon in the hall knowing the sort of punishments they could expect if they didn't give him their rapt undivided attention.

Satan scanned the hall slowly; he was their sole focus of attention, but he knew how to milk an audience and it did no harm to build up the suspense. He was faced with an almost infinite combination of demons – big, small, thin, fat, with horns and without. Some had limbs growing from unusual places, a collection of nightmare forms even Hieronymus Bosch wouldn't have dared to paint. Some had decided to attend in the forms they adopted when making deals for souls and carrying out evil deeds on Earth – gold jewellery and tracksuit bedecked rappers, scantily clad women of the night, pimps, dealers, bikers and smart business men; any human form which could corrupt a soul. For some reason, there were several demons that had taken the form of black and white Friesian cows and they stood in a herd, seeming out of place, chewing their cuds and gazing up at him with the vacant black stare unique to bovines. Sometimes, on very rare occasions, it was better if even Satan didn't ask too many questions. Demons could be an imaginative, but strange, bunch and took any form they saw fit to entice humans into sin.

He saw Leviathan, the Grand Admiral of Hell, standing at the back of the hall and guarding the door, ensuring no demon tried to sneak out until the very end of the meeting. Satan offered him an almost imperceptible nod, but it was noticed and returned with a low, sweeping reverent bow.

Satan's expression was cold and impassive as he scanned the crowd, but inside he was excited. He hadn't felt like this for a very long time and he wanted to ensure he revealed his orders appropriately, ensuring there could be no doubts or questions. He wanted them to listen and know this wasn't a joke, or a test. This was the future. No more decay, discomfort and chaos.

"Pain, torture, punishment. That is our business and business is good," he growled.

He was interrupted by cheers from a group of overly-enthusiastic Jikiniki, corpse-eating, demons that hadn't been involved in any fights and still had plenty of energy for ill-conceived exuberance. They were soon silenced however, when Satan raised his right hand, pointed his index finger at one of them and a bolt of lightning shot out from it, blowing a rough, jagged hole in the demon's stomach. It would grow back eventually, but until then there would be plenty of pain and Satan had ensured he would have nothing to deal with but a frightened silence from now on.

Returning his arm to its resting place on the lectern he continued, his demeanour calm, as if nothing had happened.

"Hell has served its purpose, but now it is time for a change." He paused to let his words sink in. "Look around you. Every imaginable, and a few barely possible, ways of making the damned pay for their sins; the same thing for all eternity. Gone are the days where a red-hot poker could be used to cover a multitude of sins. Now we have so many different methods of punishment, but they're all just variations on a theme. Where's the job satisfaction? Where is the pleasure? We just do what we've always done."

He lapsed into silence to allow the ensuing murmurs to die down.

"Why?" he bellowed in his loudest, deepest voice. The stalactites overhead swayed under the force of his guttural growl. A millennium of dust and ash fell onto the heads of the creatures' underneath, leaving them with white and grey soot covering their heads and shoulders like demonic dandruff. The crowded ensemble stood at rigid attention as the word echoed around the hall and slowly subsided. The impact and effect of the single word surprised even Satan, and he had to suppress an evil laugh at the ashen grey horde before him. 'Who said Hell shouldn't be fun?' he thought to himself. Then he remembered that he'd made that rule far too many centuries ago. But what the hell? He was the boss and if he wanted to laugh he would. Provided it was in a demonic way, of course. If he just chortled or sniggered, he would deserve flaying for a week. And if he tittered, he would willingly jump into a bath of boiling oil.

"We do it," he continued, in a calmer and controlled voice, leaving the stalactites unmoved this time, "because this is Hades, Pandemonium, Barathrum. HELL! It has many names, but it's still the same place doling out the same punishments. And we do it because we're demons. The most wretched and despised detritus. We are just dirt on the bottom of the shoes of God and his brown-nosing sycophants, hangers-on and do-gooders. Am I right?"

The demons roared, or in certain cases, mooed their loyal agreement. None of them wanted to appear less than enthusiastic or not in total agreement.

Raising his hands to quieten them again, Satan gave his audience a knowing smile and nod of approval.

"Yes, of course I'm right. We're heaven's dustbin. We take the trash that they don't want and keep the scum of the Earth, so the streets of heaven can stay clean and fresh. But why do we torture people? Because God threatens humans with us. Be good and go to Him. Be bad and down you go. We're just his bogeymen."

A slightly disgruntled noise erupted from a corner of the hall which contained a small pocket of Bogeymen. They hated the group term as they were always seen as a joke by the other demons. Viewed as only being good for scaring little children, they also considered the term completely sexist because half of them were women. They wished they could have a cool collective name like the Alp or Succubus had. They would love to be called the 'Rippers', but Satan liked the traditional name and thought it would be too hard to get the new name to catch on. So, they were stuck with 'Bogeymen', which they thought made them sound as if they'd been sneezed out of someone's nose.

Ignoring the noise, Satan continued with his speech. "Does God, or anyone else outside of Hell, really know how we punish sinners? Of course not! He has no access or visibility in our dimension, just as we can't see into heaven. For all anyone knows, we could be making the damned lie in baths of warm custard rather than burning in the flames in the deep pits. He genuinely has no idea what goes on. As far as he's concerned, it's a case of out of sight, out of mind. He's relied on us to stick to type and trusted us to punish people for all eternity just because it's fun for us. Letting our anger and hatred rule our actions like pre-programmed robots. While all the time, we've just blindly followed His will. We're puppets!"

Murmurs of agreement erupted in the hall, so he paused to let them die down. His words were having the desired impact and they obviously understood what he was saying... so far. He wanted to believe he was milking the audience, but he couldn't get the image of the demon cows out of his mind. He knew demons were expected to have horns, but that was taking it a step too far. Shaking away the image of a cow sitting on his throne, he continued. "The time has come for change! We're not His lackeys; if He wants us to do His bidding He needs to give us something in return. He needs to accept us. He needs to let us back into Heaven!"

The crowd broke into a massive cheer. It has been a very long time since the last big battle between Heaven and Hell and the demons always thought there were some old scores to settle. Being able to invade Heaven and take over the place was exactly what they wanted. Satan raised his arms, signalling them to settle down and be quiet, and when they did he spoke again. "Therefore, I intend to contact God, set up a meeting and try and arrange for us to be forgiven and accepted back into Heaven."

The whole hall fell silent. Many of the demons stood there, wide eyed and open-mouthed. Others waited to see if there was more. Perhaps some joke without a punchline, or a precursor to some unspecified plan for war. Such a reaction had been anticipated so Satan glared at the audience, ensuring they would be in no doubts that he was deadly serious. Any dissent wouldn't be welcomed and would be an extremely bad – and painful – career move.

"I intend to leave Hell to its own devices. Let the damned come here, land in the lake of fire and stay there. That way, they all receive the same punishment and we can be relaxing in Heaven." Taking a deep breath, he surveyed the demons. "There is much to be discussed and arranged, but that's my plan. Are there any questions?"

The demons remained stonily silent, except for one slimy, green-skinned Kappa demon. He raised a long arm and shouted out in a Japanese accent, "Are you flikkin' clazy?"

A ripple of laughter erupted from some of the less wise demons, but a large space was suddenly created around the creature who'd spoken. Those standing close to him had a fair inkling that their own personal space needed to be a lot bigger, and far away, from their vocal colleague.

Satan set his eyes on the Kappa demon and raised his eyebrows. "An interesting and valid question; allow me to clarify…" He pointed his finger at the demon, and the ground beneath its feet began to shake and opened up. Flames and smoke rose from the void and as suddenly as they'd appeared the pyrotechnics, the hole in the ground and the kappa demon were gone. "I hope that answers the question." Smiling imperiously, he concluded with, "Any more questions?"

There was a quiet ripple of demons responding in the negative. The entire hall avoided eye contact with their boss and found they had a desperate need to study pieces of rubble on the floor beneath their feet, or to stare absent-mindedly at the ceiling as if searching for party balloons stuck in the rocks.

Satisfied, Satan turned and walked to the side of the stage. Sensing his approach, the Cacodemon opened the door for him and then he was gone.

As soon as they felt it was safe, the entire hall of demons broke into a mixture of loud debates, heated arguments or general spitting before they slowly filtered past the Leviathan and through the vast doorway out of the hall. They were in such a state of shock, they'd come to a tacit, unilateral decision that now wasn't the time for continuing their own private squabbles and knife fights. They would wait for another day.

Chapter 3 –A Cold Day In Hell.

As the various demons made their way to their own different rings of hell, and their personal chambers for the punishment of the damned, a few of them shared the journeys together. Discussing the import of what they had just heard and how they were looking forward to the chance of getting into Heaven after such a long period of being in their own prison of hate, anger and all the negative emotions. The option of ripping a few angel wings from the current inhabitants was always something they looked forward to. However, there was a small group of demons that were in no rush to get back to their respective chambers. They hung back, just outside of the hall, until all the other demons had gone, and then started their discussion.

"The Kappa was right, Satan has finally lost it." A tall red skinned Knight of Hell began.

"But imagine if he could pull it off?" butted in a small Daevas "we could be out of this place, no fires, no screams, no pain."

"Moooooooo" added a Demon Cow. "Moo!"

Everyone else stared at the cow. Nodding sagely, taking in the full magnitude of what it had just said.

"Exactly, I couldn't have put it better myself!" responded the Knight of Hell.

At that a slender, and voluptuous, demoness took the opportunity to speak. "Well, we can give him a chance, can't we? I for one do not fancy taking on Satan and challenging his rule" she hissed. "I have seen far too many try and fail."

There was a general murmur of agreement. It would take a very large army of strong demons to defeat Satan and they knew that they would find it extremely difficult to get enough on their side to have any chance of winning. With the price of defeat meaning they would be on the receiving end of the punishment that they had, gleefully for millennia, given to others. They liked dishing out the punishments and had no desire feel the pain of their own devices. They all knew that they had to give him a chance. Perhaps later on, if all else failed, they could have another war with Heaven, they were always fun. But now was not the time for such talk.

Then out of the shadows, along the wall of the dark corridor, stepped an Archdemon, even though he had human form, dressed in leather trousers and a greasy t-shirt, the whole group recognised him as being Balfon, one of the most senior demons and they knew all about his power and authority. He had no patience for anything, or anyone, that didn't listen to him and do as they were told.

"I think you are all being a little premature," his words were slow and precise with a voice colder than any ice. "…you have no choice but to accept *and* obey *his* instructions. If he succeeds we all succeed. If he fails, then what is the worst that can happen? He isn't planning any war, YET, so we just stay here doing the same jobs we always did. I suggest that you go along with his plans and do as you are told. I promise you that you WILL suffer if you decide otherwise". There was vocal steel adding strength to his frozen tone and he made sure that there were no doubts that there could be no further discussion, debate or arguments. He looked from demon to demon to gauge their reactions. Some averted their gaze others looked him straight in the eyes and nodded. But he knew that he had got his message across and that word would soon get around all the other demons. Satan was not alone and that those that didn't follow would have, in a very real sense, hell to pay.

By coincidence, but as if to emphasise the point, Leviathan walked through the doorway of the hall, the last one in and, now that the meeting was over, the last one out. He nodded a greeting to Balfon and looked suspiciously at the other

17

demons as he walked past them and meandered casually down the corridor.

At that cue the small group quickly dispersed, alone with their various thoughts and doubts. But they all knew how it worked. Listen to the instructions and orders, expect a trap and watch their own backs. Every demon for themselves if they had to, but until then, they knew that they had their jobs to be done. They shuffled away in silence, apart from the gentle tinkle of a cow bell.

Once all the demons had gone and the uncomfortably warm corridor was no longer occupied Stuart jumped to the ground, from a small dark ledge just below the jagged ceiling, landing in a crouching position. There was a dull squelch as he hit the ground, his knee having landed in a fresh, wet and warm cow pat. He swore under his breath as his leg became unexpectedly moist. Getting clothes clean in hell was not the easiest of things to get done; even for someone as resourceful as he was. It was a long walk to the laundry punishment chamber and they always used far too much starch and not enough softener. Besides, if Satan were to find out he would never let him forget it. Looking about him to ensure that he was alone and un-noticed he straightened up and stood upright, his trouser leg sticking to his knee. He had seen and heard enough. If he needed to report anything to his master he could and, if it was advantageous to him, he was ready to do so. But there was no rush. Satan had not shared any of his plans and he certainly wasn't going to risk his own position by sowing any seeds of concern or disquiet. No, far better to stay in the shadows and wait. He looked down at his trousers and saw that in addition to the warm and wet cow faeces they had picked up some dust from when he had landed so he casually brushed himself down. He then raised his left arm and clicked his fingers. A small wooded door appeared in the wall. He opened it, walked through the doorway closing it behind him. Once on the other side the door disappeared again leaving only the rough and hard wall and a silent and empty corridor.

Chapter 4 – Long Distance Call.

When Satan got back to his inner sanctum, he closed the creaky door and allowed himself to relax. He walked across to the large, rotting drinks cabinet situated on the side wall, opened the doors, and retrieved an oversized bottle of single malt whisky. No matter how frequently he removed it and gave it a dust, the dirt soon gathered on it again. One of the perks of the job was access to as many spirits – of the drinking kind – as he wanted. He poured a generous tot into a crystal tumbler. Savouring the bouquet first, he took a large sip. With a sigh of appreciation, he walked over to the fireplace and gazed into the flames. He always recognised the irony that he was the master of flames specifically designed to torture, yet he found so much beauty in his own log fire. He nonchalantly spoke aloud. "Stuart." He had no need to shout as he knew that the summons would be heard and he'd arrive quickly. Seconds later, there was a loud knock on the door, it opened and in stepped Stuart.

"You called sir?" A cold, phlegmatic smile adorned his weasel-like face.

"Yes Stuart, unlock the phone."

The phone was the only one in Hell and it had only one contact, and a single purpose. It was a direct line to God – sometimes even the greatest of enemies needed to talk. It was deliberately kept in a securely-locked safe, hidden behind a painting of an upside-down crucifix on the wall. The security was required due to an unfortunate incident when a mischievous Cambion demon had snuck into his office, got hold of the phone and made a prank call to Heaven, asking for room service to send him a hooker, a crate of beer and an extra-large pepperoni pizza. Satan had found it funny at first, but quickly realised it was best if the line was kept secure and all future calls were answered by Him and taken seriously. The Cambion demon found himself 'treading water', up to his neck in raw sewage in one of the less-popular chambers of Hell. It had been

19

fortunate for him that Satan had seen the joke, or he would have been head first.

In his time as Satan's personal servant, Stuart had never needed to access the telephone. He knew about the joke call and he'd heard rumours of occasional calls being made to ensure the uneasy truce between Heaven and Hell was maintained, but this was the first time he'd had to retrieve the key from his locked desk. He carefully lifted the painting down and put the key in the lock, turning it and twisting the dial. He knew the combination by heart and once he'd entered it, he pulled the handle and opened the safe door. The safe interior was small and the only item in it was the old-fashioned black Bakelite telephone with a round dial mechanism sat ontop of a dusty buff coloured folder. Stuart removed the phone and carried it carefully to Satan's desk then he looked at it, pondering its shape and design. It seemed odd having such an old, outdated device when mobile phones on Earth were miniscule, stylish and sleek. He knew Satan was very much a traditionalist and could never be accused of being a slave to fashion. Besides, if you wanted to talk to God, there was certainly more gravitas in such an archaic design. Thanks to some paradox he couldn't explain, the phone had existed long before telephones were invented on Earth and there was no rush to change the design classic now. Stuart dutifully stepped back and stood patiently in his usual pose, arms behind his back and his face expressionless. He watched Satan walk to his chair, sit down and place his glass on the desk.

"That is all, Stuart." The dismissal was issued nonchalantly, Satan not bothering to lift his gaze.

"Sir," ventured Stuart, "there is one thing. Grank, a devil in charge of the Sisyphus division on the third ring, is outside and would like an audience with you." Stuart paused for a second before continuing. "I believe he is requesting more boulders; the old ones are eroding, worn down and some are now the size of pebbles. He also wishes to request a transfer."

Satan offered Stuart a contemptuous scowl. Requests for additional punishment material were just a formality, and rocks could easily be obtained from one of the punishment mines on the fourth ring. It certainly wasn't much of a punishment to have someone pushing a pebble up a hill for all eternity! Transfers weren't uncommon either, but they were tiresome and usually made by impatient and ambitious lesser demons or spirits, wanting to destroy a superior by reporting some real, or imagined weakness. Requests to move seldom came from someone in such a position of authority and power. Satan was curious, but such things could wait.

"I will see him after I've completed my telephone call. Tell him to wait." He stared at Stuart. "Anything else?"

"No, sir."

"Then get out!" Satan snapped, releasing one last parcel of rage before he had to calm down and talk with God.

Not needing to be told twice, Stuart quickly left the room. He left the door slightly ajar and held his ear against it, hoping he wouldn't be noticed and could listen in on at least part of the conversation. He hoped to use any knowledge he gained to his advantage in the future.

Satan, however, was an old master with such minor tricks and with one click of his fingers, the door slammed shut. Stuart's eavesdropping came to a violent end when the door slammed into his head and threw him across the office

Interlinking his fingers, Satan stretched out his hands and cracked his knuckles. 'Right,' he thought to himself 'let's do it!' He'd been thinking and planning for such a long time, and now that the time was finally here he felt strangely elated. Here he was, with a slim but real chance of getting back into Heaven! He might not be welcomed back with open arms, and the positioning of his seat might be a good distance further away from God than it had been in the old days, but that didn't matter. What did matter was that he would no longer have to put up with Hell. He might have created the place, be to blame for all evils and the master of every negative emotion, but the regret he felt, right now, for a few of his choices weighed heavily on his spirit. Now might be the opportunity to change and make things better. What did he have to lose? Leaning forward, he picked up the telephone receiver and placed it against his ear. With his other hand, he dialled God's direct number; it was easy enough to remember – a single seven. God had chosen it despite the phone only being able to contact one person, and in theory, no matter what number he rang he should get through to God.

The phone rang four times before it was finally answered.

"Hello Bob." The voice at the other end of the line was loud, friendly and cheerful. It immediately grated on Satan's nerves. He also disliked the nickname. In Hell, the name Beelzebub was spoken in reverence, and any jovial shortening would have been met with his unforgiving wrath. "How in Hell are you?" The weak joke was backed up by jocular laughter.

"Hello Gordon," Satan replied with barely concealed contempt. He always tried to get a reaction from God with the use of the contrived nickname but failed abysmally every time. "I'm fine. And you?"

"I'm fine, thank you."

There was an extended pause, as Satan wasn't very good at small talk and God knew it. He was always happy to make Satan uncomfortable with an empty silence. Each microsecond seemed like it was its own eternity, forming, evolving and decaying in his mind. Realising what He was doing, Satan pushed on with the conversation. "Look, I have an idea and we need to talk. Can we set up a meeting somewhere on Earth to discuss it?"

There was another pause at the other end of the phone. "This isn't another one of your tired attempts to find a loophole in the Bible, is it? Like the time you tried to take control of Belgium, due to a misspelling of a verse in the King James version? Or how you created Portugal because two pages of Deuteronomy had got stuck together in Hell's library? I hope you can do better than that. After all, you do have virtually every lawyer that ever existed down there – can't they come up with anything better? And what about all those Catholic priests? I know they have a working knowledge of the Bible, so don't you think they could have been more help with your tricks? No, I'm sorry Bob, but I have neither the time nor the inclination to play any of your silly games."

"Hang on," Satan jumped in, feeling he'd lost before he'd even started, "this is genuine. There are no tricks, traps or games. I want a truce and I want to discuss the terms of my surrender!" The power and magnitude of what he'd said shook him. He'd had no intention of revealing his plan, especially in such a straightforward manner. But it was out there now. He held his breath, waiting for something – anything – from God. The silence was almost unbearable.

"Very funny," the response finally came. "Satan promised me his phone would be locked away and there would be no more silly calls! Now run along, and stop being so stupid."

"No, no, this is genuine, it is me! Beelzebub, Satan, Baal. It isn't a joke!" Satan's voice was louder and more rushed that he would have liked, but he wanted to be taken seriously. "Look Gordon, it is me and this is a once in 10,000 life times offer. Think about it; Earth can be a paradise again and we won't have to spend all our time thinking of ways to attack or defend against each other. What do you say? Surely it's worth giving me some time to explain."

There was another long pause at the other end of the line. "Alright, I'll go along with this, for now. I'm sure it will be another stupid, infantile trick so know that I'll be ready for you. Trust won't be given unconditionally; you'll have to earn it. I'll have a full team of angels with me and my army will be on standby. Where shall we meet?"

"How about Las Vegas?" Satan ventured enthusiastically. He'd always loved the place, ever since he created it, and thought it would give him the opportunity to enjoy one last wild time before he had to give it all up and be good.

"You've got to be joking! Do you remember the last time you spent a night there? Nobody wants to go through that again," God replied. "I think it should be my territory. How about Jerusalem? That's a suitable place if what you're proposing is legitimate."

"Oh, no. The food there is terrible and the wine is even worse, and we wouldn't be able to move for bloody tourists. And I remember all the fuss after you spent a night there; they still talk about it, even now. How about somewhere neutral? What about London?"

"No, Bob that's far too formal, the food is better, but the tourists are almost as bad as Jerusalem. I know – how about Hawaii? The food is wonderful and I created a beautiful beach on the northern coast of Oahu. We could take over the Terrapin Cove hotel, well away from Honolulu, for the duration. The most comfortable beds I've ever encountered on Earth and it's got a great sea view. And just think you could even get a great *lei*." God laughed at his double entendre, referring to the flowered necklaces given to tourists.

He hated to admit it, but Satan liked God's suggestion. It had been a while since he'd visited any of the Pacific Islands and Hawaii did have wonderful food, if you didn't count the tinned meat. "Okay, agreed. Oahu it is, then. If you send one of your lot to the lobby now, I'll dispatch one of my demons to meet him there. They can sort out the accommodation and report back once everything is arranged."

"Agreed, I'll see you in two weeks, and" God added menacingly, "*no* tricks!"

"Sure, no problem," Satan responded and put down the telephone receiver. Things were going better than he'd hoped. Allowing himself a smile, he leant back in the chair and put his feet up on the desk. "Stuart!" he called.

"Yes, sir?" said Stuart as he entered the room briskly. Having had his ear against the thick door in a futile attempt to catch some, or all, of the conversation; but all he had managed to pick up though were odd words.

"You can put the phone back into the safe and then send in Grank. If he wants a transfer, I think I have just the job for him."

Removing a long, thick cigar from his suit breast pocket, he put it to his mouth and made flame shoot out of his thumb to light it. Drawing in a few mouthfuls of smoke, he slowly exhaled, producing a large smoke ring. He smiled to himself as he leaned further back in the chair. Today was going well.

Chapter 5 – Travel Arrangements.

Despite all the wonderful attributes given to God by the many, and varied religious groups, ancient writings and devout thinkers on Earth, He was not totally omnipotent, and he certainly wasn't omnipresent. Hell was in a dimension that he had absolutely no powers over, so Satan could say, or do, what he liked. God would never be able to prepare for any possible tricks until the activities spilled out onto Earth or the hordes of Hell had set up battle camp outside the Pearly Gates. And even on Earth, the sheer enormity of being everywhere at the same time, and seeing into everyone's hearts and souls simultaneously, was impossible. When there had just been Adam and Eve, it had been easy, but for billions of people it was out of the question. He could look into specific people's minds if he selected them, and concentrated hard enough, or He could focus on a small room and scan a handful of people. Any more than that and He ran the very real risk of becoming psychotic from all the conflicting and confused voices in his head. Humans had become far too complicated and diverse. He definitely kept an eye on Earth and intervened in the bigger situations wherever He could, and providing it followed his grand design. But He understood all too well the full extent of cause and effect, as He had created it. Tragic events had to be allowed to run their course, so lessons could be learnt and good could come out of them. He appreciated that His believers wanted to believe and have faith that he was there, steering every single person's destiny. That He was benignly watching over them, every minute of the day and night – but if they knew the truth, they'd have been sorely disappointed. There was also the fact that some of the other powers He seemed to have been involuntarily imbued with were very creative, but not very practical and as He'd created evolution, he often let that take its course.

God stood there for a moment, looking at the small grey mobile phone in His hand. From long experience, He'd grown used to Satan trying to play mind games and tricks on Him, but deep down, He was an eternal optimist. In fact, Earth had been created because of that positive trait. And there was something different about this phone call. However, irrespective of anything else, He was curious and even if it was yet another trap He enjoyed foiling Satan's plans. It was like reading an Agatha Christie novel, trying to recognise who did it, and why, well before the last page.

Placing the phone down on the large white desk He settled in His blue office chair and took a sip of warm black coffee from a mug with 'THE Big Boss' printed on it. He didn't really need the drink, but he had to admit He liked the buzz that really strong coffee gave him. Letting out a sigh of appreciation He leaned forward and pushed a red button on the intercom. "Angelica, could you please come into My office for a minute or so?" He sat back again and surveyed the room. Everything was neat and tidy, as it always was. The paintings Raphael and Monet had painted for him on their arrival in Heaven hung on the walls. Beethoven's 15th Symphony was playing softly in the background. God had always found that a favourite and was glad Ludwig kept composing long after he'd stopped decomposing. Three recliner chairs were positioned around a small glass coffee table and sunlight shone through the office window, illuminating a fish tank where clown and yellow tang fish swam happily around bright coral alongside long extinct prehistoric grey Knightia and brown-speckled Dipterous fish. A deliberate paradox God had made as a private joke; both creationists and atheists alike would have their arguments and belief systems blown out of the water if they'd entered His room and seen it.

The cream coloured office door opened and, Angelica walked primly into the room. She was five feet two inches tall, with a slender build, long raven black hair and olive coloured skin. In life, she'd been the owner of a large haulage company in Southern California and had some success as a romantic author. She'd died in a tragic accident when she was handing out surfing trophies after a competition and one of the airhead surfers, too busy checking out her cleavage and slender legs, had slipped and impaled her with the tall and pointed trophy. Upon her death, and subsequent entrance into Heaven, she'd immediately requested a secretarial position working for Saint Peter and worked her way up the ranks to become God's personal assistant and trusted friend. "Hello Mighty One, how can I be of assistance?" she enquired. Her voice had a soft west coast American accent and whenever God heard it He could understand why so many of the male angels and younger saints fell so easily in love with her, tried their luck, and ended up heartbroken. She never led them on, but her kind manner and beautiful smile would have many in Heaven cutting off their wings and risking the fires of Hell for just one night with her. Sometimes, God made things just a little too perfect!

He smiled kindly before He began to speak. "Yes, thank you Angelica. I've had a very interesting telephone conversation with Satan, and he wants to set up a conference. It will be in two weeks' time and we've decided Hawaii would be a nice place to have the meeting. Could you get in touch with Dedan and brief him? I need him to go to Oahu and book the whole of the Terrapin Cove Hotel, on the north side of the island, and ensure security is tight. Satan is sending one of his demons to assist in dealing with arrangements, but obviously, I don't want him to take command and play any silly little tricks. I can imagine Satan trying to make my room a broom cupboard, or, be facing directly out onto a tree so that all I could see was foliage. So, make sure Dedan knows he has to take full control, and watch his back. He also needs to ensure I have the penthouse suite, facing the ocean. If you could arrange all the relevant paperwork, and money for him that would be wonderful. Have him tell them the whole building is needed for a top-secret conference of world leaders, chaired by the President of the United States, and I'll ensure he's believed and his requests are met. Also, organise for the portal to be opened so he can get there. Once that's been done I can brief the top angels, so they're up to speed and ready for the meeting and I'll also need Michael and his SWAT team on standby, just in case the talks take an unexpected turn. He knows the routine; certain modern weapons should be avoided. I doubt they'd use dragons this time, so please, no nuclear or chemical weapons." God had a soft spot for the chain of islands and remembered what happened to Atlantis after the last great battle – very unfortunate.

"Of course, Mighty One. I'll get things organized right away. Will there be anything else?" Angelica's smile was big and happy.

"Yes – could you bring me another cup of coffee?"

"Of course, Sire" she replied cheerfully.

God passed her His cup and watched her walk gracefully out of the office, closing the door behind her. Yes, He had to admit, that was one creation He was very proud of. He smiled to himself when He picked up the phone and began to dial…

Chapter 6 – Good? Meet Bad!

Grank stood uncomfortably in the lobby of the Terrapin Cove Hotel. He hadn't been on Earth for a very long time, and everything seemed so strange and different. Things had certainly moved on since the Bronze Age. When he'd decided to ask for a transfer, he hadn't expected this. He could see the well-stocked bar and smell the aroma of the fresh flowers mingling with the heady odour of freshly-brewed coffee. This certainly wasn't what he'd asked for, but he wasn't complaining. Looking around he saw the comfortable beige sofas strategically placed around the room, interspaced with teak wooden benches which had cushions made of the same material. There were a handful of guests, mostly in shorts and wearing garish shirts, sitting and talking or working on laptops while they drank cocktails. 'Bloody tourists' he thought to himself. He glanced at the window and caught sight of his reflection in the glass. He had to admit he liked what he saw. Satan had ensured he looked the part of a rich and influential business man. Six feet tall, his lean, muscular body was dressed in a discreet charcoal grey suit. Very smooth and sophisticated, which helped put him at ease. He felt awkward without his long, twisted horns, but he couldn't have everything. Not being able to impale enemies made him feel vulnerable. He'd been briefed well and knew exactly what to do, but he also knew the repercussions if he got anything wrong. He'd overseen punishments for long enough to appreciate that even for demons, it was better to give than to receive. He walked casually to the bar, sat on a vacant stool and perused the drinks menu. He had no idea what any of them were, so he chose one he liked the name of. Ordering a large Devil cocktail, he watched in amazement as the barman mixed the drink. Once the concoction was poured into a glass, he took a sip of the sweet red liquid and smiled. Oh yes, he was going to enjoy this mission. He would immerse himself in his role and play it to the full – a true method actor. Grank perused the cocktail menu while he continued to sip his current drink. So many choices, and he was interested in all of them. In the interests of purely scientific research, he should test them all.

Turning to the page with the ones starting with the letter 'A' he smiled. Today was going to be a very good day, indeed.

*****

Dedan had materialised on Oahu several hours earlier, but he'd been cautious and decided to reconnoitre the grounds of the resort before he entered the main building. He doubted there would be any traps, but there was no harm in making sure. The large golf course didn't look any more suspicious than any other golf course did. The golfers themselves appeared to have obtained their clothing from a tailor who was already destined for Hell, and no longer cared about style or panache. But he saw no Sabbia demons lying in wait for him in the sand traps or Umido demons in the water hazards. He'd surveyed the stables and admired the horses. He was relieved to discover they were calm when he observed them from a distance. They had a sixth sense for recognising angels and demons, so they started to get a little bit skittish when he approached, but he soon calmed them. The simple fact that they were calm before he got to them assured him there were no Bajang demons – disguised as cats – lurking in the shadows. He'd even taken the opportunity to take off his shoes and socks and enjoy the sensation of the sand between his toes on the beach. It was a simple pleasure, but he enjoyed it greatly and he seldom had time to appreciate such things in Heaven. There were so many delights; the little ones often went unnoticed. There was also the added benefit of lots of slim, tanned, bikini-clad women. Such sightseeing wasn't forbidden in Heaven but being such a high-ranking angel meant he was expected to set a good example and behave himself – not an easy thing for him. He was far from being a stickler for maintaining the rules, and he could have happily taken off his jacket and shirt and spent the rest of the day admiring the many views, applying suntan lotion to any willing female and swimming in the warm blue ocean – but he had a job to do. So reluctantly, he'd put his socks and shoes back on and made the short walk to the main hotel complex, happy that everything seemed as it should be.

31

Neither angels nor demons had specific powers to recognize their natural enemies when they'd taken on human, or animal, forms on Earth. They had to look for tell-tale clues and hope for the best. Sometimes it wasn't too hard – if a human wasn't doing something wrong, ever, he could be an angel or destined to be one. If a human was more destructive and vile than even the normal low standards of humanity, then he was worth a closer look to discover if he was a devil in disguise.

As Dedan walked past the swimming pool and into the hotel itself, he was met by a strange sound which made him suspect the demon he was looking for wasn't too far away. The sound he heard was a war song, coming from the direction of the lobby bar to his left. That would have been a pretty good indication a demon was probably responsible, but as this particular song was being sung in Sumerian, it was a pretty safe bet as to who was responsible. Languages which had been dead for nearly 4,000 years didn't tend to be heard in Hawaiian hotel lobbies, no matter how expensive they were, or how good the karaoke was. As Dedan approached the bar, he saw a tall, smartly-dressed man sitting on a stool slouching over the bar. He was holding a cocktail glass half-filled with green liquid, with a paper umbrella sticking out of it, and he seemed to be trying to teach the bemused barman the words to an ancient song which could best be described as a take on 'Eskimo Nell' – if she'd visited Sumeria and carried out a lot of lewd acts, some involving being run through with long, thick spears. However, his intepretation did lose a lot in translation. It seemed he was trying to sing a duet, but the barman's linguistic skills were letting him down badly.

The barman knew that drunken business men could make excellent tippers and this particular one had been very generous, but he had to maintain certain standards and besides he struggled with most of the words of the language he couldn't understand. With the accent and drunkenness, he just assumed it was a very smart tourist from New Jersey being nostalgic for his homeland. He got a surprisingly large number of those at his bar.

Although Dedan was able to choose any shape, or form, he wanted he wasn't vain and preferred to stick with the same appearance he had while he had first been alive. He managed to make his presence known without all the over bearing, and imposing, sizes that most demons seemed to opt for. He approached the drunken figure cautiously and gently tapped him on the shoulder. Grank hurriedly spun around on the bar stool, the contents of his glass spraying across the bar and floor in an arc. Leaning forward slightly and screwing up his eyes to focus, he looked directly at Dedan.

"Yes?" he demanded. "Wadda ya want?"

Dedan spoke to the barman. "It's alright; I hope my friend hasn't been too much of an annoyance. Please excuse us."

The barman smiled politely, nodded, and promptly took that opportunity to clean the other end of the bar.

"I presume" began Dedan, in a quiet and weary voice, "that you're here on behalf of a certain powerful person wishing to arrange a meeting in two weeks' time?"

These words seemed to sober up the demon and make him remember his purpose for being there wasn't to annoy the guests and work his way through the cocktail list, even though he'd managed a respectable effort and reached the letter 'T'. "Aargah! Yes," he blurted "I am Grank. And you are?" He held out his hand in half-hearted expectation of shaking the hand of the angel.

"The name is Dedan," he said, ignoring the proffered hand. "We don't have all day, so I suggest you do whatever you need to do to sober up, make yourself look something approaching presentable and I'll meet you at the reception desk area in five minutes. Do you think you can do that?"

Grank leaned back on his stool and saluted slovenly. "Yes sirrrrrr". He watched Dedan raise his eyes to the sky, mouth the words 'Why me?' and turn and walk off in the direction of the reception desk.

No matter how much alcohol had been consumed, sobering up was never a problem for the majority of demons. When they were trying to make deals for a person's soul, the ability to handle their liquor was a distinct advantage. But he decided it would be best to maintain appearances and disappear into the bathroom to smarten up a little. He checked his watch and made sure he didn't leave the bar for eight minutes. He'd be damned – or damned again to be more accurate – if he was going to rush around for an angel and give him the satisfaction of being on time.

Walking towards Dedan, he took the opportunity to observe his opposite number. He had to admit, the angel wasn't what he'd expected. He wasn't particularly tall, perhaps five feet eight inches, slightly stocky build but not fat, with neatly-cut brown hair which was thinning on top. He had a large, sharp nose and an angular, clean-shaven chin with a cleft. He wore a dark blue suit and carried a black leather briefcase, similar to Grank's, and the bottom of his trousers appeared wet, as if he'd just stepped in a deep puddle, yet his black leather shoes were dry. For some reason, he'd expected someone more like a Hollywood movie star. But he supposed angels were just like demons and came in all shapes and sizes; however, he certainly wouldn't have chosen that particular body for a trip to Earth. As Grank approached the massive white square block in the centre of the room, a clean and neat area of worktop manned by awaiting and cheerful staff, with 'Registration' in golden letters emblazoned above the check-in desk Dedan instinctively turned around to face him. He knew enough to never let a Demon sneak up behind him.

"Here, take this and don't say *anything*!" he instructed sharply, shoving a small black wallet into the demon's hand. "I'll do all the talking, and you just back me up."

"Of course, *sir*," Grank replied sarcastically. "I'll be as quiet as the grave." Which wasn't much of a promise, as Grank knew exactly how noisy graves could get if any Necrophilia demons happened to be in the area.

Dedan gave the demon a stern look, sighed and turned around to speak to the reception clerk. He gave the clerk, whose name tag revealed he was James, a warm smile and pulled out his own black wallet and opened it.

"Hello, errr, James. I'm Special Agent Dedan of the Secret Service and this here is Agent Grank of the FBI."

Grank flashed his badge nonchalantly in front of him, giving the clerk a withering and contemptuous glare. James was taken aback by such a frightening encounter. He'd only seen such things in the movies and in his mind secret government agencies meant only one thing – trouble. He just wished he hadn't smoked that 'pakalolo' joint last night. What if they'd found out and come to arrest him?

"How can I be of assistance, gentleman?" asked James, trying to keep the terror out of his voice and avoid slipping into the local Pidgin English.

"Relax, James," a smiling Dedan replied, "we're not here about you and your joints. It might be illegal, but it's not a sin which will send you to hell."

Obvious to the two guests James's tanned face turned ash white, as he swallowed heavily. The sudden urge to urinate was not so evident but equally powerful.

Dedan could read human's perceived sins as if they were name tags. A useful trick if he needed to unsettle someone, but he wasn't a Judgement angel, so didn't concern himself too much with what he saw in their souls. If he could put them back on the right path he would, but he wasn't trained in that line of work. Demon killing was normally his specialist talent.

"We're here on a more important mission. Could you please call the hotel manager? It's imperative that we speak to him." Dedan paused to let his words sink in. "And please, we don't want a big fuss, or our presence to become an issue. So we'd appreciate your discretion in this matter."

"Do we make ourselves clear, junkie boy?" demanded Grank sternly, enjoying the power the fake ID badge had over the obviously terrified clerk.

"Y-y-y-y-yes, sir. Err, sirs," he stammered. "Of course. I'll call him right away."

He picked up the telephone handset in trembling fingers and proceeded to dial a five-digit number. "Hello, Mr. Knight. Sorry to bother you, sir, this is James Kalau on the registration desk. Yes, I know procedures and rules sir, but there are two important law enforcement officers here and they're asking to see you straight away." He paused to listen for a moment. "No sir, Secret Service and the FBI." He paused again. "Yes, they do have badges, and no, they don't have any guns drawn. Very good, Mr. Knight, I'll let them know."

"Gentlemen, the hotel manager, Mr. Knight, will be with you shortly." James tried to offer them a casual smile, but the fear gripping tightly on his chest and sphincter made it look more like he was constipated. He couldn't help wondering how on Earth had they known about the joint.

"Thank you, James, you've been most helpful and I'll be sure to mention it to Mr Knight." Grank's tone was far from reassuring and did nothing to help calm James's nerves. It did however; create the opposite of constipation on his bowels.

They were joined by a short man, dressed in a smart suit and tie. His face was flushed and he seemed nervous. Knight prided himself on keeping a respectable and well run hotel, and the idea of undercover law enforcement officers wanting to see him as a matter of urgency filled him with dread. But at least they weren't uniformed police officers. That would have really disconcerted and upset the guests. And that would never do. "Good day, gentlemen, I'm the manager of the Terrapin Cove Hotel, Mr. Knight. Scott Knight. How can I be of assistance?"

Grank, seeing a chance to annoy Dedan, spoke first. "Mr. Knight, so glad to meet you." Shaking his hand firmly, he continued, "I'm Agent Grank and this is my assistant Mr. Dedan of the Secret Service. We're here on a matter of national security, so perhaps it would be better if we could talk somewhere a little more private. Your office, perhaps?"

Dedan inhaled sharply and chewed his lip at being called Grank's assistant but remained silent. Such slights would be remembered and he'd bide his time so he could regain full control of the situation. After all, he knew Satan was the one who wanted this meeting, so if he walked away, and advised God he shouldn't proceed, it would be Grank that would suffer in hell, not him.

"Of course, gentlemen, if you would please follow me." Quickly leading the way to a door at the opposite end of the lobby, Knight opened it and allowed the two men to enter ahead of him.

They found themselves in his secretary's office, where a middle aged blonde woman in a floral dress was sitting primly, working on a computer. On seeing her, Knight paused. "Er, gentlemen, perhaps you'd like something to drink while we talk. Coffee, perhaps?"

"Why thank you, Scott" Grank smirked, obviously enjoying the discomfort he was creating. "I would love a milky coffee with six sugars."

Dedan smiled. "No, thank you, Mr. Knight. I'm fine."

Mr. Knight spoke to his secretary. "Cynthia, could you please arrange for the drinks to be brought as quickly as possible? I'll have my usual."

Before she could reply, he'd ushered the two men into his office and closed the door.

"Please be seated, gents. And how can I be of assistance? I hope nothing is wrong." He scurried around his desk to sit down.

Pulling a piece of paper from his inner jacket pocket, Grank unfolded it and placed it on the desk in front of the bemused manager. "Before we start, it's important that you sign this document. It's just a formality, but we need a legal undertaking from you confirming that whatever is discussed here will be kept in the strictest confidence and that you won't impart any information to any foreign nationals."

Dedan coughed and quickly butted in, hastily getting to his feet. "I'm sure, Agent Grank, that there's absolutely no reason for Mr. Knight to sign the document." He grabbed the paper and shoved it in his jacket pocket. "You've been vetted by a higher authority and we know you're a good and honest man. We don't want you signing your life away, do we?" Turning to Grank, he stared at him through narrowed eyes. Here they were, trying to set up a meeting, and all Grank could think about was tricking some poor unsuspecting human into signing away his soul. Typical demon!

Grank raised his eyebrows and smiled innocently, shrugging as if to say 'What?'

Ensuring he maintained his authority, Dedan sat down again and proceeded. "Allow me to get to the point. The President has arranged an important, highly top secret summit meeting between the top world leaders for two weeks' time. This meeting could have critical consequences for the whole planet, and for reasons I'm not at liberty to discuss, we need to requisition this entire facility for the duration of the talks." Mr. Knight's jaw dropped, but Dedan continued. "Therefore, we need your full cooperation in this matter."

"But, but, but," stammered Mr. Knight. "This is a hotel! We have guests and bookings – we just can't help you. I wish we could, but we can't!"

Just then, there was a knock at the door and Cynthia entered, carrying a tray with the coffees on it and a small tray of biscuits. "Excuse me," she said and placed them on Mr. Knight's desk and quickly left.

Dedan raised his hands to Mr. Knight in a placating manner. "Please, I understand and appreciate your concerns and problems, and I do sympathise. However, as I said, this is of a magnitude that I'm not at liberty to discuss and should this all fall through, there will be hell to pay." Grank laughed quietly at his counterpart's joke. Ignoring him, Dedan continued. "Therefore, to ensure that the reputation and profit margin of your fine hotel are not unduly impacted, I'm empowered to recompense you and the owners to the tune of one billion dollars."

Mr. Knight was taking a sip of his coffee when he heard the amount, and promptly coughed and splattered coffee all over the desk. There was a lot of paperwork and costly arrangements to be made, to ensure all guests were relocated, but even taking into account those factors, he saw a lot of profit in what he was being offered. He tried to wipe up the spilt coffee from his desk as he spoke. "I think that the Terrapin Cove Hotel might be able to help you. Being a patriot, I feel it's my duty to assist the government in any way I can."

"Of course you are, Mr. Knight. Of course you're a true and loyal patriot," Grank smiled, his voice dripping with cold sarcasm. He could see into Knight's soul and see his fear, the tax avoidance he'd carried out over the years showed how much he truly 'supported' his government.

"What we need you to do," ventured Dedan, "is ensure the hotel is empty of guests two weeks from today. All staff will be required so they can go about their usual duties and all other arrangements will be made by the relevant government agencies. Security will be our responsibility, and we would appreciate it if all delegates, no matter where they're from, are extended the utmost courtesy and hospitality this hotel is so rightly famous for. We'll be here for no more than one week and then it's back to business as usual."

"I must remind you that this is a matter of utmost secrecy, and you must do everything in your power to ensure the media is not alerted. The last things we want are TV cameras or journalists trying to sneak in," Grank quickly added.

"Let me assure you, discretion is my middle name," smiled Mr. Knight.

"Well," added Grank, "I hope it is. Because if it isn't, you'll have to change your middle name to 'Painfully Tortured'."

Chapter 7 – Parting Is Such Sweet Sorrow…

As expected by both men, their simple mission was completed quickly and smoothly. Money was always good for oiling the wheels of big corporate machines, and massive amounts of the stuff tended to have people slipping and falling over themselves to be accommodating. Grank and Dedan left the hotel manager's office and returned to the lobby, both happy that they'd successfully completed the task despite the unhelpful presence of their sworn enemy. Both would happily have taken the other to a quiet corner and returned them to their respective dimension with the aid of a knife, gun or any heavy, blunt piece of furniture which happened to be within easy reach.

"Fancy a drink?" offered Grank. He'd enjoyed his investigation of the cocktails and he still had numerous letters of the alphabet to work through; he particularly wanted to try a Zombie. "My round!"

"No thanks, I have to get back and report to the Boss. Although I'm sure He's perfectly aware of how things have gone. Perhaps you might want to do the same?" Dedan had no desire to spend another second with the surly, sneaky demon, but he also felt badly about leaving *it* to wander around and cause problems. In previous encounters with his kind, it had been simple. A fight occurred, and it would be sent back to Hell, but he'd been given specific instructions and while he had the desire to obey them, he had no intention of breaking them. In a way, he hoped Grank would make the first move, but somehow, he got the impression all the demon really wanted was to get drunk and sing a few more lewd songs.

Dedan decided it would be safe to return to Heaven. After all, once he got there he could always dispatch a guardian angel to the hotel to ensure the drunken demon made its way back to Hell in a timely fashion. With that thought, he walked out through the hotel's revolving door. As it spun, he entered the dimensional portal and was gone – any witness would have seen a strange optical illusion where someone entered one side but didn't appear on the other. Fortunately, Dedan was always careful and his use of the portal wasn't seen by anybody, apart from the suspicious demon.

From his bar stool Grank watched Dedan disappear and smiled. Thinking on it, he decided he'd better get back to Satan straight away. The bar would still be here in two weeks. He walked over to the bathroom and as he walked through the door, he too entered a dimensional portal. There was a millisecond of almost imperceptible red light, and he too disappeared.

Mr. Knight's heart was racing. He couldn't quite put his finger on it, but the two undercover agents had seemed like the ultimate good cop, bad cop combination. In fact, Agent Grank had given him the impression he was always one second away from shooting him. He concluded that he'd better tidy up his tax returns and make sure they were in order. He'd been relieved when they'd left and decided he'd try and be available to greet the foreign dignitaries, but after that, he planned to stay hidden away in his office as much as possible. He thought the best way to take his mind off Grank was to spend the rest of the day making urgent phone calls. The CEO of the hotel chain was duly informed, and nearly had a heart attack at the mention of the amount of money the government was willing to give them. Inconveniencing some guests was unfortunate, but the money would make the necessity easier.

Without going into specific details, instructions were issued to staff and the obedient employees promptly started making arrangements for all guests to be relocated and generously recompensed for inconvenience caused. If anybody complained or made a fuss, they were told that a long-since dormant volcanic vent had been discovered directly underneath the hotel and there were fears of it collapsing and swallowing the whole complex. So, for the sake of the guest's safety, it was imperative they were moved to a safer location. The threat of sinking into a hot cavern below them was sufficient to calm any angry holiday maker and make them conform. This was ironic when they tended to ignore any clergy or holy man who gave them the same warnings!

The threat of instant dismissal and the dire warning that they'd never work on any of the islands again if anyone dared to discuss the situation was enough to maintain the staff's silence; added to the massive bonus promised on the proviso that everything ran smoothly, secretly and to plan. It wasn't until late in the evening when the last of the day staff completed their given tasks and reported back to Mr. Knight that all was arranged and there were no problems. The hotel would be ready, and he had every intention of making this part of paradise a heaven on Earth for his guests.

Chapter 8 – A Quiet Highway To Hell.

Grank wasn't used to the dimensional portal. God had designed it and there were two versions – the one going to Heaven gave a smooth and relaxing ride followed by a soothing arrival, leaving the traveller feeling as if they had just gently awoken refreshed from a long and comfortable sleep. The small highway to Hell was designed to be the complete opposite, which was why Demons disliked taking the trip to Earth or back, but then again, Earth was usually better than Hell, so what was the rush anyway?

The return journey to Hell had left Grank feeling like an industrial-strength vacuum cleaner had been stuck deeply up his rectum and he'd been sucked inside out, before the bloody mess was dumped on the floor and left to coalesce back to his normal demon form. He'd enjoyed his time on Earth, especially the alcohol-soaked section, but it felt good to be back in demon form. There weren't many mirrors in Hell, so he glanced down and checked his arms and legs, ensuring they were the correct shade of dark red and the scales were as they'd been before he left. He touched the top of his head and the razor-sharp horns felt great. Yes, it was good to be back. The portal into Hell wasn't very accurate or consistent and haphazard regarding where it deposited the demons. It wasn't unusual for a confused and disorientated devil to materialise in an unfamiliar ring of Hell, and spend days trying to find their way back to where they needed to be. It was far too embarrassing to ask for directions – for the male demons, at least! It wasn't uncommon for unfortunate demons to rematerialize inside a brick wall and spend a decade or so digging themselves out.

Sniffing the air, he caught a faint whiff of burning flesh which didn't really help work out where he was. Burnt skin was a common scent wherever you went in Hell. The walls were black and steaming which didn't help either, because the internal décor was unimaginative. Helpful signs, or mats, welcoming the damned to their respective eternal torture chambers were seen as a little too ironic, even for demons. He saw a door just ahead of him and walked up to it. Looking inside, he saw a long row of damned souls hanging upside down, while wizened old female nagging relatives wagged their fingers at them, or, prodded them with sharp umbrellas whilst they nagged and belittled. Grank smiled. He knew exactly where he was, it was the seventh ring, and this was an *Aunty* chamber. Who said demons didn't have a sense of humour when thinking up punishments and names for the chambers? Then, remembering that he had to report to his boss, he sighed in a resigned manner; he had a long walk to the inner circle of Hell and Satan's office, but at least he knew where he was.

On his journey along the seemingly endless corridors, he saw plenty of demons of various shapes and sizes and he noted the way they all seemed to treat him slightly differently. Word of his promotion and special mission had spread quickly, and Demons were eternal opportunist sycophants. They saw no harm in being in the good books of anyone important and right now, Grank was *the* demon to know. Should he fail they would, of course, be lined up to enjoy his fall from grace, but until then they smiled pleasantly as he walked past. Many bowed their heads slightly, and a few even offered him cheerful words of greeting. Although one demon saying to another demon, 'You're looking good', was always open to dangerous misinterpretation in Hell.

He turned into another corridor and saw the black and white rear end of a Friesian cow slowly plodding along. As he overtook it the cow stopped and looked at him. "Moooo, Moo, Mooo!"

"Why thank you Jon," replied Grank. "Yes, it went perfectly and everything is organized."

"Moo!"

"Yes, I'm sure it will be, catch you later." And with that, he left the cow to continue meandering down the hall. 'Demon cows,' he thought. They could be dumb, vicious and sadistic, but on a good day, and when they were trying to suck up to someone of higher rank than they were, they could be polite and quite pleasant.

Eventually, Grank made it to the inner ring of Hell. The screams emanating from the numerous damnation chambers had increased significantly as he got closer to the centre of Hell and here in the epicentre, he could hardly hear himself think. The smell here was almost overpowering, but he was used to such things. You didn't last very long as a demon if you had a delicate stomach. Ignoring two heavily armed guards he pushed open a large, arched wooden door, engraved with reliefs of souls suffering various forms of punishment. He briefly marvelled at the craftsmanship and wondered at how the artist had managed to get the elderberries looking so realistic; that was one punishment he never wanted to endure. Shuddering, he walked through the doorway. Traveling through long and dark corridors he finally reached the last part of the inner sactum and the secretaries office.

Stuart was sitting at his desk, reading a large parchment. "Oh, Grank, I'd heard you'd returned," he quipped in a disdainful tone, not looking up. "I take it everything went to plan, and all arrangements have been made?"

Hatred and anger were common emotions in Hell; as if the very walls emanated the stuff, it fuelled the demon's spirits and kept them meting out the eternal punishments without losing enthusiasm. But there was something about Stuart that Grank *really* hated with a passion. He couldn't quite put his finger on it. Perhaps it was his surly attitude, maybe it was his way of getting information, as if from nowhere, and knowing exactly what was going on throughout Hell. Or it could simply be his refusal to take proper demon form. What kind of demon was he? It was impossible to tell when he insisted on maintaining such a pathetic, snivelling form. But whatever the reason, Grank would have dearly loved to stick his fist down Stuart's throat, rip out his innards and hide them is some obscure flaming pit so he'd never find them again.

"I was given direct instructions by Satan himself and *not* you," Grank spat imperiously. "I will report directly to him and if you want to know how I did, you can ask him!"

Both demons stared at each other with undisguised contempt; the air heavy with tension. Grank's retractable claws silently extended from the ends of his fingers. He was waiting for an excuse to disembowel the insolent clerk. But Stuart knew better than to allow the situation to escalate. He remained seated, gripping the paperwork in a vice-like grip. He wasn't built to take on anything that big and being a fan of Machiavelli, he knew there were better ways to teach a demon a lesson. All he needed was time, patience and opportunity.

The silence was broken by Satan's booming voice coming from the other side of the door to his office. "Grank! Stop chatting with Stuart and get yourself in here now!" His tone made it clear he was in no mood to tell him a second time.

"Coming sir!" Grank shouted and he hurried to the door, keeping an eye on Stuart all the time. His would-be adversary was ignoring him though and busy reading his document again. His passive contempt broadcast clearer than any TV signal.

The door opened reluctantly and Grank stepped inside, pushing the noisy door shut behind him. He saw Satan, his arms outstretched, leaning against the large marble fireplace and staring intently into the flames. "Well," Satan enquired quietly, "how did it go? I take it everything has gone according to plan, and the arrangements have been made?" Raising his head, he turned to Grank. "I presume you haven't failed me!" Satan's voice was calm, but there was menace in his inflection which left Grank under no illusion as to what awaited him if he'd failed.

He managed to muster a reassuring smile. "Of course, Your Satanic Majesty. Everything went to plan, as per instructions. I would have enjoyed destroying the Angel and sending him back to where he came from, but I obeyed your instructions."

Satan nodded knowingly. He'd battled with heavenly angels many times, but if all went well, such situations could be consigned to history. "Good; excellent in fact." He paused for a moment, staring down into the fireplace. "It's been a while since I was last on the Hawaiian Islands." The memory of the volcano he'd created made him smile. "Did the venue look suitable?"

"Oh yes, Sire," Grank replied enthusiastically, "the hotel is spacious and I particularly enjoyed the bar. The cocktails were—" He stopped suddenly, realising Satan was staring at him with an angry expression. He swallowed hard, realising what he'd said. "Sorry Sire! I think the place will be ideal for you. I'm still not convinced however, that we'll be able to maintain privacy, it's a small island and even with my limited understanding of the modern human news process, I'm sure that as soon as the slightest hint of an international meeting taking place gets out, the media will be all over the place."

"Thank you for your concerns but let me worry about that. I own the souls of the biggest media barons on the planet; they didn't even need to sign over anything to ensure they'll eventually arrive here! I'll get a message to them and ensure they'll ignore us completely. I can even arrange a small war somewhere to keep them happy."

Satan walked across the room and sat down at his desk. "Thank you, Grank. That will be all, you may go."

Grank beat a hasty retreat from the office, knowing his presence would no longer be tolerated.

Sitting for a few minutes enjoying the quiet of the office, Satan lifted his head and bellowed, "Stuart! Bring me Maurice!"

The door to his office was quickly pushed open and Stuart stuck his head around it timidly. "Sire, excuse me – but did you just say Maurice?" There was a pause. "Are you sure?" He knew better than to question his master's instructions, but in this instance, he felt he needed to do so for the sake of clarity. Sometimes the risk of making a terrible mistake outweighed any punishment he might accidentally receive.

Satan held a glass of whisky in one hand and a large cigar in the other. He looked up and smiled a wily grin. "Oh yes. I did say that!"

It wasn't often when Stuart felt uncomfortable, but in this instance it felt as if Satan had stuffed his hand inside his rib cage and was squeezing his heart. "Yes Sire, straight away!"

Chapter 9 – Maurice.

As a human on Earth, Maurice had once been a pious, but hypocritical preacher travelling around central Europe in the middle of the seventeenth century, spreading the word of God while simultaneously stealing, drinking and indulging in his many sexual vices – human, animal and vegetable – wherever he went. He'd fallen terminally ill from a more-than-itchy sexual disease and with his final breath, he'd tried the old death-bed-confession trick, in the confident understanding that it would give him instant access into the open arms of Jesus, and all past indiscretions would be forgiven. He didn't realise, however, that such confessions weren't 'get out of jail free' cards and he'd tipped the scales of justice and bought his ticket straight to Hell long ago. His character made him definite demon material, but his unexpected arrival in Hell had left him confused and angry. His demonic appearance, which he acquired straight away, didn't help either. His body became short and squat, while his legs and arms stretched, resembling a child's action figure toy which had been left too close to a fire and melted. The overall effect was far from imposing, and it seemed as if he'd been the victim of an over-enthusiastic Los Angeles plastic surgeon, rather than being endowed with the face of evil.

As the decades turned into centuries, his hatred and resentment continued to grow and he became totally and utterly insane. Being nuts wasn't unusual in Hell – in some of the punishment chambers it was a boon and distinct advantage – but Maurice was off-the-scale crazy. He possessed all the conditions identified by Earth's psychiatrists and psychoanalysts and had more problems than they'd even dreamed of in their worst nightmares. His schizophrenic personalities had developed their own insane schizophrenia which started massive arguments inside his head. The run-of-the-mill psychopath would have run away and hidden under a bed, if he'd tried to find a home in Maurice's head. His Munchausen personalities had developed Fregoli delusions. The paranoid personalities had disassociation fugue, and the personalities who had Tourette's syndrome were very vocal in their violent arguments with the ones with intermittent explosive disorder. All these varied and conflicting voices had taken over Maurice completely and he'd compensated for his lack of physical presence by becoming a snarling creature that could only drown out the voices in his head by violence, or appease them by eating chocolate, or failing that, the flesh of other demons. And as chocolate was impossible to come by in Hell, he was left with the nastier, savoury options. He'd once got hold of some battle axes and proceeded to barricade himself in the demon's lounge where he managed to disembowel two Archdemons, decapitate six She-Demons and emasculate a rather startled-looking Earth Devil before feasting on his own personal buffet. His rampage was only brought to a halt by a phalanx of Marching Horde demons, rushing him and pinning him to the floor. In the process, the numerous troops had sustained broken bones, crushed genitalia, bloody lacerations and even torn-off limbs.

Ever since then he'd been locked in a dark, sound-proofed, room on the fifth ring of hell. He managed to escape once, by chewing through the stone wall and promptly destroying an entire damnation chamber and allowing the damned souls to get loose. In turn it had set off the biggest game of hide and seek Hell had ever seen. On his violent and bloody recapture, he was promptly wrapped in a steel straightjacket, a small cage was placed over his head and he was chained to a wall. When the door closed, leaving him in total darkness, it was assumed he would never be released from the room. At least he wasn't lonely in his empty darkness. The voices in his head kept him company and drove him ever further down the long, pothole filled road of insanity. Despite the supposedly soundproof cell, his screams could be heard in the corridor, and thanks to their nervous dispositions, the demon cows refused to go near the place; taking long, circuitous detours rather than risk hearing him. After all, nothing leaves quite a mess like a startled bovine.

The armour-clad Marching Horde demons were skilled and vicious warriors. They were trained in the various forms of mortal and immortal combat, willing and able to rip out a heart with more precision than a surgeon, and less emotion than a traffic warden giving out parking tickets. In battle, they experienced no fear and showed no mercy, but the twelve burly foot soldiers were definitely uneasy about their designated task. They knew of Maurice and his reputation and had no desire to go up against him with such a small detachment. Unfortunately, for them, the ability to fit one hundred soldiers of Hell in such a small room would have the equivalent of trying to fit a herd of demon cows in a coffin designed for a dwarf. Possible, but you'd need a meat grinder and a compactor to do it properly. Consequently, it was left to just a dozen to enter the cell, unchain Maurice and then somehow persuade him to join them in Satan's office. All while avoiding broken limbs or parts of their anatomy, that they particularly enjoyed, getting crushed. Even demons had to have hobbies!

Straws were drawn and the unlucky loser was tasked with unlocking and opening the heavy door to Maurice's home. When the dim light entered the long-dark room, a crouched, manacled and maniacal figure was illuminated, chained to the far wall. He was having a loud and heated argument with himself regarding which was the best filling for a sandwich being eaten on a Saturday afternoon. Several of his personalities were favouring cheese, but the rest of the voices couldn't agree if ham, corned beef or chicken was tastiest. If his arms hadn't been restrained by the straight jacket, he would have been in a bloody fist fight with his caged head.

The Marching Hordes took the opportunity to enter the room silently – or at least, as silently as twelve heavily armoured soldiers could manage. However, they weren't silent enough and Maurice noticed them enter. Seeing the light and his new guests, he immediately adjourned his inner debate and proceeded to strain on his chain like a rabid dog, lashing out with his feet and attempting to head butt anyone foolish enough to get into range.

The element of surprise gone, they had no backup plan. All they could do was dive on top of Maurice and pin him to the floor, suffering through any blows inflicted on them. Once he was immobilised, one of the Horde released Maurice's chains and locked a rigid metal brace, attached to a long steel pole, around his neck. When that was done, the exhausted guards retreated to the relative safety of the doorway; sustaining more blows in the process.

Holding onto the pole, they dragged Maurice out of the cell. This battle continued along the corridors as he was dragged reluctantly toward his meeting with Satan. Several demons that happened to be passing, were indiscriminately kicked or rammed, but the Horde were unconcerned with collateral damage, just relieved they weren't bearing the brunt of the injuries.

Eventually they reached their destination. Few of the Marching Horde had ever needed to visit the inner ring of Hell, and none of them had seen the inner sanctums, but they were too busy with their unruly charge to survey much of the room. All eyes were very much focused on the figure currently spinning around in his neck brace like a whirling dervish who had danced too close to a fire and had set his costume alight and was attempting to extinguish the flames by kicking the invisible clothing.

Satan looked from Maurice to the obviously terrified guards and smiled. "Oh, so this is Maurice. Thank you, gentleman, I've changed my mind; you can take him back now."

The Hordes froze and to a man, turned and stared at Satan with open mouths.

"Only joking," Satan laughed hysterically. "Don't just stand there, Maurice; come in and make yourself comfortable."

The recognition that he was being addressed by someone made Maurice more energetic in his futile struggle. His kicks into empty space grew fiercer and his legs took on an elasticity they hadn't previously shown; making the danger zone from his kicks even wider. "Frargle, grang, arrggggg!" he screamed.

"Where are my manners? You," Satan pointed to the nearest Horde, "take off his helmet, so we can see each other and have a proper conversation."

The unfortunate demon looked at Satan with a startled expression, and pointed at his chest as if to say, 'Who? Me?'

Satan raised an eyebrow. "Yes, you. Get on with it, will you – I haven't got all day. *Idiot*!"

Not wanting to add further insults to his forthcoming injuries, the Horde ran up to the prisoner and unlocked then ripped off Maurice's visor under a continual barrage of painful blows. Unfortunately, he wasn't quick enough and lost two fingers to Maurice's razor-sharp teeth. Even before the pain registered in his brain, his fingers were swallowed. Demon physiology meant they would grow back eventually, but that didn't make the pain any less severe. His task done he ran, stumbling wildly, back to the relative safety of his colleagues.

Maurice seemed momentarily calmed by the sudden burst of increased light and the taste of the light snack. He'd always loved finger food. Maurice stood motionless, silently taking in his surroundings, panting heavily until he caught his breath.

"See? Isn't that better, Maurice? It's so very difficult to have a proper conversation with someone, when they can neither see nor hear the other person."

Recognising his host, Maurice stood and stared at Satan, eyes angry and filled with a red rage. The burning pain in his brain had him wishing he was free, so he could grab hold of the cause of his problems and tear him a new ring of Hell!

"Oh, good," Satan smiled coldly. "I can tell by the look in your eyes that those strange little demons inside your head have quietened down enough for you to recognise me. It's so very embarrassing, having to introduce myself to a long-standing resident in my own domain! Could I offer you a drink? Perhaps a cigar?"

The Marching Hordes gasped collectively, at the prospect of going anywhere near Maurice's mouth and teeth with anything other than a long spear. Nobody held a desire to lose any digits in the process of pouring whisky down his throat, or, placing a Cuban cigar between his lips.

Maurice snarled and snapped in Satan's direction. "Frraaaarrr. Arrrrrggggg, sneeeer!" he shouted. Saliva accompanying the noises from his mouth, like wet, frothing punctuation marks. He kicked his legs wildly, but futilely, in Satan's direction. All the voices in his head were still chattering and screaming, but this time they were all saying the exact same thing – 'Destroy'.

"Tsk, tsk, tsk Maurice – such a disrespectful greeting! I'd have thought that after so much time on your own, you would have welcomed some company – other than the voices in your head, of course. Perhaps you might even fancy a nice game of chess!" Satan's taunting, sarcastic voice did nothing to calm his ranting guest. "Now listen to me, you pathetic, snivelling little clown-faced maggot. If there's any of your own brain left inside that twisted little head, I think you'd better switch it on and listen to me!" Satan's voice was stern and his eyes glowed red with rage.

Abruptly, Maurice straightened up and stared Satan directly in the eye. "Yes, I'm listening. What do you want?" His voice seemed calm and controlled, far different to his previously manic reactions.

The members of the Marching Horde were taken aback by this sudden transformation, but Satan remained impassive. "Excellent, my twisted little gargoyle. I knew you were in there, somewhere. Now stand still, keep quiet and listen very carefully. I have an important job for you…"

Chapter 10 – But Some Go To Heaven.

Dedan's return to Heaven via his own dimensional portal was – unlike the one to Hell – very pleasant and comfortable. He'd landed at his designated arrival point refreshed, relaxed and experiencing the euphoria that, on Earth, was not dissimilar to being stoned after eating a tray full of marijuana-laced chocolate chip cookies – only without the ensuing munchies.

"Wowwww," he mumbled, checking himself in the full-length mirror hanging on one of the pristine white walls. Ensuring his appearance was satisfactory, he straightened his tie and flattening a stray strand of hair before he left the room and headed to Heaven's central office. He suspected that God had been observing the series of events on Earth, but it was only polite to report in and receive any further holy orders. Besides, he – along with many other of his colleagues – harboured a massive crush on Angelica, so he welcomed the opportunity to see her and try to gain a look down her cleavage. Discreetly, of course, because he was a gentleman at heart.

He took in a deep breath, inhaling the sweet, floral scented air. It was cool and soothing, and made him feel happy. As always, Heaven's sound system ensured each resident heard the type of music they most wanted to hear and which best suited their moods. In Dedan's case, he heard rock music playing softly in the background. It was always great listening to Duane Allman and it seemed as if he'd written a new tune, which sounded great.

Dedan walked past three beautiful female angels, dressed in flowing, cream silk robes. They were discussing the latest movie heartthrob who'd arrived that day. When they saw Dedan, one started to giggle mischievously. "Hello Dedan," she greeted. "Welcome back. Did you have good time on Earth? Did you bring me anything nice?" This was accompanied by giggles from all three of them.

Dedan offered them a massive smile, spreading his palms outwards in an apologetic gesture. "Emily, Roxy, Ruth. I am so sorry, ladies. Neither time nor opportunity was on my side for this trip. If I could but bring you the moon and stars, I would lay them at your feet as gifts, but alas, their beauty wouldn't compare to you three celestial bodies." He smiled and winked. His words were met with friendly laughter as he continued his journey.

"Dedan" another of them shouted to his back, "you are so full of shit, but we still love you for it. Perhaps you could take us with you on your next business trip to Earth? You wouldn't be sorry!"

Without turning, he waved his hand in the air, acknowledging the comment. "You never know Ruth, you never know. But where I go, you do not always go, and where I stay you are not always allowed. Don't forget that it's thanks to you that I'm no longer allowed in Salt Lake City!" He smiled at the memory. It was a good job that love-making wasn't considered a sin between two consenting adults – no matter how imaginative it was – otherwise both he and Ruth would have been banned from Heaven after that mission. He'd managed to fix the wardrobe, stop the leaking tap in the bathroom and paid for the damage to the bed, so he couldn't see what all the fuss had been about. Sure, they'd been a bit noisy, but sometimes such things couldn't be helped and Ruth calling out God's name had, fortunately, been ignored by God. He had enough discretion not to answer such calls when He did hear them. It had been the first time he'd been on Earth with a genuine saint and someone who had a whole book of the Bible written about them, and he had to admit the chapters and verses didn't do her justice. Unfortunately, – then as now – men tended to get the best write ups.

Arriving outside Angelica's office door he tapped gently and walked straight in. He saw her standing by a filing cabinet, sorting out some folders. She was wearing a tight white blouse, a short black pencil skirt, black stockings and black, high-heeled shoes. There was something about her look that really turned him on. He couldn't put his finger on what it was, but he would have liked to.

"Angelica, Angelica, my fair angel! Oh, how accurate your parents were when they had named you. You light up the room with your presence! Heaven wouldn't be the same without you." His smile had broadened, and his eyes twinkled as he spoke.

"Hello Dedan. You're so full of shit, if you sneezed it would be brown," replied Angelica with laughter in her voice.

"Funnily enough, you're not the first person to say something similar to that today."

"Yes, Dedan, and I'm sure I won't be the last." She offered him another sweet, genuine smile. "That sort of cheesy line might work on some of the females who go on business trips with you, or some starry-eyed angel on a fluffy cloud, but in this office, you're wasting your breath." They both laughed. Angelica had to admit Dedan made her smile, and she genuinely liked him and held a mild attraction for him, but she wasn't going to admit it. She had plenty of admirers and enjoyed the attention.

Placing his hand against his chest, Dedan spoke. "Be still my beating heart, lest it should break. How could you say such a thing? You know I only have eyes for you, my sweet angel."

Raising her chin, she looked along her nose at him. "Salt Lake City? Cairo? Manchester? Rio? Even Detroit! Need I say more? Don't forget, I get all the reports and I know what you get up to. I might get your eyes, but it's the rest of your body that's the problem!"

Dedan gave her a look of mock hurt. "For you, my love, I would gladly give up such dangerous missions. Besides, I'm in serious risk of severe injury one of these days. Anyway, I can't spend all day listening to you begging me for a date; is the Boss in?"

"Terribly sorry for wasting *your* time Dedan. I'll try and control myself in future. Yes, He is in his office and He's expecting you. Go straight in."

Walking to the big white door, Dedan tapped gently on one of the panels, opened it and walked through, closing the door behind him. Angelica returned to her filing, smiling and shaking her head in mock disdain.

Dedan always liked visiting God's office. The décor and his taste in artwork was exquisite. As always, sunlight shone directly on the fish tank and he noticed the anachronistic fish, happily swimming alongside the modern varieties. The combination of colours and shapes were beautiful, and he wished he could spend all day watching them. The therapeutic effects weren't needed in Heaven, but he could think of worse ways to pass an afternoon. Pausing, he noticed the music playing in the background; he had no education in classical music, so he had no idea who had composed it, but the power of the piece filled his spirit with serene joy.

"It's Mahler," God said from behind His desk, as if reading Dedan's mind. "Mahler's twenty-second symphony, to be more precise. He's kept himself busy since he joined us. I commissioned him to write it for Me, to commemorate the creation of the United Nations. Good, isn't it?"

"Yes," replied Dedan, "classical isn't normally my cup of tea, but I must admit I like it."

He took note of God's current appearance. He was used to Him changing His appearance, and even gender, to fit

His mood and some of His choices frequently amazed Dedan. Among other things, Dedan had seen Him as a blonde woman; a dwarf who looked as if He'd lost Snow White; a Kalahari Bushman, and a two-year-old boy with ginger hair. Today, God had gone for what could best be described as a country gentleman from the southern states of America. A white suit covered a stocky build, and he had greying white hair and a short, neatly-trimmed, grey beard. To add to the affectation, he had a pair of totally redundant half-moon spectacles resting on the bridge of his nose. A small part of Dedan expected God to use a deep-south drawl, making him sound like a cartoon rooster. Fortunately, He'd plucked for a more appropriate booming, but friendly voice.

"I saw the mission went well. Thank you, you did an excellent job. Do you foresee any problems?" enquired God. "Naturally, I'll make sure we experience perfect sunshine during our meeting."

Dedan settled in a chair opposite God, crossing his legs casually at the ankles. "As far as any meeting with Satan or his demons go, I could spend a long time going over all the possible problems. I think we'll need plenty of security and be on our guard for any of Satan's tricks. But as for the venue and the earthly aspects, I think everything should run smoothly. The hotel manager's love of mammon was enough to ensure he'd do what was needed, to guarantee we have a comfortable stay. Despite the fact we have to share the experience with *'them'*, I'm quite looking forward to it."

God nodded sagely. He fully understood Dedan's concerns, and if anyone had asked Him, He would have admitted He didn't feel comfortable with the situation either. There was always the danger of a trap. Despite many wars and tricks, however, Satan had never got the better of Him. He'd come close shortly after the Napoleonic wars, when God had intervened to help some orphans, but those were exceptional

61

circumstances and God had learnt a valuable lesson about never underestimating His enemy.

"Don't worry," God said, pausing to drink His coffee, "I'll have Michael and his army on standby; secreted along the ridges of the Ko'olau Mountain range. At the first sign of any trickery, he'll be with us, armed to the teeth and ready for battle. I want to avoid such a situation though; the paperwork alone would take years – but if needed, at least we're prepared."

"Do you think he's genuine?" Dedan enquired. "It just sounds too good to be true and I'm sure you're in no rush to let Satan, or any of his mob, through the Pearly Gates. Peter would have a fit."

God chuckled at the image of St. Peter, ripping up his book of 'Good Souls'. "I'm sure Satan isn't on the level, but no matter what, I have to give him the benefit of the doubt and listen to what he says."

"Your Majesty?" Dedan began hesitantly, "can I request that I be allowed to lead the security team? I've carried out reconnaissance of the area and identified some useful places to post guards and avoid possible traps."

"Of course, Dedan. I was thinking of offering the job to you anyway. You did a great job when you were down there. Michael has his troops ready, but I'm happy for you to select your own team for the hotel. Just tell everyone not to get distracted by the scenery and to watch their backs, unless they want some demon leaving daggers in them. Oh, and one more thing before you ask…" he added, tilting His head forward so that he could look theatrically at Dedan over the top of his glasses, "no, you can't take Angelica with you on the assignment. I know exactly what you're like and I *won't* have you getting up to your usual shenanigans with her."

In addition to being a fabulously efficient personal assistant, God liked Angelica because she had a wonderful personality and Dedan did have a habit of getting his fingerprints on all his previous female assistants. He knew Angelica could take care of herself, but why put temptation in either of their ways?

Dedan smiled sheepishly. There was no point in pretending he wasn't about to make the request. The sun, sand and sea breeze would have been perfect for him to engage his seduction techniques. And he also realised why God had chosen to wear the half-moon glasses. The look he'd been given had been marvellously dramatic and God had made His point perfectly. "Of course, your Majesty. I'm sure she'll have enough to do up here. Thanks for the job, I won't let you down."

God glanced into his now-empty coffee mug absent mindedly. "Yes, I know you'll do fine, don't worry about it."

"Is there anything else, Your Majesty," Dedan said, peeking at the door and contemplating a few more minutes chatting up Angelica and, if possible, admiring her legs.

God put his cup down on his desk "Ask Angelica to bring me another cup of coffee."

Chapter 11 – This Is Shinola.

God did have his own army but they were more a collection of reservists rather than a permanent standing force. They'd come to heaven across the millennia and happily maintained their training, ready for any eventuality. While they hadn't been kept busy, what they lacked in modern warfare experience they more than made up for with enthusiasm. Although they all wore the same, standard-issue one piece black jumpsuits, Roman Centurions rubbed shoulders with Boxer Rebels and English Red Coats, and they were all eager to fire their standard issue sub-machine guns in battle, instead of mock exercises. Such exuberance was a concern to God and, sometimes, he suspected deploying them on Earth would be like searching out a gas leak with a lit match; but in certain cases he had no choice and it was better to have them, rather than risk letting Satan win.

St. Michael was known as the Taxiarch, or 'Brigadier' and he was directly in charge of God's vast army. He had exceptional medical skills, which could be applied to both mortal and immortal alike, and he'd defeated Satan before, but he was also aloof, boring and had absolutely no sense of humour. His troops joked that the injured never needed anaesthetic when Michael was treating them. All he had to do was talk in his monotone voice, and they'd be fast asleep within twenty seconds. Ever since God called him into His office and told him about the meeting with Satan, St. Michael had been busy rallying his troops and preparing them. He was in his element and had come up with an almost endless list of possible scenarios should he be called into action; each one requiring detailed plans and confusing, or conflicting, battle strategies.

Although angels and demons were immortal, they could be 'killed' and in the ongoing skirmishes which had been erupting since long before the Book of Revelations, both sides had suffered every imaginable form of death at the hands of their eternal nemeses. Similarly, to humans, at the time of their

64

death's, they went to their respective dimensions, but unlike humans who tended to either go straight to Heaven or Hell, the angels and demons killed on Earth found the process of re-entry to their normal home a much longer process. It could take up to five years for their souls to rematerialize, painfully, and even then they had to wait before they could even think of returning to Earth. God had created the system to operate deliberately slowly, so the combatants didn't get killed and instantaneously reappear on the battle field to continue fighting, like a character from an action video game. The safety measure made both sides maintain an element of self-preservation and not just rush around, killing enemies and quickly being killed themselves. Thanks to the enforced attrition it also stopped all subsequent, genuinely holy wars from lasting forever. Michael had drilled this danger into his troops and felt certain they would be alright on the day. He just wished that, for once, God would issue him with the 'Sword of Uncreation'. It had been forged eons ago, by a skilled Sadducees priestess and part-time swordsmith and was the only weapon which could truly destroy an enemy and consign them to total and utter oblivion. But God had quickly seen the danger in such a weapon should it inadvertently fall into the hands of Satan, or some skilled demon, so he'd safely hidden it on Earth and resolutely refused to reveal to anyone where it was ever since. With the sword in his hand, Michael felt sure he could end the conflict between Heaven and Hell once and for all, without the need for all the peace talk nonsense. He refused to trust Satan and he was convinced there would be several regiments of the Marching Horde lying in wait for God as soon as He walked through the hotel door. How that many demons would fit, unnoticed, in the hotel's lobby wasn't something he'd really thought about, but in his head, he was sure they would be somehow hiding behind the sofas and lampshades. The best thing would be for a squadron of winged angels, armed with bombs, to carry out a pre-emptive strike and blow the hotel off the face of the Earth, minutes before any of God's negotiating team got there. Any collateral damage done to humans was unfortunate but would ensure them their place in Heaven. Michael saw that as a win-win situation.

He had row after row of troops lined up and was meticulously inspecting each and every one of them. He'd be damned if he'd let any of his soldiers go into battle with a top button undone, or less than shining boots. Discipline and smartness were his mantra and he was convinced those points were half the battle. To him, the demons were slovenly and undisciplined and no match for his men. What good were dirty horns when up against trained soldiers in clean footwear?

After hours of standing to attention, carrying their weapons and full battle kit, waiting for Michael's inspection to end, the only mantra his troops could think of was 'this man is an arsehole'. They all hoped he'd take the first bullet, regardless of whether it was friendly or not, so they didn't have to put up with his pompous, self-righteous, gung-ho attitude to war. They were trained and ready for the dangers and horrors of battle, but they'd rather not put up with this first.

Chapter 12 – Blunt.

Blunt wasn't the name he'd had when he was a human on Earth, pre-death and damnation days. On his arrival, it had quickly become apparent to the other demons that he wasn't the sharpest tool in the box, so he'd acquired his new sobriquet for all eternity. It was true, he'd have serious difficulty spelling 'IQ', never mind telling anyone what it meant. His lack of intellect was more than compensated for however by his fearless approach to fighting. Someone once said courage was being afraid and still carrying on. Any definition applied to him was more likely to suggest that Blunt was too stupid to see the danger and just carried on obliviously. His talents had been recognised immediately and he'd been made a member of the Marching Hordes. Whenever they had a mission, Blunt was usually selected to be part of the team as he could be relied upon to rush straight in and fight until he eventually collapsed from exhaustion. This tenacity allowed him to rise through the ranks without needing any military skills, foresight or talent. So in many ways, he wasn't dissimilar to many army officers on Earth. His presence on a battle field usually spelled trouble, although not for Blunt as he couldn't spell the word. His victories, despite his total lack of any tactical skill, had made him a hero to his fellow soldiers, so they'd gladly follow him anywhere.

Although Satan had reservations about putting Blunt in charge of the Marching Horde, and the rest of the army, for such an important mission he was certain if he put enough skilled generals under his command, they'd focus his energies and point him in the right direction so he fought against angels, rather than a random troop of cub scouts who'd accidentally hiked into his field of vision. Consequently, upon the announcement of his ultimate promotion, the foot soldiers met the news with cheers and drunken celebrations which Blunt happily joined in with. The overlooked generals hadn't been so gracious and took the news with a great deal of resentment, anger and jealousy. But they knew better than to question Satan's orders or share their emotions with fellow officers, in case it gave others an excuse for backstabbing, both real and figurative. They'd been in Hell for a long time and could have written the book on how to bide their time. A book they felt sure that, if it did exist, Blunt would not have been able to read; even if it did have lots of pretty pictures which he could colour in with children's colouring sticks.

After the initial drunken celebrations finished, Blunt stood before his loyal, and reasonably attentive, army. They could hardly be accused of standing to attention; most were sitting on the hard, stony ground in one of the more comfortable chambers of Hell. The flames flickering over the walls gave plenty of light, the smell of sulphur wasn't so obvious and the screams of the damned in adjacent rooms were hardly audible. Some soldiers laid on the ground, either watching him or sleeping off the effects of having consumed enough alcohol to not only destroy the livers of a ship full of Royal Navy sailors, but also to drown them in the process. But those who were conscious were transfixed by their leader, who was built like the proverbial stone-constructed outside toilet. He might make an easy target for any enemy, but he certainly made a great defensive shield for a whole battalion of his troops. He'd never been fond of the idea of losing his human form, so he'd demanded to keep his almost-simian shape and no bureaucratic demon wanted to risk arguing with him.

Currently Blunt stood in front of the various shaped demons, looking very out of place. He'd searched his brain trying to find some words that might inspire his troops. His craggy face, furrowed mono-brow, and, dark squinted eyes, gave the impression he was straining to remember a complex Shakespeare soliloquy. His features morphed into a pained look which gave him the expression of someone constipated and trying not to be. His mouth opened then closed again. Whatever elegant words had come to the front of his brain had either found it too lonely a place, or just not recognised the scenery and gone back home. All this facial gymnastics had his audience mesmerised. They were just willing him to speak, something, anything just to break the suspense.

Finally, a few, almost random, words joined together like a chaotic daisy chain and escaped from his mouth. "Thank you. My head hurts!"

At those words, the gathered, conscious, army gave out a rapturous cheer. To them, such utterances were the ultimate recognition of a fantastic night of drinking. To get Blunt past the inebriation state, so his head hurt, was high praise indeed.

Encouraged by the reception his initial words had engendered, Blunt was confident enough to continue his in-depth monologue. He smiled and then added, "I want to fight. Anyone else fancy ripping the wings off some angels?"

Those words had the demons on their feet, cheering. Their attention span wasn't long anyway, so brevity was definitely the wit in their souls. Such mental and verbal exertion had taken Blunt to the edge of his intellectual limits, so even if he had more to say, he wouldn't have been heard above the din of the appreciative and enthused multitudes in front of him. The noise had woken up the sleeping demons and, despite missing the speech, they joined in the general cacophony as they thought it was best to be seen to be excited by whatever they'd missed. The generals standing uncomfortably behind Blunt glowered at the back of his head. In just eighteen clumsily formulated words, he'd managed to inspire and motivate the entire army of assorted demons in a way all their military skill and cunning could never have done. They would have droned on for hours about 'falling for the greater good' or 'the glory of battle', but they'd never have injected so much energy into their audience, and certainly wouldn't have received such loyalty. They didn't know whether to join in the cheering, in recognition of Blunt's achievements, or just allow their hatred and resentment to continue to seethe and boil. Opting for a middle option, they smiled painfully and clapped politely. Although being an officer in a demon army was no guarantee of loyalty or protection from becoming the target of their own side the generals looked out at the sea of cheering demons and felt assured that the scent of the right blood was filling their nostrils and if the fighting started then they would blindly charge in roughly the right direction and protect them rather than making them the initial fatalities.

The vast army, on the other hand, couldn't be bothered with their supposed betters. To them, most officers were only good for starting the fight; after that, they'd best keep running ahead or just get out of the way, as they might get trampled by the real soldiers. There was no particular loyalty to any of the generals and they would just as readily eviscerate them, as an Angel general. The troops would probably enjoy it more as well. The head of a decapitated demon general decorating the end of their spears would have made a great trophy going into battle, and certainly made any Angel soldier think twice about challenging that particular demon warrior.

Blunt was totally oblivious, and apathetic, to the hidden animosity looming behind his massive back; he was just overwhelmed by his loud reception. He turned to face his generals, giving them a naive but genuine smile and the double thumbs up sign. "Right, when do we get tooled up?" he enquired.

The generals glanced at each-other, all of the same mind. None of them fancied trying to sort out the mess left by their hungover, but over-excited army, if they got hold of weapons too early. Perhaps in hindsight, it would have been better if Blunt had given his motivational speech once they'd set up camp on Earth. They quickly looked from at each other, faced Blunt and simultaneously shouted *"Later!"*

Chapter 13 – Nice View; Now What?

St. Michael had to admit that God had chosen a beautiful, if tactically flawed, location for his encampment. The view from the top ridge of the Ko'olau range was breath-taking and he could see the hotel in Kuilima Cove clearly. He could also spot the road going around the range, and the tranquil blue ocean beyond Kahuku Point. Any approaching demon army would be spotted easily and should they attack, the angels would have the definite advantage of higher ground. There were plenty of steep cliffs to take aim and destroy their foe. But there was one strategic disadvantage of being in such a place – how was he supposed to get down from the mountain and come to God's assistance in the hotel if there was an attack? The winged angels could be there in a matter of minutes, but not all his troops were in the winged section. They had to get down the hard way and that would take several hours, leaving them all exhausted in the process. They'd need several more hours to catch their breaths and prepare for battle and even worse they'd have dirty footwear. By that time, he suspected, the entire contingent of angels in the hotel would be slain; God would have been dragged into Hell and already be suffering multiple tortures. The thought made Michael's blood run cold, and he tried to avoid imagining them. He'd seen what the demons did to many unfortunate prisoners during the wars of the Apocalypses, it was no way for a soldier to go and ever since then, he hadn't been able to look at watermelons and potatoes without his eyes watering.

Looking northeast of his position, he saw a broader stretch of land, free of houses and holding very few buildings. It looked verdant, an ideal place to relocate to and the hotel looked easily accessible from the position should they be required. He could always leave a small detachment of winged angels up here for reconnaissance; they could keep watch and notify him of any enemy movements. He turned to his subaltern, a bespectacled angel named Bernard. "What's the name of that place down there?" he asked, gesturing to the flat low area.

71

Bernard perused the small map in his hands. "Er, it's the James Campbell National Wildlife Refuge."

"Fine, muster the troops. We're relocating and our new camp is going to be there," Michael announced grandly.

When the new order was communicated to his army, crowded along the narrow ridge, they showed mixed emotions. Relief because they would no longer have the risk of accidentally falling over the steep, high cliff, but also frustration, because they had a long dusty march and climb down the mountain to reach the new camp. They knew that when they got there, before they had a chance to pitch their tents, they'd have to spend ages cleaning their boots!

Like all armies throughout history, the common soldier's right and prerogative has been to complain and grumble about anything and everything. Similarly, it's been the right, and necessity, for officers to ignore them. This was no different for St. Michael's celestial troops. Freedom of speech was met with the equal freedom to ignore. A perfect balance which was also adopted by most of the leaders in democracies, on earth when the people spoke to them.

The heavenly soldiers, having once been human, knew how to gripe. It was too hot. Their kit was too heavy. Their boots were too tight. Their main grumble currently was having to march down the hill instead of using the portal to transport them quickly, efficiently and safely to their new base. Using that method of transport would have been the simple, easy option, but St. Michael hadn't thought of it so consequently, it wasn't a great idea.

When the troops finally marched into their new encampment, they were disconcerted to see the grassy area was already teeming with an enormous collection of 'people'. Dressed in blue denim dungarees or boilers suits, they were carrying a selection of weapons ranging from obsolete flintlock pistols, muskets and blunderbusses, through to high tech laser-guided rocket launchers, sub-machine guns and AK47's. They were sitting beside shabby tents, drinking beer and barbequing local wildlife.

Despite both armies being in human form, they immediately recognised their counterparts for what they really were. The chance of a human redneck convention being on the same island as a ninja outing, at the same time, was highly improbable. Both groups immediately snatched up their weapons and froze, waiting either for orders, or for somebody to loudly break wind so they could start fighting.

St. Michael wasn't averse to fighting demons, but he had his orders and decided, that discretion was wholly better than valour. He marched up to the nearest demon, one wearing a baggy boiler suit and sporting a greasy mullet and spoke in a booming voice. "Bring me your leader!"

Unaccustomed to being ordered about by a saint, the demon stood open-mouthed and stared at St. Michael vacantly. He recognised authority, but he was certain he shouldn't be responding to it, and certainly not obeying.

Silence persisted for several minutes, before one of Blunt's generals, dressed in a blue suit, casually walked up to St. Michael.

"Yes?" he enquired. "What can I do for you?"

"Who are you? Are you in charge of this scum?" Michael demanded pompously.

"I am General Mara. Field Marshall Blunt is indisposed. Who are you?"

"Me? I'm St. Michael, leader of the Heavenly army of God, protector of the sacred light, defender—"

"Yes, yes, I'm sure you are. Well done and congratulations, but I didn't ask for your life story. Now, what do you want?"

Used to more respect and a civil attitude, Michael was taken aback by the interruption and sarcastic response was momentarily silenced. But he soon got his mind back on track. "I demand that you immediately leave this place and go elsewhere. This is our chosen location for encampment and I insist you vacate it *now*!"

"No. Sod off Mick, we were here first!" Mara wasn't going to kow-tow to this show of bluff and bluster; he'd seen it all before. He had squatter's rights, and he wasn't going to step down in front of his leader or troops, and especially, not in front of his fellow generals. "If you want it, you'll have to take it from us."

There were no doubts in Michael's mind regarding exactly what Mara meant. Both sides raised their weapons again and readied themselves for battle. Some of the demons even put down their cans of beer; a sure sign they were serious. Although he wanted a fight, and this was as good a place as any, St. Michael had a firmer grasp of God's instructions than this general did of Satan's.

He casually looked around and sniffed the air, reacting as if noxious gas filled his nose. "You're right, General Mara; I think I'll allow you to keep your camp. Looking at it, it won't meet the high expectations of my men. I've decided my troops will set up camp over there." He pointed to a patch of open ground next to a small wood, a hundred meters away from where they stood. "Oh, yes. That looks an imminently better place."

With that, St. Michael turned and started to organise his army to set up their camp and line up their sentries, right next to the demon camp.

At that precise moment a winged angel, who'd been on lookout duty on top of the mountain, swooped down next to St. Michael. "Sir, sir!" he ventured breathlessly.

"Yes?" St. Michael demanded impatiently. "What is it?"

"I wish to report that I believe I've spotted the demon army!"

Chapter 14 – A Blunt Instrument.

The unseen border between the two forces was well guarded, and each side stood armed and ready, waiting for any excuse, no matter how small, to attack the other side. There was no opportunity for the element of surprise, and both sides looked evenly matched but the animosity was so intense that the lack of that advantage didn't matter. Demon and angel alike wanted war and were sure their side would be the victor. Even the soldiers who weren't on sentry duty weren't exactly resting. It made the demilitarised zone between North and South Korea appear like a happy holiday camp.

Blunt's generals had tried to keep him occupied and oblivious to their new neighbours. They feared his gung-ho attitude, and unrestrained blood lust, would lead to him ignoring Satan's instructions and declare war without the slightest provocation. If he jeopardised Satan's bigger plan, they knew Satan's vengeance and punishment would be severe and very uncomfortable for Blunt. That thought alone made the generals smile, but they also suspected his anger and rage would behave like a mortar shell. It would be painful to more than just the titular head of the Hawaiian army. They'd all taken a lot of care to lie and cheat their way into their relative positions of power, and they had no desire to let someone they saw as little more than cannon fodder ruin everything.

Even though Blunt could be distracted, it was inevitable that he eventually looked up from the incomprehensible maps placed in front of him. He noticed the sudden arrival of lots of black-clad soldiers, with raised weapons, lined up facing his men. In his brain, even Blunt recognized they weren't part of his army when he'd arrived from Hell.

When he asked General Mara what was going on, he got a reluctant, but honest response.

Mara had expected an outburst of rage, and instant orders for a pre-emptive strike. But all Blunt said was, "Oh, good," with a vacant smile on his face as he left his tent.

His actions left his generals confused; it was one thing to predict the base actions of an idiot, but not so easy for those of an enigmatic idiot.

Blunt was totally oblivious to the consternation he'd caused. To him, things were very simple and there was no need to overthink; even if he'd had the capacity to analyse the situation. He was loyal and obedient and had been given definite orders from Satan. As he understood them, he mustn't start the fight unless Satan specifically told him to do so. It was that simple. As the angels hadn't attacked, he saw no need to start the war. Instead, he walked directly to the demarcation line and blithely approached the nearest angel.

An exceedingly large, and unarmed, Neanderthal-like soldier dressed in faded blue pseudo-battle fatigues bearing down on him made the angel distinctly uncomfortable. Despite all his expectations and the stereotypical views of demons and their tactics he'd never visualised a Blunt. Horns? Scales? Teeth? Dirty boots? Yes, they were all part of the enemy DNA. The idea of a lumbering soldier, with a face carved in granite, a single long eyebrow resembling a fat black caterpillar and a disarming smile was just wrong.

Blunt was unaware of the mental turmoil he was creating. Such emotional nuances had never been part of his limited experiences. To him, if he wasn't fighting someone, they were a potential drinking partner – and being an angel didn't preclude them.

"Hello, I'm Blunt," he volunteered. He paused to allow the next jigsaw of words to enter the space in his brain, left by the evacuation of the previous sentence. Not recognising the cliché – not having a clue what a cliché was, in fact – he proceeded. "Take me to your leader!" On a roll after managing two consecutive, and coherent, sentences in a row, he decided to go for a third. "Does your boss like beer?"

The angel was reasonably certain that St. Michael wasn't a massive beer drinker, although he liked the idea of seeing him staggering around the camp in a drunken stupor. He could imagine him singing lewd songs, and hugging every soldier he bumped into, telling them, 'You're my best mate, you are. I bloody well love you, mate!' Consequently, he rated the chance, no matter how slight, of some random demon getting St. Michael drunk as too good to miss.

"Right, sir. If you'd care to walk this way, I'll take you to him." He stood back slightly, so Blunt could pass through the defensive line. As the two opposing soldiers walked towards St. Michael's tent, they chatted as if differing ranks, uniforms and ideologies didn't exist. They talked pure soldier talk, which even Blunt could participate in. Similar views on poor food, pointless discipline and the tedium of waiting for battle were shared. It seemed some things were common with everyone.

Word of Blunt's presence in the angel camp quickly spread and his progress had quickly acquired a large, heavily armed and suspicious audience. To them, this interloper must be very brave and clearly didn't understand the meaning of trepidation.

Blunt didn't see his actions as brave, he was just seeking out his counterpart to discover if he could scrounge some better beer than what was in his own camp. But in one respect, the angel soldiers were perfectly correct; he didn't know the meaning of trepidation. He knew the meaning of fear as a concept, but not from experience. In fact, he would have struggled to spell it!

When he reached the vast command post marquee, St. Michael had already received word of the approaching demon and stood expectantly inside. He wanted to make a dynamic impression, so he stood by a trestle table, staring intently at a large map of Oahu, determined to ignore Blunt's entrance for as long as possible and ensure he maintained the upper hand.

Knocking on the flap of a tent is a futile action, at best sounding like someone shaking the dust out of a coat and at worst, totally inaudible. But that didn't deter the soldier, his knock akin to sound of a pigeon flapping its wings twice. Pausing briefly, he stepped into the tent. "Field Marshall Blunt, *Sir!*"

The announcement was greeted by his commander in chief's continued study of his map.

Blunt walked into the tent casually, and ignoring his counterpart's posturing, approached a bottle of wine on the table. He picked it up and took a long gulp straight from the bottle. Wine wasn't something he was particularly familiar with, but he had a soldier's nose, and radar-like senses, for any liquid which contained alcohol. Draining the bottle, he placed it back on the table and released a large belch. "That was good. Got any beer, mate?"

St. Michael had nothing to draw on in his age-old log of experiences which allowed him to react properly to Blunt. In his ordered world of discipline and polite deferential respect, he didn't know what to say, or do, to this caveman who had walked into his tent and proceeded to gulp down his fine vintage wine as if it were water. "Errr, I'm not sure," he blustered, desperately trying to hang onto his dignity. "I'll ask. Captain Hellewell!" he snapped.

An angel, in a black boiler suit and sporting a Sam Browne belt and pistol holster, rushed into the tent. "Yes sir?" he asked, giving Blunt a brief but suspicious glance.

"Ah, Hellewell. Do we have any beer? It seems our guest is thirsty."

"Beer, sir?" Hellewell was unaccustomed to his leader requesting something so simple and low-brow.

"Yes, Hellewell, beer. I assume you do know what beer is?" snapped the saint superciliously.

"Of course, sir. I'll go get some." He promptly left the tent. He'd wanted to respond that while he knew what beer was, he was amazed that St. Michael did as well. But he knew better than to display any obvious insolence to his boss. So he just released a very un-angelic expletive under his breath, and proceeded to requisition a crate of beer from the nearest soldier's tent. He suspected it was going to be a busy night.

He dropped the beer off in the command tent, saluted crisply, and departed. He'd had enough sarcasm for one day, and saint or no saint, he didn't like St. Michael's pompous attitude. 'Damned officers,' he muttered, momentarily forgetting his own angelic military rank.

With the arrival of beer, Blunt quickly set about emptying the large cans. He had to admit, heavenly beer was much tastier than any demon brew. Hell's beer tended to taste like Armadillo urine, but it was strong stuff. He'd already drained three cans before he realised that his host was standing empty-handed; staring at him in pure amazement.

"Sorry, Mick." The beer lubricating his brain cells allowed him to string more sentences together. "Here, get this down your neck." He handed the saint an unopened can of beer.

"Thank you. Er, cheers," St. Michael said uncomfortably. He opened the can, raising it in salutation and taking a sip of the contents.

Blunt belched loudly, laughed and then proceeded to empty another can of beer. It was good stuff and he wanted to make the most of it.

"Field Marshall Blun—"

"Just Blunt!" interrupted Blunt.

"Alright," there was a pause, "as you wish… Blunt. What can I do for you? I presume you're not here to tender your unconditional surrender, and I assume you're not expecting me to reciprocate?"

Having no idea what reciprocate meant, Blunt just smiled again, raised his beer can and cheerfully replied, "Yeah, probably. I just want to know if you wanna fight?"

The question made St. Michael survey the tent wildly; he was sure he'd left his automatic pistol somewhere. He hadn't expected such a declaration of war, and if it wasn't war and just a one-on-one punch up, he was at a definite disadvantage against Blunt.

As usual, Blunt was totally unaware of the effects his words, and presence were having. "How about a fight this afternoon? Your champion against ours? Last one standing wins their weight in beer?" Despite his lack of higher level intellect, and his inability to fully articulate his thoughts, he was a foot soldier at heart and knew his men. A tense soldier with a gun was a dangerous thing and a trigger finger could quickly get itchy as nerves grew tighter. There was nothing like a good old fashioned, traditional brawl between two men to relieve some tension. Besides, he had just the demon in mind and he'd love to see an angel get his wings ripped off while still maintaining Satan's primary order.

Details were quickly thrashed out and the remaining beers placed in his pockets before Blunt casually walked back to his own lines. It had been a pleasant meeting and he looked forward to the forthcoming fight. The match was to be conducted in a circle, half in the demon camp and the other half in the angels. St. Michael had insisted on the 'Marquis of Queensbury Rules' to which Blunt had happily agreed. He had no idea what they were but assumed they didn't apply to his champion. Being a demon fighter, he'd have been totally correct anyway!

Chapter 15 – A Day Like No Other.

Officer Charley Palakiko of the Honolulu Police Department had started his shift an hour before. Having left the Kahuku Police Sub-station and set off north along Highway 83, he hadn't really expected to come across anything of any real interest. His designated patrol area wasn't a hot bed of crime. There were the occasional petty thefts reported, but it wasn't the most densely populated part of the island. His normal day usually involved pointing lost tourists in the direction of the golf course, or the Polynesian Cultural Centre, and driving along the roads enjoying the sunshine and the views. Like many police cars outside the city of Honolulu itself, his car was unmarked and only had blue lights on top of the roof as a method of identification. So the presence of a police officer was often a surprise to the unwary, or uninitiated. But mostly, his normal day could best be described as routine, bordering on the mind-numbingly dull.

Although he didn't know it at the time, today wasn't going to be his most normal of days.

Driving along the highway, he saw an unusually large number of people at the James Campbell National Wildlife Refuge in the distance. Even in the height of summer, it could hardly be described as the island's top tourist destination and many local inhabitants, born and bred on the island, barely knew of its existence. Consequently, it was rare to see more than a few cars and a handful of people there at any one time; especially as the gates were usually kept locked and entrance was by appointment only.

But now, there was a whole army of people there. Getting closer, he could clearly see two groups of people, one half in thick blue clothing and the other half wearing black jumpsuits. Neither was the most suitable attire for enjoying the island's warmth.

He stopped near the edge of the black clad group and got out of his car, fingering the holster containing his Glock pistol for reassurance. Smiling broadly, he approached one of the jumpsuited men, who saw him and returned the smile. "Aloha, brah. What's going on here?" requested Officer Palakiko, maintaining the broad smile and using the traditional Hawaiian greeting.

Before the soldier could answer, an angelic commissioned officer quickly ran to meet him. Putting himself between the policeman and the soldier, he butted in breathlessly. "Hi there," he said in a heavy Texan drawl, flashing a military ID card. "I'm Major Johnson, how can I help you Officer…?"

"Palakiko, sir. Officer Charley Palakiko. I was just wondering who you are and what you're doing here?"

"Well, Officer Palakiko," the Major began, "I'm sure you've been informed of the situation and you're aware of the need for secrecy, so I won't bore you with the details. All I will say is that you maintain your discretion in this matter and do your duty."

Officer Palakiko had no idea what this Major was talking about, but like most people in uniform, they suspected a conspiracy if they weren't kept in the loop regarding any piece of information. But to admit ignorance would have indicated to the military that he, and the police force as a whole, were insignificant and not worth being informed about what was going on. He decided the best course of action was to bluff it out and if that failed, just lie through his teeth. "I understand the need for secrecy, sir, but the details from my superiors have been a little *contradictory*, so I'd appreciate it if you could clarify for me. Straight from the horse's mouth, as it were."

The Major knew he had the poor police officer hooked on his line of deceit, so he decided to reel him in slowly. He walked over and placed a conspiratorial arm around his shoulder

"Charley, I'm sure you're aware of the highly secret international meeting taking place at the Terrapin Cove Hotel in a few days' time. A total media blackout is in force, and strict instructions have been issued to the local law enforcement agencies to stay well clear. As far as jurisdiction is concerned, it ends at the entrance to the hotel. No police officer will be made welcome and they'd be risking both their career and pension if they tried to get in and photo-bomb the *President*. I'm sure you understand that?" He paused, to let the word 'President' sink in. "Despite the need for secrecy, I'm sure you'll be able to discretely clarify the situation with your supervisors. After all, it'll be their heads on the block, as well as the ones in the patrol cars."

The obvious menace was applied as heavily as a teenage girl applying makeup and wasn't lost on Officer Palakiko. He'd already made a mental note to patrol elsewhere for a few days. He had several days leave due to him, so maybe a trip to one of the other islands would be good? He had an old aunt on Ni'ihau Island – perhaps it was time to surprise her with a visit. But even then, it might be too close, and he wished that he had a distant relative, in both senses, living on the far away island of Nihoa.

"But sir, I understand that – but who are all these people and why are they here, and not at the hotel? Surely they're very conspicuous?"

"Well, Charley, that's a very good question and I'm glad you asked. Do you see all those strange looking men way over there? The ones in the blue overalls and workmen's dungarees? The ones who look like they should be playing banjos, flying the Confederate flag and applying sunscreen to their burnt necks?"

"Yes," the bemused police officer replied, glancing in the direction of the demons.

"Thanks to the presence of the Russian Premier at the conference, they have insisted, in the strongest of terms, that they provide their own military and security cover so they've forced us to accept the presence of an extremely large contingent of the Spetsnaz – their special forces – on US soil. Embarrassing enough just for that fact, and even more important that secrecy is maintained! Those fine-looking troops in the black are a contingent of the 19th US Special Forces Group. We need that many here to keep an eye on the Russkies."

Charley was feeling as if he'd walked into a minefield wearing clown shoes and wished he'd never stopped his car. "Major," he ventured hesitantly, "why are they dressed like *that*?"

Major Johnson smiled, his mind was racing, trying to be creative with the story he was making up. Why the hell were they dressed like that? Sometimes though artistic improvisation, no matter how implausible, is enough to appease a confused human mind which isn't given enough time to think over the explanation. "A damned fine question, Charley. It seems the head of the Spetsnaz came from cold, remote Kamchatka, which is as far from Moscow as you can get while still being in Russia. Consequently, he's had very little contact with the West and especially America, so his main education regarding our culture came from watching old episodes of 'The Dukes of Hazard' and the movie 'Deliverance'. So, he thought those clothes were normal attire for looking inconspicuous!"

While Johnson was unaware of the truth, the true reason for choosing the demon's attire was equally bizarre. The demon charged with choosing an appropriate uniform for the mission had been, in life, an Alabama member of the KKK and died at a relatively early age when a burning cross fell on him. His racism, virulent anger and hatred had gained him instant access into Hell. Experience of anything outside his small southern community had been extremely limited, and he assumed his normal clothing could be naturally extrapolated across the rest of America. If anyone didn't dress like that, they must be either stuck up city slickers, or damn Yankees. In both cases, they were unimportant in his eyes and didn't count. So, in hindsight, it was lucky the demon army weren't all carrying Confederate battle flags and wearing white pillow cases over their heads. And they were additionally lucky, as the quartermaster's assistant had been, in life, a Nazi officer. If he'd had his way, the entire demonic army would be sporting jack boots and black uniforms covered in death's head skull insignia and swastikas. That would have been a lot harder to explain away to any curious human.

The Major gently led the bemused police officer back in the direction of his patrol car. "I suppose it's a good job he wasn't a fan of John Wayne westerns, or God only knows what they would have been dressed like."

Officer Palakiko had heard enough – he was confused and worried that he'd walked into the middle of an international incident just waiting to happen. He didn't want to be anywhere near when it all kicked off and WWIII started. He was glad to find himself back at his car and didn't hesitate to make his excuses and say goodbye, driving away as fast as he could go until the nature reserve and the cold war warriors were no longer in his rear view mirror. Some things were best left out of reports, and he doubted this would have been believed, anyway. He certainly wasn't paid enough for this sort of thing.

Chapter 16 – War By Other Means.

The circle for the fight had been cleared quickly, willingly and eagerly, by both armies. The temporary encroachment out of the small strip of no-man's-land onto their separate areas had been welcomed and the soldiers on both sides were frantically scrambling to secure the best vantage points around the ring. None of them wanted to be stuck at the back of the crowd, unable to be part of this unique occurrence. Demon rubbed shoulder with angel; the angels' beer was shared with the demons, and barbecued Hawaiian duck and moorhen was shared by the demons. The endangered status of the birds was made even more precarious, thanks to the new-found bonhomie – and the misfortune of the meat tasting so delicious. It was fortunate it was the wrong time of the year for the rare Hawaiian Monk Seal to be on the coastal shore; otherwise they would have become a culinary delicacy as well.

As the alcohol and fresh meat were consumed, all past animosities were ignored. Perhaps not forgot and certainly not forgiven, but for the duration of the fight they were put to one side. This fraternisation was much to the disgust of St. Michael. If he'd realised his discipline would break down, he never would have consented to the fight. But he was confident good would prevail – after all, surely good always overcame evil!

Although the belligerents were required to maintain human form during the fight, under this superficial skin they maintained the same physical structure they had in their own dimensions. A demon might have a human form twice the size of Blunt, but wouldn't be strong enough to punch their way out of a paper bag. Inversely, they could be built like a weedy, fourteen-year-old computer nerd and be able to smash through solid brick walls and wrestle wild rhinos without breaking a sweat. Consequently, human appearance wasn't always an indication of what odds a bookmaker would give.

Everyone had to admit, however, that the demon approaching the ring – wearing only boots and cut-off blue denim shorts – was huge. It appeared he'd somehow managed to meld his body with an elephant and his head would be susceptible to permafrost.

A large section of the cheering demon crowd vacated their optimum viewing positions, so he could enter the ring, and once he'd gone past, there was a mad scramble to either regain their prime vantage point or move their position closer to the action.

As he walked around the ring, arms raised in a gesture of defiance, his fans started to chant his name repeatedly, "Abaddon, Abaddon, Abaddon…" One of the demons standing at the edge of the ring handed him a metal sword, which he swung through the air several times before bending it into a U shape, as if it were nothing more than a plastic children's toy. This only encouraged his frenzied fans to chant his name even louder.

The angels, witnessing the showboating, fell silent. Each of them was glad they weren't the heavenly champion who'd been selected to go up against this wall of flesh and muscle. Faintly at first, but growing stronger, the angels began to rhythmically chant the name of their approaching hero. Geburah – or Geb as the crowd were calling him – was, at first glance, a mismatched opponent to Abaddon. He was tall, but slender, and his muscles were tight on his frame. He wore a one piece, figure hugging leather outfit and dark glasses. The angels reverentially cleared a way for him and he nodded, almost imperceptibly, to the cheering crowds. He silently removed his glasses and passed them to a nearby angel, flexed his arms, then shook his shoulders to loosen his muscles in readiness. A small demon stepped into the ring and stood between the two combatants. He raised his arms and spun around, looking at the crowd. They slowly fell silent and waited for his words.

"Last man standing," he croaked in a loud, but gravelly voice. "Last man standing, last man standing." His fists punched the air in time with the words. The new chant was quickly adopted by the entire crowd, and only then did the diminutive demon casually swagger to the side of the ring so the fight could commence. His explanation of the rules might not have been complex, but it was effective. The two fighters looked each other up and down before they started to circle, maintaining their distance from each other.

Abaddon raised his arms and roared, as if he was about to attack, and Geb tensed up in readiness. This reaction made Abaddon laugh at his adversary. In his mind, there was no contest and he'd soon be the victor, having smashed the angel's head like a melon and sent him back to Heaven.

There was no such complacency in Geb's head. He was sizing up Abaddon and seeking any possible weak spots, biding his time and letting the demon make the first move. That move was quick to come, when Abaddon lunged at Geb, his arms flaying like a demonic windmill. Having the benefit of agility, Geb side-stepped using his leg to trip his opponent, sending him sprawling into the crowd. He landed on a couple of beer drinking angels, who sat at the edge of the ring, unable to get out of the way of the toppling giant in time.

The demons in the crowd jeered and shouted words of encouragement to their hero, while the angels – or at least the angels who hadn't been knocked unconscious by the falling fighter – cheered and volunteered boxing tips to Geb. He didn't have time to take notice of their advice as Abaddon had quickly got back on his feet and decided another full-frontal attack, at top speed, would take Geb by surprise. As he ran forward, he soon realised he should try another tactic. A single fist impacted with his square jaw and the powerful punch sent him spinning back into the crowd, this time knocking four demons to the ground.

In an act of bravado, he got back to his feet and snatched a piece of cooked wild fowl out of the hand of one unconscious demon. He bit into the meat and then threw the remainder into the baying crowd. But he'd learnt his lesson and decided Geb wouldn't be such an easy target. A more calculated approach was needed. Walking slowly towards the angel, he raised his fists and adopted a more traditional boxer's pose. Geb mirrored his stance. When Abaddon was within range, he jabbed and impacted with Geb's right cheek. This attack received a massive cheer from the demons in the audience but failed to have the desired effect. The angel was pushed back slightly, but he merely shook his head and returned to his original position.

The fight had begun in earnest and each blow was met with blows and kicks that were either blocked or countered. Despite the disparity in sizes, and the difference in fighting styles, neither seemed to gain the upper hand to deliver the coup de grâce. There were no three minute rounds, just a non-stop onslaught. As the minutes stretched into hours, the increasingly inebriated crowd lost none of their enthusiasm for the entertainment. If you hadn't been able to discriminate by their clothing, you'd have been unable to distinguish demon from angel. The fight had long since stopped being about good versus evil – it was now a battle between two determined people. It wasn't very angelic behaviour, but the angels baying for blood was primal and instinctive. Any dainty sensibilities of human civilisation had been put on hold for the moment. This was all about the savage scent of sweat and the adrenaline pumping through everyone's bodies. Voices hoarse from the shouting, ears filled by the noise of fists impacting on faces and torsos. Eyes were mesmerised by the blood and the sight of two people refusing to yield to the other.

As if by some unspoken consent, both fighters suddenly separated, and breathing heavily, walked to diametrically opposed edges of the circular dirt ring. It didn't matter if it was demon, or angel, it was no longer important or relevant. They were each handed beers, which they drank appreciatively, and then turned to face each other again. They both nodded slightly, as a sign of mutual respect and then Abaddon was running, as if he'd experienced a total recharge of energy. He wanted to end the fight and end it quickly. He knew his reserves were running low, but he was sure his opponent must be feeling the same way.

Geb remained standing as if rooted to the spot. Closer and closer Abaddon ran, but still Geb didn't move. It wasn't until the charging giant was within inches of grabbing hold of his thinner opponent that Geb acted. Falling backwards, he swiftly raised his left leg and his booted foot made direct contact with Abaddon's groin, as his right fist made simultaneous contact with Abaddon's chin. Momentum had the forwards tumbling hulk unable to do anything about it, and ended his battle against gravity. He barrelled over Geb, who'd fallen to the floor, and continued to topple. He finally fell onto a mixed group of drunken angels and demons. He painfully attempted to lift himself up but the effort was too much. Abaddon's body rose slightly but he quickly collapsed again; as unconscious as the spectators he'd landed on.

Both sides knew they'd witnessed a spectacular tournament and no longer cared about sides. Winner and loser alike had gained everyone's respect, and as the cheering crowd surged into the ring, Geb quickly ran over to his foe and checked he was alright.

Rolled onto his back, Abaddon opened his eyes groggily and gave Geb a smile through a swollen, bloodied mouth. He knew he'd been beaten and despite losing and being knocked to the dirt in front of his own army, there was no dishonour or shame.

Geb was lifted onto the shoulders of some elated angels and carried back to his tent, so he could recover and have his battered and bruised body tended to. Abaddon was returned to his tent, in the same manner, and neither resisted the unconsciousness that the ensuing sleep provided. The prize of beer, for the winner, could wait.

Although the relevant parts of temporary ring in the dust were quickly reclaimed, by both sides, the tension between the potential belligerents had been released. Defensive lines were resumed, but weapons were no longer raised. In small sections along the boundary, angels and demons sat together in the setting sunlight, sharing a beer and enjoying barbecued duck wings. The day had gone well, and despite some noisy drunken revelry in both camps, there would be peace between the two sides during the night.

Blunt didn't care about the lack of passive hostility. He'd enjoyed the fight, and despite his low IQ, knew there was no longer risk of any loose cannon starting an unwanted war.

St. Michael, on the other hand, wasn't happy with the flagrant and inexcusable breakdown of discipline. But even he could see his job had become a whole lot easier, and the most unlikely of truces had been forged.

And deep down, he'd enjoyed the fight just as much as everyone else. He might be a saint now, but he'd been human once.

Chapter 17 – Apathy Rules, But Who Cares?

Like an itch under the pot on a broken leg, something was wrong and he couldn't quite put his finger on it.

The sight which met St. Michael when he left his tent for his first inspection of the day didn't start him off on a happy note. It looked as if discipline had disappeared and anarchy had taken its place. It was already mid-morning and the vast majority of his army were still fast asleep, many lying unconscious on the ground. Those who were awake were huddled around fires, keeping the mild morning chill at bay, quietly talking, laughing and joking together. He even saw a scattering of demons, inside his camp and sleeping off the previous night's partying, or, keeping the angels company around the ambers of the camp fires. He sniffed the air and his nostrils were immediately filled with a mixture of stale beer and the faint whiff of marijuana. Looking across the field at the enemy encampment, a similar sight met his eyes; soldiers of both sides in various state of consciousness. There was so much wrong, he wanted to shout and scream at someone – anyone – but he knew a gentler approach was needed to regain any semblance of control and military order.

He finally realised the thing that was missing; the most important symbol of good against evil – his own personal statement of power. There was absolutely nobody on sentry duty.

The invisible line which differentiated his idea of 'Us' and 'Them' was unguarded. How could he feel superior, and prove he was looking out for any tricks, if he didn't have heavily armed troops ready and pointing guns at the demons? Without the defended border, all they had was a large grassland area and wooded nature reserve – all-be-it depleted of nature – but full of people sleeping. How would an outsider know they were enemies? In his pompous military mind this just wouldn't do. He walked purposefully to the nearest tent and opening the flap, walked straight in. Seeing Major Johnson asleep, he kicked the foot of the camp bed violently. "Get up and get dressed, *now*!" he barked at the blurry eyed officer.

Struggling to focus, and get his bearings, after a late night and uncomfortably insufficient sleep, the Major attempted to formulate an appropriate response to his superior officer and failed abysmally. "Wassa, err. Yerrrr?"

"Oh, wake up man," the saint snapped. "I want you to come with me. Now!" He stomped out of the tent and returned to his frustrated surveillance of his camp. Definitely not a happy angel.

A fully dressed Major Johnson came stumbling out of his tent, attempting to obey orders and be with St. Michael, but still struggling to put on his last boot at the same time.

St. Michael offered his underling a look of disdainful contempt. He needed to blame someone for the breakdown of law and order, and until he could wrestle back his authority, Johnson would be the brunt of his irritation. Once Johnson's boot was fully on, and fastened, he stood to attention, awaiting further orders from his commander. "This will not do," muttered the angry saint, "this is disgraceful!"

The bemused Major had no idea what Michael was talking about. He looked down at his uniform to see what was amiss, but seeing nothing specific, he decided ignorance was bliss and he'd allow events to unfurl at their own pace. Hopefully he'd catch up on the one-sided conversation at some point. "Yes sir," he replied, opting for the standard military response.

Turning towards the enemy camp, St. Michael began to stride determinedly in its direction. Lifting his arm, he waved his finger in a grand gesture and pointed towards the big marquee in the middle of the demons section of the field. "Come with me." He continued walking, without checking to see if his latest instruction had been heard and obeyed.

The Major obediently ran to follow, as Michael pressed ahead. He was still tired, hungry, and had a mild hangover – and he could do without rushing around a field without knowing what was going on. Stepping over recumbent bodies, they ignored the utter mess around them. St. Michael would have loved to 'accidentally' tread on some of the bodies as he walked but restrained himself. He might not have a full understanding of 'winning hearts and minds' but stomping on sleeping soldier's heads probably wasn't it.

Reaching the enemy's marquee, the Saint lifted the door flap and walked, unchallenged, into the tent. He had no idea what to expect inside the command centre of the demon army, but he definitely hadn't expected to see four generals sitting around the main map table and playing poker. This sight was compounded by the Field Marshall sitting in a chair, his feet resting on the edge of the table and casually sipping a can of beer.

"Hey, Mickey. Come in," Blunt greeted on seeing his new guest. "Come. Sit down. Want a beer?"

The generals unanimously decided the game of chance could wait, and placing their cards on the table, went to stand respectfully at the back of the tent. They'd also witnessed the breakdown of demarcation and discipline, and it irked their sensibilities. They were curious to see how their angelic counterpart reacted and dealt with the situation. Satan had given specific orders about avoiding any overt conflict, but they were not sure such a lax and peaceful coexistence would be acceptable to their overlord. If blame and anger occurred, they were happy for Blunt to bear the brunt of it.

St. Michael walked forward and sat gingerly in the nearest vacated chair, taking stock of the inside of the tent.

There were empty beer cans scattered over the table and floor. Against a side wall was a dartboard, with darts in it. Hanging on another wall was a painting of Satan, complete with cartoon moustache added by marker pen. There was an almost overpowering smell of urine and he was sure he'd spied abandoned marijuana roaches at the Field Marshall's feet.

"Fancy a beer?" Blunt asked once more, in a nonchalant voice.

"No, thank you," St. Michael replied in a superior tone "You don't happen to have a sherry, do you?"

Quiet laughter erupted from the generals behind him. Blunt's eyebrows naturally had the appearance of an overhanging rock face, but now they appeared as if a landslide was about to happen. He mouthed the word 'sherry' to himself, as if he'd been asked to solve a complex algebraic equation. He decided the question was far too complicated and stuck with what he knew.

"Lager? I think we have that."

"No, thank you. Do you have any port?" Michael enquired.

Now Blunt suspected he was on better mental territory. He knew and understood what a port was. His brain couldn't understand what relevance it had to this conversation, but he recognised there was much in the world he didn't understand. But he could find out later from his generals if he needed one, and if so, he'd organise one. "I don't need it. We have the dimensional portal!" he volunteered helpfully.

The laughter from the generals became uncontrollable. They were enjoying this and couldn't wait for the next instalment in the clash of smug intellect hitting a brick wall of total, blithe, ignorance.

St. Michael turned to face them and shot the generals a withering glance.

It had no effect on their amusement whatsoever; the morning show was too funny to keep straight faces. Besides, respect for angels wasn't something which came naturally to them.

Realising that his glare, no matter how stern, wasn't going to change the generals' behaviour, St. Michael decided it would be best to carry on with the surreal conversation with Blunt and ignore everyone else.

"Look, Field Marshall Blunt, yesterday's fight was entertaining and it was definitely beneficial. It alleviated the risk of conflict and de-escalated an extremely tense situation. I must salute your idea, it was a work of genius," he said, ignoring the louder laughter behind him, "however I'm sure you'll agree that things have gone too far. The casual, lazy attitude which is permeating the whole camp isn't conducive to military order."

Blunt had no idea what on Earth, Heaven or Hell Michael was talking about. He recognised some of the words, but the few which did make sense were quickly buried by the ones with too many letters – never mind syllables. He could tell from Michael's face that what was being said was important, but the gravity was lost on him. Clutching at straws, he grasped on the part of the conversation which made sense and decided on what he thought was the most appropriate answer.

"Yes, it was a great fight!" To emphasise his joy at the eloquence of his response, he raised a can of beer in a salute and took a long drink from it.

He wasn't sure what was wrong, but St. Michael had the definite impression his message wasn't getting across to his demon counterpart. He might just have to dumb it down, so he could be understood and get the discipline returned without the tension returning.

"Yes, exactly," he started, "as I said, a great idea and fantastic result." He turned to briefly look at the demon generals, ensuring he'd been heard and daring them to laugh at the idea of their champion losing. Satisfied by their lack of laughter, he felt more comfortable continuing. "We're two separate and enemy armies. Right?"

Blunt nodded slowly in agreement. The new track of conversation was just within his area of understanding.

"Therefore, we need to make sure the two armies are kept separate and apart. Can I respectfully request you to order your troops to stay on their side of the camp borders, and I'll tell my soldiers to do the same? Then we can keep the peace, but from our own sides of the nature reserve."

Letting the sentences trickle slowly like a viscous liquid through his mind, the words came to a standstill in some lonely part of Blunt's brain. He understood what had been said, even if he didn't understand why people couldn't keep drinking beer and getting stoned until it was time to fight. But he'd never tried to understand angels – too much like hard work for him. His previous encounters with angels had always entailed lots of violence, so this was a genuine education for him on many levels. He'd have preferred a good old beating as opposed to the pain being inflicted on his mind right now, but to him war was out of the question - for now. Orders were orders.

"Okay, Mick." His reply was strong and confident. "Whatever you say. Our men, our side, your men yours!"

St. Michael had to admit Field Marshall Blunt was a man of few words, and some of them were gibberish, but when he did make sense, he had a knack of hitting the nail on the head.

Standing St. Michael, adding, "Thank you for your hospitality, Field Marshall." His salute wasn't returned by Blunt but was met with renewed sniggering from behind. "I trust you'll issue your orders without further ado?"

"No Mick, I'll do it now," replied the demon leader.

St. Michael eyed Blunt, trying to catch even the slightest glimmer of irony or sarcasm on his face, but all he saw was a blank stare from the granite-like features.

With a "Good day, sir," he pushed his way past the grinning generals and left the tent. He pretended he didn't hear them laughing uncontrollably, like hyenas on drugs.

Major Johnson was standing nearby with a small group of demons, genially chatting and enjoying a shared breakfast of barbecued Hawaiian Moorhen washed down with beer. When he saw his leader storm out of the tent, he quickly dropped the pieces of bird meat, passing the beer can to a neighbouring demon. He rushed over to St. Michael and waited for either an admonishment or some orders. To his relief, it was the latter.

"Johnson. Oh good. I want the order issued that with immediate effect, all angel soldiers will no longer be allowed to fraternise with the enemy and must, under no circumstances, cross the demarcation line into the enemy camp without specific orders from higher up. The demon scum is to be escorted from our encampment and won't be allowed back again, without specific approval." He glared at the nonplussed Major. "Do I make myself clear, Major Johnson?"

"As crystal, sir" the Major responded promptly. His compunction to disagree, and point out the benefits of the unusual truce, was weaker than his desire to be the brunt of more verbal abuse from a high-ranking officer, unwilling to accept contradiction or criticism.

With that, the self-satisfied saint strode off towards the moral, emotional security of his own side's ground.

The Major stood to attention while he watched St. Michael walk off into the distance. Once he'd disappeared, he relaxed and looked around him. The demons he'd been chatting to merrily, were staring at him with impassive faces. They'd heard the discussion and understood the ramifications. Without any further discussion, it was mutually accepted that the holiday was over and they'd have to get back to being soldiers again.

He bowed his head in sadness; demons or not, on this field they weren't vastly different from his own soldiers. Simply pawns, waiting their turn to move into the front lines. They would fight like the demons they were in a battle, but he knew his own men would fight equally well and mercilessly. His gun could do just as much damage to them, as theirs could do to him. He didn't see a real need to fire up the hatred, ignorance and distrust between the sides, just so they could destroy each other faster when the time came.

But such was the existence and purpose of a soldier. When his time on Earth had ended and he'd died in the Second World War, he'd hoped being a soldier in the angelic army would be different. More simple and clear – a battle between good and bad; obviously with the good always winning. Unfortunately, he'd soon discovered that even in the afterlife, some lines would always be blurred. Sighing, he noticed two angels sitting on the ground, looking up at him.

"Well?" he snapped. "What are you waiting for? You heard our beloved leader; get your arses back to our camp!"

Not needing to be told twice they stood up, and walked sadly to their own lines.

'Ours is not to reason why' thought the Major philosophically, as he slowly walked back to his tent.

Chapter 18 – A Time In Paradise.

When the devout entered heaven, they often put their holy knowledge to use and went on a pilgrimage to meet, get autographs and be photographed, with as many Biblical or canonised people as they could. It came as a shock to them to discover that some of the celebrities they sought didn't actually exist, or their achievements had been exaggerated, or altered, by historians so they'd gone to Hell instead of Heaven. At first, this heavenly tourism was nice for those holy people who were name checked, but over the millennia, it got to be an annoyance and took away the privacy of many saints. Matthew, Mark, Luke and John found it difficult to achieve any privacy and got writer's cramp from autographing so many copies of the Bible. In the end, they started adopting disguises when they walked about Heaven. St. Mark often ended up walking the streets of paradise looking like a wizened old cobbler, who answered to the name of Stanley.

Dedan was mentioned in the Bible, and even had an ancient city named after him, but he tended to be well off the radar to all but the most extreme religious zealots. He didn't mind shaking the odd hand, and if he was being honest, enjoyed the small-scale fame, but overall, he could walk around Heaven and avoid getting mobbed by adoring fans. He was good friends with Elvis, and always felt sorry for him.

Having been in Heaven from relatively early days, he'd seen the place grow and liked it, but he always felt more at home on Earth. Sure, it could be too hot or too cold, the food couldn't compare and try as he might, no matter where he went, he could never find a bed as truly comfortable as his own in Heaven.

But the people! Even the good ones could be secretive, dishonest and devious. On Earth he was privy to all the other things which made people human; and he just loved them. When he was among them he could sense their sins and see their goodness, and each had their own aura which filled his spirit.

Even when he was on a job and got murdered by a demon, or shot by a jealous husband, he didn't mind the long, frustrating time it took to return to Heaven and resume duties. Most other angels didn't mind going on missions, but they recognised that Heaven was a far better place to be and given the choice they were happy to stay there – but not Dedan. Whenever there was an opportunity to volunteer for a mission he would always be the first to step forward. He didn't mind what he was being asked to do, or where on the planet he was sent; if he could be on Earth he was in his element. In all the centuries of using the dimensional portal, this operation he'd been put in charge of was definitely the most important of his career. Satan's real intentions were a mystery and there was a good chance it would be a convoluted trap, but he didn't care. Hawaii was a beautiful island and ever since God had given him the responsibility of ensuring all the heavenly things ran smoothly, he'd been kept busy. There had been several return trips to the hotel and he'd ensured Mr Knight was keeping the best rooms reserved for God and his retinue, the meeting room would be available 24/7 and that room service was prepared to provide whatever was requested by either side. He'd also made sure he had a lavish room right next door to God's, so he could be on hand if required. He liked to see himself as God's bodyguard.

God, on the other hand, didn't think he needed any such protection. Dedan had only been back in Heaven for a few hours and he was already missing the hustle and bustle of Earth. But he needed to be here, as he'd arranged an appointment with God, all the heavenly delegates and the security angels, so he could brief them and ensure everyone was ready for any eventuality. For reasons known only to God, the temporary meeting room he'd created on a nearby celestial cloud had the internal appearance of a WWII British RAF bomber command briefing room. Each element was exact in every detail. The chairs were metal, framed with hard brown canvas. The walls were bare brick and the single glazed windows had khaki curtains and X-shaped tape on the glass in case of Luftwaffe bombs shattering them. There was an old wooden table at the end of the hall and there was a Union Jack flag in one corner and a picture of King George VI on a side wall. The only anachronism in the whole set up was the giant map at the end of the room. Instead of it being a map of 1943 Europe, displaying dams in the Ruhr Valley, or French railway lines – it was showing the Hawaiian island of Oahu. Honolulu could be seen in the south-east corner, but the northern tip was shown highlighted in yellow and an enlarged section had also been added and placed in a section where only the Pacific Ocean had been before. Dedan was a few minutes early but was glad to see that when he entered the room, carrying two large white folders, most of the rows of old seats were taken and the occupants were merrily chatting to each other. They'd heard rumours but knew nothing specific and were eager to find out more. He looked around and couldn't see God, but he wasn't surprised. God liked to make a grand entrance and Dedan half expected Him to enter the room having taken the form of a WWII fighter pilot, complete with pipe and handlebar moustache, or perhaps secretly disguised as a 1940's tea lady. In this guise He would no doubt serve drinks and biscuits, and then transform into a more recognisable form and scare the life – it they had lives as a human might understand the concept – out of some of the newer angels. There wasn't much room to manoeuvre in the hall, so he had to squeeze his way through the crowds. When he finally reached the table at the front, he placed his folders on the desk and sat on a chair behind it. Just as he sat down, a door appeared in the nearest corner and God walked in. The entire room immediately jumped to attention, accompanied by loud scraping noises as chairs were simultaneously pushed backward by their occupants. A beautiful sight and noise – and Dedan immediately understood why God had chosen to recreate such a setting for the meeting. Pure theatrics, but he had to admit he loved every bit of it.

God had opted to maintain his appearance from his previous meeting and he'd added a large Cuban cigar in the corner of his mouth as an extra prop. The tip was glowing, but no smoke was being released. God took the cigar from his mouth, raised his arms towards the crowds, and with a broad grin, gestured for everyone to sit down.

"At ease, ladies and gentlemen. Please be seated." He was obviously enjoying the amateur dramatics. Why have a meeting in a neat, dull white room, full of heavenly light, when you can sit and talk in a detailed replication of history? Not relevant to the mission, but still an interesting idea.

Upon the command, everyone obediently returned to their seats. After all, who wanted to disobey a request from God made in Heaven? All eyes were on Him, eagerly waiting to get more details of their mission and receive holy orders.

Clearing his throat, God stood up. The audience were about to stand up again, but He quickly raised his hand and gesticulated for them to remain seated. He scanned the crowd and began. "Thank you all for coming here today, I'm sure you've heard rumours and would like to know why you've been chosen for this mission. Allow Me to get to the point. Satan has been in touch and from the sounds of things, he'd like to close down Hell and be allowed to return to heaven, or at least come home and let Hell go to…. well, Hell!" God was interrupted by a cacophony of muttering from the audience. The enormity of what they'd been told had solicited an immediate, shocked response. Undeterred, He continued. "Please, everyone, settle down. Yes, I'm sure it's just another one of his tricks or traps; he can be very convincing and I'll never forget how long it took Me to straighten out the mess at Cadiz, after that poker game I had with him." This was met by a murmur of agreement from the listeners. "But nevertheless, there was something in the tone of his voice which made this request sound genuine. And I think we need to at least play along with him for now and see what happens. Therefore, I have agreed to have a conference with him on Earth, in a hotel in Hawaii, and you've all been chosen as part of the team to ensure everything goes well and everyone remains safe."

The noise from the audience grew louder as they tried, and failed, to discuss this revelation quietly with the person sitting next to them. God coughed loudly to regain their attention. "As I was saying, this will take a lot of planning and it's imperative that everybody knows their roles and responsibilities while we're down there. For the angels responsible for security, you'll need to be extra vigilant considering the status of our guest. It's *Satan*, ladies and gentlemen – not some jumped-up devil or a self-important Archdemon. Although, there will be a fair few of those there with him." Looking at Dedan, He added with a wry smile, "There will probably be a few Succubi as well, so you'd better be careful, Dedan!"

This brought loud laughter from those in the room who were familiar with his reputation. Dedan smiled back at God, revealing a little embarrassment; he had fond memories of a wild fling with Lilith that would have put a contortionist in traction. But that was before he'd sent her back to Hell with the aid of an axe and a burning torch. It always made him uncomfortable, however, to be reminded of it by God.

God continued. "Therefore, I'll now hand over to the mission Commander, Dedan, who will give you more specific details."

Dedan stood up. "Right, you lot," he started, "there are lots of details and it would take weeks to cover all the areas of responsibility in any detail. There will be briefing folders for each of you at the end. So, I'm just going to go over it briefly now." He picked up a long thin cane which lay on the desk and started to point at the map. "This, for those of you who don't know, is the Hawaiian island of Oahu. In exactly three days' time, we'll be taking over the whole of the Terrapin Cove Hotel and Resort. This will be under the guise of a top secret, international peace conference. We've ensured that we won't be asked too many awkward questions by humans. We'll take the dimensional portals and materialise a few miles away from the

106

hotel, continuing the rest of the journey by human transport. Those posing as dignitaries will go by limo or helicopter, and the rest of us will arrive in Hummers." He carefully placed the pointer back on the table and leaned forward so his chest hovered over the table. "St. George, where are you?"

A muscular man, sitting on the penultimate row from the back, stood up and gave Dedan a wave. Dedan smiled and waved back. "Hello, George; looking good. St. George over there will oversee security in the hotel and grounds. St. Michael is already on Earth with his army and I'm sure he'll have them chomping at the bit in anticipation of coming face-to-face with some demons."

Knowing what had happened on Earth God palmed His face but remained silent.

Dedan continued. "If required, he can be called upon to provide greater support. I can see St. Jude there." He waved to a man on the front row and had his gesture of greeting returned. "He will be in charge of all the angels who'll be in the guise of politicians. So, you'd better get practicing with the false smiles and lies!" This comment was met with polite laughter. "And finally, the lovely Emily will be responsible for all liaisons with the demons. As the sole point of contact, this will prevent any risk of them giving contradictory information to anyone else and reduce any possible confusion should this be a trap." Emily was a pretty blonde and buxom angel, sitting on the third row, and when she heard her name she automatically stood up and gave the crowd a slight bow before sitting down again. Dedan stared, giving her a little smile and conspiratorial wink. If he was going to have an assistant helping him out, why shouldn't he have a beautiful one? "Right, I won't delay you any further. If you have any specific questions, I'll be available after the meeting. Otherwise, meeting adjourned and I'll see you at the dimensional portal at the times specified in your personal briefing documents. Thank you."

With those words the people began to filter out of the room. Small groups formed outside to discuss what they'd heard in the meeting, but each and every one of them had to admit to a sensation of unease. None of them liked Satan, or thought Hell was a great holiday destination, but the idea of having their nemesis back in Heaven, rubbing shoulders with them after so long and so many violent wars, filled them with terror and resentment. Many of them remembered the original disagreement over power and the wars of the Apocalypse – and no one wanted that to happen again.

Chapter 19 – Could It Be Magic?

There were many things wrong with Hell, which wasn't surprising given it wasn't designed to be a pleasure cruise; providing free drinks and an all-night cabaret to its occupants for eternity. It was meant to be wrong, in so many ways. Sure, let the damned souls suffer – that was par for the course and they deserved what they got. But Hell had problems, far beyond its chambers of torment. The plumbing seldom worked, and entropy rapidly affected everything making items in Hell quickly fall apart. The one thing that did work, after a fashion, was the internal public address system, but no matter what it was programmed to do, or who tried to change it, all it ever played was Barry Manilow songs at full volume whenever it was switched on. This was quite often, as the off button had a mind of its own and would belt out 'Copacabana' or 'Mandy' at the most inappropriate times. Not bad songs, if you were in the mood for them, but after the 15,000th time of hearing the same tunes, it did tend to get on the nerves.

Now was one of those times when Satan was *really* regretting having the whole system fitted. It had seemed a good idea at the time, but in hindsight, he should have known better. His office was filled to bursting point with demons of all shapes and sizes, pushing and shoving each other so they could be seen by Satan, perhaps gaining something from him acknowledging their existence. Voices rose in argument and rage, and the atmosphere was tense. Satan knew two demons in a room was usually one too many – or even two too many – and now he had hundreds of them in his office. The sight wasn't pretty and the smell was worse. Hygiene wasn't top of the priority list in Hell, especially when the brimstone odour tended to permeate every pore. There was also the added hint of cow dung, which Satan knew he wouldn't get out of the carpet once everyone left. If the odour could have been reproduced on Earth, some malevolent dictator could have used it as a weapon of mass destruction

Satan was getting fed up with waiting for his audience to notice that he was ready to speak. Good manners weren't expected in Hell but respecting him was. Taking in a deep breath, which made a sound like a tornado trapped in a cavern, he released a bright tongue of flame that left the first three rows of demons smoking and smouldering. *"Shut up!"* he bellowed, as if he needed to reinforce the statement made by the flames. All chatter, and moos, had instantly ended.

In that precise moment, the public-address system decided to fill the quiet void left by the silenced demons. 'It's a Miracle' proceeded to float around the vast room. Some demons recognised the song immediately and saw the irony in it but stifled any laughter they might have normally wanted to be release. The new backing track did nothing to brighten Satan's mood. If there had been a demon in the room that hadn't been needed for the mission, he would have gladly vented his fury on it by ripping its head off and eating the brain. His red eyes scanned the crowd, willing one of them to crack a smile or avoiding giving him eye contact. But not one demon gave him the slightest provocation.

Lacking a vent for his rage, he decided to press on and hope he could dismember something later.

"Maggots, parasites, scum!" The idea of winning his audience to his side with kind, happy words was a concept Satan knew of – and used frequently on humans to win their souls – but it wasn't a method he needed to use with his own staff. "Listen to me! You are all going to Earth and you will obey me, *without question*! If this mission fails because of any of you, I'll personally create a new ring of Hell especially for those responsible, and probably the rest of you. You'll think that the damnation chambers you were once in charge of were happy hours in the Savoy Hotel."

Even the PA system seemed to take in the gravitas of his words and reduced the volume of the song. Satan noticed and was taken aback. He'd always tried to block out the music as much as possible by ignoring it, but the sound system always fought back and grew louder. This time, it was working with him, despite the choice of music. He just wished it would play some heavy metal or something slightly different for once; a song appropriate for the occasion rather than a chirpy, sing-along tune.

"You've already been personally instructed by Stuart as to what form you will take on Earth and what your roles and responsibilities will be. You'll have to put up with angels, and we're not there to collect souls, so any fighting will just be you battling against your normal urges to crush some do-gooder!"

There was a murmur; some muffled words and mooing of mutual, but reluctant, agreement from the assembled demons.

"God and I have conducted several telephone conversations and confirmed which dignitaries each side will be playing in front of the humans; no point in them being party to what's really going on. In our high-powered human guises, we won't be asked too many awkward questions. Make sure you don't walk around the hotel in your demon form, as that would make them suspicious. Just ensure you take orders from me and ignore the angels." He paused, surveying the room.

"However…" his voice grew stronger and he punctuated the word with a long, attention-holding pause, "if things go badly, or they should attack us, then I will not hesitate to issue the instruction to attack and *if* that happens; remember God will be there. So tantalisingly close." Satan held up his hand, making his fingers contort as if he had the deity trapped in his grasp. "Forget angels, archangels or saints – go for Him! With Him as our prisoner in Hell, Heaven will be defenceless and Earth would be ours for the taking! And the *oh,* so pompous and pious St. Peter will have no choice but to open up those precious gates of his and let us in."

The assembled crowd obviously liked the image and cheered rapturously. Each mind imagined their own favourite form of torture being inflicted upon the tender and sensitive parts of Jehovah's person. Shouts of "Yes!", "Alright!", and "Moo" punctuated the air. Even with the PA joining in by blasting out 'Could it be Magic' at full volume that wasn't enough to drown out the demons' joy.

Satan remained standing in front of his assembled hordes, arms folded across his chest and a smug grin on his face. If all went well he'd be able to return to Heaven and this? This would be history. Of course, some of the demons wouldn't be allowed back up there. Some might not adjust and would need to be sent back to Hell, others might not want to go to Heaven in the first place. He understood that there were some demons who could never relinquish their sadistic pleasures and would rather stay in Hell, inflicting pain on the damned. He could grudgingly see the joys of that. What demon couldn't? But to be back in Heaven, with the decent plumbing, and the manna instead of the muck he usually had to eat! The beds without springs always escaping and no bloody Barry Manilow songs piped at him at the worst possible moments? Bliss!

Chapter 20 – It Isn't Happening.

"Thank you, Charley that was very useful and interesting information. I'm sure if what you're saying is true, then my Christmas present to you will be very generous, reflecting our friendship and how long we've known each other. Yes, we'll have to meet up for a beer some time. Take care, buddy."

Ed Mercerator sat staring at the receiver, which he'd just placed back on the cradle on his desk. He chewed pensively on his lower lip as he collected his thoughts. The information he'd been given, very unofficially by a serving police officer, had sounded valid and genuine, but how could it be true? He'd seen it on the news that morning; the President was busy at the White House, greeting the Queen of England as she was on an official state visit and she would be spending a lot of time with him. She was even due to address both the Senate and House of Representatives, and surely the President wouldn't be able to just slip away for a week, stay at the best hotel on the island and then return without it being noticed?

Ed's left elbow rested on his desk, and he placed his head in his hand and drummed his fingers against his cheek. Surely someone was winding Charley Palakiko up? Maybe he'd just got the wrong end of the stick? What if it was just a scam? But Charley was only a patrol cop. He'd never supplied any massive leads in the past, but he had been useful and he'd never steered Ed wrong before. Perhaps there was some mileage in making a few calls and checking out a few basic facts. Ed had been a reporter for the last twenty years, working on various newspapers on the mainland. He'd seen it all and watched as newspaper's stopped being one of the key sources of information and became a quaint thing, irrelevant to increasing numbers as electronic media took over. He'd adapted and with a nose for a good story, and the tenacity to grab hold of a lead like a dog biting a postman's leg, made himself invaluable and not a dinosaur as many of his colleagues had become. He'd enjoyed his work and managed to do well working in Chicago, until he'd been forced to move to the warmer and sunnier climes of Oahu for health reasons. A high-powered politician and part time gangster had been arrested thanks to a story Ed unearthed about him. Despite being acquitted due to a legal technicality and several key witnesses mysteriously disappearing, the politician had made Ed a very generous offer. Leave Chicago quickly and possibly live a long and wholesome life, or remain in Chicago and live a very short life punctuated by a messy death; one where he would be put into an industrial meat grinder and made into hot dogs. The population of the city could digest him in a different way and he might not be as wholesome. Ed was a courageous journalist, and loved his name on a story, but if the story involved his name being the lead and reported the disappearance of a top reporter, discretion would be the better part of cowardice.

He had to admit living in Honolulu had its benefits. The weather was a lot better than Chicago, the people were friendlier and he could get a tan without having to become a tube steak and cooked for twenty minutes by gangsters. The one massive drawback was that the island was relatively small and it wasn't the way it was portrayed in Hawaii 5-0 or Magnum P.I. Crime wasn't rife and the petty larceny or mugging of tourists didn't excite him or the vast majority of the island's inhabitants. There were more murders in one week in Chicago, than there were in a year on Oahu. But at least he wasn't one of those statistics.

Consequently, this story had his wholehearted attention. If it was true, he could get a front-page story online, rather than some tale about a paperboy getting his bicycle stolen or a drunken trail of damage left by marines on weekend leave. He could be on people's lips and not need to worry about onions and mustard being involved. He got on his computer and checked a few basic facts. There it was online – photos of the President, grinning like a vacuous bumpkin, standing in the oval office next to the Queen. It was taken that morning and the page also listed her itinerary while in DC. Much of it was with the president. All fancy dinners, expensive dances and plenty of photo opportunities for a leader struggling in the polls and seeking re-election. There was no mention of any important conferences and no windows of opportunity for him to come to Hawaii for some top level secret talks. To Ed, it seemed almost impossible; people would notice and the story would soon leak and be front page news. But that's what had his nose twitching. What if it was true? He could have a real scoop. There were always ways of checking a few details without having to leave the desk. He'd always been friendly with key people dotted about the island and had met Mr. Knight a few times. As the manager of the hotel, he would be able to give him a quick yes or no. Checking contact numbers on his computer, he quickly found the right telephone number and began to dial. Knight's secretary answered promptly.

"Hello beautiful," he began on hearing her voice. "It's Eddie Mercerator from the Honolulu News, long time no see. How are you?" He was struggling to remember her name, but he could charm the birds from the trees so little details like that didn't matter at the moment.

"Hello, Mr. Mercerator, it has been a while. I think the last time you were here was when we had a spate of burglaries. How can I help you today?" Her voice was polite, but the friendliness seemed a little forced. As he remembered it the story he'd run had been favourable to the hotel and didn't offend.

"I'm good, thank you my dear. Is Mr. Knight in? I really need to speak to him."

After a few seconds the call was put through to the hotel manager.

"Hello Edward, how can I help you?" Ed was used to Mr. Knight maintaining his air of superiority, but he could sense a hint of tension in his voice.

115

"Hi. I've had a little dicky birdie tell me something big is about to happen on the island. Not just on the island, but at your hotel. Have you been holding out on me?"

"I, I, I don't know what you are talking about Mr. Mercerator. Everything is normal here. What have you heard?" There was a hint of panic in Knight's voice and Ed could hear it. "I assure you, there's nothing going on here!"

"Okay, sorry about that Mr. Knight. Obviously, I've been misinformed. How about a game of golf sometime?"

"Oh, yeah, Edward." Knight's voice was regaining its composure. "That would be great. It's a busy tourist season so I'm snowed under at the moment, but can I take a rain check?"

"Of course, I'll get in touch in a few weeks! Have a great day." Ed put the phone down. Something was wrong; he knew Mr. Knight hated golf with a passion and last time he'd picked up a club, he'd dislodged a divot that left a hole which could have created a new course hazard. The ball itself had hit a nearby tree and bounced so far, it was further from the hole than it had been when he teed off. Ed paused, thinking for a minute and then looked up another number online. He dialled it and heard a voice on the other end.

"Hello Terrapin Cove Hotel, how can I help you?"

"Hi there, I'd like to book a double room for two nights from Wednesday of next week. What have you got available?"

"I'm sorry, sir. We're fully booked all of next week and we have absolutely nothing available." The voice at the other end of the phone sounded confident and polite.

"Oh. Okay," Ed continued, "in that case could I book a slot, sometime next week, to play a round of golf? I've heard so many wonderful things about your course, I simply must play a round there."

116

"No sir, I'm terribly sorry but the golf course is also fully booked for next week and there are no slots available."

"Really? Oh, I'm so disappointed, but never mind. Thank you!" With that, he put the phone down again. He didn't know what was going on, but there was definitely something afoot, and it wasn't just something inside his shoe. Tales of US Special Forces troops keeping an eye on a Russian regiment, on a nature reserve, seemed ridiculous but a simple drive-by would soon verify their presence. And the fact that the hotel receptionist knew straight away, without having to pause and check, about the hotel being fully booked next week seemed strange. It wasn't the busiest part of the high season just yet, and there were always a few free rooms available. And not one slot free on the golf course? Highly unlikely.

He could smell it. Right in front of his nose there was a story. He had no idea what it was but it was big.

Ed got up and walked across the open plan office and knocked on a glass door at the far end. He opened it and walked straight in. "Boss, I think I have a really big story. Not sure what it is yet, but I need to take a quick drive up to Kahuku Point and see what it's all about. It's a few hours' drive, so I'll pop up there, see what's going on and be back in the morning"

"No you won't, Ed," his editor replied without looking up from his computer screen. "I've heard rumours too and I've already checked it out. It's just a waste of time. Just a dull birdwatchers' convention and it doesn't even warrant a paragraph, never mind the cost of the gas to drive up there. I've heard whispers of drugs being openly used by the Warriors football team and I want you to spend some time checking that out."

The optimistic smile on Ed's face froze. He got the impression he was being fobbed off, but he had enough experience not to let his boss know that. "Sure thing. I'll go and start looking into it now."

"Good," the editor responded, taking his eyes from the screen and looking directly at Ed. "There's no need to go running up to the Terrapin Cove Hotel. There's no story there!"

"Okay, boss, sure thing. No point in me rushing up there, then." He closed the door and walked back to his desk. Now he knew there was a story and it was getting even better. He'd never mentioned anything about the Terrapin Cove Hotel but he'd been told quite specifically not to go there. His opinion of his editor wasn't particularly high. He had no idea about basic grammar or punctuation and wouldn't know a good story if it was a hole, he'd fallen into it and couldn't get out again, necessitating a Collie dog to go for help. Perhaps he was trying to prove his worth by keeping the story, whatever it was, for himself. Or there was a conspiracy and the spineless editor was covering things up for higher powers, but Ed knew he was going to investigate the story. What did he have to lose? If he was wrong, he could check out the drug story soon enough. But if he was right, it could be big. He allowed the words 'Pulitzer Prize' to shoot across his mind. He opened his desk drawer, removed his car keys and left the office. It was a good day indeed and he was going to take a little drive up the Kamehameha Highway and do some proper journalism. It had been a long time.

Buckowski watched Ed walk out of the office and breathed a sigh of relief. He was convinced his lie had been swallowed hook, line and sinker. He'd started off his career sweeping the print room floors. He'd requested the chance to be a cub reporter and been given a break and quickly shown his superiors he had the journalistic aptitude to remain a floor sweeper for the rest of his life. The few leads he had been given, and followed up, had been enough to send the then-editor to sleep. When he'd been given one last chance, he'd missed a scoop about a famous rock singer dying of an overdose in a brothel – he'd gone to the wrong address and ended up in a warehouse instead. It wasn't until he'd made a deal with a friendly devil in a bar one evening that he'd swiftly, and inexplicably, begun his meteoric rise to his current position. Of course he had to lie to his staff occasionally when he got specific instructions from his unholy contract holder, but if it delayed his journey into Hell, he could live with that. Even if there was no story about drugs he was sure that Ed Mercerator, his star hotshot reporter, would be more than capable of finding some story which would make good copy and provide him with a few column inches.

Chapter 21 – There Are Just Three Steps..

Any human who happened to be out and about early that morning and happened to be looking at an out-of-the-way field on the island of Oahu, would have witnessed the spontaneous arrival of a large contingent of angels. They wouldn't however, have been able to make sense of it. The dimensional portal was disguised as a small, orange four-man tent and the angels came to Earth and materialised inside it a few at a time. It was more like a supernatural railway station, but hardly New York's Grand Central Terminus. A few got there, and walked out of the tent, quickly followed by a few more. After half an hour, God, archangels and angels had all materialised in human form and were mulling around the waiting vehicles and preparing to set off. Any human witness would have no clues who all the people were. They'd also be confused about how so many smartly dressed people managed to walk out of such a small tent, without anyone walking into it. They might also have been curious regarding why one of those people bore a striking resemblance to the President of the United States of America. All those sorts of occurrences were rare. Even in Hawaii, where virtually anything goes. Fortunately, there were no such witnesses. Angelic visitations were seldom believed, especially if the person involved mentions seeing the President and Marine One, his personal 'Whitehawk' VH-60N helicopter, and what appeared to be a large contingent of secret service agents. The total lack of heavenly light, wings or halos tended to add to the camouflage and subterfuge.

God glanced around, and seeing that everything was working, decided it was all good; as it usually was with angels. He was dressed in a light blue suit, white shirt and a red and pale grey striped tie. He looked every inch the exact replica of the president. Even the bits nobody would see were identical, right down to an old scar on his waist, from when the real president had fallen from a tree in his youth, and a mole shaped like a relief map of Italy on his left thigh. Such things were usually only seen by the First Lady and starstruck, but foolish, interns. Like a well-oiled machine, the angels disguised as Secret Service Agents – complete with black suits, dark glasses and discrete ear pieces – were getting into their sleek black limos and setting off on the three-mile drive to the hotel. They had plenty of time, but needed to maintain appearances and arrive before God so they could keep up the pretence that they were there to protect Him. God patiently watched the dwindling number of vehicles leave the field, and disappear along the adjoining highway. Once the last one was out of sight, he glanced at the four remaining agents standing with him. He enjoyed the theatrics and found it funny that here He was, God pretending to be President instead of the other way around, which was usually the case.

He smiled at his totally pointless bodyguards. After all, any would-be assassin would fail to hurt this particular celebrity and He gestured towards the waiting helicopter. "I needed to pull a few strings within the White House to get hold of all these cars and this helicopter, so I think it's appropriate we use it. After you, gentlemen." He gestured towards the open hatch of the waiting vehicle.

They boarded the small military helicopter and took their seats. It took off gently, the complete absence of pilots obscured by the darkened windows. Once off the ground, it turned and headed in the direction of the hotel, leaving only tracks in the ground as evidence of any vehicles having ever being there – along with a single, forlorn-looking orange tent which had managed to remain standing, despite the buffeting it had received from the helicopter's downdraft.

It wasn't a long distance for the helicopter to travel, but God was in no rush; the ersatz Security Service agents needed to be in place and ready to greet him when he left the helicopter. It was all about keeping up appearances for any human observers who might happen to be there. Besides, He enjoyed looking at his creations while He was on Earth and God had to admit, He'd done a fine job of it here. The Pacific Ocean to His left was beautiful and tranquil and the verdant mountains, drawing closer to his right, were majestic. After His Garden of Eden hadn't worked out to plan, He'd decided to have another try, without humans messing it up this time, and this had been the result. It wasn't until a lot later that man colonised the place and by then, He'd moved on and was paying more attention to the Middle East, ensuring the Bible stories were working out correctly.

Despite the added soundproofing in the small passenger compartment, the noise of the rotor blades was still loud, but it didn't matter. The angels knew their roles and God wasn't a great fan of small talk. So, they sat in silence, gazing out of the window. It was unlikely Satan would have sent any winged demons to intercept, but there was no harm in extra vigilance. Eventually, the imposing structure of the hotel came into view. A multi storey Y-shaped building, it was built on an outcrop of land jutting out into the ocean. Approaching from the west, above the golden sandy beach, they could see the angelic honour guard of black-suited guards congregated on the grassy lawn in front of the hotel, in position and ready to welcome the Presidential Helicopter, and the head of Government, sitting onboard. Standing among them God could just make out the shape of Mr. Knight, his shorter shape and white suit out of place among the burly guards. There was also a female in a red floral dress standing next to him. As they got closer her once beautifully coiffured long black hair became a victim of the downward draft of the helicopter's blades.

Once on the ground, the rotors stopped spinning and the exit door was opened. Secret Service agents quickly took up position to welcome the President and then Mr. Knight, and the slim lady, approached the door. The doppelganger President stepped out of the helicopter and gave the assembled people an obligatory wave and a broad, toothy smile.

Mr. Knight walked up to him with an obsequious expression on his face. "Mr President, please accept my heart felt welcome to the Terrapin Cove Hotel." He offered his hand, which the President shook vigorously. "The facilities are at your total and utter disposal and if you require anything all you have to do is ask and we'll move Heaven and Hell to ensure your stay is as comfortable and memorable as possible."

God smiled at Mr. Knight's incorrect, but accidentally ironic, turn of phrase. 'If only you knew' he thought, 'Heaven and Hell had moved to be here'. He was also sure his stay here would be memorable for reasons the fawning hotel manager could never imagine. Perhaps His welcome would have been even warmer, if Mr. Knight knew the true identity of his star guest, but not so friendly if the real names of some of the other meeting attendees were revealed. The marketing team, in charge of populating the hotel's promotional website and tourist brochures, would have a field day boasting about it being God's favourite vacation spot, but a five-star recommendation from Satan might not attract the type of guest they really wanted. Moonlit virgin sacrifices on the golf course at midnight, or pentacles on the sandy beach would never replace the more traditional lu'au.

Mr. Knight continued his well-rehearsed welcoming speech. "Mr. President, if I may, please let you introduce you to my daughter, Caroline Moore. I hope you don't mind, she was dying to meet you." Mr. Knight stepped to one side so the young lady could move forward and shake her country's leader's hand. She was tall and slender, but thanks to the effects of the helicopter's approach she looked as if she'd spent five minutes in a tumble dryer. Her hair was windswept and half covering her face and her once-pristine dress was dishevelled.

"Pleased to meet you, Ms. Moore." God shook her hand and He could sense the excitement in her soul at having met someone so powerful. He was glad it wasn't the real President here today, Caroline was very attractive and her evident admiration of the leader of the free world, and innocent naivety, would have left her vulnerable to the President's manipulative advances and seduction. His secret agents might

123

have been proficient at arranging for secret trysts and then covering up his many subsequent indiscretions; but God knew all about them. He gently brushed the hair away from her face. "I hope you'll be voting for me?" It was an unnecessary question, but He liked to stay in character as much as possible. He also sensed she had early stages of a rather strong and virulent form of cancer in her liver, so he quickly made that disappear. He could now see a long and fruitful good life ahead of this girl.

Totally oblivious to the miracle she'd received, Caroline giggled and replied, "Oh yes, Mr. President, I certainly will".

The greetings completed, Mr. Knight escorted the President to the hotel, closely followed by his daughter and the cadre of angels in the guise of Secret Service agents. Dedan had been standing by the nearest hotel wall, casually leaning against it with one foot resting on the concrete behind him. He was well away from the showy arrival of his deity, observing the goings on, but also keeping a wary eye out for any unexpected surprises. As the procession walked past, Dedan stood to what could best be described as slovenly attention. God glanced at him and offered him a slight nod in a gesture of recognition and acknowledgement of a plan going perfectly: so far.

Dedan returned the nod and went back to scanning the surroundings. Satan had made use of grassy knolls before, so he wanted to ensure no demon repeated that tactic. Once the long line of people had walked past, he casually joined the back of the procession and walked into the hotel. After standing outside for so long, wearing a suit in the glorious sunshine, the air conditioning in the lobby was refreshing. He watched the manager's daughter, admiring her slim figure, but then looked at the President and saw Him looking at him, His eyebrow raised. That one gesture said all Dedan needed to know. *Hands off and behave yourself!* Dedan returned the look with a shrug of his shoulders and a mocking look, as if to say *'What? Who? Me?'* but he'd got the message and would obey.

While they waited for the other angels, disguised as world dignitaries, to arrive, God – ever the consummate performer, stood in the foyer chatting amiably to Mr. Knight. His daughter and various hotel staff were close by standing at attention and ready to provide for His every wish. He glanced outside and saw more of the black limos arrive and one car at a time, a long list of the great and the good of fake international leaders stepped out. First to arrive was the Prime Minister of the United Kingdom, then the president of France. Numerous other luminaries filtered into the hotel, the last of which was a dour-looking President of Russia. The angel playing him didn't particularly like his given character, but he was acting it out with aplomb – all sullen grimaces and scowls, with an expression like a Rottweiler chewing a wasp. The mock contempt for his earthly host was there for the world to see. God graciously shook the hand of each leader and once they were acknowledged and escorted to their designated rooms God was taken to his penthouse suite by Mr. Knight, who was enjoying his fifteen minutes of fame as the escort to the leader of his country and titular leader of the free world.

Dedan saw Emily sitting at the lobby bar, drinking a large cola with ice. He hadn't seen her enter the hotel, but he was pleased to see her. She was stunning in her tight yellow dress and high heels. She offered him a joyous smile and gestured to the bar stool next to hers, inviting him to sit down. He didn't need to be invited twice when given the come-on by a voluptuous, attractive woman, so he sidled up, gave her a quick hug and polite kiss on the cheek and took his place by the bar. Ordering a large vodka from the barman, they started to talk while Dedan kept a cautious eye on the main door in anticipation of the demon contingent. He glanced at his watch; although the angels had arrived on time, the schedule given to Grank had been doctored by a few hours so that even if Satan tried to get to the hotel early, he'd still arrive well after God got to his room and settled in. It avoided any possible disagreements over who had the best room. Dedan oversaw all rooms anyway, so he'd already ensured the angels had the best views.

Chapter 22 – It Sure Beats Being In Hell.

The Earth-bound dimensional portal from Hell could be more accurate than the one that sent demons from Earth back to Hell. In this instance, they arrived in the large carpark on the complex of the Brigham Young University in Laie. No students were about in the Saturday morning sunshine, some busy sleeping off hangovers from the illicit alcohol they'd smuggled into their rooms, others already on the beach. Parking bays were occupied by stretch limos and Hummers which had been specially shipped in from the mainland for the occasion. Satan had understandings with many American politicians and mob bosses, so he was easily able to ensure they acquiesced to his request for free transportation from his assembly point to the hotel. One head of a large gangster family even offered to provide hookers to make the journey even more pleasant and enjoyable, but after some deliberation Satan decided it wouldn't be in keeping with the occasion, and the purpose of his visit, to arrive and greet God covered in gaudy lipstick and smelling of expensive perfume; having given the limo's suspension an extra work out enroute. Instead, he'd opted for a less objectionable alternative and insisted on well-stocked mini bars in the back of each car.

As the portal began to disgorge its cargo of demons, in the form of world politicians, the air began to swirl coldly around the area. Several mock humans arrived first in matching dark grey suits and red ties, looking dishevelled from their uncomfortable trip across the dimensions. Subsequent leaders appeared dressed in similar suits and in equally messy and untidy states. Finally, Satan arrived, looking exactly like the President of the United States of America, only this version was dressed in a burgundy suit and his hair was slicked back more than the regular leader usually would. He didn't mind playing the part of the guy, but Satan had to embellish on the appearance and give him more style and panache. Once his rough re-entry on Earth was completed, he checked his appearance in the wing mirror of a nearby car. Smoothing his hair down and straightening his tie, he took stock of his surroundings. All the demons had arrived now, along with a large oak steamer trunk, wrapped in chains, which stood on the tarmac rocking slightly and its contents releasing a barely audible howl.

"Come on," Satan shouted in a menacing growl, "get in your vehicles and let's get going! I'll be damned..." He paused when he realised what he'd said "Again... if I'm going to let God get there before me."

With those words, the demons proceeded to climb in to the nearest limos. Although they were all the same, in every detail, the leaders took it into their heads that they needed to have any vehicle a neighbouring demon had selected. Consequently, lots of shouting and arguing had erupted in pockets across the car park. Everyone knew Satan would take the lead car, but they all wanted to be in the cars immediately following his. A demon's ego was a hard thing to suppress.

Eventually, the dignitaries grudgingly found their designated vehicles and were sitting waiting for the convoy to set off. Most had already discovered the alcohol-filled mini bars and were doing their best to empty the contents before they'd even left the car park.

The numerous demons who'd been given the roles of CIA, FBI and NSA agents helped load up the indistinctly-swearing steamer trunk into the back of a large silver grey Hummer and then boarded their own vehicles. Two of these vehicles set off first, followed by the Satanic President in his limo, then the rest of the luxury cavalcade. The convoy making its northbound, thirty-mile journey to the hotel. Once the vehicles left the car park, no trace of any evil arrivals remained. The calm morning silence returned quickly, punctuated only by pleasant birdsong and the faint hum of distant traffic.

Satan helped himself to a miniature bottle of single malt whisky, from the tiny bar in front of him. Pouring it into a cut crystal glass, he took an appreciative sip of the warming liquid. With the exception of the foul Japanese imitations, no matter what the brand or age of the stuff, whisky on Earth always tasted far better than the stuff he consumed in Hell. He took another sip and allowed the light brown liquid to rest on his taste buds before swallowing it. Whisky had been one of his most pleasant creations, and he knew how to appreciate it fully. Other demons might swig it as if it were water, but some things had to be savoured. He held the glass up to the light coming through the window and studied the contents. He looked at Stuart, who was sitting quietly next to him. "You know Stuart, I have a good feeling about this trip. Imagine it, being back in Paradise. No more eternal fires, no more screaming, complaining, damned souls."

This was Stuart's first return to Earth since he was killed by a filing cabinet full of embezzlement records falling on him, so he was enjoying the break from hell. He wasn't confident his master's plan had any chance of working, but he knew enough to keep such thoughts to himself. "Sir," he began, his voice oily and full of dripping sarcasm which Satan chose to ignore, "I've never been in Heaven, but the brochure makes it sound nice. I was born in Lancashire, England, sir. So, this is the closest I've ever been to paradise, and from what I've seen of it so far, it looks very nice. It's good to feel the sun on my skin again after all these years of the eternal fires of Hades. I'm sure Heaven is even lovelier so any little cloud up there, that you manage to arrange for me, would be greatly appreciated".

Satan glanced at him suspiciously. He detected a hint of sarcasm in Stuart's words, but chose to ignore them, looking him up and down disdainfully. Even in a smart suit, Stuart still looked like a slug wrapped in an old cloth – the most skilled, talented tailor on Earth would have his work cut out trying to imbue him with even a modicum of élan. His personality, or lack thereof, oozed out through every pore and became his outward appearance. In Hell, Satan found Stuart a useful lackey, but he wasn't sure such a vile little creature would ever find a place in

Heaven. He wouldn't miss his personal servant if he returned to Heaven alone. Even in his days as a close friend and confidante of God, and in the time before he'd created Hell, the place had standards and many a wayward or unsuitable soul had been left in purgatory, rather than be allowed into Heaven to clutter up the place and spoil the views. Yes, after careful consideration, he'd have to make sacrifices and leave some of his old baggage in Hell, and Stuart was one such piece of his current life he'd gladly give up.

Oblivious of his master's plans for him, or more accurately, *lack* of plans, Stuart returned to staring out of the window. The scenery was pleasing and, he was making the most of it. In the distance, he saw what looked like lots of people in a large open area, mingling around khaki tents. As the limo drew closer he could make out one half of the group was dressed in black, and they were marching around a makeshift parade ground or sitting and polishing shoes, while the other half were denim clad men with terrible haircuts, sitting around laughing, drinking beer and eating what appeared to be barbecued chicken. Recognising the blue clad army, he realised what had happened and managed to suppress a laugh.

"Sir" he ventured hesitantly, his lips pulled back to revealed his stained, yellowing teeth.

"Yes Stuart, what is it?" snapped Satan, annoyed at being pulled back to reality.

"Sorry sir, it doesn't matter!" Smiling to himself, he went back to gazing out of the window and contemplating his master's rage when he discovered the unofficial truce between angels and demon forces.

"Suit yourself" replied Satan and went back to his day dreaming. If God didn't succumb to small talk, Satan despised it with a passion – and he had no desire to indulge in it just to pass the time with a contemptible underling.

Eventually, the entourage of executive vehicles snaked their casual way northwards along the scenic highway and arrived on the outskirts of the hotel complex. At the turn off from the main road the cars were waved on by two black-suited Secret Service officers. They radioed ahead to notify the angels, who had requisitioned the hotel's security office of the imminent arrival of the demonic contingent. On receiving the news, one of the angels sent the other occupant out to go find Dedan and warn him of the approaching, less friendly and more unpredictable, guests.

The door exiting from the security room – full of CCTV monitors, radios on chargers and other paraphernalia – was discrete and unobtrusive and opened directly onto the lobby area. As soon as the angel stepped out he saw Dedan's back, propping up the bar and chatting to Emily. The angel raised his eyes to the ceiling. *'Typical'*. Dedan had a well-deserved, and wide spread reputation.

He walked up to Dedan briskly and tapped him on the shoulder "Dedan, they're on their way. They've just entered the complex, should be here in a couple of minutes."

"Okay, many thanks," answered Dedan, stepping down from his bar stool. "Round up a few agents and meet me outside the main door."

"No problem." And with that, the angel went off to find any available mock Secret Service Agents he could find.

"Sorry Angel, I have to go. Catch you later." he said to Emily with a pretend sad frown.

"See you later Dedan, you horny old dog!" Emily responded as he walked away. The comment was greeted by a waving hand and a loud barking noise, but he didn't turn around to look at her. He'd already set his mind onto more important things.

Once outside, he squinted as his eyes adjusted to the glorious sunshine. It was warm, but there was a slight breeze coming off the ocean which felt good. Looking across the grassy area, past the helicopter which waited to be needed again, he saw the pale blue waters of the Pacific Ocean. Dedan had always been in awe of the sea. When he was alive, all those centuries ago in what was now a miniscule corner of Saudi Arabia, he'd never seen an ocean. He'd heard tales of them, but the only seas he'd seen were created of sand which surrounded what became known as the Dedanite kingdom; a small but significant dot on the map for the lucrative caravans on the incense trade route. But after his demise, and subsequent elevation to angelhood, he'd been able to view all the seas and oceans and quickly fallen in love with them. He recognised the raw and almost limitless power, occasional serenity mixed with pure force. The beauty overwhelmed him and he had to admire God for creating something so vast and unpredictable. He could stand there watching them for hours, as long as he didn't have to go out and be *on* them. Even angels could get seasick.

His reverie was broken when a Hummer drove past him and stopped fifty yards further down the road, disgorging its demonic cargo of suited FBI agents. They looked the part and played it well. Approaching Dedan, they challenged him and he returned their curt questions with polite, yet hard-edged answers. He had no intention of being browbeaten by self-important devils. He'd dealt with visitors from Hell many times before and knew exactly how to deal with them.

The demons took up positions next to Dedan and as the first limo arrived, one of them looked at Dedan in anticipation, as if expecting him to step forward and open Satan's car door.

Dedan tilted his head and raised an eyebrow at the demon. "Really? Come on! As if that is *ever* going to happen!"

The demon merely gave a throaty growl in response and stepped forward, opening the rear door of the limo. Satan casually stepped out and with a stretch surveyed the area around him. He was unhappy that God had given him the wrong time for arrival. He'd deliberately arrived an hour early, but still hadn't got to the hotel first and snatched the room reserved for God. *'You just can't trust anybody these days'* he thought. Walking towards Dedan, he looked every inch a slicker version of the same President who'd arrived a little earlier. "And you are?" he asked in a smooth voice.

"Hello, President Bob, I'm Dedan. I'm in charge of God's arrangement and I'm here to ensure you don't try any tricks."

"Ah, yes – Dedan." Satan's teeth clenched at the deliberate lack of respect shown by Dedan's use of his unwelcome sobriquet. It was one thing for 'Gordon' to call him Bob, but certainly unacceptable for some annoying angel. "I've heard a lot about you over the years and it's interesting to finally meet you. In the past, you've been an annoyance and spoilt a few schemes I'd invested a lot of time and planning into!"

"Really? Have I? That's wonderful to know. Thank you very much." Dedan maintained his stoic expression, but inside, he was enjoying finally officially meeting the person who'd kept him so busy for such a long time. Being recognised as a thorn in his side just added to the experience.

President Satan gave Dedan a cold smile. "Never mind, dear boy. All water under the bridge now." His voice suddenly took on an air of calm and relaxed charm. "Perhaps if all goes well, after this conference, we can put things behind us and become friends and neighbours?"

Dedan raised an eyebrow; he knew the supposed purpose of the meeting, but he found the idea of Satan actually succeeding and taking up permanent residence in Heaven –

never mind anywhere near Dedan's heavenly condo – a very hard image to visualise. No matter what, there was no chance of Satan being invited to one of his occasional barbecues – whether he brought a bottle or not.

Satan could sense what Dedan was thinking and laughed at the mild discomfort he'd generated. "Relax, who knows? I might not be as *bad* as people seem to think I am." He punctuated the sentence by giving Dedan a jovial slap on the shoulder. "So Dedan, are you going to show me in?"

"Certainly. But one thing first. What the hell are you doing here in the guise of the President of the sodding United States of America? Grank and I agreed everything in advance and what nations you and your lot were supposed to represent were clearly laid down. God has already arrived and, he is the President."

"Oh, He would be him, wouldn't He!" Satan countered. "Well, I decided the list of nations you gave me was pathetic. Andorra, Nepal, Morocco, Chad? Come on, what kind of place on the world stage do they deserve? Hardly credible for a, so called, covert and critical conference for high-powered world leaders. I decided to alter the seating arrangements slightly and make it look like it was important and I'm sure that any human witnesses will find it interesting."

"Interesting? That isn't the word I'd use. Two identical Presidents of the USA having a conference with each other to discuss the future of the world sounds downright schizophrenic. Any human witnesses will think they've taken LSD."

Satan laughed even louder. "Yes, funny isn't it?" He started to walk into the hotel, followed by his demonic bodyguard. Stuart scurried after his master, pausing to give Dedan an oily smile before carrying on into the hotel.

Dedan muttered an exasperated oath under his breath and quickly pushed his way past the demons to enter the hotel. Mr. Knight had seen, from his office window, more limos starting to arrive, so he'd resumed his position in the lobby, ready to meet and greet the new contingent of world leaders. His surprise and confusion was apparent when he stepped forward, hand outstretched, and greeted the President of the USA – again. Only this time, the leader was in a dark red suit and had slicked-back hair. The mental turmoil of the befuddled manager was compounded as the rest of the VIP's – or more accurately Very Important Demons (VID's), left their transportation and walked into the hotel to be introduced to him. In a period of just over a hour, he'd ended up shaking hands with not only one too many Presidents of the USA, but another three Prime Ministers of Great Britain, two more presidents of France, one Queen of Andorra who looked more like a drag queen, and a Prime minister of Jamaica, who for some inexplicable reason carried an uncanny resemblance to Papa Doc Duvalier, only with dreadlocks and a Rasta hat. There were six presidents of Belgium, of which four were male and two were female. None of them bore any resemblance to the previous one, as no one in Hell knew, or cared, what the leader of Belgium looked like or what gender they were. The demons had been given free rein to choose the country of their choice, so they'd unilaterally picked countries at random. The fact that other demons had picked the same country didn't matter to any of them.

By the time all the new arrivals had trooped past, and gone to their rooms, Mr. Knight's eyes had glazed over and he looked at Dedan. His mouth opened and shut repeatedly, but no words came forth, leaving him looking like an exceedingly large goldfish in a white suit.

"I know this all seems a little bit strange and odd," Dedan volunteered, struggling to come up with a credible and sensible explanation, "but I can explain. Shall we talk in your office?" He put a comforting arm around the bemused manager's shoulder and started to lead him to his room. He was hoping he'd be able to make up something which would make sense before he got to the office. He opened the door for Mr. Knight and followed him in to his secretary's area. He nodded politely to Caroline and Cynthia who were gossiping together about the earlier meeting with the first president and then strode into the main office and closed the door behind him. Mr. Knight walked to the other side of his desk and sat down, his gaze transfixed on some invisible object hovering over Dedan's right shoulder.

"As you know," the almost equally confused angel began, "this conference is highly secret and of critical importance."

Mr Knight nodded in vague agreement.

"Well, news of this meeting leaked out and several terrorist groups, from around the world, got wind of it and threatened to kill some of the world leaders. I'm sure you appreciate that such threats are usually just empty words, but we had to take some highly unusual and secret measures to protect all involved." Dedan paused to look at Mr. Knight and noticed he was still staring blankly into the distance. "Consequently, we decided to create an elaborate diversion. The more confusing the number of leaders there are, the harder it is for any would-be assassin to choose the right target and obtain political capital. It's a bit like zebras!"

That word seemed to draw Mr. Knight out of his private world of swirling and spinning images of world leaders. "Zebras?" he asked with a quizzical expression on his face.

"Exactly!" Dedan exclaimed in a voice louder than intended, which made Mr. Knight jump. "Zebras!" His voice lowered to a normal tone. "They stand around on the Serengeti plains, happily eating the grass until a lion or pack of hyenas appear out of nowhere. Once they're in sight, what do the zebra do?"

135

"Do?" Mr. Knight was beginning to lose the thread of what was going on again. "Zebras…"

"They run around in all directions, Mr. Knight! All black and white stripes." He paused. "Or is it white and black stripes? Never mind, all the stripes confuse any would be predator and nine times out of ten, they're left bewildered and the poor lion is still hungry and skulks off to try and find an easier meal."

"Zebra," the hotel manager repeated in a vague tone. He had no idea what Dedan was talking about and was beginning to suspect that the next time he left his office he would walk into the lobby and it would have turned into a safari park complete with stripy horses. He shook his head to get rid of the image of a lion pouncing on him. "Zebra," he said again, as if it would help the conversation.

"So, Mr. Knight, those numerous and occasionally odd-looking bunch of so-called world leaders are actually trained decoys. We know which ones are the real ones and which are fakes. Thus, confusing any enemy."

Mr. Knight didn't know or care about any enemies, but he was certainly confused and hadn't really followed much of what he had been told once the zebras had been introduced into the conversation. His mind was on some dusty nature reserve in Africa, hypnotised by dancing black and white stripes. He was happy there and enjoying the golden sunset he'd once seen on a wildlife documentary, and for the moment, he had no desire to return to the strange reality which had taken over his hotel.

Dedan felt his explanation was sufficient for the moment and any further embellishments would have fallen on deaf ears, so he decided he'd best leave Mr. Knight in his own private world and return to his duties, ensuring Satan and his numerous demons didn't get up to any tricks. "I'm going now,

Mr. Knight; if you could stay in your office as much as possible during the meetings, it would be greatly appreciated."

"Zebras…" replied Mr. Knight.

"Exactly," whispered Dedan as he exited from the manager's office, "zebras!"

Once back in the lobby, he looked around to ensure everything appeared correct and in place. There were scatterings of various undercover supernatural beings and he wasn't sure if angel was following, and keeping a wary eye on demon, or vice versa, but he recognised the mutual suspicion and distrust between both sides. Oblivious hotel staff carried out their normal duties, unaware of the real identities of the people who'd taken over their hotel. And there, where he'd left her, sat Emily. She'd swivelled around and was facing him with a broad smile on her face. She held a cocktail glass in her hand and she was resting it nonchalantly on her crossed legs. Her tight dress revealed a small section of firm, muscular thigh which Dedan instinctively noticed. She raised the empty glass and gently shook it, inviting him to come join her. He put his fingers to his lips and blew her a kiss, then spread his arms in an apologetic, and supplicatory, gesture and pointed to the corridor leading to the lifts. He would have loved to have continued his pleasant conversation with the beautiful angel, but he had more important, pressing duties to attend to.

Emily excused his inattentiveness with a graceful smile and swivelled around so she was facing the bar again and could order a refill. She watched Dedan disappear and began to sip her drink. She'd soon have plenty to do, but for now she was enjoying being on Earth and the opportunity to get the alcoholic buzz which was always missing from the beverages served on Heaven. She really missed hangovers.

Chapter 23 – Beth.

Beth had deliberately held back from entering the hotel at the same time as her demonic colleagues. Despite her critical role as the sole official go-between and line of communication with the angels, she preferred to maintain a low profile and avoid attracting too much attention. It wasn't easy to do, however. She-devil's instinctively opted for a seductive and vampish appearance, and Beth was no exception. When she entered the hotel and strolled across the lobby floor, mortal men, angels and demons alike stopped to watch her lustfully. Her hips swayed, holding their gaze and her long dark hair bounced freely on her shoulders and across the back of her tight black dress. She instinctively gave her admirers a withering look. She knew how to manipulate men and break their hearts, but that wasn't her job here, so she was determined to pay them as little attention as possible. Her focus was on other things – for once, she was looking for a woman.

Scanning the area, she saw her target sitting at the cocktail bar. Her briefing had been to seek out a female angel who would meet her in the bar and be the single point of contact for issues relating to angel and demon peace and cooperation. This didn't extend to Satan's talks with God, but that didn't bother her. She had power over male demons and that was her raison d'être. Dominating and controlling men was what she did best, whether by leather and whips, her body, or in this instance, words and withering looks.

Walking towards Emily, she deliberately added an extra swing to her hips, which resulted in numerous onlookers having to hide the resulting groinal appreciation of her figure behind trays, folders or cupped hands. All attempts to look inconspicuous failed abysmally, their excitement obvious to anyone who had a habit of looking at such things. "Hello boys," she whispered, pleased by the awkwardness she'd created.

When she got to the cocktail bar, she settled on the stool next to Emily. The barman was ready and waiting; one attractive woman had already captured his attention and as his only customer he'd enjoyed serving her, but now he had two beautiful women in front of him he was experiencing the same problems as the other males and was glad he was wearing a white apron to cover his arousal. Beth gazed directly into his eyes and gave him a look which made his heart race and had him suspecting he was, if not in love, at least in lust. Beth had exactly the same effect on many men. "I'd like a 'Slow Comfortable Screw against the Wall," she requested in her most suggestive voice.

"Yes, of course Ma'am" he replied in a high-pitched squeak, as his hormones diverted blood from his vocal chords to his crotch.

Emily heard what was happening and without looking directly at Beth, smiled at the obvious act. "I take it you're the director of communications?" she enquired, holding up her glass and pointing at it so the barman would give her a refill.

"Yes. I'm Beth."

"Emily" replied the other woman.

Both women turned on their seats so they could study their opposite number, in a way only women do. It involved recognising and being instantly jealous of the other's beauty while seeking out any physical blemish. The blemish could be split ends, a flaw in their makeup, or signs of cosmetic surgery – anything that would enable them to find fault and feel superior, while simultaneously being friendly to their face. Like some biological radar, they scanned each other's appearance and both failed to find any fault, so they resorted to the traditional fall-back position of making up one.

'*Skinny trollop*', Emily thought, while Beth decided Emily tried too hard with her makeup and was a little too big on top. Once the obligatory faults had been found and pigeon-holed, they could get on with the job of becoming the best of friends and ensuring they did their jobs properly.

Over the ensuing hours they casually chatted. Once the lines of official communication and procedures had been discussed and agreed, they were free to talk of other things. How useless and ego-filled men were, their past conquests and also shoes. Beth enjoyed the fact that she'd been mentioned in the Bible and happily went into great detail regarding how useless King David was in bed, and how Solomon was actually fathered by a willing bodyguard.

Emily wasn't so old but, as the numerous drinks began to affect both their brains, she gladly shared tales of her exploits. Despite being theological and moral opposites, by the end of the night they'd become firm friends, sharing a common disdain for men. The barman had cottoned on to the theme of their conversation early, and decided to retreat to a safe distance further along the bar, only approaching when they needed more drinks.

Eventually the two women decided their conversation had run its course and sufficient alcohol had been consumed for one day, so they mutually agreed to retire to their rooms.

Leaving the stools, they leaned on each other for support. Beth hadn't checked in, so they staggered to the reception desk to allow her to book in and collect her room pass. Giggling loudly all the way, they proceeded to the lifts. When the doors slid open, they half fell, half walked into their respective elevators, the doors sliding behind them. They both heard the lift muzak playing a tinny version of 'The Girl from Impanema' and immediately laughed rowdily, despite being in separate lifts. Although in different wings of the hotel, they were on the same floor number, so the elevators arrived simultaneously. Emily was met by two angel Secret Service agents and Beth by two demon NSA agents, both agencies responsible for protecting their respective leaders. Each set of guards recognised their own drunk and dishevelled head of communications and allowed them access.

Emily squinted at the agents and offered them a drunken greeting. "Hi! I bet you've got some *really* big weapons hidden inside your suits," she announced, with a further bout of laughter.

Once out of the lift, Beth zig-zagged in the direction of her room. After several attempts at getting the pass key into the lock slot, she entered the room. Collapsing fully dressed on her bed, she went straight to sleep.

Emily managed to open the door to her room, with the willing assistance of an angel guard. Once inside, she walked unsteadily toward the bed, but collapsed just short of it. On hitting the floor, she hazily contemplated a second attempt at getting in the bed, but in the end, decided to sleep where she was.

Chapter 24 – From A Distance.

When Ed arrived outside the property belonging to the Terrapin Cove Hotel complex, he'd attempted to turn off the highway and onto the road which went past the golf course to the hotel, but the way was blocked by two men in suits and wearing dark glasses. They flashed United States Secret Service identification badges and sent him on his way, making it abundantly clear he wouldn't be allowed access and his presence wasn't welcome.

Ed apologised profusely, saying he didn't realise and was only looking for a game of golf and then proceeded to drive away. He stopped half a mile further down the highway, out of sight of the complex and its grounds. *'No President?'* he thought to himself. *'Secret Service?'* The USSS had two roles; one being to investigate fraud for the treasury and the other to protect presidents and their families. He doubted they were guarding a hotel because of money laundering or counterfeiting. His senses were buzzing and he knew that no matter what his boss said, there was a story here and it was big.

As he was about to cross the road and begin his long walk to try and gain access to the hotel, he was delayed when a long cavalcade of black limos with darkened windows drove past him. He had no idea where they'd come from, but he was certain he knew where they were heading. Once they'd driven around the bend and were out of sight, he ran across the road and into a densely wooded area. If he continued in a straight line, he would eventually reach the beach and hopefully get closer to the hotel that way. Walking cautiously, he had to dive to the ground a couple of times when he spotted suited guards.

He heard the loud juddering noise of a helicopter and looking up saw a helicopter, bearing the seal of the President of the USA. His resolve renewed by the sight, he pressed on with his slow journey toward the beach. Eventually, through a clearing in the woods, he saw the sea. Carefully he skirted around

142

the grassy area and surveyed the golden sand. "Damn," he swore under his breath when he saw more suited agents standing on the golden sands. He could see the hotel jutting out in the distance and the helicopter resting on the lawn in front of it, but he had no easy way to get any closer. He'd have to try and head eastwards through the woods as best he could and then try and crawl closer once the cover ran out. He was too old, fat and out of shape for such exertions and in his shorts and blue patterned shirt he wasn't exactly inconspicuous, but he had to try.

At the edge of the wood he saw the golf course, where lots of sentries patrolled. It seemed that there were two distinct groups of undercover agents and they seemed more preoccupied with watching each other than seeking out any unwanted interlopers. For some strange reason, what appeared to be a herd of black and white Friesian cows was busily eating grass and chewing the cud at the eighteenth hole. Ed had never seen such cows on the island before and had no idea how they'd got there or why they were being tolerated on the golf course. Regardless, there was little chance of him making his way across the fairways in daylight, without standing out like a Ku Klux Klansman at a Mississippi gospel choir concert. He glanced down to the beach again and saw a slim chance of getting closer to his target. There was a slight sand bank between him and the agents on the sand. If he was quick and kept his profile low, he might just be able to run, bent double, and remain out of sight. He waited for a good opportunity and ran. His imagined his squat figure looked more large, awkward, waddling duck than Navy SEAL, but luck was with him and he managed to get to the blind side of the sand bank without being seen. The soft sand left his footprints visible, but not too obvious, and he hoped by the time they were noticed he'd be close enough to his destination that he'd be able to find a better route.

Maintaining his ape-like posture, he ran as fast as he could, having to stop frequently to catch his breath. He had to dive to the ground a couple of times when he saw people, but he finally made it to some stone steps leading up to the hotel.

He had no idea why, but they were unguarded. Perhaps no one expected an intruder to have got this far with all the guards. Maybe the guards were just out of his line of sight, but he took the opportunity anyway and ran, expecting to hear voices challenging him at any second, but none came. He reached the top of the stairs and paused, breathing heavily. He could see the helicopter on the grass to one side and on the other was the hotel entrance, but there were more guards by the door and he could see others patrolling around the perimeter of the building. They were heading his way and he was running out of options. He could go back, or he'd be captured as he skulked by the hotel wall.

He suddenly had an idea. Why hide? Someone running around and trying to hide would stand out like a sore thumb, especially someone of his shape and size – so why not bluff it out? He stood up, brushed any obvious sand from his clothing and proceeded to walk casually towards the hotel main entrance. "Hello," he greeted the guards as he got closer. He tried to appear as nonchalant as possible, and the ruse worked. The guards gave him a scowl, nodded reluctantly, and continued on their patrol.

The demon guards saw him but just assumed that he was one of the Angel delegates. Their orders to avoid interaction, and any possible conflict, with their enemy working in his favour.

He got to the door and used the same tactic with the guards there and was thrilled when they allowed him into the hotel unchallenged.

The angels just making a similar assumption to the other guards, this time just thinking he was probably a demon delegate out for a walk. Possibly one of the many Presidents of Belgium.

To his utter disbelief, and thanks to elements that he had no comprehension of, he'd made it. He was in the hotel's reception area. There were plenty of people milling around, but they were mostly wearing suits and very obviously special agents, or hotel staff in uniforms. As out of place as Ed looked; nobody seemed to give him a second glance. Most seemed preoccupied with two very attractive women sitting at the cocktail bar, but Ed had other things on his mind at the moment. He needed to get out of sight, so he casually walked towards a double door with a 'No Entry' sign at the far end of the room. Still no challenges were issued and he couldn't believe his luck.

Once through the doors, and out of sight again, he rested his back against a wall and took a deep breath of pure relief. He'd visited the hotel many times, but he'd never been in this area before. Taking stock of the unfamiliar surroundings he saw a plain white corridor with several closed doors lining it. The dull painted walls and plain beige carpet was in stark contrast to the opulent décor of the rest of the building. This corridor was obviously for staff only, so no expense had been wasted on beautifying the surroundings. Ed walked along the corridor, trying doors as he went along. Some were locked but those rooms he could gain access to were investigated. As expected, there were broom cupboards, linen closets, rooms full of toiletries waiting to go into guest's rooms and finally he found what he was looking for. The staff laundry was filled with uniforms, washed and pressed and hung up ready to be worn. He flicked through the long rack of clothing until he managed to find something which might fit his rotund frame. He undressed and tried on the generously proportioned uniform. It wasn't a perfect fit – the trousers were a little bit tight and the tunic was slightly too large, but when he looked at himself in a wall-mounted, full length mirror, he thought he might just get away with the charade as long as no one looked at him too closely, or, asked too many questions.

Folding his old clothes, he stuffed them out of sight in an empty locker nearby and left the room again.

He was in.

Chapter 25 – Atrophy.

Happiness wasn't usually the default emotion associated with Satan. Anger? Yes. Hatred? Obviously, it went without saying. But happy? *No!* Satan himself would admit he hadn't got to where he was today because of a cute side to his nature. But he could on occasion be happy, and not in the sadistic, 'let's skin a kitten for fun' sense of the word. A fine whisky or a working nefarious plan were ideal opportunities to see Satan displaying his razor-sharp teeth in a genuine smile. Although if you were hoping that finding him in a jolly mood meant it was wise to ask for a day's rest, you'd have been greatly and quite possibly painfully, disappointed.

Satan was currently pacing his room. God had beaten him to the hotel and had the best pick of the rooms. Sure, he'd also got a penthouse suite, and had a beautiful view of the ocean and sandy beaches, but he instinctively suspected God had a far superior room and by default, he wanted it himself. If God had accidentally been allocated a broom cupboard, Satan would still have coveted it, because it was in his nature to want what others had. Envy was, after all, one of the deadly sins he'd created. Seven of them, in fact, just to show God that bad things, as well as good, can come in sevens.

Despite is paranioa Satan's room was identical to God's. It was spacious and had everything he could possibly need; a giant, comfortable bed, expansive desk, and most importantly, a fully stocked mini bar – but this was immaterial to him. He'd been seething ever since he got to his room and only now was he starting to calm down and fully appreciate the place. The most important fact, in Satan's mind, was that it wasn't a room in Hell. The bed was comfortable. The air was clean and fresh and critically, the plumbing worked. For nothing more than the satisfaction, he went into the bathroom and flushed the toilet three times in a row, just to hear, and see, clean water flowing. Such luxuries were not to be found in Hell – at least, any flowing

147

liquids found there weren't the type you'd want to wash in, never mind drink.

Thanks to the presence of so much evil in that section of the hotel, the combined aura and essence of Satan, his demons and Archdemons had already caused items to start and atrophy. The flowers which had been placed fresh in his room that morning had already withered and drooped, dropping petals on the table. Some of the smaller domestic appliances had stopped working – not that Satan had much use for the trouser press or the hair dryer. The wallpaper had already started to develop a furry green mould and was peeling at the edges. But to Satan, who'd grown used to being surrounded by far greater decay on a daily basis, his room was a vast improvement on anything in Hell and a big step up the comfort ladder.

In the corner of the room, adjacent to the main door, the steamer trunk stood conspicuously. There was muffled swearing emanating from within and occasionally it rocked violently before settling back to an indistinct release of profanities. Satan walked up to the trunk and patted it, as if it was a pet dog needing reassurance. "There, there my friend; save your strength, you're not going anywhere. Yet!"

There was a knock on the partition door leading to the adjoining room. "Come in," growled Satan. Grank walked through the door, followed by Stuart. Both had laid claim to Satan's neighbouring room and neither of them had any intention of relinquishing it to the other. As a result, they'd ended up having to share, leaving the room one door further along the corridor vacant.

It hadn't remained empty for long though, as one of the demon Presidents of Belgium had heard it was empty and quickly claimed it as his own, an upgrade from the one he'd been issued on the second floor. The door now proudly sported a small black, yellow and red tricolour flag of Belgium. As far as any hotel staff were concerned, it was sovereign territory, complete with diplomatic immunity.

Neither Grank nor Stuart were looking happy due to their stubborn approach to sleeping arrangements, but both of them could sense Satan's foul mood and determined it would be wise not to say anything regarding their problems. Satan obviously had other things on his mind and any judgement he might make could prove to not be in their favour.

"Sir," began Grank, "the meeting is set for 10am tomorrow and I've checked out the room. If you get there early, you can sit with your back to the window and have the sun shining directly in God's eyes. I'm sure that will annoy Him."

"Sir, if I could also make a suggestion?" Stuart was determined not to be outdone by the demonic interloper who, up until recently, had only been in charge of ensuring the damned pushed rocks up a hill. "We should have as few demons in the room as possible. He'll be expecting you to have more than the agreed numbers, but if it's just you and I in there, the surprise might make him more amenable to listening to you." He turned to Grank and offered him a smug grin. "And of course, Grank can stand outside the door, ensuring we're not disturbed."

At the last comment, Grank gritted his sharp teeth. If anyone had smashed a two by four plank of wood across his shoulders at that specific moment, it would have broken on his tensed muscles. If he'd had the piece of wood himself, he would no doubt have used it on Stuart. Despite that he maintained his calm and relaxed external countenance.

Satan knew what was going on, but he didn't have a problem with a little bit of brinkmanship and inner politics. It was acceptable for demons to hate each other and try any tactics to rise above the others. It was better they squabbled between each other, rather than join together to try and steal his throne.

149

"Sir, I think it might be prudent if I'm in the room as well, for security reasons!" volunteered Grank, as cordially as he could muster.

Satan steepled his fingers and placed his forefingers against his lower lips. "Yes, interesting suggestions," he ventured pensively. "I think you're right, the fewer demons we have distracting the proceedings, the better."

At this, Grank sensed the acceptance of his idea and allowed himself to smile slightly.

Satan continued. "However, I think Stuart is right. He'd be better placed in the room with me, while you ensure security is maintained outside."

"But Sir…!" Grank spluttered instinctively, without thinking.

"*But?*" Satan roared. "*But?* Surely, you're not questioning my decision? If you happen to have a better plan than mine, then please feel free to share it with me!"

Immediately seeing the error in his outburst, Grank spoke quickly, trying quite literally, to save his skin "No, of course not sir! It's a perfect plan. I was meaning to say, what a brilliant idea it was and I'd be happy to maintain security outside. Of course, I would make myself available to join you straight away, if my presence was required."

Without even looking at Grank, Satan continued. "Excellent, I thought that was what you meant to say. There is one addition to our party which I think will be of benefit; I want Beth in there with us. Stuart, tell her I want her wearing her best classy slut outfit. She'll know exactly what to wear. I'm sure her presence will help divert some of Gordon's entourage, especially Dedan. If his reputation is anything to go by, he'll be so distracted he won't even notice me in the room."

Satan walked to the window and looked outside. He glanced across the vast Pacific Ocean to the setting sun on the horizon and then slowly brought his gaze closer to home. Scanning the golf course, he saw demon and angel security guards walking around fastidiously eyeing each other up with undisguised suspicion and contempt. Scattered among the greens were several small herds of demonic Friesian cows that seemed to be in a world of their own, happily chewing the cud. Why, he wondered, did he bother bringing them along in the first place? They weren't exactly incognito – Hawaii wasn't, to his knowledge, famous for its dairy produce and if it came to a battle, there were scarier, fiercer demons he could have brought along. In his opinion, 'Oh help, run away! They have dairy cows!' had never been heard on a battle field. Then he saw, in the distance, what looked like a very large, muscular and stocky brown cow. *'Now where had that come from'* he wondered to himself.

Turning, he discovered Stuart and Grank were still standing and waiting for him to issue further instructions. "Yes?" he demanded. "Don't you have better things to do than stand there like ugly sculptures? Get out!"

They both bowed slightly and quickly hurried toward the door to their shared room. Determined not to surrender to each other, they got stuck in the doorway as the both jostled to be the first one through. They managed to squeeze through eventually, neither having given in or given the other an advantage. Once the door closed Satan walked towards the mini bar, which was no longer fully functioning, and took out a lukewarm miniature bottle of whisky. He opened it, poured the golden contents into a glass and promptly drained it. *'It is going to be a long few days,'* he thought to himself.

Chapter 26 – The Same But Better.

God was sitting at his desk in his penthouse suite, sipping a strong black coffee from his personal mug. He didn't need the buzz of the caffeine, but he enjoyed it and even deities needed their little pleasures and indulgences. Once he'd drained the mug, he stood up and walked over to the window to get a better view of his favourite island and the setting orange glow of the sun on the horizon. Lowering his eyes, he immediately recognised the cows, on the golf course, for the demons they were. He smiled to himself and clicked his fingers in the direction of the far end of the golf course, just by the woods.

A very confused Hereford Bull instantaneously appeared, one that had, up until a second ago, been happily grazing on a windy, cold, English hillside. After the obligatory bowel movement that startled cattle are prone to, he quickly grew acclimatised to his new surroundings. The bull took stock of his new surroundings. The sun on his back was unusual, but not unpleasant. He saw humans walking about and was about to charge them when his attention was taken up by the sight of some rather attractive-looking black and white cows in the distance. Generations of selective breeding had created him to be a high-performing bull and he knew exactly what he needed – and wanted – to do. If ever there was a creature that loved his job, this bull was it. Bulls didn't have the capacity to smile, but as he trotted towards his new harem, he would have done so if he could have.

That'll teach them,' God thought to himself as he turned away from the window, allowing the bull some romantic privacy.

Dedan was sitting on the edge of God's bed, absentmindedly flicking through a copy of a Gideon Bible, checking forlornly for references to him.

"Couldn't you have chosen something different to that?" enquired God, with laughter in His voice. "After all, we were both there and your part isn't exactly given much detail. And besides that, it's the New Testament, not Old, so it's quite a bit after your time."

Dedan closed the book and looked up at God. "True," he sighed. "It would have been nice if they'd put more in the full Bible so that I'm remembered a bit better. All that's left is a few words and a lost city in the desert. Not much of an epitaph. Speaking of which, why didn't you bring along Gideon? He's pretty good in a fight."

"Yes, he is, but he despises hotels, and Gideon Bibles. He's more disgruntled about the snub than you are. Flattered that the society was named after him, but his victories and courage are deliberately ignored. Whenever he's in an Earth hotel, he always rings room service and demands a 'proper Bible'!" God feigned a pompous voice. "One with all the action included in it!"

"Well, I suppose I can see his point. I wonder what will happen to all the Bibles in the demon rooms? Anyway, your Highness, what are your plans for tomorrow's meeting? I can get a message to St. Michael to have his troops brought onto the golf course, if you want them on standby."

God offered Dedan a quizzical look. "Goodness me, no! That isn't necessary yet. He's camped right next to their army, so if they try anything, it will be seen straight away and action can be taken there and then. Besides, Satan called the meeting and we should give him the chance to say his piece first, or, make his play. No point in giving him an excuse. I think we should have a handful of angels with us, as backup, but nothing too over the top. No more than half a dozen. If you don't mind, I'll ask you to stand at the back and watch the demon's body language. I'm sure your keen eyes will take it all in. But don't be in too much of a rush to declare war. This is a beautiful island and I'd hate for it to become collateral damage."

"Of course, your Highness. I've grown fond of it here as well, so I don't want to start any trouble. As for his lackeys, my eyes will be all over them and I'll be ready and willing to jump on them if duty demands!"

Chapter 27 – Evening Calls.

The demon delegates had made the most of the VIP rooms, and all the benefits which being assumed world leaders brought them. Fruit and muffins had been quickly devoured, and the well-stocked mini bars had been emptied, then refilled by eager room service, before being emptied once again. Impatient at having to wait for the over-stretched humans to return and keep them drinking, the allure of the numerous bars lured them out of their rooms to explore the hotel in the quest for steady, consistent flows of alcohol. The numerous, identical demonic prime ministers, presidents and queens from around the globe all remembered seeing the cocktail bar as they'd entered the hotel earlier in the day and decided to make their way there. By the time the last president of France had arrived, the confused barman had been forced to call for reinforcements and the entire bar staff were hurriedly throwing their cocktail shakers about like a majorette team with flaming batons, trying to keep up with the ever-thirsty politicians. As the night wore on, and the bar was replenished from the store room, the demons began to forget their strict instructions about behaving themselves and gradually started to revert to type. Animosities began to boil to the surface and old scores were remembered as demon saw demon and natural instincts kicked in.

The Queen of Andorra had started a fight with one of the female presidents of Belgium. Two of the Prime Ministers of England were hitting each other with bottles, and leaders had started brawling with leaders in a seething mass of biting, kicking and gouging of eyes, legs and arms. The Prime Minister of Jamaica had already had half his dreadlocks yanked out by the roots and the blood of many countries was beginning to mix into the carpet.

The human staff of the bar and lobby were surprised and confused by this unexpected display of political diplomacy and negotiations. It certainly wasn't something they'd seen on televised debates in the United Nations, or their own Senate.

They were unsure how to react. Would it be an international incident if they grabbed hold of a President of France to stop him kicking a President of Belgium in the groin? Even if it wasn't, they were sure it would be more than their jobs were worth.

On hearing the noise outside his office, Mr. Knight decided he would venture out of his inner sanctuary and investigate what was going on the lobby. He'd just begun to recover from his earlier encounter with the numerous world leaders, and the sight which met his eyes wasn't something that eased his tired, frayed mind. The mound of writhing bodies resembled a giant, bloodied spider with arms and legs indiscriminately kicking and punching itself. The words emanating from the huddle certainly didn't seem like the political rhetoric he was expecting, either. His eyes glazed over and he promptly turned one hundred and eighty degrees and walked back into the safety of his office muttering to himself, "Zebras!"

Valets, barmen, reception clerks and the hotel manager were unnoticed by the combatants in the mini version of World War III being enacted on the plush carpet and in among the lobby furniture. Each demon was seeing his own red mist and enjoying themselves far too much to be bothered by the concerns of any human audience. Thanks to the need to suffer for their sins in Hell, a demon's pain threshold was high, so most of their powerful blows inflicted minor pain. It was immaterial to them, the rage coursing through their very beings helped to magnify any perceived pain meted out. Scores had to be settled, and to them, this was just another form of extreme exercise.

It was fortunate Satan had known what his band of evil brothers were like and had them searched for weapons before they came to Earth. Despite orders, each one of them had tried to smuggle knives into their luggage, several had tried to sneak in hand guns and the Queen of Andorra even tried to hide an anti-tank rocket launcher under her dress. If any of those had been deployed the already high blood quota would have been mixing with severed limbs and, quite probably, grey brain matter as demons returned to Hell sooner than anticipated, or even desired.

The angel guards in the security office had seen the fighting on the CCTV screens and been uncertain what to do. Unlike the humans, they had no qualms about attempting to bring peace to the small battlefield, especially if it gave them the opportunity to inflict additional damage to their age-old adversaries. But they had their orders and were wary regarding how it might be construed if they interfered in a purely demonic battle and were seen to be starting an unprovoked fight with any demon. No matter what they were doing to each other.

Unsure of how to deal with it, one of the angels picked up his cell phone and dialled Dedan's room number. "Sir, it's St. George, I'm in the security office," he began. "Yes, I'm sorry sir, and I do appreciate the lateness of the hour, but we have an incident in the lobby. It seems the demon delegates are all fighting one another on the floor outside the cocktail bar. No sir, no angels are involved. Oh, no sir, the humans are keeping well out of the way as well. It's just demons fighting each other. Very well Dedan, if you say so. Sorry for bothering you. And you, sir!" He switched off the phone and placed it back to the desk.

"Well?" enquired one of the other angels.

"He isn't bothered if it's just demons fighting each other. We're to leave them to it and only get involved if they start any fights with us, or it involves humans. He's also told us to keep our eyes open, in case it's a decoy and other demons try to get into God's part of the hotel."

With that, the diligent angels went back to watching the fight on the screen and scrutinizing the other monitors for further trouble.

Unaware of the televised action and the angel's concern, the demons continued their fight, but the energy was draining from the blows and kicks. Finally, exhausted, the last half-hearted punch was delivered and the tired demons lay gasping on the floor. A small number were unconscious, but the majority were awake and their focus reverted to their reason for being in the bar in the first place; the consumption of copious amounts of the full gamut of free alcohol. Those who could manage to make it onto their feet staggered to the bar – those that couldn't walk dragged themselves across the floor. Soon wounds and injuries were forgotten, or at least ignored, cocktails were served, and glasses were gratefully emptied.

Grank's emotional thermometer had been boiling over ever since his meeting with Satan, when Stuart had got the better of him. To have a mere oily clerk usurp his own perceived critical importance was stinging. He had mental images of Stuart suffering a terrible and incredibly painful accident involving a flight of stairs, lots of knives and some acid. These daydreams were helping to cheer him up, but he still had a long distance to go to find any tranquillity. To help speed up the process, he'd decided that as it was getting late, it might be an ideal time to nip down to the bar and have a solitary quiet cocktail to help him sleep. As the lift door slid open his eyes were met by seeming carnage. Some demons lay comatose on the floor in pools of blood, and others were leaning on each other for support, or lying by his beloved bar and merrily drinking as if nothing had happened. The supposed Queen of Andorra was sitting in a very un-regal manner on a bar stool, kicking her legs in the air and shouting "Yippee, I am the champion!"

Sound erupted inside Grank's head as his mental thermometer began to boil again. First there was the sound of steam whistling, and then the noise of glass and mercury exploding. Any chance of calming down tonight evaporated. Striding purposefully towards the inebriated, doppelganger world leaders, he grabbed hold of the most convenient demon, who just happened to be one of the British Prime Ministers and lifted him up by his shoulders. "What in Hell are you doing?" he screamed at the battered, bruised politician. "If the boss finds out about this mess and stupidity, he'll build a new section of Hades just to make sure we all rue the day we came here!" With that, he hurled the barely-conscious demon across the room where it landed on a coffee table and made it collapse, splintering beneath the sudden impact. The bar staff had witnessed a lot of unexpected things during their shift, but the sight of Great Britain's leader being thrown like a football was definitely the highlight. Having released a bit of his rage made Grank feel slightly better, but he still had further to go before normality was resumed. He glared at the assembled demons and was engulfed by a cooling tidal wave of despair. He didn't have a receptive audience to his fury, and inflicting violence wasn't satisfying if the recipients were in no condition to acknowledge the pain or appreciate why they were being hit in the first place. Reaching inside his suit pocket, he removed a small radio and clicking the transmit button, spoke into it. "Eight penthouse guards down to the lobby. Now!" he shouted.

"Yes boss," came the unquestioning reply.

He returned the radio to his pocket and glowered at the demons. Those who were conscious had lapsed into silence and watched him expectantly through cold, glassy eyes. Across the lobby, the elevator bell pinged and eight demonic guards exited and ran towards Grank.

"Right," Grank said, addressing those drunken leaders who were able to listen and understand, "get back to your rooms, clean yourselves up and do not come out until I tell you to. If I see *any* of you before then, I'll personally dispatch you straight back to Hell and the the boss will deal with you once he gets back." A few got to their feet unsteadily, using each other as collapsible crutches to stagger towards the elevators.

"You lot!" he snapped, looking at the bemused demon guards, "get this rabble upstairs and out of sight. I want this mess cleaned up. Come tomorrow morning, this will never have happened and anyone that says it did is lying and will have to answer to me."

As he fell silent unconscious leaders were lifted onto shoulders and the process of transporting them to their rooms began.

Grank looked at the Queen of Andorra, who had a very sheepish grin on her face. "And? What are you waiting for? Get out of my sight," he snapped.

She slowly and falteringly removed herself from the bar stool and began a zig zag walk toward the lift.

"And get some underwear on!" Grank shouted to her back, to which she responded by giving him a one finger salute. If he hadn't had other things planned, he would have run after her, ripped off the offending digit and rammed it where the underwear was missing, but some things were more important.

Eventually – either walking, crawling or being carried – the offending demons were removed. Grank had worked his way around the large room, giving a significant amount of cash to the humans who'd been working and witnessed the debacle. The money had the desired effect and ensured they all developed instant amnesia and myopia, ensuring they could remember nothing more than the fact that it had been a quiet night and they hadn't seen a thing. He didn't know it but not only had an undercover reporter witnessed first-hand the story of a lifetime, the journalist could feel the Pulitzer Prize in his hands already, having just been given a large wad of money; some stories just got better and better.

Extra cash was given to two of the hotel staff so that they would clean the carpet as best they could. If the blood couldn't be removed, the offending rug would be disposed of discretely and replaced.

Once that was done, with relevant tasks allocated, Grank righted an upturned bar stool. Sitting on it, he faced the considerably wealthier and much happier barman. "Hello, young man," Grank calmly said to the eager servant. "A quick test for you, what happened here tonight?"

Any barman worth his salt could have answered that in a heartbeat, but years of being a shoulder to cry on, or confidant to rich, powerful and more importantly, appreciative drunken guests had honed his powers for ultimate and infinite discretion. He knew how to keep silent and be rewarded for it. "Tonight sir?" he replied with a confused look on his face "I have no idea what you're talking about. It's been a very quiet and dull evening; I haven't served a single drink. And to be honest, I doubt I'll be serving any at all tonight. A bit of a waste of time me coming into work."

Grank gave him an appreciative nod at the well-worded response. "Exactly. A dull night indeed. I'm afraid I've had a senior moment and I can't for the life of me remember what letter of the alphabet or the cocktail I'd managed to try…"

The over-eager barman was about to interrupt and enlighten his generous customer, when he was silenced by a quickly wagging finger.

"Yes, as I was saying," continued Grank, "as neither of us have any idea what drink I'd managed to get up to, I'm forced to start again." Rubbing his hands together briskly, Grank smiled. "Give me a nice cocktail beginning with the letter A. But you don't have to bother with any umbrellas. I think the risk of a storm has now passed."

Chapter 28 – Darkness In The Night.

In the clear night sky, the waning gibbous moon was bathing the hotel and its grounds in a pale silvery light. The black shadows of the trees were a sharp contrast to the illuminated, undulating moonscape of the golf course. The helicopter at the front of the hotel cast a silhouette like a giant beetle caught in a spider's web. It's rotor blades swayed almost imperceptibly in the warm coastal breeze.

Guards, both good and bad, were walking their designated areas warily, eyes peeled for external intruders and monitoring the movements of their counterparts. No casual nods of acknowledgement were exchanged between the opposing sides. No recognition of a shared situation and mission. Just suspicious, challenging looks filled with undisguised hatred. Trust was never high on the list of either side's requirements and in the darkness, it was even less evident. Age old battles had taught hard lessons about what could happen to an expecting soul once sunset added a cloak of darkness to any daggers. By the eighteenth hole the demon cows had formed a giant herd on the green – all with their rumps pointing inwards. Although evolution imbued them with naturally vacuous expressions, they had looks of terror in their eyes. Having earlier been totally surprised by a frisky, virile and energetic bull, they'd suddenly become very defensive and determined not to experience him again. None of them wanted to look the other cows in the eyes. There seemed to be a mutual, unspoken, or un-mooed, agreement to never speak of such things ever again. Like the events in the bar, this was something that as far as they were concerned, had never happened. Jon, the lead cow, was slowly chewing the cud and was determined that, as soon as the mission was over, he would be seeing Satan and asking for a transfer. He wanted to change his form and never wanted to be a cow again. He wasn't even sure he'd ever be able to walk normally again and wondered how real cows managed it.

The now exhausted, but sated bull, on the other hand, was happily fast asleep. Reliving, in his dreams, a day's worth of excitement and the bovine equivalent of romance and passion. Content in the knowledge that he'd managed to complete his biological imperative with so many coy, resistant, cows. He was sure that by morning, he'd have regained his strength and be able do it, and them, all over again. It was good to be a bull.

Meanwhile, several miles down the road, Police Officer Charley Palakiko was slowly, and exceedingly reluctantly, driving his patrol car in the direction of the hotel. As he quickly drove past the encamped angel and demon armies, he tried not to take any notice of them, in the hope that they wouldn't involve him in any army games. He'd seen first-hand what damage could be done by off-duty marines from the local camp on the island and he shuddered to think what trouble the Russians could cause. Having explained the situation to his superiors and managed to convey the full gravitas of the situation, they'd promptly refused his request for immediate leave and made him the sole liaison officer for the hotel, armies and all things related to the secret conference. They'd assumed they hadn't been advised of what was going on because of bureaucracy and they blithely damned the Honolulu Police Department Headquarters for leaving them out of the loop, yet again. All this was academic to Charley, as he would have gladly swapped this duty for attending a bloody race riot. At least he knew what to do in a situation like that. Redneck Reds were out of his comfort zone and he wanted them to stay well out of it.

He saw, in the distance, the moonlit turnoff running along the side of the golf course and leading to the hotel. He also noticed shadowy figures standing in the road talking. As he approached them, he was flagged down and upon winding down his window, dark figures approached his car. "Hello, what do you want?" demanded the demonic FBI agent brusquely as he flashed his fake ID badge. "This entire complex is out of bounds

163

to any and all unauthorised personnel. I suggest you drive your angelic piggy ass out of our sight because you aren't getting anywhere near the hotel down this road." With the demon assuming Charlie was an angel that had chosen a rather plump and stocky guise for this visit to earth and he was determined to lord it over the unsuspecting officer.

Charley wasn't expecting such impolite treatment from a member of the FBI and he was also disconcerted by the reference to his ass. To his knowledge, it had never been called angelic before and he wasn't sure if it had some sexual undertone that he wasn't used to. Piggy was one thing, but FBI or no FBI, he'd never had such comments aimed at his body. Irrespective of the motivation and meaning, he decided he wasn't going to hang about and obtain clarification. Without waiting to wind up his window again, he promptly reversed his car back onto the highway. He decided he would try his luck via the dirt track leading to the hotel that ran between the far side of the golf course and the adjoining wood. He set off slowly in that direction and saw dark figures in the distance, illuminated in the pale moonlight. Without bothering to turn down the track he parked on the side of the highway and decided to wait for them to come to him. Two of the figures walked up to his car and one of them rested his arm on its roof and leaned forward so he could see inside and talk to the waiting police officer.

"Yes Officer? Officer Jones, Secret Service how can I help you?" The guard enquired politely as he flashed his badge.

"Hi, I've just had one hell of an encounter and I just need to look in on the hotel to ensure everything is going to plan and I'm not required for anything."

At the mention of Hell, the angel automatically assumed the hapless police officer was just another demon in disguise and his demeanour changed instantly. "Hell? Yes, well there are a lot of you to encounter. If you want to get to the hotel, I suggest you go back and speak to one of your *FBI* friends, I'm sure they'll be happy to let you in, but you're not sneaking down a dirt track to get there".

"But I—"

"No buts. Get your demon shit out of my sight!"

Charley no longer had the stomach for wasting time talking with vulgar FBI agents, that he suspected might be coming onto him, or equally impolite secret service agents. He didn't want to be on duty and wouldn't have to take such unreasonable abuse from civilians, so he couldn't see why government officials had to behave like that. Without waiting for further invectives about his body or bowel movements, he decided the best way forwards was a tactical retreat. He drove off with his wheels kicking up dirt onto the guard. He'd had enough and decided he needed to spend the rest of his shift parked up in a stopping point at the west side of the Ko'olau Mountain range. He could easily spend a few hours in his car, catching up on paperwork and eating his packed lunch. His report in the morning would show that he attempted to gain access to the hotel, but the security was tighter than a virgin on her wedding night and he was refused access. Not the best way to spend his shift, but tonight, he just didn't care.

Chapter 29 – Rapture? Here I come.

Dedan was in his room, ideally placed next to God's penthouse, sitting casually at the bureau desk. The lone source of light was a small lamp, illuminating the maps and floor plans laid out in front of him. Slowly he sipped on a can of cola allowing the liquid to cover his taste buds before swallowing the sugary drink. He still suspected the motives of Satan and expected some contrived stratagem. Precautions and defences had been put into place to cover any imaginable eventuality and try as he might he couldn't see any weaknesses in his operational plan. Security was tight and he seemed to be ready for anything. He massaged his forehead tiredly as he scanned the paperwork. A wild, crazy and downright strange thought entered his head briefly – ever since God had briefed him, it had been working in and out of his consciousness, but each time he came up with the same questions. What if Satan was genuine? What if he really did want to get back into Heaven? No, it couldn't be. It just couldn't work and be real. Closing Hell wouldn't work and would need God to instigate some sort of eschatological end of days' event, so that the good could enter Heaven and leave the wicked on Earth. In his spare time in Heaven, he'd studied all of the almost innumerable doomsday prophecies. The vast majority of the world religions had them. To him, it seemed as if they created them as an excuse, and a get-out clause, for not being good and kind to each other while they lived. If more humans tried it, they might get to like it and Heaven would be on Earth and Hell would become a minority destination. He pondered over all the various, conflicting views and ruminated over how the process would occur. Visions of prophets in flowing robes, riding white horses and battling each other to prove they were the most peace loving and worthy of leading people into Heaven. Perhaps God would create a divine rapture and have lots of good people floating about in the sky, waiting to be picked up, like smug, self-righteous balloons? Although he shuddered at the thought of so many pushy and opinionated 'Born Again Christian' Americans suddenly filling Heaven's golf courses, all talking too loudly and spoiling the place. However, he knew that many of the so-called good people who believed in the rapture were just cold, cynical hypocrites who would happily put a needle through the eye of a camel if it made them look kind. So it was of some relief to know that many of them would be sorely disappointed when their feet stayed steadfastly rooted to the ground. He'd always enjoyed the Jehovah's Witnesses opt out with trying to interpret any Biblical words. All they came up with was that it was beyond their knowledge and they would only understand it after it happened. The only time they had any real opinions, was when they were disparaging other Christian faiths. It seemed each age saw wars, earthquakes and famines as the signs of the imminent end and they, and their particular interpretation of religion, would be saved – leaving everyone else who didn't cowardly bow down to their form of praying, doomed to damnation. He had to smile at the thought of all the prophecies about the end of the world all happening simultaneously – now that would be a confusing and wild party to be in. He especially looked forward to meeting the Whore of Babylon. Even without existing, she had a great PR team marketing her prowess and skills and he was sure that if she were to exist, he might learn quite a lot from her. And if it was the end of time, then what a way to go.

Fortunately, God had never revealed His plans for the end of the world to anyone – mortal or otherwise – and to Dedan's knowledge, God had no plans to put an end to His creation. His flood was blown out of all proportions and greatly misreported and, He had no desire to go through all that bad press again. Much to the annoyance of many religions, even science had its own theories involving the end of reality and the reunion of the divine. Although the scientist's reports tended to use far less poetic language and far too many dull clinical terms to ever make them sound interesting. Big crunches or big freezes were the current favourite, but their timescales were so large that those who postulated such theories would be long since gone and forgotten by the time such things ever happened, so they'd never know if they were right or wrong. But despite all the ancient texts and images spinning around in his mind, he just couldn't see how Satan would sell the idea of conciliation to

God. Did he simply think God would nonchalantly change everything just because Satan wanted a comfortable bed and fresh running water in Heaven? It was too preposterous and couldn't be genuine. *'Oh, please, don't let it be real,'* he thought to himself.

Dedan's reverie was broken by a knocking sound. He heard it, but it took a moment to recognise it for what it was. His eyes stopped focusing on the desk and he turned, trying to identify where the noise emanated from.

He heard it again, it was coming from the far wall, where a door led to the room on the opposite side to God's. "Just a second," he responded, his voice croaky. He knew the room belonged to Emily but hadn't expected her to talk to him at this hour of the night. He unlocked the door and opened it.

His neighbour walked in without waiting for an invitation. "Hello Emily, what a lovely surprise. What can I do for you at this hour?" He looked her up and down and had to admit he'd seen her looking better. Her hair was ruffled, her make up smudged and it looked as if she'd just woken up after falling asleep on the floor fully clothed. In this instance, looks weren't deceptive. But for all that, she still looked stunningly attractive in the glow of the single small table lamp.

She raised a thin eyebrow. "Hello Dedan, I'm sure I can think of a few things you could do for me at this hour," she said, her voice deep and hoarse. With that, she pushed the door closed behind her and stood, arms akimbo, watching him and waiting for his response.

Never one to look a gift horse in the mouth, he didn't have to think too hard about the unexpected, but very welcome interruption. "Well in that case, make yourself comfortable," he said, gesturing to his bed. "Would you care for a drink?" He turned around and walked over to the mini bar. Expecting a response, he turned to look at Emily. In the short interval, she'd slipped off her dress and was standing there in nothing more than her black lace underwear. Dedan's smile broadened.

Suddenly her back started to ripple and move, as wings appeared from beneath her skin. The extra appendages indulged in a brief, but victorious battle with her bra before the stretched, abused and defeated garment beat a hasty retreat and flew from Emily's body with a ripping and snapping noise. It flew over Dedan's head, but he had no interest in its trajectory because he was more interested in her almost totally naked body. She stepped towards him, stretching out her wings and engulfing him with them as if he was captured prey in the clutches of a Red Kite or Kestrel. When she began to kiss his neck, he let out a breathless whisper "Oh my Angel!"

Being on Earth was always an amusing education for God. If he wanted to, with a smattering of focused concentration, He could scan the minds of all the great thinkers on the planet and catch up on the ideas that were in vogue at any given age. But He much preferred to walk amongst His creations every now and then and just entertain Himself with how they perceived Him and the world in general. He wasn't anything like the jealous and vengeful deity many firebrand preachers claimed He was. How they came to that insight was a mystery, as He tended to leave people to their own devices. Without free will there wouldn't be a need for Heaven or Hell, so there was no point interfering. He had no problem with what was said about Him, his creations or what they said about each other; they would be judged on their actions, and their hearts, once they'd stopped breathing and making contributions, good or bad, to society.

Sleep wasn't something He indulged in often while on Earth, so He had plenty of time to occupy His mind. Having searched through His bedside cabinet, He'd found, among the tourist brochures and island literature, an old copy of a scientific journal which the previous inhabitant must have left behind. Flicking through the pages, He was enjoying all the hypotheses and theories which were reported. Some were accurate and exactly as He'd created them. Some of the quantum physics stuff was spot on, even if the names of what they'd found were ridiculous; for some reason, the word *GLUONS* always made Him smile. There was one particular article however that made Him chuckle to Himself. Some glaringly obvious mathematical miscalculations had shown that there should be more matter in the universe than they could actually find. To make up for the gap in the maths they'd come up with 'Dark Matter and Dark Energy' to compensate and fill in the missing pieces and make them right in the real world. Filling their picture with theories and erroneous equations like a modernist piece of art. As a result, billions of dollars were being spent on research trying to find something with zero mass and density which neither emitted nor absorbed light or energy. God had encountered all the belief systems there were, and this was definitely a new religion, creating their own atheistic ideology and then blindly following it. Proof, evidence or even common sense didn't matter. God always thought looking for dark matter was like putting a blind man into a dark room and telling him to look for a black cat which wasn't there. The maths had a grain of accuracy, but it always made Him laugh as they already had all the answers, given by Einstein, but they were so busy looking in space, they forgot about time.

But he also knew that one of his primary rules was that He couldn't let the human race time travel, so they were unlikely to find what they were looking for. The world was confusing enough as it was, without them popping backwards and forwards changing their own history while they counted matter and anti-matter in the past and future. 'Human's', He thought; a great idea and wonderful things, but sometimes he had to wonder how they'd managed to survive so long without the whole lot of them getting confused by the concept of flushing toilets and drowning themselves as they tried to brush their teeth. He finished reading the article and lay back on the bed, arms behind His head, staring at the ceiling. He'd done, and experienced, most things while on Earth and very little was new to him. The concept of God not having anything to do on Oahu on a Saturday night might seem strange to anyone who'd visited the Hawaiian island, and He hated to admit it but He was mind numbingly bored. He tried to pass the time by counting the atoms in the far wall, but that task was soon completed. There was only one thing for it – He would be forced to watch some TV; a thought that filled Him with dread. Satan had come up with the idea, and sublimely suggested it to Alexander Bain, the early inventor, as a joke and then it had taken on a life of its own. Switching the TV on, God sat back and started watching a contrived police crime drama. The acting was terrible and the plot implausible, even to the weakest human brain, but the flickering lights had the same effect on Him as it did on many humans. Almost hypnotised, He became engrossed in the story.

Blinking, He looked up from the screen to the clock on the wall. It was 4am. The crime show had finished and He'd flicked through the channels, finding a James Stewart Western to watch, passing more time. But his concentration was broken by a loud, low and repetitive thumping noise coming from Dedan's room next door, punctuated by high-pitched groaning and screams of pleasure. He didn't need to be omniscient to know what was going on. Dedan was his best field operative, but he had far too much energy and despite his ordinary looks, he had an air about him that women loved and had them far too interested in him. Usually it resulted in some innocent piece of furniture collapsing under the strains of his subsequent exertions and creative gymnastics, but such was his personality and imagination. Dedan would try anything once – the problem was he kept trying it.

God climbed off the bed and walked over to the wall. He was tempted to make Himself appear in the room and surprise them, but decided against it. Instead He knocked heavily on the wall and shouted, "Can you keep it down please? Some of us are trying to concentrate!"

With that, the enthusiastic noises went suddenly and guiltily silent.

The sudden interruption surprised both Dedan and Emily, much to the disappointment of the angel guards in the corridor, eagerly evesdropping. It hadn't stopped their normal carnal activities, but it had forced them to slow things down, change position and avoid vocally sharing their exploits within a five-bedroom hearing distance. The deep embarrassment of knowing they'd been caught in the act by the Supreme Being made them both blush at first, and they'd looked into each other's eyes and started to giggle quietly, like naughty school children.

The mood was broken, for Dedan, by the ringing of the room telephone. It had managed to stay on the bedside cabinet, despite the shaking and rocking of the bed and the vibrations transmitted along the floor.

"Ignore it, it's probably a wrong number," offered Emily, laughing at her own comment although she knew that it would have been for him.

Rolling over, frustratedly Dedan picked up his phone. "Hello?" he snapped. "Do you know what time it is?" Sitting up, his attention grabbed, he listened intently for a few seconds before he continued. "Good grief. I hope none of our lot initiated it, or got involved... Well, that's a relief... Any humans dragged into the fight and injured? Okay, it doesn't seem like too much of a problem if you ask me. If it's just demons letting off steam, I don't think it's something we need to dive into the middle of. Just leave them to it and don't get involved unless they try and start anything with any of our angels, or if it looks like humans will be injured. Leave it for Grank to sort it out in the morning and have to explain to Satan. Oh, and keep an eye on the other monitors, in case it's some sort of diversion. Yes, thank you St. George, good night." He replaced the phone receiver and turned to face Emily again.

"Anything wrong, darling?" asked Emily, as Dedan reclined on the bed and she draped her arm over him.

"Well Em', it looks like some of the demons are having a different kind of fun to us." Turning to face her, he smiled conspiratorially. "Right then, where were we before being so rudely interrupted…"

Chapter 30 – Just Like Old Times.

The early morning light began to reveal the state of Dedan's suite. Sitting on the edge of his bed, he groggily surveyed the mess. Emily had returned to her room before he'd woken up, so he was left alone to take in the full extent of the previous night's entertainment. Bedding and his clothing were strewn randomly across the floor, ornaments were overturned and for some reason, that he couldn't quite understand, the mini bar was upside down and five feet away from its original position. Rubbing his face and stretching he looked up and did a double take at the ceiling. Something large and black, with what appeared to be lacy frills, had managed to wrap itself around the main light fixture and was hanging down from the high ceiling like a double-D cupped pirate flag. He was tempted to keep it as a souvenir but decided to retrieve it at some point and return it to its rightful owner, although he suspected the clip mechanism hadn't survived its forced removal.

He checked the time. It was still early, but he had a lot to do. First though, he needed a shower; he could tidy things up later. The warm water felt good against his skin and helped him fully regain consciousness. It had been an active night and he was still tired, but he knew he'd need to be fully alert if he was to properly fulfil his role as head of security.

Once shaven and dressed, he double-checked his appearance in the mirror. He was wearing a smart cream-coloured suit with a pale-yellow tie. He'd be surrounded by dour, plain angels and demons, so he thought it might be good to stand out from the crowd. Besides, it was Hawaii – plain dark suits were far from traditional clothing. *'When in Rome...'* he thought to himself. There was a knock on the door leading to God's suite, which he promptly answered, stepping over the items still covering the floor.

"Good morning, Your Majesty. Are you well?" he enquired politely, knowing full well that God was unlikely to be unwell.

"Yes, thank you Dedan. And you?" God was in the clothing and guise of the President and looked every inch the world leader. He scanned the messy room and offered Dedan a knowing smile. "It looks as if you had an interesting night." Dedan squirmed slightly under God's amused scrutiny. Looking upwards, He pointed to the light fitting. "It looks as if someone hoisted a battle flag. I do hope the eventual surrender didn't come too easily or quickly?"

"Well, err, yes, err, well." Dedan's discomfort got hold of his voice box and left him floundering, uncertain regarding the correct response.

God grinned. "Relax Dedan. I understand and I don't mind. You know very well that I never made love-making a sin. Just try and keep the noise down next time." He accompanied the words with a kind wink.

Dedan appreciated being let off the hook in such a light-hearted way. "Thank you, sir, I'll try and be much quieter next time."

Slapping Dedan jovially on the shoulder, God laughed. "Come on, we have work to do. Do you want to bang on Emily's door to wake her up, or did you do enough banging last night?"

"I'm sure I have no idea what you're talking about," replied Dedan, getting into the spirit of the conversation. He always thought any pious humans hearing their God make rude double entendres would be totally shocked. "Anyway, she's very efficient and I'm sure she'll be ready and waiting for us. We can go down together." And with those words, he just hoped God wouldn't find a joke in there as well, or if he did, He'd keep it to himself.

175

They walked across his room together, avoiding standing on any ornaments which might be hidden under the discarded clothing. Arriving at the main door, Dedan opened it and allowed his Boss to exit first, quickly following Him and closing it again. Outside a dozen Angels were assembled, all dressed in matching suits. At the back of the entourage, Emily stood, wearing a dark grey business suit. Her skirt sat just above the knees and her legs were covered with black stockings. Any traces of the previous night's drinking session with Beth and subsequent horizontal, occasionally vertical, and gravity-challenging diagonal activities were now gone. Dedan saw her and had to admit, although she'd looked amazing earlier, she definitely looked a lot better than last night. Memories of their nocturnal exploits filled his mind and he had to suppress a grin which would have made him look like a cat that had fallen into a vat of cream. As the procession began to walk along the corridor, Dedan took his place just behind God and Emily joined him there.

"Good morning Dedan. How are you? Sleep well?" she casually enquired.

"Yes, thank you Emily. I'm good and I slept like a log. Nothing like a quiet night's sleep to leave me refreshed and ready for the joys of the day."

Even though the two of them couldn't see it, both God, in front of them, and the angel escorts behind them were all grinning at the civil, mock innocence and ambivalent tones in their voices. Thanks to their intense fun and getting lost in the moment neither Emily nor Dedan realised how loud they had actually been and how rapt the guards had been as they listened to the groans and screams in the corridor and they knew that Dedan's night was anything but quiet. Everyone knew of Dedan's reputation and, in many quarters, he was admired; especially as none of his male colleagues could see how he did it. He was far from the tall, dark and handsome type. But that just helped enhance his reputation and made women curious.

The lift doors opened, allowing God, and half of his party to get in while the remainder waited for the next one. In the cosy confines of the elevator Dedan had inadvertently positioned himself so he was in front of God and facing Emily. Trying to avoid eye contact Dedan looked down at his shoes, but only ended up giving the impression he was studying Emily's breasts, so he ended up staring at the ceiling with intense concentration on his face while Emily looked down at the floor.

As the descent began, the piped music started, a feeble rendition of a hit tune played on pan pipes. God's eyebrow's furrowed. "I don't think so!" He said lifting His left index finger and pointing at the ceiling. Immediately the music changed to a stereophonic rendition of a soft and lilting piece of classical music which seemed to be produced by a live orchestra above their heads. "See?" He asked of no-one in particular. "That's better, isn't it? There should now be the appropriate music for everyone, good or bad, while we are here."

The elevator reached the ground floor and disgorged its heavenly passengers. This time Dedan led the way. He took them along a corridor and opened the doors of the conference room so that God, Emily and three of the angel Secret Service guards could enter. He gave the remaining guards a knowing nod and entered the room, closing the doors behind him. The conference room was long, airy and well-lit, with a window lining the far wall allowing in plenty of sunlight. In the middle of the room was a long rectangular boardroom table in dark oak, lined with dark brown leather chairs. God proceeded around the table and sat in the middle chair of the imposing table, his back to a large window overlooking the golf course. Checking the clock on the wall, which revealed it was 9:05am, God smiled. He knew how Satan worked and planned things – he'd have wanted to be in the room first, sitting nonchalantly with his feet on the desk, the sun on his back, and a look of arrogant smugness as if he owned the room and God was an unexpected guest. It was worth getting to the conference room early, just to piss Satan off and see the expression on his face. He knew Satan would be early and estimated his arrival to be at 9:28.

He decided to make himself at home, changing from his Presidential form to his 'Southern Gentleman' appearance, before he pushed himself back on the chair, put his feet on the table and placed his hands behind his head.

"Emily. You did tell Beth the meeting would start at 10am, didn't you?" He asked casually.

"Of course, Sire. I passed on all the details exactly as instructed. Is there something wrong? I told them 10am, so we're the ones who are far too early." Emily looked concerned, in case she'd been meant to pass on some covert hidden message.

Sensing her disquiet, He smiled gently. "No, I assure you everything is perfect. Today…" He paused for emphasis, "today we're first and that's what's important. I'm happy to wait half an hour."

"Half an hour? But…" Emily was silenced by the kind, but indulgent look in God's eyes. Sometimes it was pointless to question His actions. Although He might frequently profess not to be all knowing, and thanks to free will, the future was as much a closed book to Him as it was to everyone else, He still seemed to have an unerring understanding of what was likely to happen.

Looking at the company with Him, in the room, God offered a simple explanation. "Satan might think that he can play mind games, but he's taken on the wrong opponent. He'll be here at 9:28!"

There is a popular expression with humans – 'Satan never sleeps'. There might be an element of that in Hell, because the beds, even his, are not conducive to slumbers. They were uncomfortable, like lying on rough concrete rubble in a Hessian sack lined with razor blades and infused with the odour of a dog's stale urine. However, on Earth the aphorism wasn't as apt. The beds, even in less salubrious locations, tended to be a blessed relief compared to those in Hell. No spring could ever be as uncomfortable, no bed bug as vicious, and apart from a specific hotel in Birmingham, Alabama, the smells were a distinct improvement. Consequently, Satan had definitely made the most of the sleeping arrangements upgrade. This was how he remembered the beds in the good old days, before he'd decided to take over and lost the gamble. Upon lying down, sleep came quickly and he'd rushed into its warm and welcoming embrace. No nightmares, no screams from the damned and no disturbances. He could certainly get used to this.

In his unconscious state, he allowed himself a smile of contentment. If people didn't know better and were ignorant of the fact that he was the ultimate evil, they might have viewed him as having an angelic countenance.

The knock on the door took time to register in his mind, seeming like a distant echo. He tried to ignore it, hoping it would go away, but it continued and grew louder and more intense as his mind relinquished its hold on slumber and began to acknowledge the real world. Eventually, begrudgingly, he opened his eyes and took stock of where he was. The knocking continued, louder and more insistent than ever. Finally, the peaceful feeling, or as peaceful as he could ever know, evaporated and he forced himself to acknowledge the noise. "What?" he bellowed.

The noise stopped abruptly and the silence was just as annoying to Satan as the unwelcome knocking had been to his resting in the arms of Morpheus. Slowly, the door to the adjoining room opened, as if the door itself were afraid of some tongue of flame licking off its paint work and melting the gold-plated handle. Eventually, the hesitant head of Grank appeared. Satan let out a frustrated sigh, realising why he was being disturbed.

"Yes?" he said, more calmly. "What is it, Grank?"

"It's time for you to get ready and go down to the meeting room, oh mighty one."

Satan threw off the warm covers and swung his legs over the edge of the bed. Standing, he stretched, his bones creaking and cracking like crushing skulls. He gave the bed a last, longing look and transformed from his normal human Satan form, to that of his version of the President of the United States. He was identical to the real thing; only with an indefatigable air of panache, sophistication and relaxed arrogance the real one could never capture, no matter how hard he tried. Satan walked to the wardrobe and studied himself in the full-length mirror. His stylish, made to measure, silk lined burgundy suit seemed totally out of place for the normally austere, conservative and dour leader of the free world. But one of the benefits of being the President was nobody would openly question his fashion sense. He turned and looked at Grank and Stuart, who'd entered his room and were standing obsequiously by his bed, awaiting further instructions. "Come on then," he instructed, yawning, "let's go get the best seats and welcome Gordon when he arrives."

Racing each other, Grank and Stuart ran to the main door. The muscular demon in charge of security had the strength and agility and reached it first, quickly opening it for his satanic master. He gave Stuart a broad grin over his tiny, insignificant triumph; as if he'd just won a major victory on a battlefield.

Satan saw the display of toadying and ignored it. The gesture having the opposite effect with the childish antic not impressing him. He wasn't in the mood for such things and, besides, he knew how to open a door for himself. He walked past them both and went into the corridor. It was crowded with hard-faced, mock FBI agents, pressing up against the demonic versions of other world leaders, all suited up in anticipation of a meeting which would possibly re-write history and add an unexpected chapter to the end of the Bible. After Revelations, the Book of Reconciliation? At the front of the dark multitude stood Beth, dressed in a short, tight black dress. Her long dark hair flowed down her back and her slender legs were supported by black leather high heeled shoes – a vision of pure seduction. Satan looked her over and gave her his most wicked smile. She looked every inch the temptress, as per his instructions. She was a woman who knew her role and played it well. As distractions went, he couldn't think of a better one. Turning his attention away from his chief of communications, he looked across the bustling corridor. Letting out a long, slow, resigned breath. "What are you lot doing here?" He turned to Stuart "You did pass on my instructions, didn't you? Three in the meeting and the guards outside, with the rest not getting in my way – no more world leaders will be required!"

"Yes, of course, my liege. I think they're hoping you might have changed your mind. Strength in numbers, and all that." Stuart surveyed the expectant crowd "You heard the boss. Back to your rooms and keep out of the way!"

There was a collective disappointed groan from the world leaders. Various presidents of Belgium and France looked at each other accusingly, as if the overabundance of duplicate leaders was the reason for their exile to their executive suites, with room service, and mostly empty mini bars. Begrudgingly the demons turned and filtered back into their rooms. As banishments went, they knew from experience, that there were far worse alternatives but they still resented not being able to witness, or participate in, the main event. Many hadn't been in Hell for the previous battles with Heaven and they wanted to see what God really looked like.

Without waiting for the crowd to disperse, Satan turned and started to walk towards the lift, closely followed by his retinue. Before Stuart or Grank could rush past him and press the button summoning it, his finger was in place and the button lit up, indicating it was on its way. The corridor was too crowded and he had no desire to put up with the jostling lackeys, trying to press a button for him. The doors eventually opened and he stepped in, closely followed by Beth, Stuart, Grank and the determined cohort of undercover FBI demons, none wanting to be left behind and having to take another lift. The small cube quickly filled to overflowing, so Satan was squashed against the far mirrored wall with Beth in a similar predicament next to him. Summoning the deepest and most menacing tone from his arsenal of voices, Satan inhaled and then bellowed "Guards! Guards, *get out now!* Take another elevator, take the stairs or jump out of the friggin' window. I *don't care* what you do, but you can't all take this lift to the ground floor!"

Those demons still pushing to get in ceased their struggling and stepped back, closely followed by the demons who'd managed to find a space in the crowded elevator. The more astute of them had already set off down the stairs, running to get to the ground floor in advance of the elevator and be ready and waiting for their master. The others just stood and watched vacuously as the lift doors closed on the four figures left inside the elevator.

Grank pressed the button for the right floor and the descent began. Then it started – the sweet, crystal clear musical tones of Barry Manilow singing 'Mandy' could be heard coming from the sound system. Satan gave himself a double face palm. "Gordon!" he mumbled in an exasperated voice. "There was no need for that!" His companions studiously stared at their shoes to avoid his glare, and in doing so, be less likely to suffer any accidental consequences from his pent-up rage. Eventually the uncomfortable silence was broken by the elevator reaching its destination and the doors sliding open to reveal a handful of breathless, rosy-cheeked demons who'd managed to run fast enough to form part of Satan's renewed escort and bodyguard. They greeted him eagerly like a long-lost prophet, with compliments and words of welcome. Satan was beginning to have serious misgivings about some of his choices of guards, both for quantity and quality. Hell was full of cunning, shrewd and exceedingly intelligent demons. People that, when on Earth, had done their best to make it a hell and to garner as much power for themselves as they could by careful thought and planning. But somehow, he'd totally overlooked the necessity of having demons with him who were more than just raw brawn imbued with a puppy dog's desire to please. He was sure if he'd had a ball or a stick handy, he could have thrown it and most of the demons would have rushed off to retrieve it and come back with it in their teeth. He shuddered at the thought of his tough, elite bodyguard being so pathetic. He filed away a mental note to himself. Next time he'd initiate some form of intelligence test into the selection process. He didn't need a platoon full of tormented astrophysicists, but he *really* expected more than idiots jostling for his attention. He stepped out of the lift and the crowd parted to allow him to get past and walk down the corridor, falling back into close formation behind him. Any real threat to Satan only existing in their paranoid minds. It would have taken a determined assassin on a unique grassy knoll, or book repository, to take out this particular president and even with the best telescopic sights, it would take more than a bullet to send him back to Hell if he wasn't ready to go. A place where so many other world leaders, throughout history, had already gone. The mock FBI, NSA and CIA agents were more for show and self-aggrandisement, rather than to provide any real protection to their leader. Turning the corner of the corridor he was met by a large number of smartly-dressed Secret Service agents congregated outside the doors of the conference room. Immediately he recognised the situation. God – his eternal nemesis – had once again beaten him at his own game and got there before him. He silently swore and wondered if anyone could be trusted. Anger at being thwarted rose in his stomach like acid, which would have dissolved any mere mortal. However, he knew better than to show his emotions to the angels who stood waiting for him. Instead, he just continued at the same pace and maintained a look of casual ease. When he got closer to the door a waiting angel politely stepped forward knocked on the door and then, without waiting for an answer, pulled the doors outwards and stepped out of the way allowing Satan access. Ignoring the overt gesture of showy politeness, he walked directly into the room followed by Beth and Stuart. Grank reached the doors and stopped abruptly, causing the hurrying demons, directly behind him, to walk into him; pushing him forward several feet. The watching angels' undisguised laughter and sniggering made Grank's flesh crawl.

The clumsy demons quickly stepped back, pushing against the demons behind them who were still intent on pressing forward, unaware of the need to come to a more dignified stop. Eventually, the momentum came to a halt and they came to a standstill, awaiting some instructions to be given. Grank just ignored them – for now, he had the angel audience to contend with and what dignity he had left needed to be maintained. He casually closed the doors, so his master could have his meeting. Then he nonchalantly turned to face the demons behind him and calmly announced, "Make yourselves useful, lads!"

With that he took a stance in front of the door, feet apart, arms folded and face cold and expressionless. Standing stock-still like an evil sculpture, impassive and impassable, his purpose was obvious – none shall pass.

Inside the room, Satan stood looking at God. His 'Southern Gentleman' façade was unfamiliar, but he could easily identify him among the people already in the room. Even if he hadn't been sitting in the most prominent seat, his bearing and aura gave him away.

God was facing Emily, seemingly deep in conversation and didn't react immediately to Satan's entrance. Slowly He turned slightly, so He could face him directly, and then glanced up to check the clock on the wall and smiled. The second hand was just about to complete its ascent and change the minute hand so the time was almost 9:29. He offered Emily and Dedan a self-satisfied smile and they returned the smile with a nod of acknowledgement at the accuracy of his prediction.

Returning His focus to Satan, He gestured grandly to the seat opposite him. "Hello, take a seat Satan. It's been a long time since you and I last sat at a table in peace."

"Thank you, Gordon." He paused at the realisation of what he'd just said. He looked at God's face and saw a raised eyebrow and a look which implied *'really?'* "Sorry, old habits die hard. Thank you, God, it has indeed been quite a while. Good old days." The last words were said without a hint of irony. "Allow me to introduce my assistants. This is Stuart, and this lovely creature is…"

"Bathsheba?" Dedan interrupted. "Is that you? Long time, no see. God, it has been a long time." He noticed the glance from God at his minor blasphemy. "Err, my apologies, Mighty one. It's just that I had the pleasure of meeting Bathsheba in the old days, when I was more corporeal. She showed me her palace and treasure trove."

"I bet she did," Emily muttered sarcastically under her breath, but loud enough to be heard by everyone in the room. On hearing that remark, the joyful expression on Dedan's face immediately evaporated; leaving a more serious and professionally detached look. A cold silence took over that ran the risk of confusing the thermometer on the air conditioning system.

God, having no desire to allow his trusted aid to suffer in the Hell he'd created for himself thanks to his open and friendly personality, decided to step in and lighten the mood.

"So, Satan. Before we get started, shall we have a drink?"

Satan's dark mood lifted at the suggestion. His thoughts immediately sprang to the idea of a large, very old single malt whisky but then he realised that perhaps it wasn't the kind of libation God had in mind as being appropriate for the occasion.

"Stuart," he barked, without taking his eyes away from God. "Be a good man and do the honours for everyone please."

This unexpected and uncharacteristic display of borderline good manners took Stuart aback for a split-second. He was used to Satan barking commands at him, but the use of a 'please' wasn't something he'd heard escaping from his master's lips on frequent occasions.

"Of course, my Dark Lord," Stuart responded, emphasising the title for the heavenly audience. "What would everyone like?"

Not wanting to risk the resultant drink from one of Satan's aides all but God, from the good side of the table, declined the offer and God requested a black coffee, without sugar. Beth declined as well, but Satan asked for a milky tea without sugar.

Stuart promptly made the drinks, resisting the strong urge to spit into both cups, and then served them. God casually took a sip of His coffee and gave the cup a disgusted scowl.

"Satan, I know it's your job, but did you really have to persuade the Americans they know even the slightest thing about coffee?"

Satan tilted his head slightly and gave God a grin. "Come on. You've got to admit their smug, superior attitude towards the stuff is funny. They go pay a fortune at coffee shops for large cups of stuff that tastes like super heated elephant's piss, and because it has a continental name and someone told them it's a great taste, they swallow it with smiles on their faces. You should taste it nearer Halloween – now that is dire."

God pouted and nodded in acquiescence. "Yes, I suppose it serves them right for being so gullible." He accepted the reasoning behind it, but still thought it a cruel joke. To him coffee was one of His top ten culinary creations, and the liquid in front of him was sacrilege. Not one to allow earthly pleasures to get in the way of His happiness, He turned the cup into his own special mug and the contents into a strong European blend that was more befitting his stature. He took a sip to ensure it was perfect and released a loud sigh of relief. "Ah, bliss".

Now that He'd had his first caffeine hit for the day, He was ready to take on his erstwhile second-in-command. "Okay, Satan, let's get down to business. What is it that you *really* want? What is it that you're up to?"

Satan put his cup down. Americans were even more clueless about tea than they were about coffee, but Satan wasn't bothered, it still tasted infinitely better than any of the Earl Grey or Darjeeling he got in Hell. Taking a deep breath, he began. "It's simple really, as I originally said on the phone; I want to be allowed back into Heaven. I want to do whatever it takes, so that all past sins are expunged and forgiven and then I can be allowed to sit at your table once more." He saw that God was about to interrupt, so he gave him a placatory raised eyebrow. "Yes, I know it sounds incredible and like it's some sort of ploy, but I'm totally genuine. I would gladly close the earthly exit doors and portals into Hell and let the damned stew in their own juices, or whatever punishment they happen to be enjoying, and then it would be a simple case of free will. Be good and up they go to you and bad, then bingo! Hell doesn't need me or my demons to be there; let the damned go directly to chambers and they're ready to pay for their sins. Neither I, nor any of my army, would be on Earth trying to tempt the humans, so all the stupid battles between good and evil will be resigned to the level of Hollywood horror films. Consider how easy life would be without having humans worry about me trying to buy their souls for a sports car or a successful political career? Look into my soul, and you'll know it's true."

Even if he had wanted to, God wasn't able to look into the soul of Satan. It had been part of the punishment after he'd been banished, his soul would be forever in torment and too ugly even for God to view. But God did hear an element of sincerity in his voice. Even so, the words didn't make any real sense and the argument seemed to be extremely naive.

"Satan, Satan, Satan. At the risk of letting my Southern Gent appearance become My character, are you out of your cotton-picking mind?" The last part of the sentence was spoken in a Southern drawl. "Without temptation, there is no free will. People will just do the right thing because they don't see an alternative. Yes, they might be tempted to eat a cream cake while they're on a diet, or even commit a bit of adultery, if they get the chance, but without you, and your lot whispering in their ears, how will they truly prove themselves? Hearts can change from good to bad, but not without being tested!" God paused and looked around at His entourage. Despite their rapt, attentive expressions and outward appearances, He could tell they were interested in the proposal, but not that interested in the full details of the debate. He looked at Satan. "I don't think Satan here is going to do anything silly, so if it's alright with him, I think it will be perfectly acceptable for everyone else to leave the room. What we need to discuss can be just between us two."

At this proposal, the atmosphere in the room seemed to change completely, the relief and escape from the potential boredom obvious, especially on the faces of the angelic bodyguards.

"Of course, God, I'm sure Dedan and Beth have a lot of catching up to do and Stuart can occupy himself productively elsewhere. Stuart, Beth, you may leave."

God gave His escorts a quick glance and a nod and they also began to leave the room silently. Dedan was tempted to protest but thought better of it. After all Satan, on his own, was no threat to God and he would be close by, in case he was needed.

Dedan was the last one through the doorway and into the crowded corridor. All eyes were on him when he closed the doors behind him. He ignored their expectant stares – if the time came for them to be told more details, they would be informed. Until then, it was none of their business.

He thought it was a bit too crowded to stay there, so looking at Stuart, Grank, Beth and Emily he spoke with an optimistic smile on his face. "I know it's very early in the day, but I think we've all earned it. Fancy a drink at the bar? Hell will pay!" He glanced over at a nearby angel Secret Service Agent. "You – when the meeting is over, please invite God and Satan to the bar. I'm sure they'd enjoy a drink before they go back to their rooms."

This suggestion was met with enthusiastic approval, and the small group – from totally opposite philosophical and moral positions – set off to the cocktail bar. To the outsider, they looked like five people having a laugh as they walked through the hotel. All emotional guards were down and they were going to have a few drinks. No good, no evil – just friends.

Grank got to the bar first and remembered where he'd got to in the alphabet from the previous late night's tidy up, and subsequent wind down drinking session. He ordered five Queen's Necklace cocktails and took up position on his customary bar stool. As the hours passed Grank's accompanied journey down the alphabetical cocktail list continued. The letter R was polished off very quickly, as was S. The conversations ebbed and flowed over such topics as favourite missions they'd all been on, what cities on Earth most resembled Heaven or Hell. Even sexual conquests were discussed, although Stuart kept conspicuously quiet on the subject. Being an accountant, and a slimy one at that, his personality was enough to protect him from too many sexual encounters with anything more than his right hand or the occasional farm animal.

Eventually, the long and often fraught and heated meeting came to its end. Despite all the arguments and numerous ideas Satan had proposed – and thought were perfectly valid – God had been able to find objections; not only on theological points, but also on statistical and logistical perspectives. They both agreed that as it was now mid-afternoon, it would be best if they both resumed their human Presidential forms and adjourned until the following day. They left the room to be met by a corridor full of guards, all standing crisply to attention, as if it were a competition. Demon and angel, sticking their chests out proudly in an act of superiority, hoping for some sort of inspection and acknowledgement of who was the smartest. Both God and Satan looked at each other, smiled and nodded their heads as if to say, *'well it wasn't my idea'*.

The Secret Service agent tasked to invite God to the bar by Dedan stepped forwards. "Your most Majestic Highness. God, sir." He stumbled, unused to addressing his deity, especially on such a conversational topic. "Dedan has invited you both to join him and his guest at the cocktail bar in the lobby." With relief that he'd managed to speak to God, and deliver Dedan's invitation, he gestured down the corridor as if there were different directional options to be taken to get to the bar.

"Thank you – Colin, isn't it?" God looked at the angel with a gentle, understanding smile. "I think a drink would go down rather well." He glanced at Satan. "Mr. President, would you care to join us?"

"Well, Mr. President, I think that would be an excellent idea."

With that the two, mock American leaders, proceeded down the corridor, closely followed by angel and demon guards, jockeying for position to see who could be behind their respective bosses. At the front, and on the outer perimeters, the jostling was minor and not obvious to any outside observer, but inside the crowd it was like a scrum, as good and bad swung low level punches into ribs and kicked shins like frustrated school children in an assembly hall with no teachers watching.

The long cavalcade of leaders, and followers, reached the bar and laying his hands on the shoulders of Dedan and Emily, God smiled broadly. "Hello, boys and girls. Missed me? It looks, and smells, as if you've all been busy. All peaceful, I hope? Right, which one of you is going to buy two thirsty Presidents of the United States a drink? I think, if I remember correctly, that the other President would like a large malt whisky, straight up, and I'll have a Russian Mule."

The attentive barman nodded, uncertain whether he should be talking to the President of the USA while he was on duty, and if so, which one. After all, it wasn't something he'd ever been trained for. Deciding discretion was the better part of valour, he silently served the requested drinks and stood back, looking at the strange collection of leaders and their assistants who sat or stood directly in front of him, not to mention what seemed like a small army of pushing, shoving security personnel lined up several yards away.

Emptying his drink, in one go, Satan released a satisfied gasp and set his glass on the bar. Looking directly at God, he smiled and laughingly enquired, "So God, another? Fancy a Virgin Mary, or do you remember what happened last time you had one of those?"

Chapter 31 – Taking Stock.

Stuart and Grank were relaxing on the single sofa chairs in Satan's suite, as they watched their leader pace the floor with his arms clasped behind his back, silently chewing his lower lip. Stopping occasionally, he looked from one assistant to the other before averting his gaze to a position in the middle distance, as if there was something he could see, which was invisible to his two guests. A couple of times, Stuart opened his mouth as if to say something, but thought better of it. The silence seemed oppressive and fragile, but he wasn't going to be the one to break it. Grank experienced no such compunction; having spent centuries hearing the screams and groans of tormented souls under his control, he appreciated the full value of peace and quiet. If it were up to him, all day, every day, would be like this. He was bemused by Satan's pacing, but he didn't try and analyse it. As far as he was concerned, his Dark Lord was thinking about the day just gone and more than likely planning for the next. Perhaps formulating some more cunning ideas to back up his argument with God and inevitably persuade Him of the value of his case. His resentment over being precluded from the meeting had left him with the warm and comfortable knowledge that Stuart's presence had very quickly become similarly redundant and he'd been unceremoniously ejected from the meeting. Schadenfreude was not a word he was familiar with, but he definitely felt it deep in his being. He would bide his time and then, perhaps, gloat when he got the chance. A long monologue of invective sarcasm had already been prepared in his mind, ready to be launched, as if it were grapeshot from a catapult. He could see it now, Stuart defenceless against his withering verbal onslaught. His planned insults weren't of Oscar Wilde's quality or intellectual calibre, but for a resident of Hell, any victory over an enemy was to be savoured.

Satan finally stopped and turned. His face was impassive, framing a distant look in his eyes. "What was I thinking?"

The question caught both Stuart and Grank off guard. They'd been expecting some sort of 'Eureka' moment, some revelation about forthcoming strategy or an insight into his mental machinations. This test of their non-existent psychic abilities left them perplexed and all they could do in response was remain seated, giving him blank expressions.

"The bloody, Bloody Mary joke!" he began. "Stupid, just pure and simple stupidity. Said to anyone else it wouldn't have been a problem. It just came out, I couldn't help it!"

"But Sire, you were…" ventured Stuart, but he was cut off in mid-sentence.

"It could have destroyed everything. All my planning, every argument, the working plumbing, comfortable beds and flushing toilets. All gone in an instant!" Satan's seemed to want answers, but by not asking a direct question, his audience came to the mutual conclusion it was better to remain silent until they got a better understanding of the direction the monologue was going. "But did you see his face? If only I had a camera, I'd have been able to print it off and have it put on every wall of every chamber in Hades. Proof of what I can do."

"Yes, Sire." The penny finally dropping in Stuart's head regarding the theme of Satan's ramblings. "The silence that enveloped the room was monumental. After the sharp intakes of breath from his angelic scum, you could have heard a metaphorical pin drop."

"Yes" interjected Grank, not wanting to be left out of the conversation "God looked, momentarily, like he'd turned to cold stone."

"Exactly." Satan spoke, his voice now full of energy. "He kept me on the hook, the bastard, dangling like a man on a noose. But eventually, he laughed, and oh what a welcome laugh." Satan's mind went back to that moment. He'd realised just a split second too late what he'd said and what damage it could have done, but then God had decided to see the funny side and laughed.

Everyone there had recognised, with collective relief, how volatile the situation had been and how another possible apocalyptic battle had been averted. Even the human bar staff had joined in the laughter, despite having no real idea what they were laughing at. It could easily have become the 'Battle of the Poor Taste Joke'. A small corner of some Hawaiian island flattened by vast armies; all because of Satan's sense of humour. But thankfully, the laugher had let him off the hook and tomorrow's meeting would still take place. Satan's smile was broad now when he looked at Grank. "No matter what happens in the meeting, I think we should give any communal drinks a wide birth. No point in pushing our luck is there?" At that, all three of them burst into loud, raucous laughter, the tension of the day released. And although it was, in reality, only muffled angry swearing coming from the giant trunk in the corner of the room – it seemed to be joining in the mirth, rocking and swaying like a bellicose, asymmetric clown. However, the occupant wouldn't be invited out so that he could join in the fun.

Chapter 32 – It's Going To Be A Long

And Hard Night.

Dedan had returned to his room, having visited God's suite and ascertained if there were further instructions for the next day's meeting with Satan. It was due to start at 10.00am and God was planning to arrive in the room at 09:59 and 58 seconds. He knew that this time, Satan would be in the room first and he would be there waiting impatiently. He planned, once again, to share the conference room with Satan alone, so Dedan would be free to ensure security in the hotel, and its perimeter, was maintained. Other than that, God hadn't shared any more of His plans for the day, and Dedan hadn't asked. He assumed God had a strategy and was ready to counter any points made by Satan, but he knew better than to question the Supreme Being over such matters. Dedan had been dismissed for the night, so he'd taken the opportunity to sit down and contemplate the events of the day. He too, had experienced the cold tension after Satan's joke and he'd been relieved when God decided to see the funny side of it. The ramifications of a bad-tempered walk out and the abrupt cessation of talks could have been catastrophic for the hotel, its staff and probably for any inhabitants in a five-mile radius. As for the nature reserve, and the armed campers there, the endangered and defenceless animal residents would have moved up the classification of species from 'vulnerable' to 'extinct'.

Battles between good and evil didn't tend to be contained in a small area. He remembered the brief but violent battle of Tunguska in 1908. Fortunately, due to its remote location, no humans had been involved and they were able to make it look as if a comet hit the place, but if it had been a densely-inhabited part of the planet the loss of life would have been large and hard to pass off as some freak 'act of God', or 'something falling from the heavens'. It was strange how people seemed to blame God for all those sorts of things, instead of pointing fingers at the real culprit. But then again, perhaps it was better if they didn't know the truth. Easier to live a normal life when everything is wrapped up in weak religious dogmas and myths, and the truth was often stranger than any fiction.

Dedan ran his tongue over his teeth and gums. He had no idea what it was, but a strange green, blue and orange cocktail had left him with an unpleasant lingering taste in his mouth. It was as if he'd been drinking industrial slurry mixed with surgical alcohol and sugar. He could understand demons wanting to drink such filth – they would drink each other's urine if it was mixed with vodka and you put an olive in the glass with it, but why did humans so willingly subject their taste buds, and livers, to such obvious abuse? In his time, even as a human, he'd drunk some dodgy looking and smelling concoctions, but that was usually out of necessity – not as a hobby and for pleasure. Perhaps he was just too old school, from a time before schools, but people didn't need much educating as to what they should and shouldn't eat or drink. Learn and live or just die, there was no multi-coloured rainbow of possible alternatives in between. He decided if he was invited to another drinking session tomorrow, he'd stick with wine or beer and leave the poisonous spirits to those who deserved them, the ones whose spirits were poisoned. There was a knock on the door leading to Emily's room. The gentle noise was a reminder of the existence of his beautiful colleague and abruptly brought him back to reality with a happy smile. "Come in, my angel."

The door opened silently and just a hand appeared around the edge of it, the index finger wagging and curling slowly. It was instructing him, seductively, to join the owner of the pale hand in her own room. Rubbing his hands gleefully together as he rose from his chair, he smiled. "With such an invite, how could I refuse?" He brushed his hair down with his hands before he walked quickly to the door and stepped into Emily's room. It was dimly lit, with just one small bedside lamp switched on. Its subtle yellow glow providing more a warm ambiance, than illumination, to the spacious room. "I wasn't expecting a—" his sentence stopped as he made out the shape of another person in the room, sitting on the edge of the bed behind Emily.

"Hello Dedan," said the voice. The figure stood up and only then was he able to recognise Beth. "Emily and I have been talking, and it seems we have something in common." She smiled devilishly, her eyes twinkling in the faint light as if they were touching his heart and playing with it coquettishly. "We've decided it's been a long day and we need to let off some steam. But first, we need some heat."

Dedan's smile was broad and perhaps conveyed more of his salacious mind than he intended to reveal. Too late to play it cool now, even if he could be bothered to try. He knew where this was going and was happy to light some fires and stoke a couple of boilers. Closing the door behind him, he looked first at Emily and then at Beth "Of course ladies, more than happy to oblige." Even in the poor lighting, the contrast between the two women was startling. One was blonde and voluptuous and the other dark haired, tall and slender. Both, however, were stunningly beautiful and their shining eyes or coy smiles alone would have driven any man wild.

Without turning, he pushed the door which obediently closed behind him leaving the three of them in the semi-darkness. He stepped towards Beth and as she started to undo his shirt Emily moved up behind him and wrapped her arms around him, gently kissing his neck. He released a sigh of pleasure and dived onto the bed causing the two women to fall with him. The sudden action made the bed move six inches to the right, hitting the bedside cabinet and simultaneously knocking the lamp onto the floor and extinguishing what little light had lit up the room. The darkness went unnoticed by the three giggling bodies however, as six hands blindly, but efficiently, worked to remove whatever clothing they came into contact with. Once released from the owner's body, the items were carelessly discarded. Hurled chaotically about the room; finding their own random places for the night.

197

Outside the room, in the brightly lit corridor, the guardian angels on duty had seen Beth go into Emily's room and hoped for some aural entertainment to occupy the night and help the long, otherwise silent, hours to pass. The anticipated entertainment had drawn a large contingent of off-duty angels as well. All were keen to enjoy the voyeuristic sound show. Many had dragged comfortable chairs from their rooms and were sitting together casually, chatting and drinking bottled beer as they waited for the show to start. If an unsuspecting stranger had happened to walk into the corridor, they would have been met by a sight reminiscent of a busy, but narrow, bar filled with people relaxing as they quietly talked and enjoyed a drink.

A less-than-totally-angelic angel who had been pressing his ear to Emily's door suddenly gave a frenetic hand gesture to the gathered crowd, indicating they should be quiet. The show was about to start and they didn't want to miss a word – or more accurately, a guttural noise.

They all seemed to collectively hold their breaths as the noises from the other side of the door, began to emanate out to the audience. The initial assault on the bed, and sound of the light crashing signalled the start, but as the night continued they were treated to other noises from exuberant voices vocalising the pleasure they were experiencing, the groaning noises and sounds of moist bodies rubbing against each other combined with the noise of various pieces of furniture being utilised for things the designers hadn't contemplated, or the manufacturers had not factored in when building. Any warranties immediately invalidated. Chairs creaked and groaned under the weight of three imaginative, creative people. The wardrobe rattled as more than clothes briefly took up the space and the poor bed gave up the ghost completely, its legs collapsing like a marathon runner crossing the finish line having just beaten his personal best. Limbs gone from underneath, body laid helplessly on the floor. The carnage done to the room, and furniture, or the entertainment provided to the assembled and appreciative crowd outside, was not noticed by the trio. The wild ménage à trios being their sole focus making them oblivious to everything but themselves.

Eventually the almost endless reserve of heavenly and demonic energy was spent and silence returned to the hallway. Angels put their chairs back where they belonged and tried to fill the remaining few hours of night with sleep, or resumed their pointless vigil in the corridor, ensuring nobody disturbed the peace and quiet of the place. But all minds were filled with similar thoughts of admiration, respect and a large amount of jealousy for Dedan. None of them could work out what he had that allowed him to succeed, when in their view, he shouldn't even manage to gain a smile from a beautiful woman. Each of them had the same phrase running through their brains.

'You lucky bastard'.

Which was sheer coincidence because as Dedan laid in the, now beaten and broken, bed looking up at the ceiling, invisible in the night, with the two exhausted and sleeping women resting their heads on either shoulder and draping their arms across his chest he was thinking the exact same thing. Nights like this didn't happen everyday, or night for that matter, but when they did they were treasured.

Chapter 33 – Ready And Waiting.

It was 6am and Satan was dressed and ready. He paced the room impatiently; there were many things he hated and being kept waiting was high on the list. It was nothing to do with manners or etiquette, he just preferred to make others wait for him. Being on the receiving end of it, even if it wasn't planned, made his blood boil – which ironically, was a punishment he often applied to people who tried to make him wait. He'd gruffly called out Grank and Stuart's names and they'd sent indistinct, muffled and panicked responses through the closed door. He could hear them squabbling as they rushed to get dressed, neither of them wanting to get out of the other's way and both determined to be the first ready to present himself in front of their grumpy master.

"Get a move on you pathetic maggots, or I'll have you shovelling and eating shit for all eternity in Hell," Satan growled.

Such threats were never idle or merely crazy metaphors when issued by Satan, and as invectives went, he was hardly touching the surface of his abusive vocabulary. He stopped pacing across the room and stood in front of the adjoining room's door, legs akimbo and arms folded tightly across his chest. He adopted an almost blank expression, only his glowing, blood red eyes revealing any perceptible emotion. Even his body language screamed rage. If a stance could spit, snarl and swear, he'd found it. The welcome awaiting the first sycophantic servant to fall across the threshold into the luxurious suite probably wouldn't be the one hoped for, and whoever it was, would probably regret being the first to see their master.

In the other room, whose ownership was contested by Grank and Stuart, there was panic and chaos. Both recognised the urgency and annoyance permeating from next door. The more they rushed to get ready, the more they fell over trying to put on their trousers. Left legs slipped hurriedly into right trouser legs, and were quickly withdrawn again, causing the garments to turn inside out. Partners for single socks were hunted down and quickly slipped on. Shirts were buttoned up, out of order, necessitating a second attempt with slightly more attention to detail.

All the time, the racing pair kept a vengeful eye on the other, relishing any mistake made by the opponent whilst also adding to their own mental pressure. Both desperate to win the competition to be the first to be presentable to their sovereign master. After his third attempt, Stuart finally managed to fasten his tie in a Windsor knot. With the final piece in the clothing jigsaw puzzle completed and after a quick check in the mirror, he was satisfied his appearance was immaculate.

Grank still struggled with his tie – not that it was really needed in Hawaii, where aloha shirts and shorts were standard issue garments, even for meetings – but if Stuart was wearing one, Grank refused to appear underdressed in comparison. The main drawback was that ties weren't something he'd had much experience of. He'd garrotted people during his time as a human, prior to going to Hell. In fact, he'd even tied knots to make nooses for hanging enemies, but the fiddly requirements of ties were far too complex for his less-than-dexterous fingers. Each frustrated attempt ended up resembling a red silken lettuce protruding from his shirt collar. The smug smiles he was receiving from Stuart did nothing to ease his vexation, but he recognised defeat when he saw it. The battle had been lost. Slipping the crumpled garment from his neck he threw it onto the bed, unbuttoned his collar and moved towards the door.

His journey was blocked by Stuart who'd already reached the door and had his hand on the handle. Turning it, he threw open the door theatrically and with a large, self-congratulatory smile on his face entered Satan's room.

Grank followed closely behind, fastidiously staring down at the carpet trying to avoid his master's eye and hoping the absence of a tie wouldn't generate a stream of insults. He needn't have worried too much.

As the first person through the door, Stuart encountered the full impact of Satan's waiting pose. The smile on his face quickly morphed into a more appropriate expression of abject terror when he saw Satan's stance and rage-filled eyes. He gulped instinctively. He'd seen the look many times before, aimed at some hapless demon who'd failed to please, and he knew the omens weren't good. His next words, if he got chance to say any, could easily be his last. He opted for obsequiousness. "My mighty Lord, my humblest apologies for my tardy timing. Such lateness is inexcusable. Unfortunately, Grank was delaying me and blocked my progress!"

Grank's eyes rose from the carpet to the back of Stuart's head. He had a quick glance around for a heavy, blunt instrument, suitable to smash Stuart's skull and introduce his brain to the open air. Seeing nothing within easy reach, he clenched his teeth, fists and even toes. Yet another slight which would be remembered and provide him with an excuse to mete out violent and gory vengeance when the time was right. Perhaps he could conceal a knife in his jacket pocket and eviscerate Stuart unobserved in some dark corridor and leave the body to be discovered by someone else. The assumption being that the murder was carried out by some random, but unidentifiable, demon bent on settling an old score or even some less than saintly angel that had decided to fight the good fight on a one to one basis.

On hearing the blustering apology, and shameless attempt at passing the blame and witnessing the accompanying expressions on first Stuart's and then Grank's faces, Satan was consumed by the humour of the situation. Being on Earth hadn't softened his two main assistants, and he liked that they were still as oily and rage-filled as they were in Hell. Unable to maintain his hard manner, his eyes lost their red fire and returned to a more human appearance and his folded arms relaxed. A smile spread across his face and he released a loud, guttural laugh.

This reaction took both servants by surprise. Stuart was seeing a side of his master he hadn't encountered before and it confused his defences. He'd been expecting some form of painful punishment. Humans had a medical comparative pain scale, used to ascertain what a person was enduring, and of course Satan had a similar thing. Both ranged from very mild to unimaginable only with the highest reaches in Hell being far more unspeakable. Eternal agony wasn't something humans had thought of when they created their little list.

Consequently, ribald laughter wasn't something Stuart had been bracing for. As the merry howling, at his expense, continued for what seemed like an eon, he began to wish the punishment *had* been more physical. A short sharp shock from a lightning bolt would have been preferable to this.

Grank was listening to the laughter and watching Satan but he too, was totally confused. He'd been expecting some form of punitive punishment, but assumed he'd missed some joke and would catch up later if he kept his ears open and his mouth shut. Unlike Stuart, he wasn't used to being in Satan's presence, so had no frame of reference with which to interpret any nuances so just accepted the situation as normal. After all he had no intention of asking for an explanation and risk spoiling the mood. Stepping forward, he took up a position next to Stuart and waited patiently for the guffawing to subside.

Eventually, Satan regained his composure and the smile vanished when he spoke. "Alright, I don't have the time nor the inclination to mete out punishments right now – perhaps later? Stuart, make a note to remind me!" He paused. "You should just hope today's meeting goes well, so I'm happy and forget about the tardiness and lack of respect. I expect you to do better tomorrow. Shall we go?" The question was totally rhetorical, as they were hardly likely to disagree. "Oh, and Stuart, you might want to do up your fly before we set off. I don't want any angels having a cheap laugh at your shortcomings. They're expecting large horns, not unimpressive stubs!" Then, turning, he walked towards the door.

This time it was Grank's turn to suppress a laugh at Stuart's expense. The sight of Stuart, trying to nonchalantly zip up his trousers almost made up for the earlier insult. The homicide he'd planned was still an option, but there might be some comedy value in allowing Stuart to remain on Earth for a little longer. Maybe he should let him be the first through the door every morning and avoid being a target of derision.

Satan's progress to the conference room was better organised than it had been the previous day. Despite their lack of intelligence, the demonic guards had learnt the lessons of the day before. A safe distance was maintained as Satan walked to the lift and only when the door had closed behind the three occupants, did the charge down the stairwell commence in an undignified attempt to beat the elevator to the ground and be there ready to meet their master with an air of composure and trying not to look like they have raced down several floors and were now totally out of breath.

In the elevator, the dulcet tones of Barry Manilow rang out. The song sharing its name with a place in Rio was determinedly ignored, and the desire to obliterate the sound system was resisted. Satan needed to maintain his composure, despite the justification to destroy everything he encountered.

When the elevator door opened on the ground floor, Satan was met by red-faced, breathless and dishevelled bodyguards. Ignoring their appearance, he strode past them and walked towards the conference room. He regally swung open the double doors and made his grand entrance.

The show of grandeur was unnecessary, as the room had no other occupants. He closed the door behind him, leaving

Stuart and Grank outside with the demons and a contingent of angel security who were already there, casually talking to one another, and determined to give the demons as little acknowledgement as they could. Just because they were there didn't mean that they mattered. Devils could keep their distance and all would be fine.

Inside, Satan glanced at the unadorned clock on the wall and noted it was 6.18am. He allowed himself another smile and selected the chair with its back to the window, overlooking the already sun-drenched golf course. In the distance were a few demon cows, which looked on edge and were moving their heads around as if seeking out some imminent danger. Unaware of the unwelcome romantic tryst which occurred the previous day, Satan assumed they were being diligent in the execution of their duties and were on guard against any angelic tricks. As far as he was concerned they had no reason to be unhappy in their work. The vacant look on Jon's face was unable to reveal the pain that his rear end was feeling at that moment.

After appraising the view, he settled in his seat of choice – let God have all the sunlight in his face for a change. More importantly, he'd beaten his foe to the meeting room. In the grand scheme of things not a massive victory, after all he was trying to get back into God's good books, but in the age-old war between vice and virtue he'd take whatever wins he could get.

Chapter 34 – A More Casual Approach.

In God's vast, bright penthouse suite, the sun was streaming in through the window and bathing the room in a bright golden glow. Although He hadn't specifically made the sun so bright this particular morning, the effect was as if He'd waved His hand and banished all the morning clouds. As God lay in His bed, He felt the warm sunlight on His cheeks and it seemed even the rays had come to worship Him. Stretching, He looked at the alarm clock by the side of His bed. 8.30am – a suitable time for getting up and ready for the start of the meeting at 10.00. He could sense Satan was already in the conference room and had been there for quite some time. Let him score a goal – it didn't matter to Him what time Satan got there and which chair He sat in, He wasn't childish and bothered about where he sat.

Making his favourite mug materialise in his hand He sniffed the contents. Fresh, strong black coffee, a perfect blend which would have made any human coffee connoisseur weep with both sadness and joy to smell its rich aroma. Taking a sip, He let out a sigh of pleasure. Removing the covers, God swung out of bed, His white silk pyjamas reflecting the sunlight. Stretching, God gave His buttocks a very un-God like scratch which would have shocked any devout believers witnessing such an occurrence. To them, God wasn't the type who needed to do that. It was probably for the best that they'd never heard Him belch or break wind either. Both natural occurrences, even for a deity, but not something any follower of the Judeo-Christian faiths wanted to think about when they made themselves comfortable and prayed for whatever miracle they thought their faith would bring by simply asking for it. It might have been true that His farts smelled fresher than anybody else's, but that was scant consolation to the faithful. To them, such things were the acts of Satan.

Oblivious – or more accurately apathetic – to such small minded metaphysical opinions God proceeded to undress, shower and then dress in His Presidential suit. He could have just as easily transmogrified from 'God in PJ's' to 'President God in Suit' – but where was the fun in that? He was on Earth and wanted to make the most of the normal experiences the place had to offer, and that included the basic mechanics of ablutions. A warm refreshing shower, the sensation of a soft towel as he dried off and the feel of His fresh, clean, smart suit. Simple pleasures perhaps, especially for Him, but still things to be loved.

Once God was ready, He went back into His bedroom and studied Himself in the full-length mirror on the wall. He changed His face to that of the President and there it was, the reflection of someone who was, externally at least, a perfect copy. Even the President's mother wouldn't have been able to tell the two apart. He glanced at the clock again and saw it was 9:30, a perfect time for him to take a leisurely stroll to the meeting.

He was in no rush, and decided to take a slight detour and say good morning to the hotel staff working in the foyer. A nice gesture and one which would enable him to time His entrance to the conference room perfectly.

Striding to the door leading into the corridor, he paused; hand hovering over the handle. He considered giving Dedan a knock on his door, to wake him up and invite him to join him, but He decided against it. He knew exactly what he'd been up to last night. Despite Emily's room being further away, the crashing furniture and vocal excitement had made its way into His room and ears. Let Dedan sleep – it wasn't as if there was any need for extra security and protection.

He smiled softly, chuckling to himself and headed to the lift. The angel guards escorted him to the short distance and radioed down to the guards stationed on the ground floor, advising them that He was on his way. The journey down was pleasant, as the air was filled with classical music never heard on

Earth, or by mortal ears. Beethoven's 15th piano concerto poured out of the elevator's normally bland and ineffective sound system. Majesty and power, a magical mix of feelings all designed to make the piano sound like it had become a new emotion to be felt in the heart and soul. Then, all too briefly, the elevator reached its destination, the doors opened and the music ended. Stepping through the doors, He was greeted by happy, smiling guards. Good mornings were exchanged and they parted to allow God to walk towards the conference room. The pace was casual, with no need to rush.

After His slight detour to say hello to staff working in the lobby he set off for the meeting. As he got closer he saw the obvious line, a physical and emotional partition between the good and bad guards outside the room. It was an invisible iron curtain, a mini invisible Berlin Wall of distrust, fear and anger. Neither side wanted to lower their mental, or physical guard, and accept that the other side wouldn't cause any trouble. Well, not here and certainly not now. Too many battles, tricks and traps had made everyone far too cynical to believe there could ever be a peace, even a temporary one, between the two sides. But perhaps, He mused, Satan was genuine in his desire. After so many eons. there could be harmony and mankind could be allowed to find its own humanity without being led astray by demons whispering in their ears, offering things they didn't need. Fleeting happiness in life; often meting out pain, death and destruction to others, led only to suffering eternally in the afterlife. Earth without a hell? Was it really possible?

He could imagine humans with unblemished souls. Hell no longer on Earth, and no souls going to Hell either. Could it be real? Such things were out of his vision. He created things, but since the creation of free will he no longer had the power to know the future – there were far too many variables.

Reaching the guards at the door, God halted and offered a genuine and disarming smile to everyone, irrespective of background. He paused to shake a few hands and indulge in small talk like a member of the British Royal family at a theatrical command performance, meeting actors. They were bland pleasantries, but words that would mean everything to the recipients and be cherished forever. He even extended a few compliments to a handful of demons, shaking their hands warmly and deliberately taking the hatred and rage from the heart of Carsten, a Comprachicos demon. God felt the anger and knew it was out of place; however, he also knew that the love that he had left in its place would soon die and the vacuum it left would quickly get filled with all the poisonous emotions that were there originally.

Once the inane pressing of skin was over, He turned to the door leading into the conference room. Walking towards it, two angelic guards who were smiling with pleasure at having shaken hands with God, promptly opened the doors for him. He nodded and thanked them as He passed and paused inside as the doors were softly closed behind Him.

Satan was sitting in front of Him, in his sinister version of the President. Even from where God stood, He could sense the mixture of frustration, anger and a sense of victory emanating from the dark leader. His glee at getting to the room before God, and getting the best chair, had been tainted by the suspicion he'd been played for a fool. Sitting in the room for hours on his own had given him plenty of time to think and stew. Thinking he'd somehow been manipulated into getting there far too early, only to have God sweep in casually scant moments before the meeting was due to start. This suspicion was inflamed by the fact the clock was just above the doorway and it told him there were only a few seconds until the appointed time. However the knowledge of his goals enforced calm on his words and actions. Politely, he stood up and bowed slightly to God.

"Good morning, God. I hope you had a good evening? This hotel was an ideal choice, and it's always great to sleep on human beds, rather than the things we have in Hell."

"Yes, thank you Satan, I slept well and yes, the beds aren't bad at all," God said, ensuring he applied the description of the bed just to see if it solicited a response. "Not the comfort of Heaven of course, but I'm sure they're a world apart from the bunks you're used to in your place."

Wincing at the thought of the discomfort and pain even the best beds in Hell produced, Satan nodded slowly and sat after his display of courtesy to his former, and hopefully future, leader. "Perhaps I could invite you around, as a guest sometime, and you could experience them for a few nights?"

"Why thank you, Satan, that's very magnanimous and generous, but I think I'll decline your kind offer." God took the words in the spirit of a joke, rather than some off-hand snide comment. "Besides, if you're genuine and can persuade me, perhaps the offer would be moot?"

Satan wasn't sure how to take God's comment. Was it His turn to joke, or was it an indication that his aims could become a reality and God was actually open to listening? "Well, Your Holy Majesty," he said, reverting to one of the titles he used to apply to God before the schism and war, "I do genuinely hope you can see my point of view and accept my words in the spirit they're meant." Realising he was not being an ideal host, he decided to up the charm offensive. "Would you like a coffee?" He began to rise so he could make God a coffee if required.

"Thank you, but please, remain seated – I can get it myself. Would you like one?"

"Yes please, as it comes," replied Satan. The mantle of manners seemed strange. Words of politeness he hadn't used for millennia, or if he had used them, it was only to camouflage some deceit or snare some unsuspecting human prior to getting a signature and their eternal soul.

God went to the bureau and poured two cups of hot coffee from the percolator, black for Himself, and remembering Satan's tastes from old, adding a dash of milk for the Dark Lord. He handed Satan his drink and sat down opposite him. The sun was at the wrong angle and shone directly into His face. "Excuse me a second, Satan" he said. He gently moved his left hand and out of nowhere, a small cloud appeared in the otherwise beautifully clear blue Pacific sky and settled directly in front of the sun removing the glare. "There, that's better."

Satan knew his little ploy had been seen and bested, but he didn't mind. What was the point in getting angry? Today wasn't the day for the one-upmanship he'd planned. Instead, today seemed to be holding infinite possibilities, if only he could keep calm and control his long-ingrained baser emotions. That would be his battle for the day.

They took sips from their coffees simultaneously and both paused, studying the other. "You know something, Satan?" God said, with an expression akin to a bear sitting on a spike. "You've been guilty of committing many great evils on Earth. I could spend a century listing the worst, and it would still only be the tip of the iceberg."

Satan glanced up from the cup of hot liquid, and he had to admit, the coffee in Hell was actually better. He indicated the cup with an incline of his head. "Could I ask for a minor miracle?"

God laughed loudly and with a click of his fingers, the liquid in both cups was converted into the most heavenly of coffees. Satan sniffed the liquid and smiled at the aroma. Sipping it, he released an almost orgasmic moan of pleasure. "Thank you, God, a nice touch."

God, feeling that He'd lightened the mood a little bowed His head graciously. "You're welcome. A morning without a decent coffee is so uncivilised. Right then Bob, shall we get down to business? What exactly are you up to?"

Chapter 35 – The Great Not There?

In the cramped corridor, outside the conference room, the two sets of similarly-dressed guards continued their silent vigil. Eyes remained focused on their opposite numbers, stares concentrated, watching for any sudden moves. The tension in the air like the expectant hours before a thunderstorm, the electricity almost tangible. Hands poised, ready in tense anticipation of the person they were watching making some surprise move. Eyes watching for any sign of a hand nonchalantly slipping inside a jacket and possibly gaining an advantage by pulling out their pistol first. It was like a stand-off, in some spaghetti western. All that was needed was Ennio Morricone to add a soundtrack, and perhaps to have Clint Eastwood standing in the middle, chewing a cigarillo. Any outsider would have known that a blood bath would occur, if they waited for the right note in the music.

Of course, such social references were lost on the angels and demons who were too focused on watching for warning signs. An excuse to draw their guns first and somehow eliminate all of the opposition quickly and be the victorious side. The fastest left totally unharmed and safe surrounded by the blood splattered, lifeless bodies of the foes. But they also knew that they were being watched as eagerly as they were watching and that any move that they made could give the enemy the excuse to make the first, and possibly quickest, draw.

The only one in the confined space who wasn't in a state of high alert was Carsten. The demon who'd had his heart cleansed by God was experiencing a state of confusing, but blissful euphoria. He knew his enemies were standing in front of him, and that he should hate them with all his being. Anger should be pulsing around his brain, squeezing it like a ripe melon. Rage should be strangling his heart and making his blood burn. But all he felt was love. It was an emotion which was alien to him, but he was experiencing it at such an extreme level it was probably unknown to most of the angelic guards as well. Due to the rapidly growing population on Earth, God seldom took such direct intervention with a human's soul, or Devil's soul for that matter. The feelings would soon fade. Even the most beautiful of flowers might bloom in a desert in a sudden freak rainstorm, but once the baking sun comes out again, the petals shrivel up and the verdant green withers to dry brown and is quickly blown away in the wind. Such was the soul of a demon, which held no fertile ground for love to flourish. But fleetingly God had given one random box of evil on legs a gift. A small amount of time free from its own natural state; a taste of what it felt like to be truly happy. A happiness that didn't rely upon disembowelling kittens or eviscerating goats to, somehow keep his master appeased. There was no real motivation for it, and perhaps it could be seen as being more cruel than any punishment given out by Satan; a fleeting scent of happy goodness which would fade leaving anger to rule once again.

Ed Mercerator had not just been sleeping overnight, he had been busy planning and preparing, having heard guards talking about a meeting he had assumed that the conference room would be the focal point and he would need to gain access. New found hotel staff colleagues had been bribed, props had been acquired and guests had been watched. A great news story had to be worked on and this one needed a lot more than most. Especially as he had no idea what exactly was going on. He was now stood at the far end of the corridor, he'd managed to acquire a trolley full of cream cakes and had every intention of trying to bluff his way into the conference room on the pretext of delivering the un-requested treats as a complimentary gift from the management. Then, once in the room, he could blow his cover and perhaps have an exclusive interview with the room's residents and maybe even get a few photos taken with his hidden camera before the security guards could drag him out and kick him out of the hotel. Although any such interview, however exclusive it might be, would probably be very brief and incoherent. But the sight that met him made him pause and rethink his simple plan. The double phalanx of opposing guards didn't exactly make him think that a chocolate gateau or a vanilla slice would be a welcome discussion point and besides, the atmosphere that met him as he got closer to the guards made the ample hair on his arms stand on end and made him shudder. With the tiny camera held between his hand and the trolley handle, he quickly took a few shots of the wall of testosterone blocking his way. As suspicious eyes started to focus on him, his courage and resolve were leaching away and he was coming to the definite conclusion that this plan might work at another time, but certainly not today. Without any words being spoken he knew any attempt to access the room, or even any ludic words injected to lighten the mood, would be met with at best, silence, and at worse, severe personal injury. But, being a professional journalist, he knew he had to try so he pushed forward hesitantly; continuing his journey towards the door. His concentration was suddenly broken by the sounds of heavy breathing and even heavier running feet on carpet from behind him. Just as he turned to see who it was, he was unceremoniously pushed to the left by a red-faced, panting, Stuart, and just as promptly pushed back to where he'd been by an equally puffing and out of breath Grank. Neither seemed to have noticed him on their unstoppable course. Even if they had seen him, they wouldn't have delayed their journey to go around him or stop to apologise. In fact, they would quite happily have pushed him onto the floor and ran over his face, sending desserts and cakes flying in all directions. Social niceties were never Stuart or Grant's strengths, and at this moment they weren't even a consideration. Grank's attributes were his build and core strength. His stamina and the ability to use his feet, fists or head to inflict pain on any poor soul who looked like it would make them even more sorry for being in Hell. Running any considerable distances wasn't usually part of his health program. Stuart, however, had a weasel-like build to match his personality. He wasn't muscular or particularly strong. Filing documents and lifting ledgers didn't require the body of a heavyweight boxing champion, but the lack of bulk made him a surprisingly fast sprinter. With this advantage, he reached the bewildered crowd of guards first and pushing both Angel and demon out of his way, he got to the double doors leading to the conference room well before Grank. Once he got there, he raised his left fist as if to knock then paused, mouth open, initially a way to take a deep breath but then he abruptly realised that he had no idea what he was going to say. His whole facial expression took on a look that one of his bovine brethren might have adopted when they'd first been surprised by the amorous bull.

This pause in his movement gave Grank the opportunity to catch up; his pace rather too much for his bulk and the momentum too great, so deceleration was only made complete when he ran directly into the back of Stuart.

Stuart, in turn, hit the door with his head, therefore removing the requirement to knock. His head made impact loudly enough that it was audible not only inside the conference room but also all along the corridor. This unexpected spectacle gave both groups of guards a common focus and broke the tense atmosphere as they laughed at Stuart and Grank who resembled an evil version of a Laurel and Hardy film.

Twisting slightly to partially face Grank, Stuart offered him a dark look and raised his fist as if to throw a punch but in the last moment thought better of it and gave the door three rapid knocks.

Sensing that something must be seriously wrong for such an interruption to take place, the guards suddenly lost their humour and lapsed into silence. Even Ed stopped in his tracks, convinced his presence wouldn't help the situation. He figured that if there was a story he might be able to pick it up from where he was currently stood.

The atmosphere inside the conference room was certainly warmer and more convivial than outside in the corridor. The day's meeting had begun well. Casual good

216

humour and many interesting points had been made by both parties. There still was much ground that Satan wanted to cover but on the whole, it had been a success.

Satan, being closest to the door, happily volunteered to open it in response to the unexpected interruption. He'd assumed it would probably just be some member of the hotel staff, providing some late morning snacks, or bringing in lunch. Which had Ed been a few minutes earlier, it would have been. With a welcoming smile on his face he opened the doors just enough to reveal the worried faces of first Stuart, and then Grank who stood directly behind him. The way they were standing it made Stuart look as if he'd acquired an extra head. On seeing this far from welcome sight, Satan quickly reduced the opening of the doorway so that it prevented God from seeing who was causing the interruption. Not one muscle on Satan's face moved, yet his happy expression suddenly lost all warmth and charm as though a sunny day had been lost to a random thick black cloud. "Yes? *What* is it?" Each word enunciated and uttered through clenched teeth.

"Err— err—, its— its Mau—Mau—Maurice, Sire!" Stuart stammered, terror filling his voice.

"What about him?" snapped Satan. His eyes narrowed. "This had *better* be important!"

Stuart paused, aware that the guards around him were craning their necks eagerly to listen to the conversation. He raised his eyebrows meaningfully at Satan and opened his hands, palm upwards, in a gesture designed to highlight the awkwardness of talking here in the corridor.

Sighing heavily, Satan turned to God. "I am so terribly sorry, Your Highness," he said, the smile on his face warm, betraying nothing of the inner rage starting to build up in his chest. "I'm afraid something has occurred which necessitates my presence to give guidance to my assistants. Could you excuse me for a few minutes, while I discuss things outside?"

God had heard part of the demonic conversation, and He'd picked up on the urgency of the situation, even if His powers didn't allow Him insight into the Demon mind, or the hotel to see what the problem was. "Of course, Beelzebub, take as long as you need."

Thanking God, Satan left the meeting room and quickly followed Stuart and Grank down the corridor, away from earshot of the curious guards and past the even more nosey and, as yet, unrecognised undercover reporter.

Once around the corner and out of sight, Satan stood in front of Stuart and Grank and grabbed each of them firmly by the throat, lifting them several inches off the ground. "This had better be good, or you two morons will find yourself carrying out some very painful and disgusting tasks in Hell. I have no idea what they'll be yet as they haven't even been created. But trust me; they'll make every other inhabitant in Hell happy, if only for the fact that they're not you." With neither of them able to move they were robbed of their usual habit of looking at each other as a form of tension release or just simply to read the opponents actions.

Grank managed to speak first, through Satan's vice-like grip. "It's Maurice, Sire." His voice sounded strained against the force placed against his windpipe. "He has escaped!"

Loosening the pressure, Satan lifted Grank higher into the air and drew his body close, so his face hovered just above Satan's. Looking deep into terrified eyes "What do you mean, *escaped?*"

"He has got away, Sire. We went to your room to check all was well. Stuart and I got into a discussion over whose fault it was that we were late. Obviously, he said it was my fault, but as usual he was wrong and—" The grip on his throat began to tighten and made speaking impossible.

"I do *not* give a flying fig about what you two dimwits talked about. I don't care if you had a fight or covered each other in whipped cream and licked it off one another. If I wanted such banter, we could all hold each other's hands and skip merrily into the woods and sit around a camp fire chatting as we toast marshmallows. *What* happened to Maurice?"

This time Satan lifted Stuart higher into the air and brought his face close, staring into his wide eyes. "Well? Do you think you can be a little more succinct?"

"Yes Sire, of course. After we finished talking, we noticed Maurice had escaped!"

"You mean to tell me that you two buffoons stood in my room and happily argued and didn't notice my special guest had made good his escape?" Satan's exasperation was evident in his voice. "I imagine that the destructive force of Maurice would have resembled a mini tornado devastating his makeshift prison cell, my room, the entire floor and quite possibly the entire wing of the hotel."

"That's just it, Sire," offered Stuart. "There was no damage, and the trunk had simply disappeared."

"Disappeared?" Satan roared, louder than he'd intended. The single word echoed along the narrow confines of the corridor. "You mean to tell me that Maurice, the most destructive creature to ever be part of Hell or to touch the Earth, simply found a way out of his box – but instead of leaving his trademark tsunami of destruction in his wake, he inexplicably develops a loving attachment to his wooden box and makes good his escape by calmly walking out of my room carrying it with him?"

"Yes, Sire," Stuart agreed, although after listened to Satan's description of the events, he was no longer convinced regarding the accuracy of his account. "He must have. Unless…"

"Unless?" Droplets of hot spittle escaped Satan's mouth and landed on Stuart's face when he spoke. "Unless… he didn't escape. Perhaps someone else came into the room before you two clowns – or for all I know, while you two were standing there, playing a game of who's got the biggest cock – and stole Maurice, box and all. Did that cross your stupid, pen-pushing mind?"

"Yes, Sire that's what I was just about to add! He could have been kidnapped!"

"Kidnapped? Who in their right mind would kidnap Maurice and expect a ransom? Besides, who even knew we had him?" Satan paused. "Hang on! Surely the guards in the corridor must have seen something?"

"That's part of the problem, Sire. There were no guards in the corridor. They were all down here, guarding you in the conference room. I doubt anyone could have anticipated someone breaking into your room and making off with anything. Especially something as large as Maurice and his 'special office'. It would just be too ridiculous for words."

Satan dropped Stuart. "Yer think?" He glanced swiftly from one cowering assistant to the other. "Whoever has taken him can't have got far. Take half the guards from the conference room entrance and have them search every room in my part of the hotel. If it's one of my demons having a laugh, or some perverted party, I want them sent back to Hell in the most painful way imaginable and I'll deal with them on my return."

"And if we don't find him in our part of the hotel?" Grank ventured cautiously.

The look he received was answer enough, but Satan reinforced his message. "Find him. Tear the sodding hotel to pieces if you must, but I want him back in my room where he can't cause any trouble unless I allow it. But…" he added quietly, "do it as discreetly as possible. Thanks to all the evil forces in this place, God has no idea that I brought any extra little weapons such as Maurice, so if he finds out it won't do my case any good. I want a covert approach taken. Do you understand?"

Both Stuart and Grank nodded eagerly, although both were confused by the task at hand. Getting demons to tear a hotel apart searching for a large trunk seemed simple enough, but getting them to do it in a subtle manner so nobody noticed made the task seem almost impossible. But they knew obeying was the only real course of action. They were painfully aware of Satan's imagination and sadistic creativity, and he would come up with something extremely nasty if they failed to find a suitable course of action.

Satan strode back to the conference room, pushing past a very bewildered Ed Mercerator. The hardened journalist wasn't sure what he'd just witnessed, but without a shadow of a doubt, he knew he had the biggest story to hit the island since December 1941 when Japan decided Pearl Harbor was the ideal place for a bit of target practice.

The President of the United States was rushing around the corridor in an obviously agitated state, looking as if he wanted to push some button and make all his troubles go away. Ed's first instinct was to break his cover, run up to the President before any secret service guards could stop him, and ask some pertinent questions. But something made him pause. The timing was wrong and he was sure there was a tastier story to be had, if he just patiently waited.

Satan was totally oblivious to the mental turmoil he was causing in Ed's mind and even if he'd had an inkling, he still wouldn't have cared. There were plenty of reporters in Hell and their devious skills for creative lying made them useful demons but as was the case with most demons, he cared little for their opinions or mental state. He was more focused on getting back into the conference room. His steps were widely-spaced and his pace fast as he hurried by the curious guards. Pausing at the doors, his entire facial expression changed. The hard, angry scowl disappeared in a microsecond and was replaced by a casually amicable look, as if the distractions of the past few minutes had never happened. Taking a couple of deep breaths, he opened the doors, walked into the conference room and closed the doors behind him.

"My humblest apologies, God," Satan smiled. The happy act came as naturally to him as a crocodile trying to whistle, but to the outside world he pulled off the task amazingly well. "You have no idea what it's like. You'd think with all the world leaders, politicians, lawyers and accountants I have at my disposal, I'd be able to find two *good* men to leave in charge while I'm busy! It seems my left and right-hand demons, Grank and Stuart, can't stop squabbling like little children and needed me to make a judgement over all matters of authority between them. Pathetic really, but what can you do?"

The oily sincerity on Satan's face didn't fool God, but there was no point in trying to make a point and asking Satan lots of questions. He knew from experience that unless it was part of Satan's plan, he wouldn't volunteer any information.

"While it isn't really a problem in Heaven to find good people to help out or deputise," the smile on God's face didn't reveal any suspicions, "I can understand your problems. It's never a good feeling knowing people you want to trust only want to stab you in the back and take your throne."

The sarcasm dripping from the less than subtle statement didn't miss its target. The pointed reference to Satan's own fall from grace was obvious, but he accepted that no matter what, that chapter of his existence would always be the defining moment in his history. Obviously, God would always have it in the back of His mind, draped in His memory like a giant Bayeux tapestry. Stitched onto the cloth in delicate thread, the image of Satan stood behind God with the Sword of Uncreation raised, ready to deliver the coup de grâce into His back. One moment of hesitation, one single doubt, and he'd lost the opportunity, and as a result suffered many eons of torment and suffering.

"Yes, I suppose Heaven is still well organised and you've brought your best team with you. Dedan seems supremely competent and able to handle anything that pops up or comes in his way." Both laughed at the joke. It seemed that Dedan's reputation extended far beyond the Pearly Gates and his heavenly colleagues. Taking his seat again, Satan continued "You know I hate to admit it, but he would have made an excellent demon and I can't deny that I've tried to entice him onto my team on more than one occasion. For all his indulgences, he's a good person, damn him!" Satan's laughter was genuine but it wasn't so much on God's behalf. He liked Dedan and knew what a dangerous demon he would have made, if a few of his life choices, in Biblical times, had been made differently. "Anyway, your Majesty," Satan continued, "where were we?"

Outside in the corridor, the Angel guards were treated to the strange spectacle of Satan's two senior adjutants collecting up their demon guard counterparts and leading them down the corridor, where they proceeded to conduct a heated, but hushed discussion. Both Stuart and Grank had marks on their necks, resembling five giant purple love bites. 'Demons!' they thought collectively. Depraved was one thing, but there was a time and a place for such practices and they all knew it wasn't here.

Oblivious to the inaccurate assumptions being made regarding their friendship, Stuart and Grank were far too busy trying to explain the situation to the large demon contingent. The biggest problem they encountered was that the vast majority of the demons had been selected for their strength and power, and only had enough mental capacity to obey direct orders and not start trouble. The need for a 'softly, softly' approach was unusual and the practical execution of the act as alien to them as the skill of juggling was to a snake. Even if many of them didn't know what had been in the big wooden box emanating angry growls, they'd all seen it when they'd been transported to Earth. Some had heard rumours, but they knew better than to investigate too closely. To some, Maurice was just a myth, a kind of demonic bedtime story. 'Be evil or share a cell with Maurice' but the idea of being in the same building with something worthy of such a reputation made even the most heated of fiery hearts beat cold. So, the task of explaining what they were looking for wasn't difficult – but the directions beyond that were slightly more complicated. Each element of the plan had to be explained slowly, with lots of pauses to allow the information to sink in, and then more time for each step of the process to be repeated back so Stuart and Grank could be certain they weren't being misunderstood.

Stuart was quickly losing patience with the situation and suspected some of the demons were acting dumber than they really were, just to wind him up. Which, of course, they were. Stuart wasn't the type of character people took an instant liking to; in fact, he had the type of personality that nobody ever took a liking to; no matter how long you gave them. All smarmy insincerity and supercilious condescension – they were traits not appreciated in Heaven, on Earth or even in the bowels of hell.

Being a demon who'd worked his way up through the punishment system of Hell, Grank was more in tune with their audience. Seeing the opportunity, he grabbed the initiative from Stuart with undisguised glee and proceeded to calmly get the demons on his side. "Look, you lot, if we don't find Maurice – hopefully still in his big locked shoebox – the big red one, who at this very moment is sitting in that nice, cosy room eating cakes and drinking coffee with God, will not be happy. The last thing he wants is his special assistant getting loose and possibly eating most of the hotel staff and probably a few angels, as well."

The demons liked the idea of angels experiencing the notorious jaws of Maurice, but they understood enough to keep quiet.

"Work in pairs and start by searching every room in our section of the hotel. Search every suite, linen cupboard and stairway. If a demon doesn't want his room searched, then tough luck! You have my permission, as a last resort, to send them back to Hell. Just don't do it in a public manner so the humans see you. And whatever you do, do *not* let the Angels know what's going on." Pausing to let his words sink in, he surveyed the group. "Once you've finished, a couple of you should remain in the corridor of each floor and the rest of you report back to me at the cocktail bar in the lobby. I'll be controlling things from there!" Thanks to alcohol his nerves were included within the scope of being controlled and less nervous.

Leaving only a dozen demons to guard the doors to the conference room, vastly outnumbered by the Angels. The rest of the demons left to perform their task. If not exactly optimistic, they were certainly enthusiastic about the thought of kicking in doors. The prospect of one or two higher level demons who'd managed to wrangle roles involving comfortable luxury rooms, mini-bars and room service being obstructive would give them an excuse to inflict severe, and more importantly, sanctioned violence on them. Being a demon wasn't always fun and games, but occasionally had its entertaining perks.

The lifts were quickly filled by eager guards, wanting to carry out their tasks as quickly as possible. Some more patient and sensible demons opted for walking up the stairs instead. The idea of finishing off at the cocktail bar sounded good, but they knew if they took their time to get to the floors, a lot of the hard work would already have been done for them by the other demons, so they'd be able to enjoy drinks in a more conducive mood for the location.

Instead of Stuart taking Grank's interruption to heart he was relaxed and recognised that the action had been beneficial, obtaining better results, hopefully far quicker, than he could have done. He looked over at Grank with his arms folded. "Come on, it's my round." With that, he began the short walk to the cocktail bar, silently followed by Grank.

Ed Mercerator hadn't surrendered his spot in the corridor while all this activity had been going on, but now that relative calm had returned, he surveyed the contents of his trolley, picking up a custard cream bun. "What the hell," he announced aloud and took a large bite out of the sweet treat before he began to push the trolley back to the kitchens. Maybe he'd find out more tomorrow. Right now, he just needed a stiff drink. It had been a strange morning.

Chapter 36 - Knock, Knock, Who's Aaaaargh...

In the eighteenth century, when Debrett's began their guide to modern etiquette, they probably didn't think their rulings on good manners and taste would become a must-read for members of Hell, and in many ways, they would have been completely correct. After all, some demon in charge of an infernal torture chamber, whose sole purpose was to inflict suffering on some poor soul, wouldn't need to be overly familiar with contemporary social manners. The right time to applaud at the opera, or the correct way to eat a canapé at a picnic would be social skills that at best would be totally redundant and at worst, liable to get the stuck-up demon beaten to a pulp by the less polite demons; in other words, everyone else! The damned souls suffering the tortures were equally unlikely to need being kept up-to-date with what should be worn at a polo match and to date, Satan had yet to devise a punishment chamber where some low-brow sinner would be forced to read up on, and practice, gracious manners for all eternity. So the various residents of Hell had no real interest in such formal, and often pretentious, rules designed for predominantly snobbish English people, trying too hard to impress other equally snobbish people. There were a select few demons however, who judged the appreciation of the highest manners and refinements as critical tools in their knowledge base. These small groups were the demons whose main purpose was to visit Earth and try to seduce people, so they'd exchange their souls for some random item they were too lazy to work for, or too greedy to realise they didn't need.

It had to be taken for granted that the demon cows didn't need to practice any special skills other than being a bit seductive to a certain type of perverted person. But for a field operative demon who was assuming a more human form, there were surprisingly frequent occasions where the ability to ingratiate themselves into a high-powered social event could garner valuable rewards. A soul vacillating on the cusp of signing its future away could often be persuaded by a smartly dressed, good looking demon if that demon could show how graceful and sophisticated they were. The knowledge regarding which spoon to use when eating a sorbet was strangely useful at times. And knives can be more than just weapons for throwing, or, stabbing an unguarded angel or pious priest's back. Knowing the difference between a tanto point dagger and a butter knife wasn't only beneficial if a demon was caught in a street fight. On the other hand knowledge of good manners for Angels was usually taken as read, although many had to study hard to ensure that they were familiar with modern etiquette. But to Angels politeness was an obligation and not a necessary evil and the need to know the name of a particular fighting knife wasn't that much of a problem. They just needed to know how to use a knife to defend themselves and to despatch demons back to Hell. A skill that the good ones tended to be most proficient at; with the less skilled ones having a shorter stay on Earth than anticipated.

The section of Debrett's which covered how a demon should convey their need to enter and search a fake President demon's room seemed to be missing. Not a deliberate oversight, after all it wasn't something the polite human socialite really got involved in. So the actual mechanics of making their presence known, introducing themselves and gaining access was more a case of regular brute force; pretend world leader or not. As the emphasis was on the need for haste, the social niceties were mostly forgotten, or deliberately ignored. The demonic version of a gentle 'shave and a haircut' knock on the door using a knuckle was ignored, with the preference for the use of a heavy-booted foot launched at any door which wasn't already open. There wasn't even a need to check if the door was unlocked first; speed being of the essence, checking the door was seen to be a waste of time and energy. With such rampant enthusiasm, the vast majority of room doors were quickly and efficiently reduced from aesthetically pleasing, secure doors into, at best, splintered strips of wood and at worst small but expensive kindling was soon accomplished.

There were many demons who had, as humans, obtained a large amount of experience in kicking in doors. Often late at night, and the people on the other side of the doors were frequently never seen again. The twentieth century alone seemed to have its own production line of fancily-dressed dictators who hung onto power by creating enemies out of harmless, and on the whole, friendly minorities or people that were seen as too intelligent and therefore a threat to the incumbent yielder of power.

In this case, the doors might be kicked in by former Soviet GUGB members, ex-Gestapo or Khmer Rouge lowbrows, but on the other side of these doors the residents were far from innocent people. These were demons who could hardly be accused of being undeserving and unimpeachable characters. Even the most forgiving of onlookers would say it was schadenfreude and they were getting a taste of their own medicine.

The first room was occupied by a demon in the form of one of the far-too-numerous presidents of Belgium. As his door was kicked open, he was enjoying the pleasures of one of the Queens of Andorra. Having emptied his, and her, well-stocked mini bars, they'd taken the concept of diplomatic relations to the next level and he was 'polling the electorate'. And unlike most people who had to put up with politicians, the fake queen was enjoying being screwed by an elected member. Their happy coitus was unceremoniously interrupted by exuberant demons in the guise of Presidential secret service agents.

The anger and embarrassment could have been ignored by the two interlopers, but that wasn't part of their nature. The glee of spoiling other people's fun – even fellow demonic fun – was a natural reaction and their resolve was strengthened when the naked President foolishly tried to stand up to his uninvited guests. Not an easy task for someone out of breath and trying to conceal his less-than-impressive, now-flaccid penis. Standing up impressively, in either sense of the word, was never going to be an option. As his first words of protest and indignant profanities came out of his mouth, the closest demon delivered a rib-cracking punch to his thoracic cavity. In pure demon form, such a blow would have, at worse, winded him and left him catching his breath for a few minutes, but in human form his anatomy, despite still being stronger, was susceptible to the same weaknesses as any normal human. Down he went. Lungs stabbed by his own ribs on their own would have led to a quick death as blood filled the gap and drowned him, but his demise was hastened further by his sternum giving way under the force and his broken ribs skewered his heart. The passing on was almost instantaneous and in this case, he went straight back to Hell; his brief but enjoyable holiday on Earth at an end. The return to Hades was made all the more uncomfortable by his materialisation in the middle of a fire punishment chamber, where the chamber master refused to believe his story about being a fully-fledged demon returning from a mission on Earth.

On seeing her lover despatched in such an abrupt manner, the Queen of Andorra decided a less confrontational reaction might be a better approach. Pulling the bedcovers up to her chin and covering her naked body she smiled coyly at the two stern demons. "Hello boys, what can I do for you?" Her eyes all innocence as if she had just awoken from a light sleep.

Not being the most articulate, intelligent or loquacious of demons, both assumed she was giving them the come-on, and offering them the same access she'd given to the now former President of Belgium, or at least one of the presidents of Belgium. In normal circumstances, they would have both simultainiosuly taken her up on the generous offer, but in this instance their mission, and specific instructions, were fresh in their minds. They had to search for a missing steamer trunk and they had to find it quickly. Ignoring the naked woman in the bed and leaving her to squirm at her discomfiture of the situation they carried out their mission, looking for a big object by opening small bedside drawers, pulling out their contents, and closely inspecting the now-empty drawers. They examined the narrow gap under the bed and finding nothing they extended the search. While one opened the wardrobe, the other went into the en-suite, investigating the toilet bowl and then searching behind the shower curtain. Satisfied that the now less-than-pristine executive suite didn't contain the escaped steamer trunk, they walked back to where the room door used to hang. With an ironic display of manners, the tallest of the two turned to the Queen as he exited and spoke politely. "Thank you for your time, enjoy the rest of your night." With that, he was gone leaving a bemused royal to survey the wreckage surrounding her. The view was made all the worse by the quickly cooling body of her recently very warm and sweaty lover.

Even without the interrupted passions, in the other rooms, similar scenes were repeated. Doors were destroyed and the searching demons enacted their ritualistic hunt efficiently even if they lacked finesse or even common sense. A few fake world leaders were unconscious from drugs or alcohol, remaining oblivious to the whole thing. Some sat quietly, knowing that whatever was going on, it was probably prudent not to get in the way. Some residents, however, perhaps full of their own self-importance that went with the characters they were playing, attempted to obstruct the process and they suffered severe and painful injuries, but all managed to avoid the fate of the unfortunate Belgian.

Cupboards were opened and shelves emptied in the unthinking desire to prove to their un-watching leaders that they were the most efficient and effective pair of demons when it came to fulfilling their task. Room after room, floor after floor – the steamer trunk failed to appear and as the last pair of guards finished the search, it became clear they weren't going to find it in the demon section of the hotel. The ramifications of this fact were quick to sink in for most of the demons and they were unsure what Stuart and Grank's next orders would be. Despite their bulky size the demon agents seemed to lose the arrogant swagger their roles gave them. No more air of intimidation. As they slowly and hesitantly walked to the elevator or stairwell they gave the appearance of crestfallen despondence. Any human that should happen to have seen them would have witnessed the Hell version of vicious, wild and snarling wolves suddenly turned to beaten and subdued whelps. Knowing that a terrible storm was on the horizon, and even though it wasn't their fault or the problem their creation, they sensed that they could be dragged into the level F5 tornado that would spin them around as if they were in a washing machine full of daggers and when it all ended they would all be in some punishment chamber in an outer ring of Hell and no longer masters allocating the punishment but the victims rubbing shoulders with the souls that they used to be lords over. In small groups they slowly made their way disconsolately down towards the lobby. Despite the destination being a cocktail bar, none of them were in any rush to get there and give the bad news to Grank and Stuart. There would be no happy hour full of witty banter, light aperitifs and with any luck a friendly fight at the end of the evening for them. It didn't happen often, and none of them would admit it, but they were all afraid. Satan didn't have a reputation for taking bad news or failure gladly, and his usual way of dealing with those who gave him bad news, irrespective of culpability, didn't involve understanding, compassion or words of sympathy. His normal countenance was more inclined towards loud expletives, rage and the dishing out of painful punishments. And the drawback of being in human form was that they had a specific orifice which was susceptible to large, irregularly-shaped and spiky objects being forced into them.

It was the wrong time to be in the home of pineapples.

Chapter 37 – All Roads Lead To The Bar.

Drained, weak and in a haze, Dedan had managed to return to his room in the early hours of the morning, just as dawn lit up the east facing upper walls of the hotel. The unwelcome light which started to invade his room was ignored for as long as possible and he was able to steal a few hours of sleep before finally accepting that he should really get up and carry out the duties he'd been brought to Earth to perform. Reluctantly he got out of bed and showered away the dry sweat, and other residue, from his hair, scalp and skin, and got dressed. Foregoing the sombre suits of the demons and angels who were putting on an act, pretending to be serious and earnest defenders of their precious political leaders, Dedan decided today's attire should be less formal. After all, he suspected he wouldn't be invited into the conference room to witness any key discussions. At first he was tempted to go for khaki shorts and a bright blue Aloha Hawaiian shirt with a sunset depicted on it. Not classy or sophisticated, but it was appropriate for the location and he thought it was time he enjoyed the place as well. Admittedly, of all the residents in the Terrapin Cove Hotel, over the past few days it could quite safely be said that he'd definitely had the most fun.

Once dressed to unimpress, he stepped into the corridor and greeted the angels standing on guard. They returned Dedan's good mornings with happy banter and double entendres about sleeping badly and waking up stiff. Dedan smiled and accepted his colleagues humour, knowing that any reaction would only add to their fun. He merely let the words pass him by with grace and a mock uncomprehending look in his eyes, determined not to acknowledge their jokes.

Once the initial teasing had come to its natural conclusion, one of the guards advised him that God had already set off for the meeting but didn't seem to be too upset by Dedan's absence. Being aware of God's itinerary, if not His big agenda, Dedan wasn't worried about reprimand or admonishment from his Leader.

The fact that he wasn't required to stand around in a corridor crowded with angels and demons, bristling for a fight, provided a good opportunity to carry out his overarching duties. He decided to use the time to check on security beyond the small confines of the conference room. So far, he'd been given no reason to believe Satan and his horde were up to no good but he knew from bitter and painful experience that if they were anything but genuine, complacency would be a dangerous weapon which grew like a fungus over a log and before long, decay would set in unless vigilance was maintained.

He walked up and down the corridor past God's room, chatting with the guards and satisfying himself that they were alert and maintaining their focus. He repeated the same exercise on each of the lower floors under the angelic contingent's control. He did manage to sneak up behind a couple of angels, unchallenged, and promptly got their attention by kicking them in the backside. When they turned around to face him indignantly, he followed the mild physical chastisement with a far more ferocious verbal assault reminding them that, if he'd been a demon, they might have received a stiletto blade between their shoulder blades and already be slowly travelling back to Heaven.

Once he'd finished, he decided to take a walk in the sunshine and inspect the guards outside the hotel. Walking down the stairs to the ground floor, he was pleased to see angel guards posted on each level, making sure no unwelcome visitors tried to enter the heavenly part of the hotel.

Reaching the main part of the hotel, Dedan took a quick look along the corridor leading to the conference room. The demon guards seemed to be suspiciously outnumbered by the angel contingent. The disparity didn't fill Dedan with any undue fear. After all, God was the most important factor in the

234

equation, so if he was well guarded, anything else Satan tried would be a side show.

Walking through the lobby, he saw the cocktail bar was already getting custom from Stuart and Grank. Their countenance and bearing wasn't full of their usual swagger, and the blatant antagonism they generally showed towards each other wasn't visible.

Surveying the lobby, he saw a sight more worrying and uncomfortable. Sitting on the plush sofas, facing each other over a chess board, were Emily and Bathsheba. Drinking coffees, they were talking and laughing merrily. He couldn't hear what they were saying, but he suspected that men – and more specifically, him – were the main topic of conversation. Choosing the better part of valour, he walked to the security room to check on the angels in there. Seeing Dedan approaching they were ready for him, alert and ensuring they looked busy; intently watching the bright CCTV screens in the dimly lit room.

On entering the room Dedan closed the door, glancing around the dark, confined space and allowing his eyes to adjust to the subdued light coming from the TV screens. "Morning gents – anything unusual to report?"

"Not as such," one of the angels replied. He was sitting in a chair, drinking a cup of Earl Grey tea. "The demonic aura in their section of the hotel interrupts our video monitoring so, if camera's are too close, all we see is white noise from any part of the hotel where they happen to be congregated." To emphasise his point, he pointed to a screen labelled 'Conference Room Corridor'. "There could be World War Three breaking out as we speak, and if nobody radioed it in we wouldn't know a thing about it. As far as keeping an eye on them, we're blind. We can track them however, by seeing which cameras stop giving us live feeds. They don't appear to have been going anywhere that they shouldn't. This morning, however…" he paused to formulate his thoughts "there have been a lot of reports of demons having impromptu and heated conversations in the conference room corridor before a large number of them suddenly rushed off back to their area of the hotel. No idea what they're up to, but it sounds as if they're not happy about something."

"Okay, we might not know what they're up to just yet, or even if there's a problem we need to know about, but I have my radio in my pocket so make sure you contact me straight away if anything seems seriously amiss and evil expanding beyond the confines of the Demon's part of the hotel. All we can do is be on our guard and expect trouble." This was met with a murmur of agreement as they returned to the intent monitoring of the screens. A dull task that was akin to watching 30 grey paintings dry. Concentration was required but watching empty corridors, or just ordinary angels stood around doing nothing, was not the most exciting of televisual experience.

Back in the lobby, Dedan squinted under the glare of the fluorescent lighting. He was glad he didn't have to stay in the security room too long and didn't envy those angels tasked with sitting in there for long hours. Once accustomed to the light, he walked past the reception desk, greeting the human staff as he went. They returned his words with polite hellos and smiles. The staff at that desk hadn't been given much to do over the past couple of days, and had little interaction with the VIP guests after the initial rush of checking in.

They had been honoured by the calibre of the people that they had got to see and, in a few instances, even to shake hands with but since then they had just sat or stood around quietly waiting for things to happen. They had heard stories, from the night staff, about drunken exploits but the day shift had missed all the fun and ensuing financial rewards for their formal silence.

Heading out through the revolving doors to the outside world, Dedan's eyes had to adjust once again to the bright glare of the sun, and he wished he'd remembered to bring his sunglasses. The air was fresh and the breeze coming off the sea filled his senses with a sense of relaxed peace. There was nothing in the world to beat the smell of sea air. Cities built by the sea were full of pollution or humans far too busy to appreciate the sensation and magic the air gave them, but here he was far enough away from car fumes and buildings to savour every breath of it.

Walking counter-clockwise around the hotel, Dedan was alert to anything which didn't seem right. He got a few curious glances and was challenged by several guards suspicious of a gaudily dressed stranger but once they realised who the victim of bad taste was they allowed him to carry on unmolested. He didn't mind being stopped by angel or demon, it reassured him to know the angels were on their toes and also allowed him to confirm the demons were following instructions and not drawing their guns at the slightest provocation. Gazing across the golf course to the woods in the distance, he could see very little to cause concern. The relocated bull was standing contentedly on the well-watered grass of the seventeenth hole, ruminating as he watched his reluctant harem of demonic cows. They were returning the bull's glances with much less happiness or contentment. It wasn't only Dedan that had been sexually active in the night, but the recipient of the bull's attention had been less than welcoming and receptive of his fervour. All they knew was that when they finished this mission, and returned to Hell, they would be looking to change their shapes for good and requesting cushy jobs overseeing some pit of Hell, joyously inflicting pain upon any evil farmers that bred bulls. And they knew exactly what a part of the inflicted punishments would entail.

Continuing his reconnoitre of the outside world, Dedan walked past the conference room windows. Glancing inside he saw what appeared to be an elderly gentleman in a white suit with a neatly-trimmed white beard, drinking coffee and having a good humoured conversation with the current President of the

United States, who was also enjoying a cup of coffee. Nothing gave away the true identity of the two people sitting around the table. Reassured by the demeanour of his leader, and His deceitful guest, Dedan continued his meander around the hotel grounds.

Dedan walked around three sides of the irregularly-shaped hotel and finding nothing amiss he arrived at the road running from the highway to the front of the hotel. The asphalt seemed incongruous beside the beautiful grass, resembling a black scar on an otherwise unblemished face.

Reaching the front of the hotel, he decided to finish off his walk by taking a quick visit to the beach. Walking along the path to the warm, golden sand he found it empty of the bikini-clad women who'd caught his lascivious eye the first time he'd been there. All he saw were half a dozen dark suited, mock security guards who appeared as out of place as tutus on Turkish wrestlers. Without the fun ambience, he experienced no desire to linger.

He returned to the hotel. For some reason, the lack of humans playing on the golf course or having fun on the beach filled his heart with sadness. Such pleasures were pretty much human concepts and even though he couldn't see the joys of hitting a small ball around a field for hours on end, he could appreciate the fact others loved the sport. Depriving humans of such pleasures, on a glorious day like this, was almost a sin. But if the greater good could be served, it was something the humans would have to live with briefly. After all people were adapt at finding ways to occupy their spare time, so if they wanted to hit balls with sticks, dressed like clowns, or wear very little clothing and swim in the sea then there were other, perhaps slightly less stunning places, on the island, that they could do it.

Re-entering the hotel, Dedan decided to be polite and say hello to Grank and Stuart. There was no harm in chatting with them and besides, he might get a better understanding of what had happened earlier to send so many demons rushing back to their part of the hotel. When he approached, he was met with uncomfortable stares. Without saying a word, they made it clear his company wasn't wanted. Undeterred by such a greeting, he feigned obliviousness to their cold reception. "Hello gents how are we today?" he enquired, using the maximum fake bonhomie he could force into six simple words.

"Hello Dedan," Stuart responded in a cold tone. "If you don't mind, Grank and I are busy."

Ignoring the obvious brush off, Dedan just smiled more. "Of course I don't mind," he said, and sat down on the bar stool next to them. "Don't mind me, I've just been for a walk around the grounds, to ensure nothing's amiss. I'm sure it's something Grank's already done before me."

Dedan sensed Grank glowering at him and knew that he'd be filled with the desire to rip his head off. But he also knew that the demon would have to bite his lip and accept his presence.

"A Coke please, ice, no lemon," Dedan requested of the barman, who like most unoccupied bar staff around the world, was cleaning and polishing already clean and polished glasses.

"Yes, of course sir. Coming right up."

"Can I get you two anything?" Dedan asked his fellow bar guests.

"No, thank you," they both replied through gritted teeth.

"Suit yourself," he responded, enjoying the reaction his unwelcome presence was creating. Swivelling on the bar stool, he turned to face Emily and Beth who were still talking and half-heartedly conducting a game of chess. "Ladies, felicitations and

239

good morning to you both. I pray you slept well and had a good night?"

This seemingly innocent question caused them both to burst out in raucous laughter. "Yes, thank you Dedan, we're good. And are you rested?" enquired Beth, with a mischievous glint in her eye.

"Why, thank you Beth, I am good. I found it hard when I treid to get to sleep, full of tossing and turning, but on the whole, I feel as fresh as a daisy." His less than subtle double entendre was met with further laughter. "If I can drag you away from your game of chess, could I entice you to join me for a drink?"

Both Stuart and Grank glowered at Beth. She hadn't been apprised of the situation regarding Maurice, but she met their eyes and instinctively understood any additional company was less than welcome.

"No thanks, tiger," she responded. "Why don't you leave those two miserable farts and come and join us? I promise you we're far better company than them, in ohhhh so many ways!"

Certain the proposed company would be far more pleasurable than the two demons he was currently sat with, Dedan decided he could keep a better eye on them from a distance. If he stayed where he was, they might move out of range of his hearing and line of sight. If he sat with the ladies, he could study their body language and perhaps read a few lips. "Okay, ladies. I'm coming; just give me a minute."

"I'd hope you could make it last longer than that," Emily blurted, and her own raucous laughter was promptly made louder when Beth joined in. Smiling warmly at his light-hearted antagonists, Dedan picked up his drink and walked across the room to sit next to Emily, facing Beth on the other side of the table. Placing his arm over Emily's shoulders, he made himself comfortable, ensuring he had a perfect vantage point over Stuart and Grank, who still sat anxiously at the cocktail bar. His curiosity was certainly roused, but he maintained his act of being perfect company to the two beautiful women sat at the table with him.

Conscious of Dedan's presence, who despite having moved further away was probably still within earshot, Stuart allowed his impatience to boil over. "Where in Hell's name are all those idiots?" He kept his voice quiet, but his tone overflowed with rage and frustration. "How long does it take to get into some rooms and search for a box the size and colour of a grizzly bear?"

"Relax," replied Grank calmly. "It takes as long as it takes, and I'd rather they be thorough, than risk missing it." Despite his previous roll in Hell, which required endless anger, shouting and impatience, he was a master at recognising another's weak point. He appreciated that keeping his calm and being the voice of reason would give him the advantage over his despised colleague – the psychological equivalent of running fingernails over a blackboard. "Besides, I'm sure the boss will be in this meeting for a lot longer, and it gives us the opportunity to enjoy a lovely, relaxing drink before the searchers turn up and it gets chaotic."

Grank's calm and placatory tone hit its mark, and Stuart glared at him contemptuously. Enraged by Grank's smug calmness, he was even more annoyed by the fact that a demon would use 'lovely' in a sentence. "And what if they don't find it?" he hissed "What do you think Lucifer will do? Just shrug it off and forgive us, perhaps? If Maurice gets out and causes trouble, he'll more than likely send us back to Hades, care of a painful and grotesque death – and on his prompt return home, he'll ensure we both suffer some *yet-to-be-created* punishment in a new wing of hell which will be opened up just for us!" Despite his quiet voice, his apoplectic state had made the veins in his neck throb, and his demon eyes had reverted to their natural fiery red. If he'd been a human, his rapid breathing would have caused any passing paramedic to pack him off to hospital.

The silence which ensued was broken by the complete contingent of demon guards, walking slowly into the lobby and heading towards the bar and their waiting superiors. It took just one look for Stuart and Grank to know they weren't the bearers of good news. "Well?" Stuart demanded impatiently when they finally got close enough to be addressed without Dedan hearing. "I take it you didn't find it?"

"No boss, …. Errr Sir" volunteered the demon that just happened to be closest and felt it was his responsibility to speak. "We searched everywhere, under beds, in wardrobes and in drawers. Not a sign of it anywhere. Sorry."

On hearing the expression 'in drawers', Grank had to suppress an involuntary snigger. He experienced a mental picture of some mysterious, dark figure attempting to shove a large, heavy steamer trunk into a standard bedside set of drawers. Now he understood why they'd taken so long – they were all complete and utter idiots. "So other than your utter lack of success, I take it the operation went smoothly?"

"Operation?" replied the same demon, "we didn't have any operations. We were told to look for a big brown box." He smiled, pleased that he'd been able to correct his boss and confirm he'd understood his mission.

Despite Stuart's obviously increasing fury, Grank couldn't hold his laughter in. "No, no, no, no, no. The mission, the task. You know the *op-er-ation*?" Despite the gravity of the situation, Grank wasn't just enjoying Stuart's deteriorating emotional state, but also the demon circus which seemed to be in town and giving him a floor show.

A spark of recognition seemed to flash in the demon's head. "Oh, I see! Yes, well, sort of." He beamed. "We had to smash in a few doors to get into the rooms…"

"A few?" snapped Stuart. He was close to violence due to Grank's apparent inability to take the situation seriously. "Define a few. A couple? Three or four?"

"Well, when I say a few, I mean pretty much all of them." He turned to look at his fellow demons and they nodded in agreement with his estimation of the damage done. "Obviously, we didn't break the Big Red's door – that would have been stupid. But virtually everyone else's got damaged." A mild murmur and nodding of heads in agreement confirmed his summing up of the situation.

"So, the door to Grank and my room was…?"

"Matchsticks, sir," one of the other demons piped up proudly, happy at his efficient following of instructions. "It was locked, so we had to get in, as per instructions." This was met with a mixture of mild laughter and sage agreement from the other demons. They sensed that this conversation was going somewhere but were not quite sure where.

Stuart paused to collect his thoughts before responding, each word spoken clearly and with emphasis so there could be no misunderstanding. "*So let me get this straight, you've managed to destroy a whole lot of doors, turning them into firewood?*"

"Yes, sir!" The collective response came from a group of creatures that should perhaps have known better and not been so gleeful about it.

Stuart released a long, resigned sigh, accepting that some collateral damage was inevitable. He was sure the cost of the doors would be covered by the fee they'd paid to hire the whole hotel, and the manager would have seen more destruction done during a drunken toothpaste sales convention. They could be fixed with a minimum of fuss, but keeping the destruction hidden from Satan might be more problematic, but he felt sure that he could explain it to him without suffering any form of pain, or even mild discomfort. "Okay, okay. Fair enough. You followed orders and did what you needed to do. No steamer trunk found, but at least you were thorough and we can tick off our part of the hotel. Other than doors which needed opening more graciously, were there any other problems we should know about?" The hesitant mumble which followed this question didn't fill him with warm fuzzy feelings.

"We... err... err... well, some of the world leaders objected to us searching their rooms, so we had to... persuade them." A loud voice volunteered this information from the back of the crowd, safe in the knowledge that he was anonymous, and out of reach of direct violence.

"Oh, I see – well, that doesn't surprise me. I suppose a few injuries are inevitable and I'm sure they'll learn a painful lesson." A hint of relief entered his voice.

"Mostly, sir," said the distant voice.

"Mostly?" Stuart's tone hardened again. "Can you elaborate on the *mostly*?"

Fortunately, the vocal demon understood the meaning of the word 'elaborate'. "Erm, welllll, one of the leaders of Belgium was injured slightly more seriously."

Stuart lifted a cynical eyebrow. "Define the word 'slightly'?"

The demon squirmed. "His injuries will take a lot longer to heal"

"Alright, alright. What exactly happened to the Belgian emissary?" Stuart was sure any answer he got wouldn't make him happy. Judging by Grank's expression, he suffered from the same sense of unease.

"He sort of died!" a voice chipped in, hidden in the middle of the crowd.

"You sort of killed him?" shouted Stuart. The question was voiced louder than he'd intended, ensuring Dedan didn't have to strain to hear the words and Stuart saw Dedan instantly give up his pretence of listening to his beautiful company. But no slight was taken by them, for the lack of attention, as both of the women had heard the words as well and had gone silent in the hope that they could hear more of what was going on. Realising his verbal faux pas, Stuart repeated the question in a quieter voice.

"Yes, sir!" The response came in a whispered affirmation.

Before Stuart could make any further loud exclamations, Grank decided to take over. "Right lads get back to our part of the hotel and wait for further instructions. I'm sure we'll need to search more of the hotel, but if and when that happens we might need to use a softer touch." He looked at the demons standing around. "Well! What are you waiting for? Piss off out of my sight."

The demons had been looking over the cocktail bar with hopeful eyes, in the expectation that their hard work would have won them a warming libation, but none of them were stupid enough to ask their stern leaders for a drink. Angry thoughts were kept in their heads as they turned and slowly walked back to the lifts. Although they didn't speak a word, their body language spoke volumes and their silent communication was crammed full of expletives.

As Grank watched the demons disappear out of his sight, he turned to look at Stuart, picking up his drink in the process. "That seemed to go well, didn't it?" The words were deliberately aimed at infuriating his drinking partner.

Stuart greeted the words with wide eyes, and his face turned a shade of puce. "Why couldn't Satan have insisted on having this whole shindig in Las Vegas? Disposing of bodies was never a problem there. The Nevada desert is full of the bodies of humans, angels and demons that have had some form of little accident and forgot how to keep living." He wondered where the best place would be to dispose of a body on a Hawaiian island. The Pacific was handy, but if the numerous sharks failed to turn up and aid the process of disappearing, it was risky and the last thing he needed was a dead Belgium leader turning up in some fishing net or bumping into some unsuspecting surfer just off a heavily populated beach. Perhaps the woods at the other side of the golf course would be worth an after-dark visit? He couldn't just leave the lifeless, soulless body in the room to slowly decompose. Even with the air conditioning on, the stench would quickly spread far beyond the demon part of the hotel especially with no doors to keep the odour contained. And what would happen when hotel maintenance staff came to repair the door? A dead world leader, laid-out and atrophying might raise an element of suspicion and he doubted that any amount of money would buy their silence. Again, he went back to wishing he was in Las Vegas.

"What do you think we should do?" asked Grank casually, as if he were asking the answer to an unusually difficult cryptic crossword puzzle question.

"Put the body in the bath and fill it full of cold water, that should avoid any smell for the time being, and allow for the door to be fixed without any questions being asked," Stuart replied, as if still deep in his own thoughts.

"No, not the body – I've worked the arse end of Hell long enough to know a few tricks for getting rid of a corpse. I'm talking about finding that damned steamer trunk. If it isn't in our part of the hotel, it must be either in the angel part, which I find highly unlikely, or it's somewhere else in the hotel out of sight, and the thief is waiting for the opportunity to remove it without being seen by the guards outside or even worse, open it up to see what's inside."

"What makes you think the thief hasn't already opened it?" Stuart asked, his face full of puzzlement.

Grant looked at him in surprise, surveying the lobby in an exaggerated manner as if to emphasise his point "Do you see the hotel full of dead receptionists, flammable chefs running and screaming in horror, or waiters being boiled down in their own cooking pots? Are the walls full of massive holes where Maurice has taken shortcuts between rooms? I think it's safe to assume he's still safely in his box. Probably not too happy if he's been moved around in a rough or violent way, but then again, he isn't famous for ever being jolly."

Under normal circumstances, Stuart would have reached the same conclusion, but the sudden rush of bad news had overwhelmed him. He was evil and devious, but he liked controlled evil, schemes which he could plan with calculable results. This was a situation far beyond his experience or comfort zone, and he was struggling to come to terms with it. He picked up the drink in front of him and drained its contents in one go.

Throughout the whole encounter with the demon search party, the barman had made himself scarce. His sixth sense for knowing when to disappear had kicked in and he'd taken the opportunity to disappear as he went to do a quick stock check of all the bottles of rum and vodka in his store room. Now that the demons had gone, he reappeared as if nothing had happened. The smile on his face still there and eager to please his valued customers. "Another sir?" he enquired, as he commenced wiping the bar where the previous drink had been resting without a coaster.

"Yes please. Make it a large vodka and leave the bottle. Oh, and while you're at it, my colleague here will have the same."

"Yes, sir!" the barman responded enthusiastically, knowing that a drunken customer was a tipping customer.

"Time to go?" asked Grank. Both demons simultaneously drank down the large vodka's the barman had placed in front of them. Placing several large denomination bills on the bar they rose from their seats picked up the bottles of vodka before they began to walk in the direction of the conference room. It had been a long morning, full of unexpected information and incidents. Neither of them was quite sure how to break the news to Satan, but they both knew they'd need to soften the blow, rather than have him discover the path of destruction when he returned to his room. And as for softened blows – they were hoping for no blows at all.

Dedan watched them walk out of the lobby and absent mindedly chewed on his lower lip. He was deep in thought regarding what he'd just witnessed and trying to make sense of it all. He hadn't heard much, but he'd heard the word 'You *sort of* killed him' quite clearly. In fact, everyone in the lobby, and bar area, would have been able to hear Stuart's involuntary exclamation and the humans in particular were left feeling understandably uneasy. After all they were not used to such expressions being shouted out in their hotel. The snobbier members of staff might have thought it likely in one of the less salubrious hotels in Honolulu but not the Terrapin Cove Hotel. Dedan didn't need to use much imagination to realise the words weren't just some random turn of phrase and someone, somewhere in the hotel, had met a sudden death at the hands of one or more demons. Whatever was going on, it was serious and likely to escalate and, he had no desire to see a battle start on such a beautiful island. Sitting upright and extricating his arm from Emily's shoulder, Dedan looked purposefully at Beth. "Beth, this is important, and I don't want any lies, evasions or omissions of facts. Something extremely suspicious is going on

248

in your evil little camp, and I want to know exactly what it is. If I don't get some answers, and quickly, I'll be advising God to pull the plug on this whole farce and return to Heaven. I'm sure that's not what Satan wants. And from the looks of things earlier, I suspect he might not yet know what's going on either."

Beth settled back and straightened her tight skirt, breathing in sharply as she collected her thoughts. Placing her hands on the table she looked Dedan straight in the eyes. "I promise you that I'm as much in the dark as you are. Stuart's colourful expression certainly didn't sound like some casual metaphor and if there have been any killings, it's a direct contravention of Satan's specific instructions. But leave it with me and I'll get some answers and let you know the score." She started to stand up. "And it *will* be the truth! Or as close to the truth as I get; demons can sometimes interpret the word loosely and tend to miss out important points."

Dedan watched her slender figure appreciatively as she walked away, hips swaying, until he received a swift elbow in the ribs from a slightly jealous Emily. "Yes, Emily, my love?" asked Dedan innocently.

"You know…" she said coyly. "Just because you had a bit of fun with us last night, doesn't mean you should think of permanently, or frequently, entering the dark side!"

Dedan smiled at the idea. "Have no fear Emily, nothing could ever tempt me away from the heaven that is your smile, your arms and your breasts." His expression suddenly changed, the smile replaced by a look of concern. "I want you to do me a favour – as soon as God's meeting has finished, I want you to collar him and tell Him exactly what's just gone on. He might decide this game has gone on for long enough and choose to pull the plug, or He could elect to let the dice roll and see how they land – but He has to know and make that call. Do you understand?"

"Of course, Dedan. I'm just as concerned about what I saw and heard as you are. But don't you think we should wait and see what Beth finds out?"

"No., I'm sure she'll come back and tell us as much as she's able to find out and she won't change a word of any information received, but whether that's the truth, the whole truth and nothing but the truth is a matter of doubt. If I'm not happy with the answers, I want to be able to move, and move quickly without having to explain things to the Boss or convince Him of my concerns."

"Yes, you're right. I'll go and tell the guards to be extra vigilant, and as soon as God gets out of the meeting, I'll tell him everything." She paused, a pensive expression on her face. "You don't think Satan will try anything in the meeting, do you?"

"No. I'm sure he knows more than we do, but he doesn't have all the facts either. Whatever the game is, he isn't part of it. Yet!"

Reassured by Dedan's words, Emily got up from the comfortable couch and headed in the same direction the demons had taken earlier, leaving Dedan alone with an empty glass and his own private thoughts. They were full of the worst-case scenarios – attempts to kidnap God and drag Him into hell as a hostage, some apocalyptic battle starting on the golf course, or some other trick Satan could use to get back into Heaven, knock Saint Peter out, open up the gates and let all Hell loose to turn the place into a nightmare. Whatever was going on, he didn't like it and the absence of any solid facts didn't ease his suspicious mind. But without further information it made any real planning impossible. 'God, I hate demons,' he thought to himself.

Chapter 38 – Known News Is Bad News.

By Satan's definition of the word, and despite the mysterious disappearance of Maurice and his temporary home, he'd had a good day so far. His meeting with God hadn't achieved any firm results and he still had a long way to go before his sales pitch about returning to Heaven would be accepted and he could be welcomed back with open arms, but at least he felt he'd made a good impression and if nothing else it gave him an alien sensation in his stomach – warmth – not the fires of Hell kind of warmth, but a contented glow he hadn't felt since the good old days when he was good and lived in paradise, rather than existed in the Hell of his own making.

By the clock on the wall, he could see it was 4:35 in the afternoon, and despite the divine ability of them both to carry on talking for an infinite period, the meeting seemed to have come to a natural conclusion for the day and it seemed right to adjourn for the night. After all, why force the issue and push things beyond their natural place? Besides, a quiet evening would give him, and God he presumed, the opportunity to mull over the day's discussions and plan for tomorrow. Both stood up at the same time, and God waited as Satan walked around the conference table and joined him. Together, they walked side-by-side towards the doors, chatting amiably about the choice of island and hotel. God took hold of one door handle, as Satan grabbed the other and together they opened the doors, revealing the congested corridor filled with angels and demons. It was a stark and monochrome-suited reminder of why they were there.

Satan's eyes fell on the waiting forms of Stuart and Grank, catching sight of the bottles of vodka protruding from their jacket pockets, his heart sank and the warmth that had been inside him went icy cold. Without having them utter a single syllable, the disconsolate expressions on their faces told him all he needed to know. Maurice hadn't been retrieved, either in his steamer trunk or out of it. And Satan's instincts told him there was something else they needed to tell him and he wasn't going

251

to like it. He maintained his happy countenance in the presence of God; there was no need to alert him to any problems and risk ruining everything. Holding back a little, he let God proceed, followed at a polite distance by most of His guards. A small angel contingent remained outside the conference room, their sole mission to ensure no demon gained access to the room and got up to any mischief. Satan walked slowly, with his two harbingers of ill tidings close behind him and the large contingent of evil guards eagerly following them. Again, the obligatory handful of demons remained outside the conference room, not because they thought the angels would try anything devious for one minute, but appearances had to be maintained. If the Angels stayed behind, then so did they.

Once in the elevator, Satan pressed the button for his floor. As soon as it had set off and 'I write the songs' began to resonate as if playing from inside an empty tin box, he finally turned to face his assistants. "Right. From the looks on your faces, I can assume Maurice is still winning the game of hide and seek." Stuart opened his mouth to speak but was silenced by Satan pointing his index finger threateningly at him. "Obviously, the thief or thieves responsible aren't stupid and know enough not to leave their newly-acquired box where it could be easily found and returned to its rightful place in my room. Hardly a massive surprise, and I would have been even more surprised if Maurice had been discovered in one of the rooms in the demon section of the hotel. But..." he lowered the threatening finger from Stuart's face, "there is something else you're just dying to tell me and you know I won't like it one little bit. I've had a good day, so there's a sixty-seven-point eight percent chance you won't have to die after you've given me the bad news. But don't try and sugar the pill by telling me in a way you think will lessen the impact. That might not work in your favour."

Satan paused and, it seemed to last an eternity, before the elevator reached its requested floor and the doors opened. All three stepped out, providing Satan with a perfect view of the tornado-like line of destruction caused by his overzealous guards. "I'm sorry, Your Majesty," Stuart began, realising that much of what he should have revealed to Satan was now self-evident, "but the search parties took their instructions far too literally, and were keen in the use of brute force to open doors. As you can see, they left quite a mess."

Sighing, Satan reluctantly accepted that this situation was probably inevitable. Demons could be heavy-handed at times and took instructions to heart without conscious thought regarding what level of force might be required. The gauge had a default setting of maximum violence and recalibrating it to 'subtle' wasn't easy. "Alright, Grank. I suggest you go see the hotel manager and make up some cock and bull story to explain away the damage. Get him to order a lot of replacement doors quickly and get the hotel maintenance staff to repair the damage." He began to walk towards the undamaged door which led into his penthouse suite.

"Yes, Sire, of course. But there is one other thing," Grank added. "In the process of searching the rooms, it seems that one of the Presidents of Belgium took exception to his privacy being invaded and tried to obstruct the search. And in the ensuing struggle, he ended up...dead."

Without slowing down or turning around, Satan opened his room door and in an exasperated voice replied. "Just deal with it." He closed the door behind him, leaving Grank and Stuart standing in the corridor. They looked at each other and both adopted the exact same expression of relief, knowing they hadn't received any punishment, either verbal or physical.

"Right, I'll go see Mr. Knight and you can sort out the secret state funeral of the President of Belgium," said Grank, striding off towards the elevator.

Inside his room, Satan smelled Beth before he saw her. Her elegant scent was more of a delicate, subtle, yet irresistible net, trapping the senses, rather than the loud, full frontal erotic

253

assault of most human women. His attention grabbed, he looked up and saw her standing in front of the window; a slender, curvaceous and dark silhouette contrasted by a sunny, golden halo of sunshine streaming joyously into the room. Even with her full appearance lost to the glare of the light, he was still captivated by the sight. It reminded him of a long time ago, when he'd been in love with an angel. It was an emotion he'd long since lost, but he would give up all that he'd created to own it again. Turning away from the window, she stepped away from the light and came into full focus. Her long hair was draped in a deliberately free style, giving the impression it was a casual accident, but it was in fact premeditated so that a man's free will would become hers at a single glance. Such affectations were wasted on Satan; he'd experienced all types of women and all the various perversions, and after so many such thrills, even they seemed dry, tired and dull to him. But looking at Beth, he experienced a twinge of desire. He could easily have her any time he wanted – she wouldn't resist or complain however, this was something more than empty lust. He saw more than just a master of physical pleasure, he saw a woman of staggering intelligence and a degree of integrity not normally found in the residents of hell.

"Sire." The word was accompanied by a radiant, genuine smile. "Had a good meeting? All going to plan?" The casual wording sounded more like a loving wife asking her husband how his day at the office had been, rather than a demonic seductress and mission liaison officer speaking to the Master of Hell. All that was missing from making it a clichéd domestic scene were the hug, kiss and a much-needed glass of scotch.

"Hello, Beth. It seemed to go well; it was more the incidents of the outside world which took away my normal sunny and kind demeanour." The irony wasn't lost on Beth and she smiled at the idea of Satan being some happy old man, content with all that life had dealt him. "I presume you're up to speed with all that's happened?"

"No, sire. That's why I've come to see you. Unfortunately, Dedan and Emily know that something's wrong and unless they get answers, they're going to advise God to call it a day, up sticks and forget the whole thing. End of story!"

Satan rubbed his brow tiredly, seeing the whole tapestry of his plans unravelling and knowing some things were out of his control, no matter what he did. "Maurice has, shall we say, disappeared. For the rest, I think you would be best speaking to Grank, he's going to have a word with the hotel manager about getting some repair work done, so I'm sure you'll be able to catch him when he's finished there. Tell him, from me, that he needs to tell everything, and I mean *everything*, to Dedan and get his help finding Maurice."

Beth was about to interrupt, but Satan's expression kept her silent.

"I'm sure Dedan has no desire for our private little weapon to be released on an unsuspecting human populace. The damage Maurice could do to this hotel is nothing, compared to what he could do if he reached Honolulu or Waikiki. Dedan's gentle touch, which I'm sure you know all about, might just come in handy in searching areas of the hotel where the demon's heavy handed, and footed, approach might not be fully appreciated. And somehow, I suspect that if he has all the facts, with nothing hidden, he'll be amenable to being discreet, and not go running to tell tales to his Boss. Perhaps not straight away, anyway. Let's just hope he has some sympathy for a beautiful and persuasive devil."

Beth's shock and surprise was visible on her face, but Satan didn't have any compunction to provide her with further reasoning. She understood what he was hoping for and would do all she could to ensure Maurice was returned with the minimum of fuss.

255

Chapter 39 – How Can Such Lies Be Believed?

Mr. Knight was busy in his office, doing what busy managers do in their offices. The lot of someone in such a high-profile position wasn't always a happy one, and the pressures and expectations laid upon his shoulders weren't always easy to bear. As he was a systematic and ordered person, he'd long ago learnt the magic art of delegation and prioritisation. No matter what the situation, the guests should never be allowed to see, or experience, anything which might spoil their much-deserved vacation. Mr. Knight had his pride and his standards, and this summit of world leaders should have been so simple to manage. A well-oiled machine ensuring that the politicians from distant locations, some of which he had no desire to visit, could talk in a secure area and enjoy the comforts of his five star hotel. And if they wanted to get well-oiled as well that was not a problem either. Discretion was ensured, especially considering how much money the hotel was being paid to keep any news leakages under wraps. However, the assumptions he'd made about how things should run were as far from reality as his understanding of where his guests really came from. If these were the crème de la crème of the world's diplomats, then it was no wonder why the whole planet seemed to be hurrying to Hell. Which it might be, but Satan was at that very moment thinking of ways to block that highway. Mr. Knight was used to a little bit of drunkenness from his guests – heaven knows once the convention season started, the whole place seemed to fill up with men and women who had the 'what happens in Hawaii, stays in Hawaii' mentality. Once the dull talk about sales projections, or the power of the latest vacuum cleaner, had come to an end for the day, then it was wall-to-wall debauchery, with drunkenness and sexual excess with either other guests or company shared with the type of guest that isn't welcome in the hotel but is tolerated as long as the customer that is paying for their services does the entertaining in their room.

But there was something about his current residents which made him long for a good, old-fashioned convention full of drunken undertakers or even a rock band staying over after a concert. The hotel had the feel of an exclusive prison. Despite being well compensated, the staff couldn't go home, or even phone their friends or family. Even Mr. Knight had been forced to sleep in his small private bedroom adjoining his office, behind a secret door disguised as a bookcase. And he hated sleeping in there as it gave him claustrophobia.

His daughter, Caroline, had been given a spare guest bedroom on the second floor, and told to stay out of sight of the extra security. And as for the Secret Service staff, he shuddered; they were a strange mix as well. All of them were on their guard, as if they knew for a fact that trouble was staring them in the face, but that was to be expected. It was just that half of them were smiling, polite and pleasant, but the rest acted as if they'd been trained and given their social skills by Nazis; which if Mr. Knight had been aware, wasn't too far of the truth. Heinrich Himmler, was a part time member of Satan's training staff and he took to the role with vigour and enthusiasm, which wasn't surprising as when he wasn't on training duties he was returned to his punishment chamber where he was starved, beaten and tortured by demon's that had been wayward Jews when they had been human. They were definitely demons that enjoyed their work and understood the concept of irony, if not forgiveness.

Then there was the incident in the bar the previous night. So many world leaders drinking together could, and should, be a positive thing. The hands of friendship reaching out together to pick up a beverage in a civilised and cultured atmosphere. But it quickly escalated into a scene reminiscent of punch up between cavemen, only in suits. It was nation fighting nation, but instead of tanks, ships and planes, it was fists, bottles and bar stools. Perhaps it was progress, but peace still wasn't within sight. Mr. Knight had heard the noise from his office and ventured out to investigate. On seeing the action taking place in front of his eyes, he'd quickly turned around and returned to his room. If he didn't see any more, then he could deny everything if he was called to testify at a government hearing or a grand jury.

Finally, he'd just received reports from a couple of staff members who'd been working in the foyer, and they'd been uncomfortable about a snippet of loud conversation they'd heard, using words based on murder and killing. Mr. Knight had told them it was just secret service speak for dealing with a difficult situation – more of a metaphor than an actual act. Neither he nor the staff had been convinced by the excuse, but they all knew from action movies that you didn't mess with the United States Secret Service. Consequently, they'd returned to their duties and passed on their interpretation of Mr. Knight's message to their colleagues – 'Shut up, you heard nothing!'

After the initial mental trauma which set in on the arrival of so many duplicate leaders, and the unexpected misbehaviour of the Presidents and Prime Ministers, Mr. Knight had decided his office was his sanctuary. He wouldn't leave it, and the hotel would run itself, with the guests leaving him alone. He kept himself busy reading old documents, then filing them. It was a dull, but efficient excuse to stay where he was. He was safe from the troublesome but well paying guests.

Just as he was congratulating himself on the brilliance of his decision, he looked up from his desk and was taken aback to find Grank standing in front of him, a hollow grin on his face. It was a smile as out of place, as a devout Irish nun at a New Orleans Mardi Gras orgy. He'd apparently walked past Mr. Knight's secretary and let himself into the inner sanctum unannounced. Momentarily speechless, at the sight of his unexpected, and most unwelcome, visitor. Mr. Knight stared at him open mouthed, his heart beating wildly.

Grank's demonic senses could feel the rise in blood temperature and pressure but in this instance, he had no desire to make Mr Knight feel uncomfortable. His job wouldn't be made any easier if his audience was concentrating more on not having a heart attack than listening to what was being said.

"Mr. Knight, I'm so terribly sorry for startling you, I should have knocked. Please excuse my bad manners; I think my undercover field training has left me with one or two bad habits. Realising that alluding to covert operations might not be the best of themes he changed subject It's a beautiful hotel you run, Mr. Knight; you should be proud of yourself and your staff." This statement was punctuated with a full stop of a smile, which was no more convincing than the smile Mr. Knight had forced onto his face when Grank walked in.

Momentarily surprised by the tone of the conversation, Mr. Knight lost his usual keen memory for names. "Why thank you Agent…" He paused long enough to allow Grank to fill in the gap in his mind. The pause seemed to stretch, a silence that went on, and on, passing from the mildly embarrassing to downright painful.

This silence stretched out because Grank couldn't remember if he'd been issued with a field name, or he'd been introduced by Dedan under his real name. "Err, I'm sure protocol will allow you to call me Ian," he said, pulling out a name at random. "After all, we're friends, aren't we?"

'Friend' wasn't a term Mr. Knight would have used to describe his relationship with 'Ian'. But being a generous, gracious and diplomatic host was part of his character. A characteristic that had been noticed by people higher up and allowed him to rise to the precious position that he now precariously sat. He knew how to be sincere, whether he meant it or not. "Of course, Ian, please take a seat. Can I get you a drink? A coffee perhaps? How can I help you?"

Sitting in the chair in front of Mr. Knight's desk, Grank stretched out and made himself comfortable. "Thank you, Mr. Knight but no, I'll pass on the drink. As time is pressing, I'll get straight to the point." He could sense Mr Knight's heartbeat start to increase again. Grank couldn't help but think Stuart's smarmy, obsequious skills would have been better suited for this task. Putting humans at ease certainly wasn't his forte, but a resourceful demon was a successful demon, so how hard could it be? He offered Mr. Knight a big smile, baring his clenched teeth and was instantly overwhelmed by an aura of abject terror. Perhaps it was harder than he thought. Undaunted, he carried on. "Unfortunately, there was a bomb scare in the east wing of the hotel this morning," he said, noting that the Mr. Knight Stress-o-meter needle spiked into the red at the use of the word bomb. "Oh, please Mr. Knight, have no fear! It turned out to be a hoax, but unfortunately in the search process, there was some damage. In the urgency to carry out a thorough search, regrettably the security services were forced to gain access to some of the rooms by…" he paused, to allow the appropriate word to come to mind, "uh, a more than usual amount of force. I'm sure you can appreciate that many diplomats see their rooms as sovereign territory, and assume they have diplomatic immunity, consequently refusing access to secret service agents."

Mr. Knight's heart beat rapidly as the reports from his staff came to mind. Snippets of overheard conversations about killings. His mind filled with visions of assassinations and cover ups, where inconvenient witnesses disappeared. He imagined being awoken in the middle of the night as a cloth sack was put over his head and being dragged away, never to be seen again.

He was torn from his conspiracy theory daydream by Grank's falsely sweet voice. "So when they refused to let us in, we had to get into the rooms quickly so that we could, possibly, save their lives. Do you understand?" Mr. Knight nodded his head vigorously, fearing to speak. "Good. You see Mr. Knight, we had to force entry and there was an element of ancillary damage to some of the room doors."

"Oh! Is that all?" Mr. Knight's reaction was a mixture of relief and surprise. "So, nobody was killed in the process?" He instantly regretted asking the question.

"Killed?" Grank's laugh was false, but convincing. "Why would you say that? I think you've been watching too many thrillers where the secret service agents are all evil and would rather torture and kill you than protect your life." When, of course, only half of them in his hotel were like that. "No, we just damaged doors and had to do a lot of explaining to irate world leaders. But once they understood, they soon calmed down. Therefore, I'd like you to replace the damaged doors as quickly as humanly possible."

"Of course, Ian." The relief in Mr. Knight's voice was more convincing than any relief which might be trying to take root in his heart. "We have a few doors in storage, ready for unforeseen situations. You'd be surprised how often a drunken guest loses their room pass and forces entry, instead of contacting reception. If I need more doors, I can order them from a warehouse in Honolulu and they're usually delivered the same day, or first thing the next morning. Roughly how many doors are you talking about?"

"Roughly…" Grank mulled over the best way to provide him with the exact number "roughly all of them in the west wing of the hotel. Oh, all but one. No secret service agent would risk their badge, or pension, by kicking in the door of our president, especially when they had the door pass key."

Mr. Knight's jaw dropped. He made a quick mental calculation of how many doors were involved and knew his supplier would be dancing with joy when he received the order. "Of course, sir, I'll get on with it straight away. I'll instruct the maintenance staff to begin repairs, using the spare doors we have here, and we'll finish the work once the extra doors arrive from Honolulu. But seeing the time, I doubt they'll arrive until the morning."

Getting up to leave, Grank bowed slightly as a sign of gratitude "Many thanks. Your understanding, co-operation and assistance in this matter is greatly appreciated." He walked to the door and just before he left, he added, "Oh, and can you ask the maintenance people to repair the door next to the penthouse suite first?" It was bad enough having to share a room with Stuart, but not having any privacy made it unbearable.

Happy with his fairly believable pack of lies, Grank walked through the secretary's area and out into the lobby to be met by the sight of Beth, legs akimbo and hands on her hips, waiting for him. Her expression was stern and left him suspecting there was storm coming and he was a bee caught out in the open. "Come with me, you have some explaining to do." It was all she said as she turned and started to walk in the direction of the elevators at the far end of the lobby. Grant scurried quickly and obediently after her. His paranoid mind wondered what he was supposed to have done and whatever it was, how she'd found out about it. He caught up just as they reached the elevators. His concern worsened when she stood in front of the one designated for the Angels part of the hotel, instead of Hell's area. Stepping into the vacant space, she pressed the button for the penthouse floor and the doors closed. Only then did she turn around, face him and explain what he was expected to do. None of it made him comfortable. The truth was an interesting idea and concept, but not something he liked to put into practice, especially when it was to an angel, and highlighted Satan's distrustful backup plan. In fact, he was distinctly queasy about the prospect, but his unease was nothing compared to the confusion and discomfort his sudden appearance created when the elevator doors opened and the Angel guards were met by the sight of a high-level demon, attempting to gain entrance to the floor containing God.

They instantly put their hands under their jackets and their ubiquitous automatic pistols were drawn and trained on Grank in case he made any sudden moves. Before they could experience the not-confined-to-human infliction of itchy finger syndrome, Beth swiftly moved from behind him, so they could see her fully. "It's alright boys, he's with me. You don't have to pull out your weapons just for me. But I like the compliment!" The joke accompanied by a smile was sufficiently disarming, on both levels, for the guards to return their pistols back into their shoulder holsters. "Thank you. We've just come to see Dedan. And you can wipe those smirks off your faces; I'm not here for twisted fun and games. We're here to talk shop." The guards liked Beth, and not just in the groin-swelling manner. For a demon she seemed genuine and had a sense of humour which was as much self-deprecating, as it was rude and sarcastic.

Adding extra swing to her hips, just for the entertainment of the guards, Beth led Grank to Dedan's door and knocked firmly, using a fist held in a manner which could have been misconstrued as a rude gesture by those with a slightly dirty mind. That included all of the angel guards who witnessed her action. They might be angels, but they were human once.

Dedan opened his door and was pleasantly surprised to see Beth. It was less pleasant to see Grank by her side. Even if he was his demonic counterpart, Grank's presence so close to God's penthouse suite wasn't what Dedan wanted. "Hello, Dedan. You well?" Beth asked without waiting for an answer. "Can we come in? We have a problem and Grank here is going to tell you *everything*!"

Stepping to one side, Dedan gestured for them to enter. Once they were in his room, he closed the door behind them and walked over to the bed. "Okay, make yourselves comfortable. But please know that if this is some trick and you make any attempt to get into God's room, I'll be forced to stop you in a noisy and messy way." With that, he reinforced his comment by reaching under the bed and pulling out a Mossberg 590 pump action shotgun. He pointed it at Grank. "I'm sorry, I know that this is no way to treat a guest, but I'm sure you understand and would do exactly the same if I suddenly appeared in your room while Satan was next door. By the way, this little friend of mine is called the Persuader, and I'm happy for it to come into the conversation if required."

"Dedan, my friend," Grank replied casually. He adopted an obvious posture of mock hurt and surprise. "Ye of little faith. You show a complete lack of understanding of demons, and you of all people should know better. If you'd managed to talk your way past the army of trigger happy morons guarding my floor and suddenly appeared in my room under such circumstances, I would have shot you several times first, then done the monologue. We're not all tired, cliché movie villains who like to chat for hours, revealing our plans to the good guy before trying to kill them."

"Good point - well made. I'll try and bear that in mind should I ever need to talk to you in an emergency. I'll use the telephone; it might be a lot safer." Keeping his finger on the trigger, Dedan raised the rifle and rested it on his shoulder. "Guns are such barbaric weapons, anyway. In the good old days, a sword was the best way to meet your enemy. Perhaps someday you and I can test each other's skills?"

"I would very much like that Dedan, but alas, now is not the time. For now, why don't you just sit down and take the weight off your gun? I have something to tell you."

Dedan sat on the edge of the bed and listened as Grank told him everything. Grank had many sins stuck to his soul, but in this instance, it wasn't the one of omission. He told his foe all about Maurice's past sins and his long path to ultimate insanity, including his lonely incarceration and eventual visit to Satan before he was unceremoniously forced into a steamer trunk and given a not particularly scenic vacation on this Hawaiian island paradise. Grank then explained about the disappearance of the large wooden box and the subsequent destructive search. No detail was left out and even the sudden demise of one surplus Belgium leader was included in the report.

During the whole story, Dedan remained motionless as he listened to the almost incredible story with rapt attention. He realised his mouth had dropped open, revealing his incredulity at what he was hearing. He turned to look directly into Beth's eyes. "Is this all true?"

"I am afraid so. It isn't something we would make up." Beth's eyes were full of apologetic honesty.

"No, I suppose not. But why are you telling me this? Forgiveness isn't part of my duties and I have no intentions of helping you dispose of any demon corpses."

"Look, Dedan," Grank interjected, "as hard as it is for me to say this, we need your help! No matter what you might think, and despite this little extra ace up his sleeve, Satan genuinely wants this meeting to be a success and to get back into Heaven. Like it or not, that's the truth. So yes, Maurice's presence here is, in hindsight, a massive tactical error and a display of bad faith, but such is life. Or death, if he gets loose."

"Okay," Dedan replied slowly, "but what exactly do you want me to do? Demon wrangling, isn't my biggest strength and I can only use my persuader if he gets into the same room as me."

"Don't be such a dick," snapped Grank, "if he gets loose he could do more damage than you could possibly imagine. You think you've gone toe-to-toe and fist-for-fist with some tough demons? They were tickle fights compared to Maurice. He's the nuclear option of demons. You wave a shotgun about as if you think it would slow him down. You'd be lucky to get three rounds off and he would probably just feel a slight scratch on his flesh before he's ripped your head off and sating his thirst on the blood spurting from your neck. And if he escapes, and makes his way to any populated areas of this beautiful island, he'll leave a trail of destruction that would make that little party in December 1941 look like a food fight. Yes, we want your help and I suppose I'll have to suffer your gloating, but don't be a fool and refuse my request. If, as you say, you do truly love this little rock stuck in the middle of the Pacific then you'll do all you can to help find him. Run telling tales to God if you want but help us. Please!" The sincerity in Grank's voice was apparent and Dedan could feel it. The last desperate word in the sentence only added to that feeling.

"Alright, alright. I'll resist any urge to laugh, gloat or kick you out of my room. This Maurice needs to be found. But…" he paused to ensure both his visitors were listening and taking in everything he said, "when he's found, he's returned straight back to Hell. No putting the ace back up Satan's sleeve!"

"Don't worry about that, Dedan. We demons are just as uncomfortable about having him in our vicinity as you angels should be. He's the sort of demon that makes the rest of us look good. And I assure you, we're not looking forward to battling his own personal brand of crazy warrior."

Dedan sighed. This sort of honesty went against all his expectations of demonic behaviour, so he was walking into new territory blindly and without a map. He thought if he tripped, he might find himself trampled on. "Alright, but on one condition. I'll be in charge and you'll follow my instructions to the letter. Give me guidance and advise, but if you're playing any clever games and try and use this mad demon to get to God, then all bets are off and Mr. Shootie here will be put to the test. I'll see if I can get four rounds off and send him back to Hell before he uses my blood as an aperitif. And any remaining bullets will be sent in your direction."

"Agreed!" Grank said emphatically.

Once they'd left his room and were in the privacy of the elevator heading back to the ground floor, Grank let out a sigh of relief. Beth just smiled. "Well, that was fun," he muttered more to himself than Beth.

"Yes, it certainly was. Dedan is a man of surprises."

"Surprises?" replied Grank, his own surprise clear in his tone. "An angel with a pump action shotgun isn't what I expected."

"Yes, he certainly has depth!" Beth responded, stifling a private laugh.

Alone in his room, Dedan stared at the pump action shotgun lying innocently on his bed. The black metal of the weapon was a stark contrast to the white linen and silk covering his bed. He had to admit he didn't particularly like St. Michael; he found him bombastic, pedantic and cold. He also had to admit that he'd called him much worse to his face, but in this instance, he was glad the anally retentive general had collared him in Heaven and insisted he had better artillery available than a disarming smile and whatever weapon was stuck inside his pants. Unfortunately, St. Michael had tried to sound like streetwise gangster rather than a military angel several thousand years old. He'd used the expression *'Tooled up!'* which didn't have the bad ass impact he'd intended. Instead it had come across as some sudden shocking, but hilarious, vocal occurrence that demanded a stifled laugh that hurt for holding it in. It was akin to a favourite aunty having a family reunion and at lunch letting the word *fuck* slip into her conversation or the local priest coming to visit and then suffering severe flatulence as he sat on the sofa drinking a cup of tea and then trying to blame it on a dog that you don't own. Yes St. Michael was many things, most of which were not complimentary, but being one of the trendy *in crowd* wasn't one of them. However, the shotgun had certainly served its purpose and allowed Dedan to maintain control of the situation. No demon was a good demon, and that was an obvious bromide every angel would tell you at the drop of a hat but sometimes, on rare occasions, the odd one was able to be honest without it making them physically sick. Beth was one such person. She was evil but there were different shades of ungodly and she was on the lighter side of malevolent. He got the feeling Grank was evil more by nurture than nature. The earlier account of Maurice's existence, and presence in the hotel, had a hint of the 'there but by the grace of God go I' to it. Thinking of the shotgun he had so readily wielded, he thought perhaps there was a tiny bit of good in some devils, just as there was a tiny bit of evil in some angels.

Shaking his head as if to dislodge such a dispiriting thought, he went to his wardrobe and removed a suitcase so heavy he could hardly carry it. He was glad one of the burlier angel guards had placed it in his room when God arrived at the hotel, certain he'd have injured himself if he'd had to carry it very far. Fortunately, he was only moving it to the bed. Placing it unceremoniously next to the shotgun, he unzipped the case and opening it up, he surveyed the collection of weaponry. A range of automatic pistols and revolvers, carbines, rifles and sub machine guns created a mini arsenal in one small area. On Earth, some angels were happy with guns and more modern methods of depriving someone of their corporeal existence, but Dedan wasn't one of those. He was also adept with a knife, sword and spear, even a longbow felt at home in his hands. Any weapons that required a degree of skill and close proximity to the enemy, he would happily use. Guns were for those too lazy, or talentless, to use a knife. Even many demons only used guns as a last resort.

Of course, he'd been forced to use them in previous missions. His participation in a gunfight in Tombstone, Arizona on 26th October 1881 wasn't mentioned in any history books, but his role was pivotal in preventing several, equally unreported, demons from taking over the whole territory.

His last experience with a rifle hadn't been a massive success. He'd started to track a particularly vicious trio of demons who were intent on starting World War Three in the early 1960's. He'd managed to despatch one back to hell thanks to a French firing squad in March 1963, but only managed to catch up with the other demon after it was too late. He'd reached the grassy knoll with the intention of eliminating two assassins.

Catching one unawares, he sent him back to hell with the aid of a slender knife, but when it came to the third demon, his rifle had jammed and by the time it had been cleared, there was one dead president and the demon was out of his telescopic sight. He'd had to pull a few strings to persuade a cancer-ridden Jack Rubenstein to send the demon back to hell. Although Ruby was no angel, his final selfless act had earned him a place in heaven.

No, to him, rifles were best avoided unless truly a last resort. And in this instance, he was thinking even heavy artillery might not be enough. He could certainly put his own principles on hold for the rest of this mission. Rummaging amongst the mini armoury, he found what he was looking for. Picking it up, he shook the cardboard box of shotgun cartridges. The full container gave off a dull rattle as the shot in the cartridges moved heavily about. Dedan stared at the box before placing it down on the other side of the shotgun.

If he was going to start pointing dangerous weapons at demons, defending himself, and others, from what would probably be an extremely angry, fierce and quite possibly bulletproof Maurice, then at least he ought to load the rifle. Just in case. And if he was going to do some serious work, he'd better get changed into a suit. The bright clothing he was wearing suddenly seemed inappropriate and made him an obvious target.

Chapter 40- A Maurice In A Box

The heavy duty steamer trunk had deliberately been made extra uncomfortable, specifically for its incarcerated occupant. Satan's rationale was that if Maurice was kept in discomfort, then if his services should be needed his rage and anger on his release would be manifested and magnified so the maximum amount of damage could be inflicted on any angel, or human, who should get in the way. One of the demons had suggested a small spike be placed in the centre of the hard-wooden seat, so the impaled rectum would add to Maurice's rage, but Satan had vetoed that idea. Not out of humane reasoning, in fact, he liked the idea, but more from basic pragmatism – he was more concerned that any blood, and other possible liquids could make their way out of the box and leave a mess on the carpet of his hotel room.

Inside the trunk, Maurice was shackled in a semi-kneeling position with his wrists tied behind his back, arms chained to the insides of the trunk and a metal hoop fastened tightly around his neck, making any movement painful and difficult. The darkness and restraints left him with only two senses - his hearing and his nasal passage. Even through the thick wood of his confines, any background talking, or noises, could be indistinctly heard and only if the person was close enough, could he make out what was said. But after the pain inflicted by the trunk being laid first on its back, manhandled roughly as it was moved and then returned, thankfully, to its upright position, all noises had stopped. He sensed he was now alone in whatever location he was in. As for his sense of smell, the breathing holes allowed for a small amount of air and he could tell he was definitely somewhere different to Satan's penthouse suite. Before, the air was clean and fresh, but now it had a warm, humid stale feel to it and there was a heady odour he was unfamiliar with and couldn't identify. The voices in his head were screaming at each other, insults and expletives exchanged between all his personalities. They disliked the treatment they'd received and each one took it personally and blamed all the other people inside his head for allowing Maurice to be put in the box in the first place.

Despite the choking collar around his neck and agonising pain caused by his position and restraints, he let out a long scream, accompanied by a prolonged body spasm. It left him in agony but had the benefit of drowning out all the voices in his twisted mind. The pain was broadcast to them and they simultaneously quietened down. Some enjoyed the exquisite ecstasy of the pain and others were silenced when their threshold was exceeded and they couldn't take it anymore. Either way, Maurice finally got a brief respite from the chorus in his head, and he attempted to plan all the things he was going to do if he ever got the slightest opportunity to escape the box. He wouldn't need much, just a few inches of extra space and he was sure he could thrash about and break his chains. His feet and teeth could do the rest on anyone who opened the box. And once he was free, he intended to inflict carnage on anyone, or anything, which got in his way. If he should happen to see Satan, then all the better. Maurice held no loyalty and certainly no love for his demonic master, and if he could surprise him there would be a chance to inflict an agonising demise on Satan. Yes, he would just return to Hell and continue with his normal duties and routine, but Maurice would have the satisfaction of being the one to send him back there.

And as for God, he doubted he'd get anywhere near him, but that didn't stop Maurice from dreaming about what he'd do to Him. After all he had believed, even if he hadn't been the most ardent of acolytes. He'd committed sins with alacrity, convinced that his death bed confession would give him a clean passport and a welcoming handshake from St. Peter, as he casually sauntered through the Pearly Gates into the warm, comfortable confines of Heaven. He'd been misinformed by the Catholic doctrine which misinterpreted the parable of the workers from Matthew 20, so that some corrupt popes could sin and their self-deception had spread. Maurice blamed God personally for the breakdown in communication regarding the

271

correct entry qualifications. He liked to tell himself that if he'd known the truth, he'd have been a better example and a model Christian. Unfortunately, sin had been in his DNA and no matter how hard he'd have tried, he would have had a small taste of sin and wanted more, not stopping until his vociferous appetites had been sated. No matter which way you looked at it, his soul was always destined for Hell and damnation. But that knowledge wouldn't have been accepted by Maurice, either as a human or as a DEFCON Level 5 insane demon. The denial fed his inner rage and indignation. His own sense of injustice wouldn't have accepted any logical reasoning before he'd joined the elite 'Extreme Lunatic Club' to which he was Chairman, Secretary and sole member. Just to ensure he was alone, wherever he was, Maurice gave his loudest, most vicious snarling cry and, despite the pain it induced, he shook his body back and forth, shaking the steamer trunk.

Just as suddenly as he started, he stopped. Straining, he listened for the slightest sound in his vicinity. Movement, footsteps or breathing, but there was nothing. No indication that he was being guarded, or, had company which might foolishly investigate the noises and open up the trunk to investigate. With the exception of the insane congress of characters in his head he was alone and as soon as he'd assessed the silence outside, the noise inside his head started to rise as the crazy chorus started to chatter, argue and shout yet again. Maurice, or what was left of the once sane Maurice, merely sighed. Of all the people, demon and angels he wished he could destroy, his biggest enemies and taunters were the people inside his head. Other than cutting his own head off there was nothing he could do about them. And even if he was decapitated, he'd just return to Hell again, with his head re-attached, and he'd be reunited with the voices, doomed for all eternity to be the sole audience to their infernal Wagnerian opera. Some sinners had chambers for their torments in Hell, but he had his torture chamber inside his head. No reprieve, no promotion and no release.

Chapter 41 – Coming, Ready Or Not.

Inside the security room, the guards were sitting uncomfortably, watching Dedan and Grank. They were hesitant about talking candidly in front of demons, and what they'd been told by their mission's controller seemed incredible in some aspects and yet such lowdown and dirty tricks were only to be expected from demons. A steamer trunk filled with a mad weapon of mass destruction and like so many WMD's its use could mean mutually assured destruction for any demon that got in front of it as well. It didn't make much sense, but Satan's reasoning wasn't the most logical. After all, he'd thrown away Heaven to run Hell; that in the angel's eyes was a bigger insanity than some demon jack-in-a-box. But they still listened to the tale, keeping a wary eye on Grank – ever suspicious he might try some trick to send them back to Heaven earlier than intended. But he defied expectations and stood, arms folded, leaning equally uncomfortably against the wall next to the door and listening to all that Dedan said.

In mythology St. George had fought a dragon, but in reality, it had only been a Lindworm demon, disguised as a large crocodile which had taken upon itself to skip the stealing souls part of the remit and just kill medieval peasants. If it could also deflower a few fair maidens, in the process, it would. The killing of one demon had been a pleasure but given half a chance he would swap all that fame and glory for the chance to decapitate the demon which was within striking distance. One swift, well-aimed blow and he was sure Grank's head would have landed in the waste basket by the side of the display panel. He was visualising it in his mind when he was dragged back into the real world by Dedan asking him a direct question. "Well?"

"Sir?" He was shocked and slightly embarrassed by his lack of total concentration. "I'm sorry, I was visualising the destruction of a demon." The answer was true, even if the demon he was referring to wasn't Maurice.

"Did you see anything suspicious? Any demons meandering around the hotel carrying a steamer trunk?" Dedan repeated patiently. "I'd imagine that someone moving something as large and cumbersome as that would have been conspicuous."

"No, Dedan, we saw nothing and we've been watching the monitors all day. If any demon walked too close to a CCTV camera, it would have shown up because the screen would have switched to white noise." For emphasis, he pointed to the top five screens which were currently displaying a crackling electric snow storm. Each screen had a label below it identifying which part of the hotel it related to. "There are no screens doing that where they shouldn't be."

"Okay, thank you George. If you can just recheck any recordings from cameras facing elevators or stairwells. The steamer trunk must have been moved somehow, and it would be too big and heavy to be taken away by some Camazotz demon flying into the room and carrying it off."

"Certainly, Dedan, of course we'll have another look, but I doubt we'll see anything. But if we do, I'll call you on the radio."

"Thank you." With that Dedan turned and left the cramped, dimly lit room, closely followed by Grank, who was happy to be leaving. He could feel the hatred for him emanating from the inhabitants; distrust and anger tinged with a desire to send him prematurely back to hell. An angel's hatred could be just as hot and violent as any demon's.

"Come with me," said Dedan distractedly, his mind trying to put the jigsaw puzzle together. It was a mystery with several pieces missing. He knew what the picture should look like, but the more he moved the thoughts around, the less the image matched his preconceived expectations. He strode purposefully across the lobby, past the reception desk and out through the revolving doors into the warm, late afternoon sunshine, followed by a bemused Grank.

Grank had no idea what Dedan was thinking, or where he was heading, but he got the impression Dedan had a definite purpose to his movements. Perhaps there was a chance his former adversary would walk straight to the missing box and things could go back to how they were. Enemies, but perhaps with a little more respect for each other as they faced one another across the ideological battle lines. "Where are we going?" he finally asked. "It might help if you let me know what is going on. I am not here just to silently follow you."

"I just need to check something," he replied enigmatically, without stopping or turning to look at Grank. "A long shot, and unlikely, but perhaps our big parcel was thrown out of the window. Then somehow, it was carried away without being seen."

Catching up, Grank walked next to Dedan, and they looked around intently, trying to pick anything out of place until they reached the part of the hotel grounds adjacent to the demon section of the hotel. Shielding his eyes, Dedan gazed up at the top floor and realized he was level with Satan's penthouse windows. He turned his attention to the ground, surveying the area for any indication that something large and heavy had made impact with the grass. Or, even better, the remains of some demon who'd been flattened and turned into a sticky red mess as it tried to catch the falling package, dropped by a co-conspirator from above. But the more he searched the ground, the more he didn't find anything. The grass was still smooth, and immaculate and there were no traces of blood or body parts. He looked up and saw a couple of demon guards fifty yards away in one direction and a couple of angel guards about the same distance away in the other direction. "Grank, you go talk to those two and find out if they've seen anything and I'll go talk to my two over there. I doubt Maurice escaped through the window, but it's still worth asking the question."

Both headed in opposite directions and quickly returned after brief, but fruitless, conversations with the guards. Other than their hated opposite numbers none of them had seen anything to make them overly suspicious. No demons had flown overhead and they'd definitely seen no falling boxes.

"I think I need to go back to square one and visit the scene of the crime." Dedan said with a serious look on his face.

"Why? Do you think you'll find something I missed?" replied Grank, sounding offended.

"No, oh no, Grank. Relax," replied Dedan, now smiling. "I just want to look the place over, and besides, I'm sure my presence in the belly of the beast, as it were, would infuriate Satan and make a lot of demons very upset."

Laughing, Grank nodded. "That's very true. They'd be very upset, indeed. I can imagine their faces when they see you lording it over them and telling them what to do. The anger, resentment and embarrassment will be hilarious."

"I know," replied Dedan with a grin, "but no need to imagine it. You'll be standing right next to me. Doing as *you're* told and ensuring the other demons know they have to listen to me!"

Grank's laughter abruptly stopped. His eyes filled first with realisation of the need for him to be there with Dedan and were quickly replaced by a look of sheer panic. Visions of the total and utter hatred on the faces of the demons as he stood and nodded in agreement with all Dedan said to them. Seeing one of their own, not as an unwilling participant in an investigation, but as a collaborator working with the enemy of all that is bad and evil. They wouldn't be able to say anything at the time, they might snarl and grimace, but silent witness made. But if the time ever came, they would simply use it to justify some twisted scheme for revenge, or just sadistic injury, on

Grank. He might have to watch his back even more than usual when the mission was over and everyone returned to the warm discomfort of Hell. If Satan's plans didn't pan out, and maybe if he was supremely helpful and assisted Dedan with his investigations, he'd be allowed to change sides and enter Heaven. He'd heard that it happened once before, long ago, but it was more of a myth than anything else, put down to some captured angel trying to turn a demon and get an early, pain-free release. Whatever the case, the story was only ever mentioned in quiet, secretive whispers in case it was overheard and the assumption was made that the demons discussing it were planning some giant betrayal. Consequently, irrespective of the veracity of what happened, it was wiser not to carry out historical investigations to confirm what really happened. But all the same, now that he'd been put in such a difficult position, no additional harm could be created if he did leave his more sinister instincts behind and acted a lot less despicable. Dedan might be the sort who would put in a good word for him with his Boss. Besides, no matter how unlikely it was to happen, he still thought he had more chance of being allowed into Heaven than Satan did.

His fleeting daydream image of exchanging his horns for a halo, and his rough leathery ceremonial wings for the more artistic and feathered variety as he walked along the pleasant heavenly footpaths was quickly extinguished when Dedan walked past him, gently chuckling. The walk to the elevator leading to the demon section of the hotel, was made in silence, both contemplating the reactions to Dedan's sudden appearance, when he stepped out of the elevator on Satan's floor. In a little corner of his mind, Grank hoped his time in Hell would be a lot easier if the guards shot first and asked questions later. God might not be too happy, but he doubted Satan would shed any tears, and he'd be able to placate his adversary so that negotiations could continue. Not quite friendly fire, but not a declaration of intent.

The time came for the possible options in their heads to become realities as they entered the lift. The sound system gave up trying to decide on what music to play and remained as silent as the elevator's occupants. As it reached the penthouse floor, the doors opened.

The edgy and wary demon guards had now been issued with Heckler and Koch UMP sub-machine guns which were automatically trained on the elevator doors, every time they opened. The sight which met Dedan as he walked onto the floor was one of enough firepower trained on him to wipe out a small European city state. Moving his gaze up from the cold metal barrels trained on him, he looked into the equally cold dark eyes of the guards. They were uncertain how to react to seeing a lone angel appear before them. Specific orders conflicted in their minds with their primary and basic instincts. To destroy or not to destroy, that was the real question in their brains. All it needed was for Dedan to make an unexpected move and he would have been anatomised, or even atomised. Even a brief sneeze might have meant him being blown away. Standing by Dedan's side, Grank realised nobody had noticed him. If any jacketed rounds started flying about in the narrow corridor, there was a good chance he'd be on the receiving end of a large number of stray bullets. Collateral damage was perhaps inevitable, and alright, in any war just as long as it didn't involve him. Moving quickly but cautiously to defuse the situation, he stepped in front of Dedan with his arms held high in the air. "Whoa, whoa, whoa. Hang on, lads. Calm down and lower your guns. Dedan is here on official business, so let's not get trigger-happy and turn this into a shooting gallery. Especially as I'm at the wrong end of the arcade." This last comment made the demons smile and helped the tension to evaporate.

All except one lowered their weapons. Carsten's dose of goodness, given to him by God, had eventually dissipated and he was back to being the same old evil being he'd been before. The brief warm kiss of life in his heart was just a cold memory, like a long-forgotten embrace from a true love he'd eventually turned his back on. He was the odd one out and was simply fighting his own inner battle between his orders, which he fully understood, and his centuries worth of training and experience that had become instinct. He saw the humour of Grank's comment but kept his sub-machine gun trained fixedly on Dedan's head. This stoic determination to keep the foe in his sights threw the rest of the guards into turmoil. Despite Grank's words, and their specific instructions, they assumed they'd missed a memo and they started to lift their guns and point them at the target, then lowered them again, only to repeat the process like a Mexican wave of black gun metal as each demon tried to keep up with the equally torn guard next to them.

This oscillating line of weaponry carelessly pointed in his general direction worried Grank, but it was nothing to the emotions running through Dedan's mind. He was certain that at least one of the demons, would get nervous and start shooting, and all the rest would automatically join in. He experienced mental images of being turned inside out by hot bullets, and a brief searing pain as his soul was sent back to the comfort of Heaven. No longer able to bring peace to the hotel, another Armageddon would begin and in the middle of it would be Maurice.

Grank's mind didn't work on quite the same level. He could visualise the quick death and return to Hell but at least he understood the demon mind better and understood their predicament. "Will you stop waving your weapons at me? You're like a set of old men who've taken a piss and are struggling to shake their cocks dry!" He used his hands to gesticulate the 'lower your guns' sign. "If the Boss came out and saw this, he wouldn't hesitate to send you straight back to Hell and you'll spend the rest of eternity up to your necks in a pool of his excrement. And when I say up to your necks, I *don't* mean you'd be standing feet first! So just point those bloody great guns elsewhere and let us get on with what we need to do. I promise you that I no more enjoy having a lickspittle, toady and goody-two-shoes angel poking his nose around here than you do, but orders is orders."

Whether it was the threat, the mutual contempt for the common enemy or just the realisation that orders had to be obeyed, they all gradually lowered their guns and pointed them to the floor.

Both Grank and Dedan released gentle sighs of relief. Looking at each other they shared conspiratorial, and almost imperceptible smiles. Grank gave his new colleague a tiny wink as acknowledgement of a victory narrowly won, safe in the knowledge that collective idiots, with or without guns, can be a difficult force to control.

Stepping forward, Dedan decided to adopt a stronger persona than he'd originally planned. If they thought they'd be dealing with some weak, polite angel they had a different lesson in store. "Right, you toy soldiers, get out of my way. You might not be able to do your job properly but I'm bloody good at what I do and where you lot lose a big Pandora's box, only without the hope, it is left to an angel that can actually spell IQ to sort out the mess. I will push Maurice back!" Dumbfounded by this unexpected tirade, the admonished guards reluctantly stepped out of the way of this strange angel that was being surprisingly harsh to them. Any desire or opportunity to send him back to Heaven had now passed and they had surrendered to the moment, like hard-core football fans deflated after their team had suffered the biggest defeat, in history, to their most hated arch rivals.

Assuming that the layout of this floor was the same as in the Angel section of the hotel, Dedan strode straight to the door that looked to be Satan's. Grank quickly followed, determined not to lose too much face in front of the humiliated demons. Once at the door, Dedan knocked but didn't wait to be invited in. He opened the door and walked in as if he were a regular and most welcome guest.

Satan was sitting in a comfortable chair placed in front of the large window; it was open and the cooling ocean breeze filled the room with a salty sea air. Satan was enjoying the view as he sipped on a large crystal cut glass of malt whisky and contemplated the day and options for the future of the talks. In hindsight, the inclusion of Maurice in the party invite as the 'plus one' hadn't been the best decision he'd ever made. Turning his head on Dedan's arrival he maintained his composure, despite his natural urge to react savagely to this most unwelcome of interlopers. "Oh, Dedan. Come in, I've been expecting you and I'm just surprised it took you so long to get here. Never mind, you're here now. Can I offer you a drink? The scotch is exceptionally good."

"No, thank you, LUCIfer" The accentuation of the first part of his name was a mild attempt to rile Satan even more. "I don't want alcohol numbing my senses. I might end up as useless as your private army out there. No wonder you begged for my help. Your best couldn't find their arses with both hands if you turned the lights off. And why should I rush about to do your dirty work? If your little Jack had been let out of his box, I'm sure we'd all have heard about it. All seems to be quiet on that front, so I'm assuming Maurice is still secure, for the moment at least."

This arrogant chastisement of his less than forgiving master made Grank inhale deeply and loudly. The noise resembled the sound a shocked little schoolgirl might make when she witnessed a pupil back chatting to the headmaster. Grank wasn't sure how Satan was going to react, but he was certain he'd have his own little hell to pay for his association with this impudent angel. The worse thought was of the arrogant smirk Stuart would adopt when he heard about Grank's unwelcome role.

Satan remained as calm as the ocean which was visible in the distance. Instead of taking up the gauntlet and getting into a counter-productive verbal battle with the angel, he chose to treat the comments as the jokes they were intended to be. "Yes, I can't argue with you there. My choice of guards could have been improved upon. I'm sure if they'd been given the choice of signing up for this mission, they'd have signed the paperwork with a big X written in wax pencil, and even then, they'd probably have spelled that wrong as well and missed the dotted line." The smile on his face deflated Dedan's hopes of breaking the Prince of Darkness's calm composure. "The inclusion of Maurice and his subsequent disappearance was… regrettable. I'm sure you appreciate that I never expected anyone to waltz in here and steal my little friend!"

"No, you're quite right," replied Dedan, determined not to be kowtowed by his ultimate enemy. "It isn't as if there are any crooks in the vicinity. I'm sure you vetted the background of your entire cohort and checked the personal character of every one of them. I'm positive that you found them all to be beyond reproach."

"Yes, well, they are what they are. But we've searched all the demon areas of the hotel and found nothing. I genuinely don't believe it's the work of some impish little spirit, trying to cause havoc. That would require a level of intellect that you yourself have witnessed to be lacking. Plus, if it had been one of my demons, they would more than likely put the box in the elevator leading to God's floor, push the relevant button and opened the gift as the door closed. Once it reached the right floor, there would be instant redecoration of the walls with a delicate hint of Angelic blood, intestines and brain. And besides…" he paused, swallowing heavily. "There isn't one demon on this little vacation that isn't aware of Maurice's capabilities. They're all, to a man, absolutely terrified of him. But of course, none of them would admit it."

The hesitation was unintended, but far too obvious to Dedan.

Grank's jaw dropped uncontrollably on hearing such an admission from Satan. He knew it was perfectly true – the demons were dim – but they knew when someone, or something, was dangerous and capable of ripping them to pieces and eating them for lunch before they could raise their guns; but he'd never expected his master to admit it to an angel. Such admissions of weakness were unprecedented. This whole conference had been a revelation to Grank and he was seeing a totally unexpected side to his master. He was beginning to display, dare he say it, almost human traits! Satan was supposed to be all dark like an evil, all-consuming black hole – there weren't supposed to be any shades of grey in his actions.

"Okay, thank you for your candour," replied Dedan, oblivious to Grank's state of mind. "I'd gathered as much any way and I'd already concluded that Maurice had been abducted by less than demonic agents. Perhaps they intended to cause trouble but didn't realize the power of the weapon they've acquired. Or it's possibly just some opportunist thief who saw a valuable trinket and will regret opening their new prize at some point. Which it is, remains to be seen." He paused to let the air clear and allowed Grank to breathe again. "Right, I just wanted to see the scene of the crime and then I'll leave you in peace." He walked across to a large rectangular indentation in the carpet. "I presume this is where the trunk was?" He ran his fingers over the carpet. "From the depth of the compressed carpet, it looks like the steamer trunk was a pretty heavy beast."

"Oh, for hell's sake, we have a bloody Sherlock Holmes now!" Satan muttered under his breath, but still loudly enough to be audible to Dedan.

Smiling and deliberately taking the insult as a compliment, he continued as if nothing had been said. Standing upright again, he walked to the window and looked out, viewing first the area of ground directly below, where he and Grank had only recently stood, and then he looked casually up to the sky as if he expected to see winged demons perched on the ledge above him. Pausing, he squinted slightly at something, just above him, protruding over the edge of the roof.

"Satan, I assume that the dirty claw which is currently sticking out over the edge of the roof belongs to one of your winged demons? Perhaps a Gorgon or Pazuzu? But whatever it is, would you be so kind as to get its attention so that I can have a quick word with it?" The politeness in his voice was a planned contrast to his recent surly arrogance.

Walking to the window and standing next to Dedan, Satan craned his neck to look at the offending piece of demon. "Ratti," he growled, "get here now!" With that, a sallow, gaunt face appeared over the edge of the roof.

"Coming, oh mighty one." There was a whooshing as wings unfurled and flapped, bringing the skinny devil to a steady mid-air hover in front of Satan and Dedan. "Yes master, how can I be of assistance?" he said in a rich Italian accent.

"I want you to answer any and all questions honestly asked by this little Angel. Do you understand?"

Ratti's look spoke more than any words he would have dared to have used. As a human, he'd been a powerful and educated man, but discretion was something he knew and even insulting an angel had a right time and a right place. "Of course, master." He turned his attention to Dedan. "And what would *you* like to know?" The emphasis he placed on the you made it seem as if he were talking to a piece of dog excrement he'd found on the bottom of his shoe after having walked all over his brand new white shag pile carpet.

"Ratti?" Dedan's mind was working hard to recall the name; he'd heard it before, long ago, but couldn't place it. Giving up, he took in the view of the gently flapping wings of the demon. The thin frame made him appear more like a lizard which had been swooped up by a condor that wasn't very fussy about what it ate. "Ratti, how long have you been on the roof, above this window?"

"Since we came here for this meeting." His tone dripped sarcasm, as if the question was stupid and the answer was obvious. "I've been getting a suntan and waiting for instructions from my mighty master."

The suntan comment made Dedan raise an eyebrow. Ratti's skin was so yellowed and pale, he was almost translucent. He suspected that a week on a sun bed set at full would at best, only turn the demon pink.

"So, you were on duty and standing above the window all day today?"

"Of course," the demon replied tersely.

"In that time, did anyone, or anything, go in or out of this window?"

Ratti eyed Dedan impatiently. "Of course not. It's Satan's window on the top floor of a hotel; it's hardly a popular and public thoroughfare."

"Okay. And while you were up there, did you hear anything unusual in this room after Satan had gone to his meeting with God?"

The mention of God made the flapping demon tense up. "I heard whispered voices, but I couldn't hear what they were saying. I also heard the sound of what I assumed to be furniture being moved. Probably just room service."

"A big wooden steamer trunk hasn't suddenly appeared up there today?" Dedan asked in an act of sheer optimism.

"What? Maurice – up near me? Not bloody likely!" the winged demon exclaimed.

285

"Thank you, Ratti. You have been most helpful. That is all… for now."

Ratti looked at Satan, awaiting further instructions. The order to grab Dedan and claw his eyes out would have been ideal, but somehow, he doubted that direction would be given. "Very good Ratti, you may return to your position. Carry on." Satan's tone was seemingly dismissive, but he was simply trying to work out what Dedan was thinking. Angels were bad enough, but inscrutable ones were worse.

Suddenly Dedan's face changed, as if a terrible thought had been wrapped around a sledgehammer and forced into his head the hard way. Turning to face Satan, he bowed gracefully. "I've finished here, but can I borrow Stuart? I need him to run some errands for me, so I can hopefully complete my investigations."

"Borrow? You can have him for as long as you want." Taking a deep breath, Satan shouted in his most menacing voice. "Stuart, get in here *now!*"

It wasn't wise to ignore such persuasive invitations, or keep Satan waiting, so Stuart rushed through the adjoining door. His confusion at seeing Dedan, standing grinning next to Satan, was clearly displayed on his face. "Er, er, aaargh," he blustered, trying to decide what was going on. "Yes, Your Majesty. You summoned me?"

"Yes, you, snivelling, maggot. Dedan here has asked to borrow you for a little while and I want you to do exactly as you're told. Do you understand?" Satan's question was rhetorical; after all, it wasn't as if the lackey was going to decline the request.

"Of course, sire," Stuart replied.

Grank remained standing quietly where he was. The discomfort which had been on his face had now transferred to

Stuart's, the look of someone suffering from a serious case of smug schadenfreude. Grank suspected he might actually enjoy the rest of his mission. Having Stuart doing the running around and taking the public humiliation was delicious.

"Right," began Dedan, "here's what I want you to do…"

Chapter 42 -Stirred, But Not Shaken.

Maurice and his multitudinous assembly of voices were currently engaged in an intense, albeit unimportant, argument over which of the many personalities inhabiting his twisted mind had the sweetest voice. Most thought they should take the title and were screaming their respective cases, as loudly as they could. With the exception of the dismissive and fearfully avoidant personalities, all of them were willing to concede victory to another. If they'd been endowed with weapons, and the arms to hold them with, there would currently be a bloodbath in Maurice's prefrontal cortex and the basal ganglia of his brain would be drowning. As it was, noise was the only weapon they had, so they were determined to make it count. The entire congregation was suddenly silenced when the steamer trunk was unexpectedly tilted forwards, then rocked backwards so that Maurice was leaning back at a forty-five-degree angle. He was tempted to scream expletives at whoever was moving him but decided to bide his time. He sensed the trunk moving, and while he had no idea where he was going, he could feel the motion of his mobile prison cell. Every nerve and sense was tightened and stretched, trying to grasp at some tiny external hint as to what was going on. Some words uttered by the people responsible for his motion, even a grunt of exertion would be something to indicate at least gender, but there was nothing.

Seizing on the silence, like a wife seeing her husband sat quietly engrossed in a soccer match on TV and taking the lack of talking as an invitation to chatter about some inane rubbish. One of the histrionic personality disorders decided to invade the rare peace in Maurice's head and play for a victory in the midst of the truce only recently declared by all parties. 'My voice is obviously the sweetest', it muttered in a screeching tone akin to Norman Bates's mother in Psycho. His opinion was immediately dismissed by a unanimous chorus of *'Shush!'* from all the other voices. It almost sounded choreographed and rehearsed, had it not been for the impossibility of such a thing. There was too much mutual hatred and anger for any of them to actually listen to another and agree on such a thing. The resultant order to shush was so loud inside Maurice's head, he thought it was tangible and would blow his eardrums out and deafen him, the person currently moving the box and his many personalities residing in his mind. But fortunately for the movers, they didn't hear a thing. The only noise in the room and corridor that they were travelling through was the distant and low pitched hum of the air conditioning unit. This was permanently set at the same level throughout the hotel, so the monotone murmur was soon accepted by everyone and taken for granted. Making the noise invisible to everyone, unless they actually stopped and strained to deliberately focus on the sound that pervaded everywhere; penetrating the ears but not the consciousness.

Chapter 43 -Nothing Worth Watching On TV.

If Grank had been uncomfortable with his role as Dedan's assistant, especially the discomfort zone he could enter if the other demons saw his actions as treasonous and decided to make him see their point with hard and sharp objects; then Stuart's unease was off the scale. He'd been instructed, by a pompous and hated angel, to leave Satan's room, walk past the accusing glares of the demons in the corridor and take the elevator to the ground floor. From there, he had to walk into the figurative lion's den, the security office full of voyeuristic and spying angels. Despite Dedan's assurances that he'd contacted them on his radio and warned them of his impending arrival, there was always the distinct possibility that his sudden arrival would be met with surprise and a hail of painful bullets, sending him on his uncomfortable way back to Hell. After all, as he understood it, his close proximity to them caused the local CCTV cameras focused on him to broadcast angry hissing white noise on the monitors. As far as they were concerned, his movements towards them could be an army of demons, intent on annihilating them and taking over the room for their own ends. Although he struggled, at that moment, to think of a scenario where the destruction of screens that couldn't see them would be of any benefit to Satan's cause.

Arriving at the door of the control room, he paused and took a deep breath to compose himself. He wasn't a combat demon, so other than his persuasive vocabulary and sycophantic manner, he had no way of defending himself against any form of physical violence. Raising his hand, he knocked firmly, ensuring they knew he was there. Without waiting for it to be opened for him, he turned the handle.

Nothing happened, because the door was locked. A fact he hadn't accounted for, resulting in his body crashing painfully into the solid door. At the other side he heard movement and the sound of the door being unlocked. When the door opened, he got his first glimpse inside the darkened room. Instead of the expected line of raised weaponry, aimed nervously at his body, and not only his head - death by groinal shooting was not as impossible as it sounds but was just as painful. Despite this fear his greeting was far less dramatic; the occupants of the room were simply sitting casually in their chairs, nonchalantly holding cups of coffee and staring at the screens as if an insignificant underling had just entered the room. Stuart coughed gently to get their attention. He was disgruntled and upset that his appearance, even if it were announced, could solicit such a total and utter lack of reaction. He was a high-ranking demon after all, damn it. He deserved some level of suspicion and distrust.

"You must be Stuart," mumbled St. George, maintaining his gaze on a screen displaying a corridor, conspicuous by its total and utter absence of any presence, be it human, angel or demon. The snub to the guest was blatant. "Dedan told us to expect you. The radio you need is on the edge of the desk by your side. Be my guest. I assume you do know how to use it? Just push—"

"Yes, thanks, I'm familiar with the operation and use of a common walkie-talkie. I think you'll find that the use of two baked bean cans, connected by a long piece of string, was abandoned by the forces of darkness long ago. As were messenger pigeons and wrapping pieces of paper around a rock and throwing them. Although we do make exceptions to that method, if the stone can be aimed at your head!" His sycophantic trait abruptly disappeared without a trace. Putting the radio to his mouth he pressed the transmit button. "Dedan, are you there? Dedan, come in please?"

"Hello, Stuart. What took you so long? Ingratiating yourself with the security team? I hope you gave St. George some cream cakes. That's usually a good way to break the ice and make a friend for life."

Stuart released a frustrated, throaty growl. His plans for today hadn't featured being humiliated by an angel. He'd intended to enjoy Grank's discomfiture, not surpass it. "Very droll, have you been getting lessons from Oscar Wilde? Am I here just to give you a laugh, or is there a worthwhile purpose to me being here amongst…" he paused, pointedly looking at the occupants of the room, "such charming and entertaining company? At the moment, it's like being inside a monkey enclosure, only without the scintillating conversation."

Dedan's voice was full of laughter when he responded. "Yes, well, I'm sure if you throw them some bananas, they can make your stay much more entertaining. But don't blame me if they throw poo back at you. Anyway, they know they can't harm you and must obey any instructions you relay to them from me. So, there's no need to embellish on anything I tell you, as I'm sure that at least one of them is surreptitiously listening in to our conversation via an inconspicuous earpiece." At that, the angel nearest the door involuntarily put his hand to his ear, giving away his secret preoccupation.

"Yes, Dedan, I see the guilty culprit, and for once I'm happy for them to be listening in on my conversation. Although I'm sure they might look for an excuse to shoot me if they don't like what you're saying."

"Relax, they know they have to behave. Besides, I think good old George is more afraid of you than you are of him!" Letting the enigmatic element of that float around in Stuart's head he continued. "Right, get them to switch on all the cameras which are facing the demon areas."

"But that will…"

"Yes, thank you, Stuart – I'm well aware of the result and the lack of entertaining televisual experience. Just do it!" Dedan's words were forceful, but his voice was still calm and in control.

Stuart stared at the angel with the earpiece and shrugging, spoke to him. "Well? You heard the man. If you'd be so kind as to allow me to see the live broadcast."

The angel obediently flicked a few switches, pressed a couple of buttons and then sat back in his chair as the central two rows of monitors switched from displaying dull corridors and rooms to showing even duller screens full of white noise. The only indication of where they were looking in the hotel was the digitally displayed location at the bottom of the screens. The preset label, under the monitors, were now redundant and inaccurate, thanks to the change of viewing area.

"Alright Dedan, now what?"

"Can you see any screens that are showing what should be the corridor of Satan's penthouse floor?"

Straining to make out the writing amongst the scrambled white with black dots and lines whizzing about the screens, Stuart finally managed to make out a couple of displays showing the location in question. "Yes, there seems to be two. One is saying 'Lift section' and the other is saying 'Window section'. Is that what you're wanting?"

"Yes, thank you Stuart, that's perfect. Now watch them both very carefully and let me know what you see and if anything changes."

Dedan had already prepped the demons in the corridor. They didn't understand why he wanted them to do what he'd told them, but they knew they had to do as they were told. After all, none of them could see any harm in obeying his instructions. They seemed a little odd, but other than that they were innocuous enough. They were not really accustomed to military standards of marching. The usual methods for demons to get into a fight could be achieved by walking or running. Even just sitting in a less than comfortable chair could be sufficient positioning for a conflict to start. The need to walk with the same measured pace as their neighbour was an anathema to them, plainly such things were human and angel foolishness. So the requirement for those demons stood nearest to the elevator, and its corresponding closed circuit camera, to walk as one in the opposite direction, towards the window at the far end of the corridor, was more of a disorganised meander than a well-executed parade. The further they moved along the corridor the more demons were involved and were swept along in the process, none of them feeling any desire to be proactive and move in advance of the oncoming tide. So, it wasn't until the mass of demons reached them that they chose to join in with the movement. As they progressed, Dedan watched them move away from the position he'd maintained by the elevator door. "Right Stuart, how's the image on the screens now?" he enquired, via the radio.

"The images on both are still the same. What exactly am I supposed to be looking for?" Stuart replied from his viewing position in the security office.

"You'll see, just keep watching." Dedan turned off his radio and continued. "At least, I hope you see something!"

As the throng saw Dedan start to talk on his radio, they assumed they no longer needed to carry on with their walking along the corridor and stopped. Dedan noticed them. "And? What have you stopped for? Keep going." With that order, they resumed their pushing and shoving as they marched further away from Dedan.

"Dedan, Dedan, are you there?" Stuart's excited voice came over the radio.

"I'm here, what is it?"

"The screen showing the camera nearest the elevator is showing an image. It's still a bit snowy and not perfect, but I can see the demons in the distance and you."

"Excellent. Now keep an eye on the other screen and let me know what happens." The smile on Dedan's face was a mixture of glee and pain at the implications of his findings. "Right, you lot," he barked at the demons that were still moving away from him. "You all need to start walking back to me now. Away from the camera at the other end of the corridor!" They'd been told they'd probably be required to do that, but they still gave off a collective groan. Reluctant to take any orders from an angel, they were beginning to feel aggrieved at being treated like sheep. All that seemed to be missing was a sheepdog yapping and nipping at their heels, and a pen to go into, and they could be at a country show. But despite their resentment they acquiesced. It wouldn't have been wise, even for the dimmest of demon, to start disagreeing when Satan was in his room, adjacent to where they were currently fulfilling his commands and instructions. So en masse, they began to shuffle back the way they'd come. This time the group included the people nearest to the end window, who hadn't had to move in the first reshuffle. Once the furthest one away was approximately half way along the corridor and when there was nobody else near the camera, Dedan's radio sprang to life.

"Dedan, it's working. Whatever you're up to has done the trick. I can see a compacted mass of demons on the corridor and you in the distance on another screen. Now what?" Stuart's voice was back to its usual calm, oily tones, but inside he was excited. He wasn't certain what it was about, but he was positive he'd witnessed something momentous and critical to the case.

"Wait for me; Grank and I will be down in a minute." Dedan was also presenting a calm exterior, whilst controlling his inner excitement. "Grank, what are you doing in there? Get out of the crowd and come with me. I'll need you to help carry the steamer trunk back to its rightful home…"

Chapter 44 - White Noise, Black Lies!

Standing bolt upright, as if to attention in the unusually well-lit security room was a line of confused angels, with their backs to the wall facing the bank of monitors. The air of nervousness emanating from them was created by the fact that between them, and the TV screens, was a high-ranking angel who was sitting far too casually, for their liking, in the most comfortable swivel chair in the room. Not only that but he was flanked on either side by two equally highly-ranked demons. They were also sitting comfortably and seemed to be enjoying their positions of superiority. The line of angels all felt like they were a firing squad which had inadvertently mustered, only to realise they'd accidentally given their rifles to the condemned men and were about to pay the price for their mistake.

Even though neither Grank nor Stuart had a clue as to what was going on, or why they were there, they experienced a sense of superiority to the normally sanctimonious angels. Whatever Dedan was up to, they seemed to be playing an important role and from the sounds of it, he was about to crack the case and allow them to return the steamer trunk and its incarcerated resident back to Satan. And once Dedan had returned to being just another angelic lackey to God, they could alter the story slightly so that the vast majority, if not all, of the glory could be shone on themselves. Obviously, each of them planned to discredit any part the other demon played, but that was what demons did and Satan expected that sort of thing. If they were benevolent and slapped each other on the back in self-praise, he would know they were lying and up to something. Anyway, such plans and actions were just schemes in their own minds right now. All they could do was sit like the smallest audience imaginable for the most eventful play ever performed. Whatever was going on, they were enjoying the show. If only they had some popcorn and a cola to go with it.

Dedan, on the other hand, had a pretty good idea what was going on and was comfortable about it. With a look so cold it could have made an iceberg seem warm, and want to return to the arctic circle, he looked across the line of angels stood in front of him. Like an eagle deciding which succulent mouse to dine on, his eyes went slowly from one to the next, until each one had looked into his eyes and suffered the chill of uncertain fear enter them. They could sense something was coming and whatever it was, they were unlikely to enjoy the process. Eventually he decided on his first victim and offered him a brittle smile. "St. Jerome, how are you doing? It's been a while since we had time for a chat, what with you spending your time in Heaven and me being on so many missions. I hope you're finding this one interesting." The air of false bonhomie was heavy with each word he spoke; leaving the saint with no doubt that there was no geniality in Dedan's intent.

"Why thank you Dedan, I—"

"Yes, well that's enough nostalgic reminiscing for now. It's been fun, but I think we need to get straight to the point."

St. Jerome was usually extravagant with his words and being cut off mid-sentence wasn't something he was used to. Usually, in Heaven, people sought him out so that they could listen to his wise words or obtain his sagacious advice. He was distinctly offended and upset by such treatment, especially by an angel.

Grank and Stuart were equally taken aback by Dedan's manner, but they were definitely enjoying it more than the poor saint. They would have been on their second tub of popcorn if any had been available. This show was riveting.

"Let's cut to the chase, Jerome, where's the steamer trunk?" Dedan demanded, the tone in his voice serious and hard.

"I— I— I— I don't know what you mean," spluttered Jerome, his face red with indignation.

"Jerome, my old friend." Dedan's voice, taking on the properties of Janus, was now as calm as a pond in summertime and full of jollity. "Please give me a straight answer; do you know where the steamer trunk is?"

St. Jerome's eyes were wide with fear as he contemplated his answer. Swallowing hard, he studied his feet and quietly replied. "I have no idea what you mean. I have no idea what you're talking about. I don't know where the demon's box is."

Dedan absent-mindedly rubbed at his face and then looked askance at the squirming angel in front of him. "Oh, Jerome. You've always been a magnificent scholar and thinker, but you couldn't lie for toffee. It isn't a trait many angels are good at. The life in Heaven seems to wipe away that noble sin. Now, take these two sitting on either side of me. They're low life demon pond scum that I wouldn't trust to be standing behind me if there were knives missing from the kitchen cutlery drawer. Vicious, bad tempered and nasty pieces of work, I'm sure even they would agree with me on that score. However, there's one thing they're good at. In fact, if it were a form of art, there would be an ancient Greek muse for it. And that skill is lying." Turning in his chair, he faced Stuart. "Allow me to give you a demonstration. Stuart, please give me a quick lie."

Without pausing to think, Stuart smiled and looked Dedan straight in the eyes. "I think you're an amazing angel and in no way do I think you're a piece of shit. I'd never cut you open with a sharp knife and eviscerate you; offering your guts to Satan as a gift."

"See, Jerome? That's how you lie – with style, panache and humour. Even though I know the truth, I can't help but like the guy and want to believe him." He turned to face Grank. "Now sir, if you'd be so good as to demonstrate your talent to the assembled class."

"Of course, Dedan. My pleasure. I think Stuart is a brilliant and competent assistant to Satan. He is wise, helpful and admired. In no way do I want to see him cast down into one of the more painful chambers of Hades. I would hate to see him suffering every day, the look of exquisite pain on his face as his body and mind were tormented for all eternity would be a nightmare for me to witness and I would do all in my powers to persuade Satan to release him from any such punishment. In fact, I would—"

"Thank you, Grank, I think we get the picture. Such a love fest, it nearly brought a tear to my eyes to witness such fierce friendship and loyalty." Dedan turned in his chair so he could gauge the expressions on the faces of those lined up in front of him. He could see his lesson had worked and had the desired effect.

"There, you go. Two wonderful examples of the art of falsity. That's what happens to people who end up in Hell. They need talents that aren't needed as much elsewhere, outside of politics. If you tell the truth all the time in Hell you're in for a very painful time. So that skill gets polished, whereas in Heaven there is never any need to lie, so people lose the skill. Admirable in Heaven, or if you have nothing to hide, however…" he paused to allow his words to sink in, "if you do have something to hide, you're at a definite and distinct disadvantage. So let's say that there's something large to hide. Perhaps a steamer trunk, for example? If any of you had something to hide from me and keep secret, no matter how hard you tried, you wouldn't be able to say anything wily to me that would conceal the truth." He punctuated the words with a brief silence, as much to catch his breath as to allow them to think. He pulled a small book out of his pocket and rested it on his lap. "George, God has personally blessed this book so if you want, you can place your hand on this Bible and tell me that you have no idea where the steamer trunk is and that you have nothing to do with its disappearance. If your hand doesn't start to go up in flames I'll believe you, no matter how unconvincing your voice is. But I'm sure you know that I know the truth and you don't want to waste any more of anyone's time. Therefore, I suggest you just tell me what happened and stop messing about like the amateur liar you are."

"Alright," began St. George, letting out a long sigh, "I took it."

"I?" Dedan questioned.

"Okay, *we* took it. When I saw the demon scum coming into the hotel carrying the steamer trunk, I knew it was somehow important. Then, when the white noise on their corridor monitor cleared this morning, when they all went with Satan to the conference, we saw the empty area as the ideal opportunity to get one up on Satan and remove it. But I promise you that none of us had any idea what was in it; if we had, we wouldn't have gone near it. And we never opened it." St. George's face was full of terror and his voice was earnest.

"Not opened it?" interjected Stuart. "That's obvious; if you'd been that stupid, none of you would be here and we'd be having to battle with a pissed off demon, intent on blithely destroying anything that got in its way."

"Yes, thank you for that Stuart. I'm sure George and his conspirators realise the errors of their ways and wish they hadn't been so stupid. And I'm convinced that God will find a suitable punishment to reinforce their penitence. Right then, we have a confession. See, isn't that good for the soul?" Thanks to the pressure of the situation and the shame of being found out, they totally missed the rhetorical nature of Dedan's question. Consequently, they all looked directly at him and mumbled their agreement.

Giving himself a face palm Grank muttered to himself. "Schmucks!"

Ignoring the angels' embarrassed agreements and the demon's interjection, Dedan continued. "Shall we cut to the chase, so we can return the box to its dodgy owner? Where is it now?"

Looking at each other as if for reassurance that they were doing the right thing and that they couldn't try and ask for leniency if they told him where Maurice was secreted. They could tell that any such tactics would be met with anger and possible additional punishments when they finally got to stand in front of God and answer for their actions. Some courses of actions were non-negotiable. Stepping forward and holding his head high as a sign of the pride and valour he was famous for on Earth, St. George spoke up calmly and in a clear voice. "We carried it to an empty storage room in the staff section of the hotel. It's safe and undamaged."

Dedan got up from his chair and the two demons dutifully followed suit. They would never admit it to the other, or even to Dedan, but they were impressed with what they'd seen. Such devious Machiavellian tactics would have allowed a demon to rise quickly up the ranks in Hell. As Dedan stood up, the small Gideon Bible in his lap fell to the floor. Dedan looked at it and then turned his gaze to Grank. "Would you pick that up for me?"

"What?" gasped Grank. "A book blessed by God? Not bloody likely – I have no desire to go up in smoke!"

"Oh, please," Dedan groaned, bending down to pick up the book and return it to his jacket pocket. "You demons think you're the only ones any good at telling lies!" Patting his pocket triumphantly. "After all, a Bible blessed by the Boss would probably burn straight through *my* jacket and incinerate me. I might be an angel, but I'm far from angelic."

"You sly old dog" volunteered Grank with a wry smile. "But still, an interesting weapon, if someone could get hold of one!"

"Right, George," Dedan said, looking at the angel who feared that his fall from grace might take him to a place he wouldn't enjoy, "please lead the way and Jerome, you can come with us. The rest of you can stay here and do the job you're supposed to be doing. We have a box to collect."

Chapter 45 - That Trick Should Be On The Stage in Vegas...

The quintet which walked past the cocktail bar and reception desk in the lobby were a mixed bag of emotions, feelings and thoughts. Stuart was mulling over the truthful lie uttered only a few minutes previously by his demonic nemesis. He already knew there was no love lost between the two of them, but now he was certain he would have to take extra care. But being a demon, he'd always harboured similar intentions towards Grank, and if the opportunity arose he wouldn't hesitate to initiate a painful demise on him. The only difference being that he would do it with far more subtlety and a whole truck full of extra pain. He didn't get to be Satan's personal assistant without picking up a few tricks in the process.

Grank was far from thinking of Stuart; to him the clerk was an insignificant toad and any threat he might pose was negligible. He couldn't envisage any scenario where he wouldn't have the upper hand and would allow such a weak menial to draw a blade and use it on him.

George and Jerome were also pensive and deep in thought. Neither had been in Heaven to participate and assist in the battle with Satan and his hordes, which saw him cast out and create Hell for him to live in. But they both knew the full story and the minutiae of information which wasn't included in the Bible, or even in divine poetry from the late middle ages. Knowing such gory details made them shudder and the threat of such a punishment being meted out on them was something they hoped to avoid. They wanted to talk to each other, to seek or give solace, comfort and reassurance but they also knew that breaking their self-imposed silence might be misconstrued and add to their punishment.

Dedan was the only one whose mind was focused directly on the task at hand. On his many missions on Earth he'd encountered steamer trunks before. He'd once owned a beautiful one, made of teak and mahogany. But alas, he'd lost it on a messy, but on the whole successful, mission on the Hindenburg zeppelin. One of Satan's more intricate plots was foiled and assorted demons and hard-core Nazis were consigned to Hell. Admittedly, there was unavoidable collateral damage, but the good souls were gladly welcomed into Heaven and quickly availed themselves to the comfort and luxury they could only have dreamed about on Earth. But the trunk, in the here and now, was something he was looking forward to finally seeing and returning to Satan's room extremely carefully, or even just destroy it, unopened, so the occupant could quickly be sent back to Hell and no longer pose a threat to humans, angels or the Hawaiian island. A controlled explosion should do the trick. Evacuate the humans from that part of the hotel under the pretext of a gas leak, and then *boom*. Smoke and rubble, but no more signs that an insanely crazed demon had ever been there, apart from perhaps a few charred remains which could easily be disposed of without causing any suspicions among the oblivious staff.

The mix of demons and angels didn't solicit a second glance from the human staff working on the ground floor. They were used to unusual guests and carried on with their own business. There were, however two exceptions. The first was the cocktail barman who gave Grank a hopeful, expectant and greedy look as he saw him appear out of the security office, in anticipation of some custom and resultant generous tips. Only to be disappointed when his potential customer walked by without even a glance of recognition.

The other person to look at them studiously was Ed. Ever the consummate reporter, he was determined to find out what was really going on as he just couldn't get his head around the story. World leaders who stayed in their rooms all day drinking, instead of going downstairs to the conference – their presence seemed to just be an elaborate smoke screen for something bigger. Only two leaders ever took part in the talks, but the army of secret service agents were so thickly packed and uncommunicative, the idea of making his way into the talks and asking a few impertinent questions had so far been impossible. He'd decided he would take any extra titbits of information he could glean by observation alone, but he started to become slightly alarmed when he saw the group head towards the door leading to the private, staff only, section of the hotel instead of going out through the main doors. Could they have discovered his secret and be searching for him? Was his cover about to be blown? He decided to casually follow them at a discreet distance. Once they disappeared through the door, he quickly waddled to the door, as fast as his bulky frame would allow. Even that short distance had him regretting the exertion. He opened the door just enough so that he could see the other side and be certain they'd walked far enough down the corridor, so his appearance wouldn't alter their actions or destination. They'd turned the corner and he couldn't see them, so he decided it was safe to carry on and follow them. He got to the next corner and again stopped. This time he knelt, as if to tie his shoelace and casually stuck his head around the corner. He saw the five reaching the store room and his heart seemed to freeze. He had to know what was going on; he needed to hear what they were saying.

The party in front of him were oblivious to Ed's presence; they were more concerned with the task at hand. They stood outside the door and Stuart noted the ominous irony of it having a number thirteen on the door, appropriate for the most unfortunate person in Hell. When people said there was always someone worse off, Maurice was the only person you could say it to and have it be incorrect. Easy for St. George to remember which room he'd utilised though, it stuck in the mind, especially for a superstitious knight of old. Dedan stepped back slightly and gestured to George to open the door, which he did with a smile of his face, and walked into the room closely followed by the other four. His smile froze and then vanished, replaced by a look of horror. The space in the centre of the room where the trunk had been left earlier that day, neatly covered by a white sheet, was now clear. The steamer trunk wasn't there and the sheet had unceremoniously been thrown in a heap on the floor.

On seeing the empty space, Jerome's logical mind began to fog over. "George, the trunk's gone!" he offered helpfully, just in case George hadn't noticed. He proceeded to lift the sheet and look underneath, as if the trunk could somehow shrunk and was still there. Realising his stupidity, and the fact that the others were looking at him as if he were an idiot, he sheepishly dropped the sheet again. "Sorry," he mumbled.

At that same instant, a cautious Ed had reached the area of the corridor just outside the room and was flat against the wall, or as flat as his rotund shape would allow, listening intently to the conversation. Hardly the greatest spying technique, but sometimes the old ways were the best.

Inside the room, Dedan's mind was racing. Something didn't make sense. It was no longer simply a case of a piece being missing from the jigsaw puzzle, there were now too many pieces left and the picture on the jigsaw kept changing. He focused on a small, almost imperceptible mark on the floor. Kneeling down, he peered at it carefully. Quickly, he brushed the forefinger of his left hand across the tiny black smear on the floor and promptly put the finger into his mouth. Hygiene wasn't too much of a concern to angels or demons, so he allowed his tongue to dwell over it. Concentrating to recall the taste, which was vile and heavy, it took him a few seconds and then he had it. Taking the offending finger from his mouth, he quickly wiped it dry on his jacket and stood up. "Okay, whoever took him is probably a human." The others in the room stared at him. How on earth could he get to that conclusion by tasting the flooring was the unanimous question in each mind. They didn't have to ask it aloud because Dedan knew what they were thinking, but he was disinclined to volunteer such information without at least one of them asking the question. A little game, and as time was tight, he didn't want to waste that commodity explaining.

"Time is probably running out and we need to search the rest of this hotel from top to bottom, or more accurately, we'll be starting on this floor so it will be from bottom to top."

He released a concerned sigh. "If the new thief opens up the box, they'll be getting more than they bargained for and we'll have a mess to sort out. We need to find it and return it to the penthouse and return it now."

Ed had heard the words and experienced a mixture of fear and excitement. Fear that he'd be discovered and the box would be taken back before he'd had the chance to open it up and find out what it was. But he was also excited by the confirmation that he had his hands on a story to die for, and nothing, and no one, was going to deprive him of that. His imagination ran rampant with visions of what the contents might be. He began to walk, quickly and silently, to the room five doors down on the opposite side of the corridor. Thoughts of nuclear bombs or highly classified documents flew around his brain as he gingerly entered the room. Closing and locking the door behind him, he walked to the upright steamer trunk in the far corner. Rubbing his hands together in innocent anticipation, he pulled a tiny penknife out from his pocket and promptly began to pick the single and seemingly insignificant lock which was preventing him from getting into the box, or more precisely stopping the content from getting out. Years of experience in journalistic breaking and entry, in search of stories, had made Ed a pretty good larcenist. The justification, in his own mind was self-evident; a story was always the excuse. The lock was more complicated than it first appeared, but he quickly made light work of it and eventually it popped open. Smiling to himself, he quietly uttered the words, "At last!"

The surprise Maurice felt at the explosion of light in his eyes and the realisation that his prison cell door was opening, was nothing compared to the surprise Ed experienced when a large, angry, insane and hungry demon leapt out of the wooden trunk. But mercifully, the surprise was short lived. Maurice snapped the weak chains and ropes tethering him by his neck, wrists and ankles to the wood and promptly attached his mouth to the poor reporter's neck. Teeth sinking in, he ripped through flesh and severed the various muscles, blood vessels and wind pipe before his jaws clamped together, ending their destructive journey. Ed's last proper words uttered were an exalted exclamation of joy at unlocking a box, hardly historic, but coherent. His final sound before his lifeless body fell to the floor was more of a comment of surprise. The blood curdling "Aaaargh" which escaped his mouth, prior to his vocal chords being bitten through, was brief, but extremely loud and blood curdling. The irony lost on both Maurice and Ed being that he had come to Hawaii to avoid being caught by evil gangsters and turned into fast food for the masses; not turned into a hotdog but now he was a quick snack for a demon. Certainly not something Ed had considered as one of his worst-case scenarios.

Swallowing his bloody mouthful, Maurice wiped the warm blood from his mouth with his sleeve and used his finger to remove a small piece of stringy, sternohyoid muscle which had become lodged between his teeth. While he did that, he took stock of where he was. Other than the corpse of his quick snack, he saw he was alone in the strange room. After the darkness of his box, the light hurt his eyes, but not enough to stop him from seeing everything. Wherever he was, he knew there was bedlam to unleash and he needed to be out and about and certainly not here. Seeing the door, he walked over to it and tried the handle. Finding it locked, he simply pushed his strong shoulder against it, and with the sound of cracking wood, it surrendered and swung open for him. He walked into the corridor and was met by the sight of angels and demons running out through a doorway further down the corridor. They'd heard the last death scream of Ed, and rushed out to investigate.

On seeing him, both Grank and Dedan simultaneously reached inside their respective jackets and brought out their firepower. Dedan had a Beretta M12 submachine gun and Grank had a Magnum Desert Eagle automatic pistol. Both raised their guns and fired. Dedan's bullets hit floor, walls and ceiling before one round found its target and lodged into the side of Maurice's chest. Being more used to using firearms, Grank allowed himself a split second to aim properly and let loose several shots, but Maurice was too fast, so only one round hit his left shoulder as he retreated into the room he'd just left. His thick demon flesh was barely punctured by either bullet. Jacketed rounds designed for urban pacification behaved more like mosquito bites to an elephant's hide. Once he'd returned to the room, and was out of the corridor, Dedan quickly released the spent magazine and removed another clip from his pocket, placing it in the gun. Grank looked at him and smiled. "Nice," he said, "more rounds than the shotgun, but like hunting a rhino with an air rifle."

"I'm not the best shot," making a mental note to practice when he got back to Heaven, "so I thought that if I fired enough times I'd hit him enough to slow him down." He glanced at Grank's firearm. "Nice weapon you have as well. And I don't say that very often!"

St. Jerome and St. George's reflexes weren't as primed as Grank and Dedan's so they hadn't been able to draw their pistols until Maurice was out of sight, but now they had them trained on the doorway. They waited, like hunters, for a stag to appear from around a boulder; expecting a quick and easy kill of an unsuspecting animal.

Maurice, on the other hand, was no naïve creature that would stick its head out to get it blown off. He had his back flat against the wall, waiting for his own prey to stick their heads around the door. Sometimes the line between who was hunter and who was hunted was non-existent. "Is that all you've got?" he taunted. "Five people with two guns and only one of you able to shoot worth a damn? Maybe it's vanity, but I thought I'd be worth more of an army. I'm insulted."

"Maurice, you insane little piece of rat's excrement, why don't you just stick that thick brick of a head of yours around the door and I'll show you how one person can be just as effective as a whole army!" Grank's voice was cheerful as he returned the challenging banter.

"I recognise that voice from when you had this little Jack in his box. Is that Grank out there? Satan's jumped up little lickspittle security guard. So skilled you can't even keep a big box safe. Tell you what, why don't you stick your soft head around the door first? I'm peckish and the podgy little human wasn't to my tastes."

"Listen, Maurice, your little game of hide and seek has caused me no end of troubles, so why don't you be a good little lunatic and go sit quietly back in your portable prison? I promise I'll give you time out for good behaviour, perhaps in a couple of millennia or so."

"Tempting Grank, very tempting, but I think I'll decline your kind offer. Now that I'm free and back on Earth at long last, I think I'll play for a while. Cause a lot of damage and trouble, as both angel and demon fall over themselves trying to stop me." Maurice's voice was hoarse and full of menacing glee. "If you're the best I have to fear I think I'll be safe for a long time."

Dedan had assessed the situation and leaving Grank and St. George with their guns trained on the door he turned to St. Jerome and then to Stuart who was cowering, unarmed, a few feet behind him. "Look," he whispered, "we need reinforcements, and we need them now. Stuart, go see Beth and tell her exactly what's going on and get her to send every spare demon they have down here. And make sure they're armed to the teeth but not trigger happy enough to shoot me by mistake. Alright?"

Stuart nodded. "I'm on my way." He ran as quickly as he could. He was one of life's true cowards and he had no desire to be anywhere near such a dangerous confined space. If Maurice attempted a break out, he doubted Grank and Dedan would be able to stop him.

310

Turning his gaze to Jerome, Dedan continued. "Right, as for you, I want you to do exactly the same thing in our part of the hotel. Tell Emily what's going on and get as many armed angels down here as quickly as possible. Just ensure she knows there will be demons down here which aren't the target, so they're not to get trigger happy either."

"Yes, sir," whispered St. Jerome and turned to head towards the opposite end of the corridor.

"Oh, and a couple more things," Dedan muttered urgently, "get her to send a winged angel to instruct St. Michael and his troops to get here as quickly as possible and ask her to find a way of evacuating all the humans from the hotel without causing a panic. The fewer humans there are about, the better."

"Yes Dedan, of course." And also ran off to carry out his set mission.

Using very unsaintly language, St. George suddenly exclaimed, "Sod this for a lark. I can sort him out!" and with that, he began to run towards the door to Maurice's room.

"No!" shouted Dedan. "There's no damsel needing rescuing and he's far more dangerous than a big crocodile. Get back here now!" But his instructions went unheeded as George reached the wall beside the door and raised his automatic pistol in readiness to leap through the doorway and start shooting. But his position wasn't as secure as he'd assumed. Maurice pushed his muscular arms through the thin wall at either side of St. George's head and quickly pulled it through the wall, leaving his body standing momentarily in its decapitated position before his legs gave way and his torso slipped to the ground.

"And now you're even less of an army. How disappointing, I was expecting more of a fight." Maurice was utilising the new hole in the wall he'd just created, as an easier way to talk. "And did I hear you mention damsels and a big crocodile? Don't tell me that I've had the pleasure of having the mighty Saint George for lunch? Talk about good taste. I think I'll enjoy slaying and eating more angels. The brain was so fresh." With that he threw St. George's head, minus part of its devoured cerebellum and brain stem, through the doorway. It hit the open door and bounced, rolling unevenly across the floor until it came to a rest next to its own left leg. Body and head were reunited, just not in the right places and certainly not functioning.

"And it's a strike," Dedan tastelessly muttered under his breath. "Grank, if he tries to make a break for it now, we probably won't have a chance. I suggest we move back a little so that if he does rush us at least we have a bit more time to get some extra rounds into him."

"You mean you'll have more time to put holes in the building?" Grank teased quietly. "But I agree." With guns raised they walked slowly backwards, keeping their weapons trained on the doorway.

As they moved back they saw Maurice's arms reappear through the hole in the wall, this time on either side of St. George's slouched body. Grabbing it under the arms, he created a bigger hole in the wall and pulled it into the room. "Now I have a nice little pistol to play with. I think that evens things up a bit," he shouted. His rough voice was filled with unconcealed, childlike, excitement. "Please feel free to come and join me at any time you want!"

"Grank, that isn't good!" Dedan offered.

"True indeed." Grank replied quietly.

There was silence from the room as St. George was unceremoniously stripped of his clothing. Maurice discarded the ancient, filthy, stinking rags that he'd been wearing for far too many centuries and dressed himself in the blood-stained shirt and black suit he'd just acquired. It was a little bit baggy on his emaciated frame, but a few meals of human casserole would soon fill him out again.

The silence was unbearable to Dedan – he could take abuse and challenges hurled at him, but the lack of noise wasn't something he liked. He had no gauge as to where Maurice was, or what he was up to. Thankfully, there was a loud crashing noise as Maurice smashed through his room's side wall and into the room next door. On his journey, he managed to sever some power cables running through the wall with the lights in the corridor, and all the adjoining rooms, went out leaving them in darkness apart from the emergency exit signs at either end of the corridor.

"Whoops!" shouted Maurice. "Was that me? I am sorry!" With that, he kicked open the door of his new room which was instantly riddled with a full magazine of bullets from a Beretta and a single round from Grank's pistol. "Just testing lads. Well done, the darkness wasn't bed time and you managed to stay awake. And it looks like one of you has improved your aim. Perhaps you could hit a barn door if it's close enough. But the problem is, I'm not a barn door." Maurice's laughter was loud; he was obviously enjoying himself.

"Maurice, you're a disease and I'm the doctor," Grank retorted angrily. "Why don't you just pop out here into my surgery and I'll administer an automatic pistol suppository. I can pull the trigger and it will be point blank and I'll blow your brains out!"

"Tssk, tssk, such unfriendly language! I'm just playing. But Grank, I promise you that when I get hold of you, the games I'll play will make your time running your pathetic little pit in Hades seem like a holiday camp."

Even though he was used to demons and their taunting, there was something in Maurice's maniacal laughter that made

Dedan's skin crawl. He knew that, no matter what, Maurice mustn't be allowed to escape from the hotel, even if it meant him meeting a slow and painful death prior to his return to Heaven. Just then, the fire alarms started to ring.

Emily had managed to find Mr. Knight, busily creating work for himself in his room by rechecking accounts from two years ago. She'd explained that there was a terrorist threat and that he needed to evacuate all the staff, including himself from the hotel and told them to wait by the main road until they were given the all clear. And under no circumstances should any of them attempt to return to the hotel prior to that. There was ice in her voice when she spoke and there was a hint of unarticulated menace which made it sound more of a threat than a polite instruction. But it did the trick and Mr. Knight quickly hit the alarm switch and personally organised the hotel evacuation. Staff ran through exits into the late afternoon sunshine as heavily and obviously armed angels and demons began to appear and head towards the private area of the hotel. Whatever was going on the sight of so many weapons gave the bewildered hotel manager an extra sense of urgency as he ushered his staff out of the building. Once they were all gone, he quickly followed them and started to lead them up to the main road and safety.

Meanwhile, the darkness and added noise of the alarm in the corridor did nothing to relieve the tension. The volume level was increased further, and the element of surprise lost, when twenty breathless and well-armed demons, closely followed by twenty-five similarly armed angels, came running heavy footed along the corridor, stopping just as they reached Dedan and Grank.

The need for whispering no longer a requirement, Dedan took control of the potentially volatile situation. Pointing to a mixture of ten Angels and demons who happened to be closest to him, he issued orders. "You lot, get in that room," he said, pointing to the door nearest to him, "and if Maurice crashes

314

through the wall, be ready for him and don't stop pumping bullets into his body until your weapons are empty and you have no more bullets left in your pockets. Do I make myself clear?"

"Sir!" they all shouted instinctively, recognising the authority in Dedan's voice. Without need for further guidance or instructions, they filtered into the room and took up positions kneeling, with weapons trained along the wall in anticipation of a wild demon creating a new thoroughfare.

"Okay, the rest of you, he's in one of those two rooms and he has nowhere to go. He has a pistol and other than that, his teeth are his only weapon. When he comes out, be ready and keep firing until his innards are his outards!" barked Grank. The assorted security guards quickly took up their positions. Some lay on the floor, others settled behind them on their knees and close behind them was a third row standing up. All were ready with weapons cocked and pointed along the corridor.

The voices in Maurice's head were getting very excited. Some of the forms of madness in his brain hadn't existed prior to his full incarceration in Hell, so actually being free and on earth was a totally new experience for them. They instantly started to debate amongst themselves, which quickly escalated into a full-blown argument as to what should be the next course of action. Virtually all of them wanted to take the lead and a full-frontal attack seemed to be the most popular choice. Not very practical and perhaps short lived, but voices inside any demon's head weren't famous for their logical thought processes. Some were in favour of waiting for the enemy to charge them and one of the voices was in favour of calling for some beer. Even though he could do nothing to shut the opposing voices up, years of experience had given Maurice the intrinsic ability to ignore them all, no matter how loud they were. When it came to battle tactics and planning he thought it was better if he was the sole general making all the decisions, rather than leaving it to a bunch of insane voices which couldn't tell a battle plan from a recipe for peanut and chocolate chip cookies. So he ignored all their suicidal advice, which would have quickly sent him back to Hell and then incarceration, when the sweet tastes of freedom, and flesh, were far more fun. As the chatter continued he took his thoughts to a vacant, quiet part of his brain where he could gather them and assess his options. Even in his insane state, he had enough clarity to know that a full-frontal assault would be plumbing the depths of insanity; far deeper than he was willing to go right now so he had to think of another plan. His tough skin might be able to take the full-frontal barrage of more than the average number of bullets fired at it, but there was certainly a saturation point where metal would overcome rage, arrogance and brute strength. And his head certainly wasn't as bullet proof as the rest of his body. Looking around the room, which he'd entered by the most unorthodox manner, he saw a long row of washing machines lined up against the far wall. Having been locked in his dark, private room in hell for so long, he had no idea what they were, or their purpose but such details were unimportant to him. He smiled because he had a plan.

Chapter 46 - Bird of Pray V. Bird of Prey.

Emily had completely understood the message delivered by a breathless and scared Saint and knew exactly what to do. She'd promptly mustered as many armed angels as she could, ensuring there were still enough left in case Satan decided to take advantage of the lack of security. Then she'd gone to the room of Dwayne, a Seraph who was on earth in the guise of the President of Portugal and told him to fly to St. Michael and instruct him to get to the hotel, with his army, as quickly as they possibly could. Once he had the instructions, he interpreted the word 'urgently' a little too literally and opened his shimmering white feathered wings and promptly exited the room via the patio windows leading to the balcony. Unfortunately, he'd neglected to slide open the windows first, so his departure was accompanied by a loud crashing noise and the raining down of tiny pieces of shatter-proof glass. Loyalty and dedication could never be questioned when it came to Seraphim, but practicality and basic common sense were different issues and shouldn't be scrutinised too closely. Looking for them might leave the seeker surprised and disappointed by their total absence. Emily, on the other hand, wasn't that surprised. She knew from experience that the seraphim spent much of their time just flying around the head of God, when He had public engagements in Heaven, chanting 'Holy, holy, holy,' as if the audience up there didn't know who He was. The work wasn't exactly creative or imaginative, but they got a lot of job satisfaction from it and the hours were good. Emily looked at the glass-covered mess of the floor, sighed and left the room, knowing she needed to talk to Mr. Knight and get the humans away from the hotel as quickly as possible.

Bathsheba's uninvited intruder into her room was most unwelcome. Stuart's entry was badly timed, as Beth was having a break from normal demon communication duties and was being entertained, in a very physical manner, by an off-duty head of state; whose entry had been more than welcome, but he still had some work to do before he could claim to have finished and come up with satisfactory results. Stuart's urgent knocking and unrequested entry into the room stopped anyone else's coming. But undeterred, Beth acted as if nothing more interesting was going on than her watching a rather dull TV documentary on the toilet habits of Three Toed Sloths. Dismounting from the eager diplomat, she casually picked up a robe and wrapped it around herself, shaking her head to get the hair out of her sweaty face. She looked Stuart straight in the eyes. "Yes?" she asked innocently.

Stuart's attention was momentarily elsewhere as he watched her cover up her glistening body. "Errrr," he mumbled before regaining focus on the task at hand rather than the body he wished he could get his hands on. "Sorry to bother you, but something big has come up."

"Yes, I already knew that. I didn't need you to tell me!" she replied with a coquettish smile.

Stuart relayed the details of what was going on in the ground floor of the hotel and what she needed to do. While he was doing so, she casually slipped on a pair of jeans underneath her robe and then quickly disrobed so she could put on a white and very tight t-shirt. Sitting on the bed to administer the final touches to her appearance, she added a pair of bright orange and blue trainers and by the time he'd finished delivering his instructions, she was ready to carry them out. "Okay," was all she said as she brushed past him and out into the penthouse level corridor. Quickly mustering her armed troops, she sent them to assist Grank and then walked along the plush carpeted hallway and straight into one of the rooms. There on the bed was a demon who had taken the form of a very tall and muscular blonde haired man and he was happily drinking from the neck of a large vodka bottle. Hoping that Beth's unexpected visit was to give him a strenuous, but fun workout, he offered her a warm and welcoming smile.

As if reading his mind, Beth frowned at him. "Sorry to disappoint, Abezethibou, but you have work to do. I need you to unravel those beautiful wings of yours and tell Blunt to get here as quickly as he can and to bring his troops with him. I don't care if you need to draw him a map in Crayon or have to escort him personally, but make sure he gets here!"

"Sure thing, Beth babe," he said, still hoping she might reward him for his efforts later on. He walked to the patio windows, slid them open and ripped off his shirt, revealing his tightly-furled coarse black wings, and with one leap he was gone.

"Men!" she said wearily as she watched him go. To her most of them had minds like Welsh mountain railways. Dirty, dark and only one track. She was tempted to go back to bed and finish what she'd started, but she suspected her presence would soon be needed elsewhere. Casually walking to the elevator, she deliberately brushed seductively against one of the remaining demon guards and skilfully reached inside his jacket and took his automatic pistol from the holster. Her hands were so adept and delicate, and he was so focused on her body that he didn't even notice the loss. Once she was in the lift and the doors were closed, she lifted the pistol and cocked it. "Men," she whispered to herself once more, with an air of exasperation. "Always boasting about their weapons but take it away from them and they don't even notice!"

Even though he knew the gravity of his task, it didn't stop the Seraph from enjoying his set job. He was flying freely, high in the cloudless sky and from that height, he could still see the sun in the west as it headed for the horizon, and the dusk that was already taking its grip at ground level. In the distance, in front of him, he could just make out the dark shapes of the military encampments against the dark browns, light green and tranquil blues of the nature reserve. From where he was, he couldn't tell which side was good, and, which side was evil, but as the cool air brushed over his sleek wings he didn't care. He

319

knew he'd be able to hover over the camp once he got nearer and spot his side.

Just then he was shaken out of his reverie when he was dive bombed by Abezethibou. The demon had utilised his height advantage and swooped down on the preoccupied angel. He'd assumed that his message was unique and if the angel was trying to get the angelic troops to the hotel as well then, the balance of power in any possible battle would be lost. So, he'd taken it upon himself to stop the other messenger in any way he saw fit. Fortunately for the Seraph, speed and surprise had been the key part of the demon's tactic but accuracy had been lost. The demon's body had rammed into his side and hit his right wing, but other than that he was unhurt and able to continue with his mission. Now that the key element of surprise was gone, he could focus and keep a wary defensive eye on his protagonist. As he watched the angel he swooped low, building up speed, then turned upwards, flapping his long wings violently as he went higher and higher, intending to attempt another high-level attack. But the Seraph just smiled – there was more to him than first glances might reveal, so he just watched his would-be attacker get into position and allowed himself to fly lower to the ground. His shadow grew bigger and undulated across the landscape, less than fifty yards above the ground. He waited for Abezethibou to commit to what would be the coup de grâce. He didn't have to wait long. The demon pointed towards him and tucked his wings tight behind him like a Stuka dive bomber; all that was missing was the howling, terror-inducing noise. Faster and faster he fell as the plummeting demon picked up velocity. His sharp teeth clenched, eyes focused on the target and arms outstretched ready to impact on the delicate feathers of the wings and his unprotected back. Even if the blow didn't kill him it would certainly incapacitate the angel, so he would no longer be able to deliver his message in a timely manner. In a human war, he would probably have won a medal for his cunning and bravery but in the endless battle between good and evil this was just seen as, relatively speaking, a routine day in the office when it was time for a coffee break and perhaps a cream bun as a special treat. Closer he dropped, one hundred yards, fifty yards, then he was virtually on him. Then at ten yards, the angel demonstrated why Bible studies would be advantageous to demons during battle training, if they could just get a copy of the book that didn't burst into flames at their touch. He picked just the right moment to unfurl his famed extra four wings and with the enhanced flying power they gave him he was able to accelerate and jump ahead of the demon's trajectory. The mixture of limited height above the ground and high rate of knots left the hurtling demon with nowhere to go but down. The ground being fortunately placed just in the right position to break his fall, along with his outstretched arms and his nose when they met the unforgiving earth. Having been banished from Heaven at the side of Satan he'd failed his master long ago during a battle of wits with Moses and had waited an eternity to redeem himself, but he'd yet again failed to beat his chosen nemesis.

The Seraph continued on his course gracefully and allowed himself a quick glance behind him to ensure the enemy had been downed. The cloud of dust which the impact sent into the air assured him he was safe from that particular demon and looking ahead he saw his objective growing larger. One or two more minutes of rapid flapping and he'd be there. He might not have been the smartest angel ever, but thanks to the unusual number of wings the Seraphim had, he certainly knew how to fly. If only the winged evil spirit been armed with a sliding glass patio door, things might have turned out differently.

Once overhead, he was easily able to identify St. Michael's troops milling around on the ground. Some practiced drilling, others polished shoes and cleaned uniforms. All of them looked bored out of their minds. Landing delicately on the vacant ground next to the largest tent he introduced himself to the surprised sentries and was led into the presence of the pompous Saint. Michael received his instructions with the joy usually witnessed from a Golden Retriever puppy being given a new chew toy. All that was missing was the lolling tongue and wildly wagging tail. He joyously barked out orders to the soldiers outside his command HQ who received their instructions with enthusiasm too. With the no fraternising orders rigidly imposed, the camp had become a stiflingly dull place. Unless someone got an erection at the thought of boot polish on leather footwear, there was little to entertain or stimulate, either mentally or physically. Hurriedly, they ran around the camp passing on the good news and began to form ranks ready for the march to the hotel. They had no idea why they were needed there, but they didn't care. Being soldiers they assumed it involved intense, violent and hopefully bloody conflict where they could inflict as much pain as possible on demons before they were despatched back to Hell. Obviously, the thoughts of the demons possibly doing the same to them, and sending them back to heaven, never entered their chirpy, optimistic minds. Clean smart boots and black jump suits were quickly donned, weapons shouldered and the troops lined up in readiness.

Abezethibou's entrance to the demon camp was less spectacular, but perhaps more noteworthy. Deformed wings bloodied and misshapen face and his arms rendered useless after his sudden meeting with the ground, he'd managed to take flight again, but he'd certainly lost a lot of grace and elegance with his flying technique. Less the slender and swift Kestrel that would have been given amazed glances if seen by any ornithologist. Instead, more a diseased pigeon needing to be put out of its misery. But even if his pride had been damaged, as much his body had, he had an important message to deliver. He landed awkwardly in front of Blunt's tent, arms limp and draped uselessly by his sides. Squinting, he was unable to wipe the dirt from his eyes or the bloodied snot from his philtrum, lips and chin. He was a pathetic creature as he stood to a kind of limp attention before Blunt and his bemused generals. Despite their inherent desire to laugh at the strange spectacle, they all knew who he was and feared him. It was prophesised that he would regain his place at Satan's side one day, and they had no desire to be names in the book containing the list of all his enemies requiring his own brand of pent up hatred and retributions.

Blunt had received the instructions in silence. His mouth dropped open but the look in his eyes was inscrutable. It was a trait more natural than a deliberate affectation, for such an act would be beyond his limited repertoire. He understood the words as they were simple enough; go from A to B, although such an alphabetical analogy would be beyond his intellectual grasp. But the concept of marching to a location, for a possible battle, fitted his mental map of the world perfectly. The idea of mayhem, destruction and then – all being well – enough beer and food to sate the appetite of even the most intemperate and gluttonous of hungry demons. War was hell and even more so on a hungry stomach.

The Generals were given the honour of relaying the instructions to the troops who were casually lounging about throughout the camp. Those who weren't asleep were either drinking beer, or eating the last of the nature reserve's stock of fauna. A couple of species had even become extinct, thanks to the less-than-selective dining choices of the unwelcome guests. As the wave of wakening kicks and barked orders spread across the camp, the demonic form of military discipline soon returned and a sense of order prevailed, even if it wasn't totally obvious to any external witness who might have been spying on them. They lined up slovenly with their weapons at the ready, and their motto was less a case of 'march or die' as it was 'walk together to somewhere so others can die' – perhaps not as pithy, but definitely far more accurate and to the point. The Angels had already set off a few minutes prior to them, but such things were immaterial. If it was a race the angels wanted, then it was a race they would get...

Chapter 47 - Where There Is Darkness Let There Be Light.

In the corridor the assembled assault squad were tensed with fingers on triggers ready to let loose a hail of bullets on anyone, or anything, suddenly appearing before them. No time would be given to assessing whether the object bore any resemblance to Maurice. In such circumstances, the adage of 'shoot first, identify the body later' applied to both angel and demon. In their haste to form a fighting line, Dedan and Grank had noticed they were on the wrong side of this textbook military formation. Any rounds released would pass through them before making contact with the desired target.

Not liking this obvious tactical oversight, Dedan tapped Grant on his shoulder and focused his attention towards the impending danger. "Oh," he volunteered, the one word speaking volumes as he recognised the situation. They pushed past the three lines of aiming troops swiftly, so they could take up a far safer position just behind the firing line, and all being well, out of their direct line of sight.

Time seemed to pass slower than even Einstein could have predicted with one of his calculations. Each long second was like an eternity as concentration was maintained and muscles strained to keep the weapons level. Sweat formed on brows and foreheads before dripping down into eyes or trickling over temples and down cheeks before falling onto shirts that were also bearing the brunt of perspiration assaults as well. Not only had the power outage knocked out the lights it had also stopped the air conditioning units and the temperature increase caused by all the extra bodies had begun to make the whole place smell like a Turkish sauna masseuse's jock strap. The combination of smell and heat could easily have knocked a human unconscious. The odour emanating from the two corpses, in the far room, weren't adding to the general ambience of the place either.

Dedan took the remaining bullet magazines from his jacket pockets and put them into the pockets in his trousers, then removed the hot jacket. It wasn't made of a thick material but it was becoming uncomfortable and wasn't helping his free movement. It might not have given him a professional appearance, but he wished he hadn't changed out of his light and congenial Aloha shirt. He might have looked ridiculous among all the burly and heavily armed guards, but he'd rather look silly and not be drenched in sweat. Being a demon, Grank was more used to the heat, and if the corridor had been in Hell it would have been deemed a cool refuge compared to the vast majority of locations. But in human form, not only he, but all the other demons were suffering from the heat. They might have Demon souls, but they currently had human sweat glands. For the angels, it was even worse; a cool, sweetly-scented and comfortable paradise was no training ground for this type of situation.

There was silence, apart from the breathing of the massed firing squad. No one wanted to break concentration and begin any sort of conversation, and if Maurice should make any sound, which might give them some advanced warning, then they wanted to be able to hear it.

Maurice, on the other hand, wasn't even noticing the heat or the less than pleasantly scented bouquet of the whole area. He was busy investigating the strange row of metal cubes at the far end of the room. They were only waist height, freestanding and all connected by several pipes to the back of them. The purpose and destination of the plumbing was unimportant; all that mattered was that they were there and he could use them. As could the armed guards outside his room, but more for their designed purpose, but laundry was not high on their priority list at the moment.

The various secret service agents' attention was grabbed by the strange wrenching noise coming from the room where Maurice was holed up. It sounded like a metallic scream of agony, followed by a sound resembling water being forced through a pipe. Abruptly, in the near total darkness, a new hole suddenly appeared in the wall before them. It was accompanied by an explosion of plaster board and breezeblock, sending dust into the air. The creator of the hole was quick to appear as a large, chrome, cube-shaped washing machine came crashing into the hall. In the dim light, the armed guards couldn't make out what it was, but their instincts were such that they didn't pause to try and analyse what the strange object that had just come through the wall and landed in front of them was. Bullets, from three rows of weaponry, tore into its thin metal skin. The noise of the gunfire in the corridor was deafening and the clanging of bullets hitting the washing machine as it was rapidly dismantled in a very brutal and random way just added to the cacophony. Mangled piece of casing, door and drum flew at various angles as they were sent flying by the impact of the rounds. The whole sight was given a flickering strobe light effect by the almost continuous glare of the muzzle flashes.

Dedan was able to see enough to realise the target wasn't Maurice and it was highly unlikely he'd become some modern-day Ned Kelly, using white goods for armour instead of a coal scuttle and a few pieces of metal plate. Besides, even though he hadn't got the best glimpse of Maurice, he was sure he couldn't have fitted himself into the drum of the machine and found a way of throwing himself through the wall. "Cease fire!" he barked, attempting to make himself heard over the noise of weapon fire and the sound of bullet casings dropping to the floor. His instructions went unheeded, so he began to grab angel and demon in turn and bellow the instruction into the ear of each one of them until they stopped. This had the desired effect and as each row ceased fire, the volume reduced enough to allow his shouted instructions to be heard by the rest. The gloom returned, made worse by the choking fog created by the gun smoke. Suddenly, there was a faint 'plop' sound and a grey movement in the distance as a solitary piece of bullet-riddled bed linen laundry chose that moment to fall out of what remained of the washing machine's drum. The vague movement and the unexpected strange noise spooked a couple of tense angels and they started shooting again, ensuring the unfortunate bedding would never again be used by any hotel guest. It would have struggled to have been recycled as dusters or dish cloths. If there had been a Heaven for linen it would have been on its way to there, having spent a full life of uncomplaining service.

Maurice watched joyfully, through the hole in the wall, the untimely demise of the, less than lucky, washing machine and its contents. Destruction held a special fascination to him and all the shots that had been fired worked in his favour. Their supply might still be there, but it wasn't infinite and the more edgy they were, the more likely they were to waste bullets on things that weren't him. Holding the late Saint's automatic pistol, he quickly put his hand out through the hole in the wall. Pointing blindly in the rough direction of his opponents, he let off a couple of quick shots before withdrawing his vulnerable hand to safety. One of his random shots managed to hit a demon kneeling in the middle row. Struck in the chest, Carsten was killed instantly, body falling to the floor as his soul was sent back to Hell. The brief return of a caring conscience, prior to becoming totally evil again, would be punished when he got there. The other round harmlessly hit the wall next to where the unexpecting guards were lined up.

Maurice's sudden assault had the desired effect, as yet more rounds were wasted as they were sent wildly in the direction of the hole. The demolition process that had only just ceased on the washing machine now resumed on the plaster and breeze block, filling the corridor with more muzzle flashes, smoke, dust and plaster. It was beginning to resemble an ecstasy drug crazed nightclub which had spent too much on lighting effects.

Taking the new barrage as his cue, Maurice ran shoulder first towards the wall, where there was a gap where the destroyed washing machine had once stood. Even though the wall was thicker than the ones he'd crashed through before it was still no match for the impact of his body. The collision resulted in the wall giving way, sending debris flying across the corridor close to where the lifts were in the guest's section of the hotel. Brick and stucco landed randomly on the expensive carpet. The new hole provided a source of light in the darkened room and seeped through the hole he'd made in the wall at the opposite end of the room but he didn't care. It might alert the guards that he'd made good his escape, but by the time they'd decided to investigate, and plucked up the courage to stick their heads through the hole to see what the light source was, he would be long gone.

He had managed to escape from another room…

Chapter 48 - A Disorderly Orderly March!

There is a pace used by the military, of some countries, called a double-time march. It's the equivalent of a close order synchronised run, performed by troops who should know better and are trying to show off. Lousy for parades, but ideal for getting troops from A to Z, as they pass through B to Y, in the fastest time possible. All while maintaining some form of order and preventing the participants from looking like a rabble.

For a healthy and well-trained human soldier, this can be maintained for quite a long period of time before it turns into a marathon race. St. Michael wasn't familiar with the specific form of marching, or the designated one hundred and eighty paces per minute. Even if he had been, the parameters would have been too limiting for him. He was currently pushing the heavily armed angel army to the limits, and making them move even faster than that. Their legs sprinting, hearts beating wildly, and in the muggy Hawaiian evening, their lungs were only just managing to gasp in warm air. All this done so that their legs kept time with his rapid staccato, 'Left, Right, Left, Right' instructions. It was an exhausting pace for the angels having to maintain their human forms, but they carried out the orders with pride. God had finally summoned them to action and no matter what they had to go through, they would answer His call.

The demons weren't as hung up on the delicacies of close order formation marching as the angels. Yes, it ensured they all arrived at any given destination at exactly the same time and therefore, they were better placed to fight a battle as one unit, but such details were immaterial to them. The important thing, in their minds, was the simple exigency of getting to the hotel first. That task had been made harder, due to the time it had taken to rouse all the demons from their various states of consciousness and get them dressed and ready. Now that they were on the road, they could see the angels in the distance, and they had a steely fierce determination to bridge the gap and win the race. They ran as fast as they could, their human forms suffering from the same constraints as the angels had to deal with. Weapons tucked tight against their bodies they ran, snorting like enraged bulls aiming at a bloodthirsty torero in the bull ring. No respite would be expected, or anticipated, until they'd overtaken the angels and had an unassailable lead they could safely maintain. The purpose of Blunt and the Generals was academic as any bellowed invectives aimed at them, urging them to move faster, would have been pointless; as they were going at the same pace as the troops, they'd have struggled to issue any loud orders anyway. Faster and faster they ran, as the distance between them and the angels began to close. Closer they got until the troops at the rear of the angelic column were only fifty yards away. Only then did St. Michael notice them from his position halfway up the line, urging his soldiers on. His surprise and indignation struggled with one another before anger snuck up behind them and stole the lead. "Faster men, faster. Run!" he shouted. No matter how tired his troops were, he knew in his heart and soul that he couldn't let the demons catch up and overtake them. The heavy clumping sound of boots on the tarmac road changed from a rapid, but rhythmic, thud to a constant heavy thrum as any pretence of marching disappeared and the race began. The increase in pace momentarily widened the gap, but seeing the quickened pace of their enemy, the demons picked up the pace as well, so the gap continued to get smaller. Minute by tiring minute, the angels' lead was reduced. The regiment were no longer so tightly packed as the fitter soldiers found their way to the front and the slower, less fit ones, fell behind to be first caught up with and then overtaken by the demons that were fastest in their army and able to take the lead. The slower demons were left to keep pace with the less athletic angels, pride and determination still strong, but bodies unable to match the band of brothers racing off ahead of them. The stragglers still had their race that they were determined to win, but getting a gold, silver or bronze medal was out of the question. If there had been a wood or paper medal then they were going for that. Even a child's sports day sticker, saying 'I tried my best' would have been accepted as their reward. But at the front of the race the ones who had fallen behind were, for the moment, of no concern. The angels could see their eternal enemies from the corner of their eyes and allowing themselves a brief turn of their heads they saw them on the other side of Highway 2, the main road running up the island like a spine. The few cars on the road had to swerve off it in order to avoid a collision with runners who were obliviously taking up the whole road, determined not to move out of the way, and risk giving an advantage to the other runners.

Past Wheeler Army Air Field on the left and the cool and inviting clear waters of the Wahiawa Freshwater State Park on their right they ran. The Terrapin Cove Hotel was still many miles away but pacing the race, so they would be in a fit state to fight once they got there wasn't part of their reasoning. Crossing the finish line first was all that mattered. On they ran, and occasionally the demons would eke out a frugal lead which they managed to hold on to for a few hundred yards, then the angels would catch up and retake the advantage. Any soldier who fell got jumped over or trod on by the men behind him. The luxury of moving to avoid them safely was not theirs to enjoy. Those that fell behind dropped exhausted by the side of the road and caught their breath and rested until the slower contingent caught up with them and they were able to join the rear of that race. All the time maintaining tight grips of their assorted firearms; well aware that arriving at the battle without them would be like turning up for a polar expedition naked.

And still the front of the race maintained its breakneck pace. Blunt, St. Michael and a couple of the demon generals managed to keep up, but none of them had the spare energy to issue instructions, even though any such orders telling them to keep going would have been moot at best and at worst totally facile and stupid. Gradually, like an Olympic marathon race, the athletic war of attrition whittled away the front section of the runners as an ever-increasing number either slowed their pace or just collapsed on the grassy verges at the side of the road. Even the generals succumbed to the limits of the human form endurance race and gave up, no longer caring what their field marshal might think about them or report back to Satan. Blunt was totally apathetic to their dropping out of the front pack. His raw brute strength and lack of intellect were his greatest assets. The pain he was inflicting on his human form was soaked up like a sweat-filled sponge. Muscles might have been crying out in agony, but his subconscious was doing the equivalent of someone sitting with their fingers stuck in their ears, going 'nah, nah, nah. I *can't* hear you!' His pain threshold was far beyond most humans, so he continued because he didn't know the meaning of the word acquiescence.

St. Michael, on the other hand, was feeling the pain in what seemed like every cell of his body. He was fighting his own internal battle as he struggled to gulp in enough air to feed his bloodstream. He was dehydrated, his head hot and pounding, giving him the suggestion that it was going to explode. His shoulders and arms were like jelly and his legs had taken on the characteristics of lead. Each step impacted on the ground and sent shock waves of pain along his spine and into his brain. His vocabulary was considerably larger than Blunt's, so he knew many synonyms for the word 'surrender'. Be it capitulate, yield or just give in. But he simply refused to accept any of them and wouldn't allow himself to slow down and risk losing the race. He knew, from experience, that human pain was transitory and would soon end when he was back in Heaven. So, on they both ran, side by side with the elite runners on equal sides of the good and bad spectrum. In ancient Greece, Philippides was turned from mortal into legend for his prowess and ability to run and request help from the Spartans and then sprint to Athens with news about the battle of Marathon. If this race had taken place in ancient times, the front runners ran the risk of being called living gods, with all the complications that caused when trying to get into Heaven or Hell. Eventually the race reached the point where the metaphorical finishing line was in sight. The road approached the turn off, leading to Kulima Drive, and from there it was just a short distance to the hotel itself. There was however, one final obstacle in their way. The staff of the hotel had congregated at the junction. Sitting or standing and talking to each other, they waited for the all clear and instructions to return to the hotel.

Also, on the road was the vacated police car of Officer Charley Palakiko, who had reluctantly decided to drive past the hotel just for appearances sake, so he could honestly report back to his superiors that he'd carried out his duty. He was mingling with the crowd, chatting and trying to get a better understanding of what was going on. He was also playing out different scenarios in his mind, trying to decide what course of action he should take next. He knew from bitter experience that attempts to get near the hotel would be met by belligerent secret service agents, but he wasn't sure what implications his reporting a bomb alert to his superiors back in Honolulu might have. They might just ask him to keep them informed, but they could panic, pick up the phone and speak to the General in charge of the Marine Corps Base Hawaii at Kaneohe Bay and before long, helicopters filled with members of the 3rd Marine Regiment could be swarming all over the grounds, compromising the top-secret conference. Once all the dust had settled, he'd be the one all fingers pointed at to apportion the blame. Perhaps in balance, he reasoned, it would be best if he took his time to report the current situation. Perhaps a week would be long enough for him to file his paperwork via proper channels.

The approaching runners could be heard, long before they were seen by either the bemused police officer or the hotel staff. But as the racers rounded the corner, they saw that their ideal route was blocked so they tacitly decided to alter the course of the final stretch. Turning left, they took a detour over the golf course leading to the hotel. The verdant grass was soft on aching feet after the repetitive pounding they'd received on the hard, unforgiving road. With one last sprint, the few remaining runners at the front of the depleted pack reached their objective. One final, almost heart exploding burst of energy sent St. Michael the few extra yards in front of Blunt. His arms lifted into the air, as if he was passing some invisible finish line. Then without any dignity, he collapsed onto the cool ground close to the 18th hole adjacent to the hotel. Taking his adversary's collapse as confirmation that the race had ended, Blunt and the other runners stopped their sprint as well. Everyone, with the exception of Blunt, fell to the floor, bodies drained of even the energy needed to remain standing. Vital fluids no longer fed organs, with sweat glands no longer produced sufficient fluids to cool the skin down. They just had to lie down and catch their breaths and hopefully regain focus when their brains finally got a fair share of the oxygen that was slowly increasing its quantity in the blood. The ability to lift weapons and engage in a battle was something totally lacking on both sides. The only person left on his feet, bent over with his hands on his knees for support, was Blunt. His only thought was that he needed a beer or, even better, several beers. Another thought popped into his mind, joining the thought of rehydration. It was a memory only a few hours old, but it felt like a demon's lifetime ago. Reaching into his pocket, he pulled out a warm, brutally shaken can of demon beer. Opening it, the froth shot out of the can in a way not dissimilar to what happens to a teenage male secretly viewing his stash of porn magazines in his bedroom. Once the contents of the can had settled, he put it to his lips and emptied it into his mouth. Demon beer might not have been the tastiest of brews, but to him, at that precise moment, it was the most delicious drink he'd ever encountered.

Slowly, the rest of the runners caught up with the race winners, their impractical uniforms more of a hindrance than a benefit. The demons, denim dungarees were drenched in sweat, weighing them down and the nylon black jumpsuits of the angels, with no design element allowing the material to breath, retained the heat and sweat so the bodies inside the clothing took on the texture of a chicken dinner boiled in persperation. And, if eaten, would probably have tasted the same as well. Out of breath and tired, they came to a stop, demon mixing with angel, across the golf course. Two vast armies, dressed in what looked like sweat-drenched Halloween costumes. All the time they were being observed suspiciously by the ersatz security guards, and cows, which'd been stationed on the fairway. If any war was going to be staged, and the battle of Terrapin Cove was to enter the books of fable and legend, then it would have to wait until aching bodies had been allowed to rest. Heavy guns were left by the side of bodies, arms no longer willing or able to caress anything heavier than a tall glass of iced water. To many of them, sleep sounded like a very good idea indeed. If only they had signs saying 'Wake me up when the fighting starts!

Chapter 49 - Kiss, Bang, Kiss Bang.

Maurice was used to cramped conditions, so he was flexible and, he had no problem pushing his body through the rough, uneven hole he'd created in the wall. The lights in the hallway were a stark contrast to the subdued gloom of the laundry room, but he wasn't bothered by the change. His eyes adjusted immediately as glanced around, taking stock of his new surroundings. The rubble strewn red carpet, the walls covered with sophisticated and expensively patterned paper, the occasional framed abstract art print hung to break the monotony was in reality just another dull corridor; only this time, for the use of rich guests who expected that sort of thing. In front of him was a deserted passage which led up to the conference room. The usually ubiquitous guards had been removed, to help with the siege of the laundry room. To his right he saw that the walkway went past some closed doors, on the opposite side to the one he'd just crashed through, and at the far end was a green sign above a door, indicating a fire exit. Taking a brief look to his left, he saw a couple of large doors next to one another. He had no idea what they were, as lifts hadn't been created during his time on Earth as a human. Perhaps if he'd perceived their function he'd have taken one to introduce himself to God, or the other to get vengeance on Satan. But currently, the words *exit* had captured his imagination. Freedom and the chance to run and get as far away from people intent on putting holes in him as possible. He saw the doors leading into the lobby and decided that flight was better than fight in this instance. Then he paused as he saw Emily walk through the doors leading from the reception area.

She could see him through the glass but forced herself not to react. A calm exterior and display of nonchalance hid total terror. She'd never seen Maurice before, but seeing the condition of the man in the distance, with a blood-soaked shirt collar and chin, standing tensed with a pistol gripped in his hand and his arms by his side, she was able to make a well-educated guess as to his identity.

Under normal circumstances he would have introduced himself to any beautiful and defenceless woman in the vicinity, in a brutal and ungallant way, but this time he overrode his baser instincts and turned to run to the fire door and escape.

Seeing that the cause of so much destruction was planning to flee, Emily decided she needed to do something. "You must be the infamous Maurice. I've heard a lot about you. Somehow, I thought you'd be taller." She kept her voice loud and confident, which was a good thing. If her words had betrayed her true emotions she'd have sounded like a timid sheep trying to chat up a hungry wolf.

The words made Maurice stop and he turned to face Emily as she continued walking towards him. "I'm afraid you have me at a disadvantage miss." He bowed his head in an act of mock chivalry. "I am indeed Maurice. And before I have my pleasure, might I know who I have the pleasure of talking to?" Instinctively, he dusted himself down. The dust diligently refusing to leave his suit; a dirty decoration, proof of his exploits.

Without stopping her casual walk towards him, she smiled innocently like a school girl approaching a loving parent. "My friends call me Emily, but you don't have to call me that."

"Ha!" he snorted. "You have guts, or at least, you have for now. I shall soon relieve you of them."

"Such a gentleman. All that time locked in a dark room and a match box must have done something to your memory. Or are women not to your taste?"

The challenge was too much for his ego, and vanity controlled the very core of his existence. Despite a few voices in his mind issuing sage advice, suggesting he should leave straight away, the gauntlet had been thrown down and he couldn't ignore it and walk away, or in this case, run in the opposite direction. He walked up to Emily with an arrogant swagger and his chest puffed out like a Bird of Paradise on the pull. Stopping with his face inches from Emily's he placed the pistol tightly against her temple. "Foolish words, especially as they'll be your last." His breath on her face was foul smelling – Hell's version of halitosis, mixed with the aroma of human flesh and angelic brain. He'd certainly be a challenge for any advertising executive wanting to promote a brand of extra strong toothpaste or breath mints. Emily involuntarily retched at the noxious fumes emanating from his mouth. "But first, I'll grant you one last happy memory before I send you to hell. A kiss." A sardonic smile stretched his tight lips.

"Hell? Do you mind? I belong in a place you could only dream about. Anyway, I doubt your kiss will give me any happy memories."

"Who said that it would be giving *you* a happy memory?" With that, he gently planted a kiss on her lips. Then, once finished wiping it off with his sleeves and gave her a sly wink.

Maurice experienced a stirring in his groin, that he doubted was of his own sub-conscious' making and saw Emily's trembling hand pressing a Smith and Wesson J frame revolver into his crotch. "Interesting" he muttered. "Now what? You think that frightens me?"

He felt the cold kiss of another pistol against his own temple. "Now? You die!" Beth's low voice hissed in his ear and then there was an explosion of noise and a fine red blood mist in the air as pieces of hair, skin, and brain tissue decorated the far wall with a new piece of modern art that a New York collector, with more money than sense, could easily have been talked into paying a fortune for. The small, neat entry hole in Maurice's head was a stark contrast to the ragged, dripping exit wound on the opposite side. A look of surprise was permanently etched on his face. His body went limp, arms falling to his sides, gravity taking the automatic pistol away from its dangerous proximity to Emily's head. Like a tree which had been hit one too many times by a lumberjack's axe, his body fell backwards onto the floor. The blood running out of his head added to the red of the carpet, giving any upholstery cleaning service an unusual challenge.

Raising the pistol, she'd borrowed from the unsuspecting demon guard to her lips, she gave the barrel a dramatic and seductive blow. She glanced down at the small hand gun, still positioned at emasculation level. "Nice little toy, Emily." Her voice was almost an inaudible whisper. "That has the stopping power of a water pistol. But I'm sure that where you had it aimed, you'd have managed to blow his brains out!"

Emily looked at Beth, eyes wide in a shocked stare, then a nervous smile suddenly started to take over her mouth and she began to laugh, releasing all the pent-up tension and terror. This in turn, set Beth off. The noise filling the corridor as two people, separated by their past actions, shared a mutual experience. Not good or evil beings but two friends forgetting about the expected antagonism that they should have for each other and savouring the moment.

Just then, automatic weapons appeared through the hole in the wall, quickly followed by the nervous heads of suited guards, cautiously investigating the source of light and noise. Seeing Maurice's corpse on the floor they relaxed and removed taut fingers from already overworked triggers. Dedan came running to join the two women via the lobby, closely followed by Grank and the full contingent of what had until only a few scant minutes ago been three rows of disorganised but effective members of a firing squad or at least they would have been a firing squad if they'd had someone to shoot. The whole ensemble came to a sudden halt, breathless, behind Dedan as he stopped by the side of Emily and Beth. He stared down at Maurice's body, the same expression still on the demonic face that he'd adopted in the moment of death. Dedan wrapped his arms around the shoulders of the still-laughing ladies "Well done, you two. I must admit, I'm definitely impressed. Perhaps I should have just called for you two to come and help me in the first place, instead of the flange of baboons I ended up with."

Emily looked at Dedan "Yes, dear," she managed to say in between giggles. "*Us help you!* I think you'd only have got in our way." This gave both merry females the opportunity to maintain their raucous guffawing.

The merriment was disturbed by one of the angels who'd been left in the security room, pushing his way through the assorted demons and angels blocking the corridor. He studied the corpse on the floor and tried to understand the cause of the almost insane laughter from the two women in front of him. His muttered, polite, request asking if they'd let him through went unheeded. Eventually he managed to reach Dedan and Grank, bemused expressions on their faces, seemingly unable to work out what the joke was. Or if they'd realised that they were part of the joke they didn't want to let on. "Sir? Sir? Sir!" he shouted, ensuring he'd got his commander's attention.

Dedan gave him an impatient glare. "Yes? What is it?" he hissed. His pride irked at the suspicion that he might be the brunt of the humour.

"Sir, I think you'd better go outside. Now!" the angel blurted out. "I think there might be some trouble."

Dedan glanced down at the prostrate body at his feet. "Trouble?" He said the word as if it were an alien concept. "Yes, okay, lead on." He turned to his giggling companions. "Ladies, care to accompany me for an evening stroll outside?" he asked, with a mock Cary Grant accent.

"Sure," replied Emily, trying in return to sound like Mae West "But I hope it won't take long, I need to go to my room and rinse out my mouth. It feels as if I've been chewing a boxer's jock strap."

Chapter 50 - Taking Machine Guns To A

Knife Fight.

The troop of heavily armed guards obediently followed Dedan, Grank and the two still chuckling women through the otherwise empty lobby and out through the main entrance into the cool evening air. Their pace was steady as they walked in a counter clockwise direction around to the side of the hotel. Walking up the slight rise to the 18th hole they were met by the sight of two armies standing, sitting or lying exhausted on the soft grass. Their numbers had grown as the remainder of the running contingent finally caught up with them and took the much-needed opportunity to rest. The angel guards who'd been on duty on the golf course, when the runners arrived, were assisting the angel troops in whatever way they could. Giving them water when they had it or just making them comfortable. The demon guards, on the other hand, stood looking suspiciously at the angel army, refusing to deviate from their instincts and what they saw as their primary instruction. Helping tired demon brethren wasn't part of their DNA. One creative and industrious angel guard had eventually located the switches which controlled the spotlights. They were positioned nearby, up on high stanchions, there to allow late night games of golf for the very dedicated; for the fees they paid for a round of golf it was prudent profit maximisation. Activated, they bathed the whole scene with an eerie light. Shadows between bodies on the ground gave it a ghost-like hue. The blinding high intensity artificial lighting leaving the encroaching darkness stuck on the outside of a bright dome of manmade glare. All those inside the tent of luminosity left casting long umbras on the rich green grass that was already attracting the evening dew. The same resourceful angel also found the switch to turn on the sprinklers and the sudden cascade of cool water was welcomed by both demon and angel as they scrambled to quench their thirsts and lower body temperatures to a reasonable level. The simple elixir quickly revived mind and body and they were soon back on their feet, weapons at the ready, eyeing up their neighbours and identifying drenched friend from soaking foe.

Dedan and his entourage arrived at the side of the golf course and were met by the strange sight of what appeared to be a ninja and redneck party, one where they'd forgot their beer but remembered their machine guns, and then been caught in a sudden, ongoing downpour. Quite possibly it was the most disappointing party that it was possible to have, especially when there was no rock music and not even tortilla chips to snack on. Thanks to the mad rush to get to the sprinklers, the already close proximity of both groups of soldiers had become even more tightly packed, so that any discharge of the varied heavy weaponry would have resulted in full metal jacketed rounds passing through the body of their intended target and continue through a couple more soldiers as well. And their allegiances may, or may not, have been the same as the intended foe. Also, a spray of bullets would have spread wider than the person directly in front of the shooter and again resulted in a great deal of possible friendly fire. Any battle fought on the golf course would have enriched the soil and turned the grass from green to red, but the old and embedded military philosophy of shoot as many of the enemy as possible while avoiding your own troops would have been impossible to follow. But the unusual surroundings and the entire situation wasn't conducive to mutual peace and harmony. It was a metaphorical powder keg, just waiting for someone to break wind too loudly. The resultant noise and smell could be misconstrued as a tear gas grenade and it would swiftly become a mess which would be difficult for Dedan to keep secret and treat as small-scale damage limitation. Swearing under his breath, he turned to Emily and Bathsheba, who were standing at his side. "Emily, could you please get God? And Beth, would you please get Satan? I think they're the only ones who'll be able to defuse this situation and get everybody to calm down; ideally standing down at the same time." Turning to the nearest angel he continued issuing orders. "You," he snapped in a firm but quiet voice, "do you know St. Michael?"

"Yes sir, I served under him at the battle of—"

"Very good. But I didn't ask for your life story. I want you to discreetly go into that crowd and quietly instruct him that his presence is required here as a matter of utmost urgency."

"Of course, sir," replied the unfortunate angel who'd been on the receiving end of Dedan's frustration. And, before he could receive any more chastisement from his own superior, he scurried off into the throng searching for St. Michael.

Dedan turned his attention to Grank. "What's the name of the leader of your lot's army? I could do with him being here as well."

"Blunt," was Grank's simple reply.

"Blunt?"

"Yes, afraid so!"

"Okay, can you instruct one of your men to do the same thing and get him here just as quickly, without him asking too many questions?" Dedan asked in resigned tone.

"Oh, I think once he's found he'll come to see us without too many difficult or probing questions," responded Grank with a wry smile. He turned and gave instructions to the nearest demon, who promptly went off to locate the demon general, although the simple act of pulling out a six pack of beer and opening one might have had quicker results. The demon general was still thirsty and would have soon picked up that scent.

In the hotel, Beth and Emily had taken their respective lifts and were in the process of requesting their leader to join the gathering outside. Emily knocked on the door to God's penthouse suite and waited for him to bid her to enter. Once the invitation came she walked in and saw God standing on the balcony, watching the two armies spread out on the golf course below. "Hello Emily. A beautiful, but interesting night, isn't it?" Without giving her time to reply He added, "I presume you've come to request I come down to bring some order to the whole proceedings and ensure nothing more deadly than biting sarcasm and cutting remarks is exchanged between the two sides?"

"Yes, sir and errrrr, yes sir." Answering both questions just in case they were needed or expected.

"Of course, Emily. Please lead the way." Then they began to walk towards the lift, closely followed by God's small contingent of personal bodyguards. Leaving just a couple of guards to ensure no demons got lost and accidentally, or otherwise, found their way into God's room.

Beth reached Satan's room, but her knock was met by a far harsher response from the occupant. Walking into the room she was met by the sight of Lucifer lying on the bed in just his underpants, drinking a large demon cocktail of whisky mixed with more whisky, topped with more whisky, and all served in a tall glass. He hadn't had the best of days and he was beginning to realise the ace card he'd kept up his sleeve had not, after all, been a wise gamble. The drink was doing nothing to erase, or lighten, his dark thoughts. "What do you want Beth?"

"Sire, the two armies are both outside on the golf course and you're needed to keep the peace on our side."

"Peace?" Satan allowed the word to leave his mouth as if it was a strange and alien concept he'd never encountered before. He exhaled a long, tired and despondent sigh. Deflated he no longer had much interest in the proceedings and in a small part of his mind he thought a large bloody war would be just the thing he needed to cheer himself up. But despite that thought he rose from the bed, dressed and followed Beth out of the room to the escalator. His own bodyguards, eager to follow him, were simply told to wait where they were. He knew he'd be safe and if things should deteriorate, he'd be more at home fighting than trying to be a diplomat brokering some insincere ceasefire. The irony that he was displaying more trust in his sworn enemy's actions than God had shown to him was lost on the master of Hell.

The two lifts reached the ground floor simultaneously and they stepped into the corridor at the same time. Acknowledging each other with pleasant smiles and nods, or pleasant in the case of God, Satan was feeling distinctly out of his comfort zone. The uncertainty of what to say in such circumstances weighed heavily on his mind, after all, small talk about the weather would have been out of the question and starting the conversation with 'Hi, just like old times!' might have set the wrong tone. *Armageddon II – Oahu Wars* wasn't what he'd come here with the intention of starting. The army had just been a backup, the biggest assembly of bodyguards he could get. He never thought he'd need to use them and a false alarm about a now-dead demon was no reason to destroy a remote island in the middle of the Pacific. And, far more importantly, totally scupper his chances of ever getting back into Heaven.

God, on the other hand, had no such concerns; he thought Satan was genuine in his desire to get back into Heaven, even if he wasn't convinced it would be a wise move. His mind was more concerned with the armies outside. They'd been enemies for so long, the first reaction when they confronted each other was to fight and try to kill the opposition before they were destroyed. In fact, it was also the second through to the 100,000[th] reaction. There were no alternatives, which had been part of the training and experiences of the past millennia. Sitting down for a friendly chat, over a latte in a cosy café had never happened, and despite urban myths and songs He had sat down and played chess with Satan, but not to get more souls. Poker, yes once, but never chess. He was also sure Satan had never played a fiddle to try and steal someone's soul, but if he had, the soul he'd got deserved a one-way trip to Hades for being so greedy.

On they walked, followed by Emily, Bathsheba and the rest of the tiny contingent of guards who'd rushed down the stairs to ensure they could follow their leaders. Both sides walked side by side, but except for the two women, there was nothing but contempt in their eyes.

Emily and Beth felt it prudent to remain silent, but there was a gleam of shared experiences in their eyes and despite the differences in their ethical positions, they'd developed a close friendship which transcended such divides. If war happened, they both knew they'd have to fight and possibly kill the other, if the opportunity arose, but until then they were friends with the benefit of sidearms.

Despite the tense standoff occurring on the 18th hole, spoiling any would be golfer's game, the walking party didn't rush. The sight of frantically running deities didn't send the right message and could easily have precipitated the exchange of gunfire in a tightly-packed area. When Dedan and Grank were joined by God and Satan, there was nothing new to report and weapons were still raised and aimed, as best they could be with so little room, at the nearest foe. Such conditions would have made a heavy Bowie knife or a medieval spiked morning star more appropriate. Old fashioned barbaric hand to hand combat compared to modern day barbaric wars where the enemy was usually distant and remote.

St. Michael reluctantly appeared from the crowd and joined Dedan and God. He'd had his pistol trained on a particularly large demon, and he resented having to lose such a prime target, even if it was to go and talk to God. Similarly, a demon, which had been stood behind the saint, was also disappointed at having lost such a prime target. Plus many of the loyal angel troops would not have been too disappointed if they had lost their general early on in the battle.

346

Blunt had been a harder subject to find among the soldiers. He'd misplaced his weapon and was casually mingling with both sides, chatting with them as he tried to inconspicuously scrounge whatever beer might have been to hand; all done under the pretence of searching for his missing gun. Disappointed at being unable to obtain alcohol, from either side, he'd decided to observe the situation from the fairway. Despite his lack of education, he recognised that the current military formation wouldn't provide a tactical advantage and his slight distance from anyone pointing any sort of weapon at him, at point blank range, might make him the default winner and the last man standing. He could always join the fight once the pack had been whittled down to a more sensible number. But even from his vantage point, he was spotted by the demon tasked with finding him and he obediently strolled around the troops to meet up with Grank and Satan. He wasn't fazed by seeing God with Satan; he just assumed His presence was all part of Satan's battle plan. Although who would plan such a strange battle was beyond even his limited comprehension of stratagems.

The only two left in the messed-up battle formation, from opposing sides but not hell-bent on destroying each other, were Geb and Abaddon. They'd fought their long and hard battle with each other, and the seed of mutual respect had been planted, started to grow and taken root. The war between them had ended and even without any written treaty, or spoken words explaining terms, they knew they wouldn't fight each other. In amongst the throng of anger and hatred, they'd taken up their positions. Back to back they stood, weapons raised. They would obediently shoot numerous enemies, but not a friend, and if they could help it they wouldn't let anybody else shoot them either. Such brotherly fraternisation was uncommon and would have been frowned upon by everyone else, but nothing would make either of them change. They would stand together and fall together. If St. Michael had known he wouldn't have approved and might have tried to intervene, but fortunately he had bigger

347

things to think about than two enemy soldiers not wanting to kill each other.

Once both Field Marshals were present and accounted for, a brief discussion took place as to what had happened. St. Michael and Blunt were relieved of the misconception that they were required to start a full-blown war and that a mutual relaxation of tensions would be to everyone's advantage. Blunts innate blood lust and desire for a good fight was turned off like a light switch; his unquestioning obedience to his master the only factor. St. Michael was less willing to trust his enemy to have peaceful intentions, or to be able to put safety catches on. His blind obedience to God might have been unquestioning, but in his mind, he wanted to disobey instructions and allow the deadly game to be played out.

While the discussions had been taking place, Satan stood there nodding his head in agreement whenever anyone looked at him for a contribution to the conversation, but he had a concern formulating and he was waiting for the right moment to mention it. But before then, he wanted the talking to come to an end, just in case anybody else saw the problem and brought it up. Unfortunately for him, God terminated discourse with the words, "Right; anybody got any questions?" The silence that ensued seemed to destroy his urgent desire to speak.

"Just one niggling thing." He enunciated each word as if they were pebbles being spat from his mouth. Then continuing with more certainty "Who is going to blink first?"

"What?" God responded with a curious expression on his face.

"We have two armies' hell bent, if you'll pardon the expression, on destroying each other. They see this as an opportunity to score points and win a war. I'm not so sure that your angels love peace so much that they don't want to fight against my demons, and I know for a fact that my lot want to put large, painful holes, in your troops as a prerequisite to their return to Heaven. So the simple question is, who's going to trust the other side and give the order for the stand down first?" He paused, allowing his words to sink in. "After all, trust doesn't seem to be in such massive supply on either side."

God rubbed His chin absent-mindedly while He considered the question. "A valid point." He turned to face the, would be, battlefield and inhaling deeply He spoke, his voice loud and clear but somehow managing to avoid becoming a shout. His words entered every ear despite any physical obstruction or distance. "Right, everybody; I want all the Angels to lower their weapons." He paused to allow his words to have their effect. But nothing happened. Fear and hatred overrode the compulsion to obey God. "I mean *now*!" Despite the unique method of his communication, the final word managed to echo around the golf course leaving no doubts in anyone's minds that He expected to be obeyed immediately. The emphasis had its desired effect, as weapons were hesitantly lowered then placed on the grass.

The demons, seeing a weakness, awaited the final order from Satan. One word and they could have opened fire and downed their rivals without one of them getting wounded.

Satan's method of passing on his instructions was far less subtle than God's, but equally fruitful. He breathed in deeply, as if inhaling enough air to send a four-mast schooner off course and crashing on to a coral reef. His words were thrown out in a violent shout which knocked over several of the soldiers who happened to be close by and made several more, slightly further away, stagger under the physical impact. "*All* Demons! Any pausing, delay or hesitation will be met with my greatest displeasure. I want you to put your weapons on the ground. There will be no war today!"

Despite any urge to take advantage of the situation, terror gripped the demons' spleens. They all knew what sort of

349

punishment would await them in Hell if they were seen to be taking their time to do as they'd been told. There was a brief instant when the guns were clumsily dropped, and then there was an uneasy silence. The soft and well maintained grass cushioning the fall of the weapons and preventED any unfortunate discharging of weapons that had not had safety catches engaged.

Satan looked at God with relief and an element of disbelief in his eyes. There was a corner of his soul which had expected a blood bath. The outcome was a surprise to him, but he was reassured to know he'd been obeyed.

Turning to Dedan, God offered him a broad smile which hinted at His own relief. "Well, that was interesting. I think I can leave this in your safe hands." He turned to St. Michael, "Michael, walk with me." He then started to walk back to the hotel and the comfort of his suite. St. Michael followed obediently, totally oblivious to His master's tactic of removing a gung-ho leader from a volatile situation, thus leaving the troops in a more sensible pair of hands. Seeing God walking away, Satan decided his presence was no longer required either, and he looked Grank up and down before speaking. "Grank, I'll leave you to handle the rest of this. I'm going back to bed; I left some whisky in my room. And it, like me, needs to be drunk as quickly as possible." With those words he strolled away, hands casually clasped behind his back, and returned to his room. He was happy with the thought that even though his desire to re-enter heaven had been damaged morethan a parcel being handled by the US Parcel Service there was still an opportunity to talk more in the morning and hopefully turn things around.

Dedan looked across the sea of inappropriately attired spirits, both good and bad, and shrugged his shoulders. "Okay Grank; you ready?"

"As I'll ever be."

350

"Angels, atten-tion!" barked Dedan. "I've always wanted to do that," he whispered in an aside to Grank. "Angels will leave their weapons where they are and proceed to the beach where they will sit, stand or do whatever they feel like if it helps you relax. I don't really care what you do, as long as it doesn't involve fighting any demons." The angels shuffled off, muttering to one another, feeling vulnerable without their guns, but glad to be safe and unharmed. Dedan turned to Grank. "Your turn now." Despite his reluctant respect for his demonic counterpart, his cynical mind recognised there was always the danger his faith could have been misplaced and advantage might be taken.

If questioned, and should he have chosen to reply honestly, Grank would have had to admit the thought did briefly cross his mind. He might have developed a new-found love of power and authority, but he had no desire to throw it all away and risk displeasing Satan and wind up being at the receiving end of punishments he was used to dishing out. "Alright demons, your turn. Just leave your weapons and sod off to the 9th hole. I'll see if I can arrange for some beers to be sent out to you from the hotel's plentiful stock."

The mention of beer removed any hesitancy from the minds of the demons. Many had no idea what a 9th hole was, assuming it was some sexual reference, but they happily followed those who looked as if they had some germ of an idea as to where they were heading. Angels and demons were randomly despatched to locate as much beer as they could, with the strict instructions that anything scavenged would be shared equally. Then an angel was selected and given detailed instructions and sent to advise the hotel staff that the DEFCON rating on the hotel had been lowered and it was now safe for them to return, as long as they stayed in the lobby for a while. Once that had been done it was Dedan and Grank's turn to lead the rest of the remaining ersatz secret service agents back into the hotel. "Ladies," Dedan said, addressing Emily and Beth, "could we interest you in a nightcap at the bar before we retire?"

After a brief exchange of glances, and wicked smiles between the two women, they smiled together. "Of course, Dedan and Grank, I think that would be a wonderful way to end the evening."

As they strolled away from the deserted 18th hole, littered with an array of weaponry which would have made a small dictatorship drool, Dedan spoke to Grank without looking at him. "You know, Grank, this could be the start of a beautiful hatred?"

Chapter 51 – Know Thyself. You Can Always Deny It To Others.

The next morning there was a different vibe to the whole hotel, hard for many to define but it had changed. Staff, tired and drained from the late night and prospect of having to clean up and repair a lot of unexplained damage, were quiet and attempting to avoid any contact with the guests. But they didn't seem to care anymore. They sensed the conference was coming to an end and they soon would be able to relax and enjoy their well-deserved bonuses.

Despite the various remains of dead bodies having been removed, there were still strange stains on the carpet and walls and staff feared asking too many questions regarding their cause. The sudden appearance of strangely dressed people on the golf course was additional food for thought, especially considering the large arsenal left unattended on the 18th hole. As for the cows, they seemed to have disappeared completely. The demonic status of the unfortunate bovines hadn't saved them from becoming special, late night guests at a drunken demon barbecue. They proved to be the most unusual collateral damage ever, smothered in a rich sauce and eaten by their own team. Their return to Hell wasn't what they had planned.

The bull had managed to avoid such a fate; on seeing his beloved harem come to a sticky end he'd decided to make himself scarce and picked up the distant, faint scent of some feral Hawaiian cattle, and casually went off to explore the island and look for a new source of love and companionship.

Compared to previous days, demons and angels alike were also far more relaxed, as if the order for the troops to stand down had extended to them. The sight of any enemy didn't make them tense up and check their weapons were still holstered under their jackets. Smiles weren't exchanged – there was still a long way to go before that would ever occur – but teeth weren't gritted and that was a start.

In the conference room, Satan had arrived first, two minutes before 10am, the agreed time. God walked grandly through the doors, precisely as the big hand moved to indicate the start of the new hour. Casual salutations were exchanged and instead of taking positions at either side of the long table, they pulled out chairs from the side of the table nearest to the door and sat facing one another with nothing between them but their history. Satan's enthusiasm was still there, but realism was creeping into the dark rooms of his mind.

After a few minutes of casual, inane, small talk, God decided it was the right time to say what he needed to say. "You know Lucifer; you are not ready to return to Heaven."

"But—" Satan responded, but his protest was blocked by a casual lift of God's hand.

"Look into your own heart, Satan. You know as well as I do that you've found where you belong. Yes, it might be Hell, but it's your home. Heaven is a dream for you, but you'd quickly return to old ways and old ambitions. You'd never accept being just another non-entity in Heaven after holding so much unbridled power. It might take you a decade, or you might bite your lip and sit uncomfortably for a thousand years, but sooner or later you'll forget the pitfalls of Hades and try and take over again. Battles will be fought and, you'll just end up being thrown out of Heaven again. Why waste each other's time? I have no desire to spend that time continually keeping a wary eye on you knowing that someday there will be a trap set up for me. And who knows? next time you might win and, I have no intention of taking over the lease of the netherworld. It isn't a simple question of a lack of trust; I know you too well. And if you were honest, I'm sure you'll agree with me."

While Satan thought, he remained quiet for what seemed to be hours, but in fact it was only a matter of minutes. He allowed the admonishment to swirl around in his head. He was searching for valid arguments to counter the accusations, but he knew he couldn't. Heaven meant comfortable beds, copious amounts of manna, working plumbing and a diversity of piped music, but his real self would remain unchanged. The ultimate power had ultimately corrupted him beyond recognition when compared to the mildly ambitious person he'd been when he first attempted to gain supreme power. Changing into some menial, subservient angel with a vapid smile, blandly singing God's praises wasn't for him and it would be a form of de-evolution. It would be like a man deciding to change back into a monkey, eating bananas with the skins on and throwing poo at passing strangers. "I suppose you're right," he reluctantly responded. Lies or subterfuge would have been wasted breath. "So, I suppose we go back to what we were? Fighting the bad fight and me scheming to take power from you?"

"It doesn't have to be that way, Lucifer. Just because you run Hades, it doesn't mean it has to be Hell. You have the power to make it better and be good."

Satan smiled wryly. "Yes, I can see that happening." No longer having to display any reverence, he allowed dripping sarcasm to coat his words. "As if that will ever happen. Where's the fun in that?"

With that admital the need for the conference had ended. Casual talk was exchanged between two old friends who'd become enemies and grown apart. Many oceans had flowed under the bridges between them but there had been a time, so long ago, when both had shared joys and happiness.

Deciding that the time was right for the proceedings to come to an end God abruptly stood up. "One last thing before I tidy up the mess we've left here, and we all go back to our respective dimensions. Will you walk with me briefly? I want to share something with you."

"Yeah, why not! What have I got to lose? A few more hours away from my throne won't hurt."

They walked side by side from the room which had witnessed the strangest conference in Earth's history and walked along the corridor to the fire exit. Stepping outside, God stopped and, Satan came to a halt by his side. He saw God looking around and Satan began to do the same, straining his eyes to see exactly what God was looking at.

"Do you smell that Satan?" God enquired in a gentle voice.

Satan's nostrils were accustomed to centuries of brimstone, burning flesh and the excrement of endless damned and frightened souls, so whatever God smelt wasn't registering. "Nope," he responded matter-of-factly.

God smiled indulgently, as if he was talking to a small child. "Focus. It's the sea air."

"Oh, is that all?"

"Yes. It is beautiful, but you'll never be able to accept that. But I wish you could. The whole island is amazing, as is the entire planet. It could be so much more if you just let it reach its full potential. Yes, humans are fickle, stupid at times and capable of evil things, but they can also do good things, show kindness and love unconditionally. It isn't easy for them, but they can be great, if only you could step back and let them."

Satan inhaled deeply and scanned the view surrounding them. The Pacific Ocean to his right, the verdant golf course directly in front him with the woods in the distance and the Hawaiian hills far away to his left. Despite the cloudless blue sky, the magical effect was lost on him. His appreciation of nature's aesthetic gifts had been lost long ago. To him it was just water, grass, wood, rocks and air. His soul, or what it had become, was just as cold and uncaring as it had been the day he'd returned to Earth.

Even if God couldn't see into Satan's soul, he could sense the wasteland in his spirit and was saddened. He knew that mankind would flourish and go beyond their current level of inhumanity, but he also knew that Satan wouldn't be willing, or able, to help them. Despite the perceived victories of the previous day, good had somehow managed to join with bad and destroy a greater evil. Suspicion and mutual distrust had been put to one side, as demons and angels were forced to avoid their mutual destruction and find an uneasy peace. Perhaps on reflection, thought God, if beings with such extreme differences, in inherent states of being, can do it, then so can humans?

Chapter 52 - Paradise Misplaced.

The staff lined up in the lobby as the God President and his retinue of world leaders shook hands with the humans and filtered out of the hotel. God paused at Mr. Knight and as He held the man's hand He created a little miracle. It was one that would never be recorded in any holy books, but still a special piece of magic. He sensed the tumbled bricks in the manager's borderline insane mind. It was rubble that was likely to tip him over the edge and into the abyss of madness. The toll of the past few days had been too high for his ordered, regimented brain. But with His touch, all the confusion and turmoil was removed and peace entered his head. Relief that he had done a great job and all would be well.

At the very end of the line was Mr. Knight's daughter, looking far more attractive and less windblown than when they'd first met. God gently took her hand and smiled. He didn't do destiny, but he could feel she had great things in her future and perhaps he could assign a few angels to help her along the path. "Have you ever thought of going into politics, my dear?" he asked.

"No, Mr. President, I'm sure I wouldn't be any good at it," she replied, surprised by the question.

"Oh Caroline, good is what you are, and that is what politics needs!"

The words left her puzzled, but God walked away, knowing He'd pointed her in a direction that her lack of self-confidence would never have previously allowed her to look.

The helicopter flew Him back to the remote field. His tent was waiting for the army to march there and the vehicle cavalcade to turn up. He watched as his soldiers, guards and the collection of mock world leaders returned to Heaven. Once they'd left the island, He took one last look around at the scenery and was gone, leaving the island and its inhabitants in ignorant bliss regarding all that had happened and how close they'd come to becoming demon dinner.

Satan's exit from the hotel was less ceremonious. Demonic guards and politicians climbed into the waiting vehicles and drove off towards the nature reserve, the chosen location for their portal back to Hell. The army had no desire to walk back there, so they just went into the woods, as if they were going for a toilet break en masse, and then just disappeared. The absence of any angel or demon left the golf course with an eerie feeling of isolation and loneliness. The only movement being the flags, at each hole, blowing gently in the breeze.

Chapter 53 - All Done Bar the Whispering...

Well Almost...

After the unappreciated joys and pleasures of Hawaii, Hell was a shock to Satan's system. The heat was oppressive, the smells would have induced vomiting in humans and the useless plumbing was just as aggravating as always. But in retrospect, this was where he belonged and, he wouldn't have it any other way. There had been a minor insurrection by some of the lesser, but still ambitious demons, perhaps egged on by more cunning devils. Such things were expected and had been easily quashed, in his absence, by Leviathan, Balfon, the Marching Horde and his loyal inner circle. The investigation had finished, those responsible had been found guilty, then sent for trial and the punishments had been meted out. Each had been sent to different punishment chambers in the second ring of Hell, where they would spend all eternity regretting their stupidity and wishing they had stayed loyal. It was a state of mind that Satan himself no longer had for God and his time as an angel. Regrets over the past were, he realised, far too self-indulgent. His life was hell and he had every intention of making as many other people's existences hell as well. Plus, his dreams no longer reminded him of his previous mistakes. He would plan to get Heaven the old fashioned way, by war, but not yet.

The inter-dimensional portal had brought back the reluctant demons who'd accompanied him on his trip to Earth. The pleasure of tasting beer and meat still lingered in their minds and on their tongues, but such thoughts would soon vanish once the routines of Hell began to take effect again. Any good habits they might have picked up would be beaten out of them – in many cases quite literally – and the balance of power between Hell and Heaven would re-establish itself.

With the aid of a pistol the voices in his head had been temporarily silenced and his brains had become part of the hotel wall, allowing Maurice to eventually return to a random place in

Hell. He'd managed to avoid reappearing inside a wall or a punishment chamber, so he'd been free to wreak havoc along the dark corridors merrily dismembering and feasting on any demon that got in his way. He was finally cornered in a dead-end corridor by 1200 heavily armoured Abdiel demons, armed with long, sharp tridents. Thanks to the sheer force of numbers they'd managed to pin him by the neck, against a wall, between the forks of their weapons. But even then, his flaying arms and legs managed to inflict damage on several dozen of his captors before they managed to trap his limbs in a similar fashion. They left him shouting expletives and abuse as he was tightly chained up and dragged to his old, dark cell where he could do no more damage to anyone or anything. His shouting was muffled by the thick walls, but his private inner voices were free to deafen his tormented mind. His screams of anguish went unheeded, and any faint noises which did manage to escape his prison cell were lost in the day to day screams of agony that filled hell.

Carsten the demon, who'd briefly been touched by God, wasn't so lucky with his arbitrary re-materialisation. His soul had solidified so that he'd retained the contorted shape he'd acquired on death; slumped forward bent forward. Unfortunately, the landing point for his less than triumphant return to perdition, was such that his top half was stuck in a brimstone-encrusted wall and his bottom half was sticking out. It left him susceptible to the imagination of any pernicious-minded demon. Or in other words, all of them. Until he could find a way out of the tomb, encasing half his body, his arse would be an amusing focal point for any and all passing jokers. If there had been many bicycles in the underworld they would have been parked there. As it was, someone had already painted a face on his buttocks and placed a cigar in between for effect. His rear end looking like a strange, and far less kissable version of Groucho Marx.

When the demon cows returned, they immediately sought an audience with Satan. They had requested, pleaded and then begged to be allowed to take on some other form but Satan, being Satan, had refused. Their ordeal on Earth had amused him and he thought that the mocking laughter they would be subjected to in hell was a suitable punishment for the lack of military benefit they'd brought to the whole affair.

God's return to heaven was celebrated as if it had been a great victory, rather than just a tense standoff followed by a sudden stand down. Angels returned to their comfortable routines, and other than a few tired limbs, were unharmed by the whole experience. There was a consensus that the entire thing had been one massive trick on Satan's and it had completely failed, as Satan's plans had always done in the past. But there was also some relief that he hadn't had his way and convinced God of his suitability for being allowed back into Heaven. Emily looked back at her time in Hawaii with fondness, but soon returned to the daily rhythm of Heaven's routines. Comfort and luxury far beyond anything possible on Earth soon overtook any fondness and desire to stay in the plush Hawaiian hotel.

There had been plenty of loose ends on Earth for Dedan to sort out, so his reluctant return to eternal paradise had been delayed. Bodies had to be disposed of, the extensive damage to the hotel had to be repaired and money had to be handed over. Mr. Knight had received the cheque with gratitude, but he was even more thankful to say goodbye and wish the Presidents, and all their followers, a safe journey and close the hotel for a few days while it was returned to the pristine standards he expected from the place. Dedan remained for as long as he could, under the pretext that he was doing final security checks to safeguard against anything inappropriate having been left behind. In the process he ensured that every employee received a generous bonus in return for their signature on genuine non-disclosure agreements, rather than Grank's versions which might have removed their souls. The official paperwork duly headed with Government emblems and backed up with severe reminders of the consequences of any loose talk. They had been threatened with a form of hell and assumed that they would disappear and spend the rest of their lives in some cold and lonely cell in Fort Leavenworth Penitentiary but in Dedan's mind the hell he alluded to was far more literal. Eventually he had to accept that he'd run out of excuses for avoiding his resumption of duties in Heaven. There were humans quite literally dying to get in yet he resisted go there for as long as he could. On his return, he went straight to God's office. The pretext was needing to report that all was well, and apart from a few endangered species moving up the critical list, Hawaii was none the worse and none the wiser for having come so close to hosting an un-prophesised apocalypse. But in reality, his main wish was to see Angelica and invite her out to lunch.

As he entered her office, he saw Angelica sitting at her desk, busily typing up a report on the computer. Such bureaucracy seemed pointless and futile to him, but the work kept her happy, so maybe that was the whole point. Looking up, she offered him a wide smile. "Hello Dedan. Welcome back. I heard you had a lot of fun down there."

Dedan wondered how much she actually knew and if her reference to fun was what he thought it was. He walked towards her and casually sat on the edge of her desk, attempting to sneak a peek at what was on the screen, but she casually tilted it so he couldn't see it. As that view was blocked, he decided he'd try and look down at the cleavage in her tight-fitting blouse. "God has a couple of people with him, but He instructed me to send you straight in as soon as you got here."

"It's alright, I don't mind waiting. I couldn't ask for more beautiful and charming company."

"You're totally right there, Dedan" she replied, a cheeky smile illuminating her face "But God takes priority and I'm sure you'd enjoy His company more."

"Well, perhaps. Who am I to disagree? I must allow duty to reluctantly tear me away from your sweet presence, my angel. But I'll count every second until I'm back with you and I can bathe in your radiance." He chuckled. "Adieu, my fair Angelica, until I return."

"Yeah, right Dedan. You're still full of crap!"

Knocking on God's door, he was still looking at Angelica. "Own up, you wouldn't have me any other way!" He winked conspiratorially. "Oh, and coffee would be lovely. Black, no sugar!" Before she could throw anything at him, verbally or physically, he was through the doorway and into God's office. On entering, he was surprised to see two bodies lying prostrate on the carpeted floor in front of God's desk. Despite the desire for many devout religious visitors to prove their piety, such acts of subjugation tended to leave God feeling a little uncomfortable. He always insisted they got up from such a silly position and either sat down or remained standing, if they really insisted, but He always said having random people lying all over His floor made the place look like an Amsterdam squat. But in this instance, God didn't appear to be objecting to their supplication. Dedan manoeuvred around the room so he could get a better idea as to the identity of the two unusually positioned guests. Once he was close enough to them, he squatted down to see the sides of their faces. Not the best identification parade when people are laid with noses pressed into the ground and trying not to make eye contact. Eventually the penny dropped. The nearest one was St. Jerome, but he couldn't place the other. He certainly wasn't an angel he'd been in charge of at the hotel and he certainly didn't look like one of St. Michael's warriors.

"Hello, Dedan." God seemed to be in a jovial mood, despite the two new temporary rugs He'd acquired. "Glad you found time to join us here in heaven. I'm sure the Earth will continue to revolve without you holidaying in the sun."

"Hello Sir. Yes, I think I left the place in good order. Or at least, in the same state as we found it. You know humans; they usually find ways to mess things up."

364

"Yes," God sighed. "Too true, many a word spoken in jest. Anyway, allow me to introduce these two to you. You might recognise St. Jerome. He is here so that he can hear his fate. Being party to the theft of Maurice's mobile prison might have been done out of naïve best intentions, but it was still a sin and his actions could have caused a lot of deaths on a small island."

"Sire, please forgive me. I beg you." St. Jerome's voice was full of fear and regret.

"Oh, shush. For a learned man, I would have expected more thought from you before you just blindly followed St. George. Your punishment is being sent to Alaska for demon hunting duties for as long as I deem necessary. Once I feel you've learnt your lesson, I'll recall you and in addition, you'll lose your saint's status. Now get out; Angelica will make all the arrangements for your return to Earth."

"Thank you, oh thank you, Sire!" The grovelling and relieved ex-saint scrambled to his feet and left the room, bowing like a Texas derrick pumping oil out of the ground as he went.

"Don't worry, Dedan, Jerome is no field agent. He'll probably bump into a demon by accident and be killed within a few minutes of the meeting. Give him a week and he'll be back in Heaven. Then I'll forgive him and he can return to his beloved library and read to his heart's content. But naturally, I won't be letting him go on any more missions to Earth."

Dedan smiled. Jerome was normally a wise person and was well-liked in Heaven. Despite everything he was a good man, and didn't deserve too severe of a punishment.

"And allow me to introduce you to Ed Mercerator," God casually continued. "An ingenious reporter who managed to evade your security and infiltrate the hotel in search of a story. It was also him who stole Maurice's box from the original thieves and opened it, getting far more of a story than he expected. Fortunately, he had very little time to report it to the mortal world."

"Hello," Ed muttered from his unusual position.

"Anyway," God said quickly before Dedan had the opportunity to respond. "Despite his actions, his motivation, in his own heart at least, was genuine. He might have an ego the size of Carnegie Hall and lusted after a Pulitzer Prize, but he does have integrity, decency and kindness in his soul and his belief in social justice is certainly refreshing to see. So, Ed, you are forgiven. Please feel free to leave and enjoy the privileges on not having been sent to Hell."

Ed recognised that he'd had a close call and left the room in the same fashion as the former Saint. He was tempted to ask for an interview, but realised he was no longer a journalist, and he doubted there was a newspaper in Heaven. Old habits die hard, even for the dead.

When Ed had left, God gestured for Dedan to sit down in one of the comfortable chairs by his desk. Sitting down, the angel finally spoke. "Sir, can I ask something?"

"Of course, my boy, but I can guess what it is. St. George?"

"Yes Sir. **Where** is he now?"

God sighed. "He is currently in limbo, going through the process of purgatory. That will decide if he will return to heaven, minus his Saintly title, or just go to Hell. Now it is all up to him."

Dedan had never visited limbo, but he'd heard many stories about the place from those who'd been through its doors and managed to make the right choices, tip the scales of judgement and prove themselves worthy of Heaven. It could be a close call as to whether he ever saw George again. He was about to speak when the peace and quiet of the room was broken by loud, urgent hammering on the door. Without being invited, a flushed faced angel entered the office. Out of breath, he ran to the front of God's desk.

"Please forgive the interruption, my Lord, but I've got bad news. It looks like the demons might have found out the whereabouts of the Sword of Uncreation and got hold of it."

God was about to pick up His favourite coffee mug, but His hand hovered just above the handle. He looked at the angel, a pained expression on His face.

"Dedan" His voice was distant, as if he was still formulating what he was going to say, but a hint of panic was mingled in his tone. "I hope you haven't unpacked your bags. I have another mission for you…"

To be continued… on Earth.

Credit Where Credit is Due (Others have to pay cash).

In the writing of this book there were people that understood and supported me, those that tried to and those that didn't. All encouraged or pushed me forward in their own ways so should be thanked. However, there should also be a spotlight pointed at specific people for all they did for me.

First, and definitely foremost, my family for the patience when I got lost in my writing and for rescuing me on the occasions when I was stuck in the jungle of my mind. There are lots of monkeys in there.

Emily Gaither, fellow writer and cherished friend, you pulled some strings and put me on the path all those years ago and also made me believe that I could actually write. I owe you more than I could ever say. Now you need to believe in yourself and write your novel (s).

Rossana Condoleo, thank you for stating the obvious, switching on that light and saving me from eternal creative darkness. A wise life coach, great writer and definitely my harshest and most honest critic.

T.A. Garcia for proving to me that the love for a story is what matters and recognising that a story starts in the heart before it gets anywhere near to the mind.

Then there is thanks to the Honolulu Police Department for patiently answering my questions and then giving me facts that I promptly played fast and loose with and occasionally ignored. You are a credit to your State and Country.

There are many more that I owe thanks to and if I were to name all of you this page would end up longer than the rest of the book, but I hope you know who you all are. If you really think I should specifically have included you, then please add your name here

....